A SAVAGE LAND PLAGUED
BY MONSTERS

They'd all heard rumors of what dwelled in Chult, the
feral monstrosities that had survived for ages hidden in
the tangled undergrowth that covered most of the island:
yuan-ti, carrion crawlers, purple worms,
plaguechanged horrors too terrible to consider.
"The colony is just a mile inland," Harp assured him.
"Once we find the path, we'll be in and out before nightfall."
The men spread out along the beach,
searching for what should have been seen easily
Listening to the distant, unfamiliar sounds,
Harp felt like he was faced with a creature he'd never
encountered before. It was vicious and feral
with only one purpose—constant growth
toward the heavens.

MORE THAN ONE THING LIES
FORGOTTEN IN THE DARK HEART
OF THE JUNGLE.

THE WILDS

The Fanged Crown
Jenna Hellend

The Restless Shore
James P. Davis
May 2009

The Edge of Chaos
Jak Koke
August 2009

Wrath of the Blue Lady
Mel Odom
December 2009

FORGOTTEN REALMS

THE
FANGED
CROWN

Jenna Helland

THE WILDS

Wizards OF THE COAST

The Wilds
The Fanged Crown

©2009 Wizards of the Coast, Inc.

Cover art by Erik M. Gist
Map by Rob Lazzaretti
First Printing: January 2009

9 8 7 6 5 4 3 2 1

ISBN 978-0-7869-5093-5
620- 23957740-001-EN

U.S., CANADA,   EUROPEAN HEADQUARTERS
ASIA, PACIFIC, & LATIN AMERICA   Hasbro UK Ltd
Wizards of the Coast, Inc.   Caswell Way
P.O. Box 707   Newport, Gwent NP9 0YH
Renton, WA 98057-0707   GREAT BRITAIN
+1-800-324-6496   Save this address for your records.

Visit our web site at www.wizards.com

To Nancy Helland

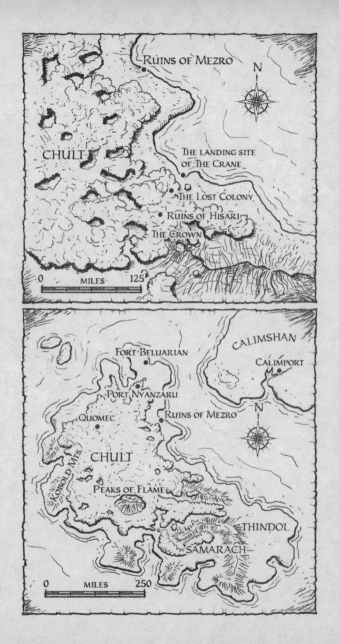

CHAPTER ONE

29 Kythorn, the Year of the Ageless One
(1479 DR)
The Crane, *the Coast of Chult*

With his face squashed between a boot heel and the deck of his ship, Harp could see scores of grain seeds that had fallen into the tiny spaces between the planks. And it made him angry. In addition to being laid out under a filthy boot, there was evidence of what a negligent caretaker Harp had been. After a decade of humiliations, looking at the seeds germinating in his beloved ship made Harp wonder if he could sink any lower. Grabbing at the man's calf, he tried to push the boot off his face, but the foot didn't budge. The boot had a wooden heel, and as "Bootman" ground it into Harp's cheekbone, the pain was excruciating.

As he heard the sound of a man unsheathing his short sword above him, Harp had an image of the broken hull of his ship battered in the shallows with a field of wheat sprouting from her boards.

Four years before, Harp and his friends had broken just about everything—their code, their pride, their backs—trying to get their hands on the *Crane,* a one-mast, rat-infested galley with warped planks and a heroic history, at least according to the fat man at the docks who owned her. The *Crane* would be their passage out of the dingy waterfront district where they had lived.

But after they'd signed the writ of sale on the ship, the currents of life had swept Harp along. Soon his dreams of freedom on the open water had been swallowed in a sea of debt. The *Crane* became nothing more than a run-down vessel hauling wheat and barley from port to port.

Harp owed her more than that.

The expedition to Chult was supposed to end the cycle of hand-to-mouth with a healthy payment of Tethyrian gold. When the shores of Calimshan had faded from sight—but before Harp could see the shadow of Chult on the horizon, or the unfettered motes that hung above the isle—and nothing but the rolling waves and the endless blue sky surrounded him, he felt something relax in his chest. For one carefree moment, Harp felt like the true captain of his ship, not some merchant for hire, or worse, a man simply biding time in the world.

The orders had been simple: check on some colonists who had gone to Chult to pursue a timber venture for Queen Anais of Tethyr. All correspondence with the colonists had ceased, and some members of Anais's court were concerned for the safety of the venture and its participants. Harp told his men that the colonists had most likely hopped the first boat out of the hazardous jungle.

The prospect of adventure had cheered the crew. The pay was enough to cover their debts, replace the *Crane's* rigging, and purchase a new golden sun-sail. The hull was glossed to a shine, and there were new bunks in the crew's quarters. The *Crane* had never looked so good.

Harp hadn't lost her to his debtors. There was no way he was going to lose her, not to this Bootman and his sneaky little ship.

"Captain!" someone shouted from the bow of the ship. Both Bootman and Harp turned toward the noise. At least Harp would have done so if he had the capability of movement in his neck. With Bootman momentarily distracted, Harp felt around for a discarded weapon, specifically the dagger that had gone flying out of his hand. But Harp's straining earned him nothing but extra pressure from his vanquisher.

"Stay still, dog," the man said, shoving his foot against Harp's already throbbing ear. "The more you move, the more cuts it will take to remove your head from your neck."

Less than an hour ago, the *Crane* had glided through the narrow mouth of a picturesque cove. Sparkling blue water lapped onto a white sand beach with the edge of an emerald jungle beyond. Bootman's ship had been hidden behind an outcropping that curved out from the east end of the cove. A slightly larger ship than the *Crane,* with a narrower beam and lighter rails, the *Marigold* had easily overtaken Harp's vessel as his crew busied themselves with landing preparations. When the enemy boat cast its shadow on their deck, Harp and his men scurried frantically for weapons while the crew of the *Marigold* tossed gangplanks onto the *Crane's* newly polished railings.

Harp stretched his fingers out as far as he could and touched the cold metal ring that tethered the mast rope. The ring was securely fastened to the boards and was about as threatening as an old sock. But the ring told Harp his precise location on the deck. The mast was six paces away from his foot, and the steps to the cabins were eight paces from his right shoulder. . . .

"Are you looking for this?" Bootman laughed, dangling the dagger in front of Harp's nose. Not only had Bootman put him down, but the man had Harp's favorite dagger in his hand, the one with the nice vine-and-flower etching that the pretty girl in Waterdeep had given him after a couple of lost days in her—

"Your ship's a disgrace. Still, she'll be worth something in Nyanzaru."

"Keep your filthy . . ." Harp mumbled, but his lips were too squished to properly form the words.

"What's that?" Bootman asked. That the man was taking time to torment him made Harp worry that things weren't going well for his crew in general. He could hear the clash of swords and shouts all along the deck. And while Harp had faith that his crew would do their best, it had been quite a while since any of them had fought for anything more than a barstool.

"You're taking too long," Harp said, trying to enunciate. If their positions were reversed, Bootman would be in two bloody pieces and Harp would be killing the next filthy cur that had boarded his ship uninvited.

"I'm taking too long? I didn't know you were in such a hurry to die."

"It's just . . ." With his fingertips, Harp traced the edge of the planks until he found the one he wanted, two boards to the left of the ring. Contorting his body to reach the board made it feel like his neck was going to break, but as he felt the distinctive knot in the oak plank, he smiled. Or he would have if his face weren't folded in half.

"You're giving me time to . . ."

"Your pitiful crew should never have left Tethyr."

". . . find the right plank," Harp finished, slamming his fist into the deck. Because of his prone position, he missed seeing the loose board swing up and clock Bootman in the face, but he heard the satisfying thunk and felt the pressure lift off his head. Harp leaped to his feet while Bootman stumbled backward from the impact, clutching his face and—oh, even better—dropping his short sword. Harp grabbed it before the blood started gushing from Bootman's nose.

"Kill quickly," Harp said as he adjusted his neck, wincing as pain shot down his back. His head felt like it was sitting on his spine wrong. "Or you'll lose the chance."

Still holding Harp's dagger, Bootman backed away, his eyes darting around for another weapon. Harp quickly took a head count of his five-man crew. His men were all on their feet, and several of Bootman's men were dead on the boards, two of them with crossbolts in their throats. Harp saw the old warrior Cenhar swing his battle-axe and slice a man from shoulder to sternum as the man crept toward Verran. Verran, who had been pushed back against the railing, looked up at Cenhar with relief as his sword trembled in his hands.

"Stay with Cenhar," Harp called to Verran just as one of the sailors charged down the steps toward the his two men. Another of Harp's crew, Kitto, leaped down from the rigging into the man's path. Casting a quick look over his shoulder, Harp saw Kitto stab his opponent in the abdomen and vault over the man as he fell to his knees clutching his belly. Satisfied that the boy could handle himself, Harp looked for his last two crew members.

The rigging partially obscured his view of Llywellan, an older man who handled a sword adequately if not particularly well. Llywellan was more of a thinker than a fighter, but he was on his feet and forcing back a prune-faced sailor swinging a rusty blade. Harp didn't see Boult anywhere, but the dwarf would manage to take care of himself and find some way to be particularly annoying while he did it.

Harp turned back to his opponent, an unremarkable man of indeterminate age with black hair and pockmarked skin. No longer the self-assured vanquisher, Bootman looked like a run-of-the-mill fellow, someone to have a drink with in a tavern. But as Harp had learned, every man had it in him to inflict pain on the weak and, more often than not, enjoy himself in the process.

"Was there something you wanted?" Harp demanded as he backed Bootman against the wall of the cabin. "Something you felt you couldn't just ask for?"

Unable to find a better weapon, Bootman made a half-hearted swipe with the dagger. Harp knocked it out of his hand. Ramming his forearm against Bootman's throat, Harp shoved the man into the wall. Suddenly, hot anger filled Harp's chest. Why did people insist on taking things that weren't theirs as if power gave them justification to possess whatever they wanted? And why did they always do it with that smug look of triumph on their face?

"Why us?" Harp demanded. "Why go after us?"

"You're dead already," Bootman growled.

Before Harp could respond, Bootman's eyes rolled back in his head and his skin turned ashen. Startled by the rapid shift in the man's coloring, Harp jerked his arm away and took a step back. Bootman clawed at his own throat as if he were being choked. Thinking the man was faking, Harp kicked Bootman in the stomach. His body clattered against the wall like a rag doll.

"What the . . ." Harp said as the man's skin turned from gray to a sickly yellow. As his fingers went slack and the dagger fell to the deck, Bootman opened his mouth to speak. But whatever words he was about to say were lost in burbles of blood as a crossbow bolt lodged itself in Bootman's throat. The man slumped to the ground, dead.

"Boult!" Harp yelled, turning in the direction that the crossbolt had come from. He saw the dwarf perched in the rigging above his head. Harp reached down and yanked the bolt out of Bootman's neck, freeing a stream of thick blood. "Is that your bolt?"

"Who else's would it be?" the dwarf replied, sliding down a shroud line and landing in front of Harp. Boult was the leanest dwarf Harp had ever met, and the only one he had known who shaved off all his facial hair, including his eyebrows, which accentuated the webbing of lines around his wise eyes. Not a natural sailor, he was sinewy and fast, and easily the best fighter on the crew. He had the long, muscular arms and short, powerful legs of a dwarf, but because he was beardless, his own race shunned him, and many others stared at him, unable to figure out what sort of creature he was.

"Damn it all, he was about to talk."

"No, he wasn't," Boult said, loading another bolt and firing a shot into the back of the last of the boarding party from the *Marigold* who was fleeing across the gangplank. The sailor grunted as the bolt hit him between the shoulder blades, and he fell into the water with a splash. They heard thrashing for a moment, followed by nothing but water lapping against the hulls of the boats.

"Everyone all right?" Harp asked as he crouched down beside Bootman's corpse. The man's yellowy flesh hung on his frame loosely, as if it had been partially melted. Harp checked the captain's pockets, noting that the man's sweat-stained shirt had been grubby before it was bloodstained.

"Everyone who isn't him," Cenhar said, dropping his axe unceremoniously and inspecting a deep gash across his own bare chest.

"Or his crew," Boult added.

"So everyone who matters," Llewellyn said.

"What happened to him?" Harp asked.

"It must have been a spell," Cenhar said, looking down at the body with distaste. Cenhar had been with Harp since their days sailing on the *Marderward,* and the graying warrior was uninterested in anything he couldn't touch or hack in half.

"Who cast a spell?" Harp asked to no one particular. A

shadow fell across the body. Verran was standing behind him looking down at Bootman.

"Maybe there's someone still on the other ship?" Verran said.

"But why kill their own captain?" Harp asked.

"Maybe they're not a crewman? Maybe a captive did it?" Verran said, blushing.

"Whoever did it, they did us a favor," Boult said. "And they're keeping to themselves now."

"We'll search the ship," Harp said, "but not until we take care of the *Crane*. Drag the bodies to the mast. Verran, get started cleaning up some of the wreck."

Harp looked across the waves at the *Marigold*. Her dirty white sail snapped in the wind, and an empty jar rolled aimlessly up and down the boards. There was no sign of life.

He and Boult helped the rest of the crew clean up the *Crane* and search the bodies, none of which had anything more interesting than pipe weed. As they tied ballast stone onto the corpses and prepared to throw them overboard, Harp saw Boult taking a particular interest in Bootman's body.

"They were waiting for us," Harp said. "Someone told them we were coming."

"Did you just work that out?" Boult said sarcastically, lighting some of the dead captain's tobacco in his griffon-head pipe.

"Well, you can't expect me to be smarter than you," Harp said amicably.

"Yes, but I can expect you to be smarter than a loaf of bread," Boult retorted. "Why are we here, Harp?"

"In the spiritual sense?" Harp asked. "Or here in the jungle?"

"I want some answers," Boult demanded. "I know who hired us for the job."

"Of course you do. I told you," Harp replied. "Avalor."

"But do I really know why Avalor sent us to Chult?"

Boult prodded. "Or have you just shown me the tip of the arrow?"

"I told you why," Harp said evasively. "He wants us to check on the colony."

"Shouldn't the missing colonists be an official Tethyrian investigation, not some personal request from the only elf on the queen's privy council?"

"Avalor is a personal friend—"

"No, he's not," Boult said. "He's the father of a personal friend."

"Liel is *not* a personal friend," Harp said.

"Right, she's a damn sight more," Boult snapped. "It's time to confess, Harp."

Under the unwavering glare of his friend, Harp tried to sort out his jumbled thoughts. He didn't want to lie to Boult, but he had promised Avalor he would keep some things secret, at least for a while. The *Marigold* and her waiting captain only proved Avalor's fears: there were people who didn't want answers about the lost colony. An ill-considered comment could find any number of ears in a crowded tavern, no matter how dearly Harp trusted his crew. But Boult had traveled with Harp for years. After they had got out of prison, they had weathered hurricanes, gambling debts, and every manner of drunken idiots in pubs from the northern edge of Waterdeep to the southern border of Tethyr.

Still, the *Marigold's* attack had raised questions that Harp wasn't sure Boult would like the answers to.

"You know what the *Crane* means to me," Harp finally said.

"She's a fine ship, all right," Boult said. "And she's survived some seriously stupid moves on the part of her captain."

"Trust me for the moment, all right?" Harp said. "You know I would do anything for the *Crane.*"

"Give me something, and I'll let it lie," Boult said.

"So much for trust," Harp said, and he smiled faintly. "I

told you that the colonists vanished, Boult. Maybe they got eaten by beasties in the night, or maybe there's something more sinister happening in the jungle."

"Like what?" Boult demanded.

"Things that were set in motion a long time before the colonists arrived," Harp told him. "Avalor didn't give me all the details. But I trust his instincts. He isn't the kind of elf to mistake storm clouds for evil spirits. We can trust him."

"Really?" Boult said, giving the *Marigold* a significant look. "Who else knew to look for a ship in this cove?"

CHAPTER TWO

30 Hammer, Year of Splendors Burning
(1469 DR)
The Winter Palace, the Coast of Tethyr

Neither revolt nor act of state could remove Evonne Linden's portrait from the wall of the Winter Palace. Despite her husband's murder at the hands of royalists, the uprising she led in his name, or the decree that declared her to be an enemy of the Queen, Evonne continued to smile at the drafty corridor from inside a mahogany frame. Her likeness was just one among many paintings in the ancient castle that chronicled the bloodline of the royal family of Tethyr.

Painted by a master artist several years before she became notorious, the portrait showed Evonne as a shapely nineteen-year-old in a cornflower blue dress sitting on a bench, before she came into her full magical and political power. A leather-bound journal rested on her knee, and a stand of tulips bloomed riotously in the background. The artist had captured Evonne's blonde ringlets, but not her feral smile.

A black drape had hung over her portrait during the time of her uprising, but the aristocracy of Tethyr had accepted Evonne back to the Court of the Crimson Leaf with a minimal hand slapping and the loss of a single, paltry estate.

It had been a month since Declan Cardew had seen Evonne, but she was due at the Winter Palace to attend the High Festival of Winter. Cardew's agenda for the evening revolved around Evonne, the mage who had captured the imagination of the country as she led a hardscrabble array of nobles and warriors to avenge the murder of her husband.

"The queen's sister," Cardew said, fully aware that it was the last thing the dwarf wanted to talk about. "Do you know Evonne?"

The dwarf's eyes widened at the question. "What's that got to do with the missing groundskeeper?"

"What is your name, soldier?" Cardew asked, trying to keep an amicable tone as he stared down at the glowering dwarf. As a Knight-Confident in the Order of the Dark Sparrow, Cardew knew appearances were crucial. For instance, it gave him an air of gentility to act congenially toward anyone he encountered, no matter the person's station or birthplace—or how unreasonable they were being.

"Amhar, sir," the dwarf replied, his dark eyes flashing with contempt.

"And you are stationed in . . . ?" Cardew probed, taking a close look at the dwarf's regimentals in the hope that there was some irregularity that he could call out. But the dwarf's quilted acton was perfectly appropriate for guard duty within the castle grounds, his sheathed sword was belted at his hip, and the insignia of his order was displayed proudly on his shoulder. Most infantry carried an ash spear, but certain orders allowed dwarves to carry axes instead.

"In Darromar. I am a member of the Order of the Tempest Stahl. Queen Anais's Court of the Crimson Leaf," Amhar recited tonelessly.

"Really? Why aren't you with your queen?"

"She's your queen too," Amhar replied.

Cardew prided himself on his tolerance, but the dwarf was pushing him perilously close to his limit. A caravan of high-ranking dignitaries had arrived just before an abnormally thick fog had settled on the countryside. The guests had requested to see someone, and as ranking officer in the palace, Cardew was the man to talk to. Or he would be if Amhar weren't blocking his way to the guests' quarters in the Griffon Wing of the palace. It wasn't the first time he and the dwarf had crossed paths that night. But if Cardew had anything to say about it, it would be their last.

"I am well aware that Anais is ruler of the realm," Cardew said tersely. "My question is why are you separated from your regiment?"

"Didn't you hear?" Amhar asked in disbelief. "A scout arrived with the news a while back. The queen and her entourage were forced to stop in the village of Celleu due to the fog. The horses lay down on the ground and refused to continue blindly."

"If it's so bad, how did the scout make it back without peril?" Cardew said testily.

"Listen to me," the dwarf growled. "There's something wrong. There's a plot underway, and you're too stupid to see it."

As Cardew looked down at the angry dwarf, he had an unpleasant thought: if Evonne were traveling with the queen's entourage, she would be delayed as well.

"Your concern has been noted," Cardew said brusquely. He wanted to be away so he could check on the status of Evonne's arrival.

"You're risking everyone's lives," Amhar said harshly. "I told you about the groundskeeper—"

Cardew cleared his throat, interrupting Amhar and giving himself time to consider what punishment would be acceptable for a soldier who so brazenly insulted a Knight-Confident. But it would have to wait until morning. The number of soldiers at the palace was unfortunately small. If Cardew locked up the dwarf for insolence, it would mean one fewer soldier on duty. And Cardew intended to dine with the dignitaries, not spend the night on watch.

At that moment, a door behind them burst open, and three young girls barreled out the door. The blonde cousins were nearly identical except for their size and the fact that the youngest, Ysabel—Evonne's daughter—still toted a grubby poppet.

The redheaded governess followed close on their heels—the same redhead that Cardew had enjoyed in the stable loft earlier that afternoon. The flustered woman barely had time to give Cardew an appreciative glance before hurrying down the corridor after her charges.

"Girls, come here," she called, waving a pair of silk slippers while Cardew tried to recall the governess's name. Lilabeth or Lizabeth, or something else entirely. Cardew had never been good at remembering women's names.

The girls paid no attention and scampered down the hallway like spoiled little brats. Cardew had the same trouble with his own charge Teague, Evonne's only son.

Cardew turned his attention back to the dwarf, who was gripping the handle of his axe like he was about to chop down a tree. Cardew raised an eyebrow.

"If the night's festivities will continue without Queen Anais, it's safe to assume that they will continue despite the mysterious disappearance of your groundskeeper," Cardew said.

"It's not just him," Amhar said. "There's the load of wood, delivered unexpectedly. In a fog such as that outside—"

"Did you check the wood?" Cardew asked sarcastically. But Amhar took him seriously.

"Yes, I checked it. There was no writ of sale. And there's the question of the fog itself. In all my years, I've never seen anything like it."

Before Cardew could reply, a young soldier hurried around the corner. Unlike Amhar, the soldier wore the hauberk and helm of a guard on perimeter duty. The crest on his shoulder was a white and green diamond, an insignia Cardew didn't recognize. There were soldiers from too many regiments at the palace that night. It was causing havoc with the lines of authority.

"There's a disturbance on the road, a mile north from the gate," he told Cardew breathlessly. There was a wet sheen on the young man's face and hands as if he'd been outside during a heavy rain.

Cardew sighed. "What happened? Did a goat cart run off the road?"

Amhar shot Cardew an angry glance and turned to the soldier. "What kind of disturbance?"

The soldier shrugged helplessly. "The patrol sent a single scout. He caught me at the North Lion's Gate and told me to find the ranking officer. I sought you out right away."

"How many soldiers are at North Lion's?" the dwarf inquired.

"Only seven on the gate, sir. We sent a dozen to meet the Queen on the road before the fog set in. They haven't returned."

"What about the southern and eastern gates?" Cardew asked.

The soldier looked pained. "Unmanned, sir. The orders were

to secure the ballast-doors and group in the north field."

"There're only eight guards in the palace itself," the dwarf reminded Cardew. "We should cancel dinner and set a guard on the guests."

That was the worst idea Cardew had heard all night. Even if Evonne was delayed, Captain Landon Bratherwit had already arrived and was, in fact, the man who had requested to see Cardew. There were rumors that the Captain was looking to fill a post in Darromar. Cardew had never met Bratherwit face-to-face before. And face-to-face was Cardew's specialty. If he wanted to have any influence on the maneuverings between Evonne and her sister, Queen Anais, Cardew had to be awarded the Darromar post, not escorting Evonne's son to lesser nobles' estates in backwater provinces and seeing to overturned goat carts.

"It is worth checking out," Cardew said to the soldier, ignoring the dwarf's suspicious glance in his direction. "I'll bring the guests to the Grand Library. We'll keep it quiet until you get back."

The dwarf hesitated, obviously not sure what to make of Cardew's sudden change of heart, but he followed the dripping soldier out of sight. There was no way Cardew was going to cloister such important people in the library or terrify the children with such nonsense. As Cardew headed down the corridor to the Griffon Wing where Captain Bratherwit and the other guests were lodged, his mind flitted away from the annoying dwarf and back to Evonne.

In the four years her son had been his charge, she had barely cast her topaz-colored eyes in his direction. He had always believed that if he just had the chance to spend a relaxed evening in her company, she would find him as intriguing as he found her.

A month before, Cardew had chaperoned Teague to the Masque of the Siren, a costume ball for children at Queen Anais's palace. When he had brought the boy home, the doorjack told him that Evonne wanted to see him in her private study. His heart pounding, he had climbed the grand staircase and rapped lightly on the door.

"Come in," she said in her distinctively low voice. She was seated behind a desk carved from dark wood. Bookshelves filled with leather-bound tomes lined ther walls, and a fire burned brightly in the open fireplace. Cardew had never met a woman who had a study of her own, but then he'd never met a woman who'd lead a revolt against the throne either.

"Lady Linden," he said, bowing. "You requested me."

"Yes, Master Cardew," she said, gesturing to the chairs in front of the desk. The cut of her black dress was casual, but she wore blue silk gloves that covered her slim arms up to her elbows. "Please sit."

"Thank you," he said, choosing a chair covered in supple red leather directly across from her.

"You escorted Teague to the palace?" she asked. She had been writing something on a scroll, which she rolled up and placed in a drawer. Evonne had a reputation as a powerful wizard, and as a man with a martial bent, Cardew had little use for the arcane arts. But Cardew never underestimated the potential of an intelligent woman. Under the right circumstances, self-confidence could be as pleasing in a lover as innocence. "How were the festivities?"

Cardew hesitated. He felt an odd tension running between them. In the presence of another woman, he would have dismissed it as attraction and begun calculating the steps to get her into bed. But with Evonne, the standard formula was too prosaic. Besides, he wanted her to come to him.

"Enjoyable," he said carefully. "There were a few surprises, but most seemed satisfied with the affair."

She tipped her head to the side and scrutinized him openly. He could see her eyes travel over his face and down his body. It was a brazen move, and after an uncomfortable moment, Cardew found himself very much enjoying her attention.

"I've been watching you," she said with a little smile. "I believe you have a . . . good eye for detail. I was hoping you would be able to be more specific."

Cardew knew exactly what she meant. While the children stomped around the dance floor dressed like animals and mutilating the simplest dances, Cardew spent the evening analyzing every nuance of conversation and connivance of the adults in the hall. Most of the members of court thought like sheep, bestowing loyalty on whoever was popular among the rank-and-file nobles. But Cardew knew that the power struggle between Queen Anais and Evonne still simmered. And he knew which nobles were smart enough to be waiting patiently in the proverbial middle ground between the sisters to see who would ultimately prevail.

"Rase Lahame talked to Captain Yohns for quite a while on the portico," he began. "The Captain was most uncomfortable and kept checking over his shoulder." Cardew talked for a long time. When he finally finished, Evonne gave him a bright smile that made him shiver pleasantly.

"You do not disappoint, Master Cardew," she said, standing up.

"Please, call me Declan," he said.

"I look forward to another discussion sometime soon," she said. Unexpectedly, she slipped off her glove and extended her bare hand. He stepped forward and grasped it, noticing a faint network of red scars branching across the back of her hand and up her wrist. They fascinated him, but he was clever enough not to let his eyes dwell on them too long. He let himself briefly enjoy the touch of her warm fingertips, bowed formally, and hurried down the stairs. The scars stayed in his mind for days. It was the first time that something other than perfection had appealed to him.

The night's festivities at the Winter Palace would be the first time they had seen each other since that tantalizing encounter. He sincerely hoped Evonne had arrived ahead of the fog.

CHAPTER THREE

29 Kythorn, the Year of the Ageless One
(1479 DR)
The Marigold, *the Coast of Chult*

Harp crossed the gangplank alone and stood on the deck of the *Marigold*. Looking at the thick grime coating the deck, the yellow mold growing up the walls of the main cabin, and the barrels leaking white slime, the seeds between the *Crane's* planks seemed like a minor sin.

Harp looked back at the deck of his ship, at his crew busy with their chores. While Kitto secured the knots on the mast ropes, Llewellyn sewed a small tear in the bottom of a golden sail. The ship's tailor, Llewellyn was a quick-witted man in his fifties who wrote fiery philosophical treatises by candlelight and left copies at the various ports where they set anchor. Most of Llewellyn's ideas exhausted Harp, but Kitto seemed to enjoy them. He was listening intently to Llewellyn as they worked side by side, a small knowing smile on the boy's impish face.

On the other side of the deck Verran held a spare board steady while Cenhar sawed it in half. The loose plank had splintered when it smacked Bootman in the face and needed to be replaced. Without being asked, Cenhar was showing Verran how to fix it so the boy would know what was expected of him if he wanted to find a place among the close-knit crew.

Harp's family.

Perched on the top of the railing, Kitto spotted Harp and raised his hand in a silent offer of help. Harp shook his head slightly, and Kitto nodded. The boy turned and walked along the narrow railing as the rhythm of the choppy waves rocked the ship up and down. His arms hung loosely at his sides while his body effortlessly adjusted to the motion of the *Crane*. Harp had known Kitto since he was small and scrawny, indentured on the *Marderward*. Even then, the boy had had an uncanny sense of balance and coordination that amazed Harp.

Kitto had been with him the night they'd fled the *Marderward* with Liel, an elf who was being held prisoner by the brutal captain. It was Kitto and Liel who had rowed the little skiff away from the burning ship. Delirious from pain, Harp curled up on the bottom of the boat with a broken hand and a split face watching the showers of hot cinders spark across the night sky. Kitto had been with him during the halcyon months hiding on the Moonshae Isles when the three of them—Kitto, Harp, and Liel—had lived in a safe haven and formed the closest thing to a family that Harp had even known. Then he'd lost both Kitto and Liel.

It was several years before he saw Kitto again, when the boy miraculously showed up in the derelict port town where he and Boult had found lodging in the months after they were released from the Vankila Slab. The sight of Kitto's small, dirty face on his doorstep made Harp weep. Finding the boy was the first thing he'd planned to do, just as soon as he had enough coin to buy a ship. Harp never got the full story on how Kitto managed it: an eleven-year-old kid walking barefoot from Tethyr with just Harp's name scrawled on a piece of paper.

Kitto gave his last coin to the beggar on the corner who pointed him in the direction of Harp's decrepit hovel, just one of many in a street of hovels. He'd been so quiet that it had taken Harp and Boult a tenday just to get him to talk about the weather, or the gruel, or anything at all. Those were the days when a strong wind could split Harp's scars open, and he wondered if he'd ever stop feeling like a walking dead man.

At least they had a plan: to buy the *Crane*. The ship had given them a singularity of purpose, probably the last time in Harp's life that was true. Every night after smashing rocks or killing rats or whatever petty job they took instead, they counted their gold and went to sleep hungry under a roof that provided only slightly more shelter than sleeping rough under the stars. They might have lived out their days in the waterfront district, never earning enough to get out—the plight of most of the denizens that shared the refuse-slick streets with them.

But the day Harp showed up at the dingy tradeshop with his latest payment on the ship, the owner of the *Crane* met him at the door. The man must have been the last honest person at the port, because he refused Harp's coin and gave him the writ of sale, saying a mysterious benefactor had paid the debt. He wouldn't say who had done them such a favor, not even when Boult, suspicious of the good deed, returned to the shop and offered him a reward for the information.

They sailed away from the port on the *Crane* that very day, with Boult, who had never been on a ship before, heaving into a bucket. Harp leaned on the railing beside Kitto, who was actually smiling at the sight of the wretched city disappearing in the distance. The scars on Harp's arms had split that morning, and there he stood, leaking blood onto the boards. As long as he never saw the inside of another prison or had anything remind him of a copper-haired elf named Liel, maybe everything would be all right.

But it hadn't been, of course. Boult and Kitto had hauled him out of more than one cell where'd he'd been tossed after a night in the wrong pub or the wrong bed or the wrong whatever he couldn't remember. And Liel was the first thing he thought of when he woke up in the morning and, unless he was drunk enough, she was the thing he couldn't put out of his head at night.

Some days, he burned with anger at Liel for letting Kitto set out on the road by himself, although there was little she could have done to stop the boy if he had his mind set on it. But she had promised to take care of Kitto even after she married Declan Cardew. Hatred didn't come naturally to Harp. He'd give a man more chances than he deserved. But the power-hungry, ambitious Cardew had been a thorn in Harp's foot for years. No, that was too gentle a comparison for the role he'd played in Harp's life. Cardew was poison in an already mortal wound.

"What a dump!" Boult's voice came from behind him.

"Nine Hells!" Harp swore. Engrossed in thought, Harp had wandered down to the lower deck, moving aimlessly between crates and barrels as if answers would be waiting for him in plain sight. He was so distracted that he hadn't heard Boult come down the ladder into the hold. "Who knew dwarves could sneak like cats?" Harp said.

"I could've cut your throat, and you wouldn't have seen me coming," Boult said. "Lingering in the past like a pig rolling in slop. You get that look in your eye, you're thinking about a certain ambitious, underhanded elf named Liel. When are you going to start using your head?"

"I've made it forty-two years so far," Harp replied. "No use starting now."

"Did you find anything?" Boult asked, lifting the lid of one of the crates and closing it quickly when the smell of rotting meat drifted into the air. "Bitch Queen, spare us. They must have been waiting here a long time."

Grates in the low ceiling allowed light into the stuffy space, and they could hear rodents scurrying in the dark spaces along the edge of the hull. Harp brushed aside a coil of thick rope hanging from the ceiling. There was a door at the far end of the hold. Covered in gilt-leaf, the door was surprisingly ornate compared to the rest of the ship and glowed faintly in the dusty light. "That must be the captain's quarters," Harp said.

"My, the captain must have been a man of fine taste," Boult said, jabbing his finger at the gaudy decoration.

"Nothing says high class like shiny foil," Harp agreed as he gingerly pushed the door open. Glass lanterns hung from the ceiling, and their low flames cast swaying shadows in the dingy, sour-smelling room. There was a cot bolted into the floor, a large chest against one side of the room, and a table with papers and brass navigational scopes. It looked very much like Harp's quarters back on the *Crane*. Only bigger.

"Laws of pillage say she's ours now," Harp said as he moved into the room to check the maps tacked to the wall.

"We sail her to Nyanzaru and sell her, chances are we make more coin than doing the job we came to do," Boult said.

Harp looked over his shoulder at Boult. "We can finish the job and still sell her at the port. I committed to Avalor."

"And what exactly did you commit to?"

"You're not going to let it go, are you?" Harp asked. "It might not even matter."

"We're here because of Liel, and that doesn't fill me with joy and hope," Boult said.

"You're wrong about Liel," Harp told him, pulling the maps off the wall. He rolled them up neatly and laid them on the cot. In his early days of pirating, Harp learned that if you could only take one thing from an enemy vessel, you should take the maps. "And it's not like you to even think about reneging on a job."

"And it's not like you to lie," Boult said. "Especially not to me."

"Since when?" Harp asked. "Our friendship would be so much less interesting if we only told the truth. I'm pretty sure you lie to me all the time."

"Have to do something to keep you conscious."

Harp knelt down in front of the heavy wooden chest and stared at its brass lock. It didn't look too complicated—or trapped—but Kitto was the true lock expert. Harp sat back on his heels and thought about fetching Kitto, who could open the chest much quicker than he could. But Harp wanted to get off the *Marigold* and onto shore as quickly as possible.

"The captain was Alon Merritt," Boult said, reading from the log on the table. He ran his finger down the page.

"Sure," Harp replied, his full attention on the chest.

"Not much in the way of personal information about Captain Merritt, just weather records and land sightings," Boult continued. When Harp didn't respond, he glowered down at Harp who was prone on the floor with his eye looking under the chest for springs or other traps.

"Did you hear me?" Boult said.

Harp grunted as he pulled his picks out of his pocket and peered into the keyhole for a better look at the locking mechanism. But the hole was too small to see the components, so he just stuck two hook picks inside and hoped for the best.

"I bet a mage could open that," Boult said grumpily. "We need a spellcaster. I've told you that a hundred times."

"We had a spellcaster. Remember Andia?"

"Of course I remember her. And the one before that. What was her name?"

"I don't know who you're talking about," Harp told him.

"Etienne. You chased her away too."

"She left of her own accord," Harp protested.

"In tears," Boult pointed out.

"Well, love hurts."

"Only when you love a bastard."

Harp twisted the picks harder than he would have thought necessary. Kitto coaxed a lock open with feather touches while Harp always relied on brute strength. However, he heard a satisfying pop, and the box sprang open. Inside the chest was a bundle of papers sealed with red wax.

"What's on that seal?" Harp held the papers up to the light to try and decipher the waxy imprint. It was a circular mark with something lean curled around a hexagon shape that might have been a cut gemstone. But heat had smeared the wax and left it too damaged to decipher. Harp showed the seal to Boult.

"An otter?" Boult suggested. "Or a serpent?"

"Whoever Bootman got his orders from, they used the stamp to verify them." Harp broke the seal and opened the bundle, but the pages were blank.

"Enchanted," Boult said smugly, as if he had known they would be all along. "Promise me that you'll keep your hands off the next spellcaster we run across."

"I promise no such thing," Harp said automatically.

Harp ran his fingertips along the bottom of the chest, pushing gently on the seams of the planks until he felt one bend under the pressure. Using his dagger, he pried up the wood, revealing a tiny piece of rolled parchment tied with a ribbon.

"Laghessi Cove. Second Ride, Summertide. D. Cardew."

As Harp registered the name Cardew, the blood flowed to his head in a rush of anger. Of course it was Cardew who had sent the mercenaries after them. As Harp stood up and brushed off his knees, his anger turned to bitter amusement. Harp handed the parchment to Boult, who unrolled it.

With an uneasy chuckle, Harp began packing up the maps. But Boult crumbled the parchment violently in his fist and glared at Harp with a deadly look in his eyes. Harp had seen that look on Boult's face a few times, but it had never been directed at him. At people trying to kill them, yes, but never at him.

"Easy, Boult," Harp said, puzzled by the intensity and anger coming from his friend. "What's wrong?"

"What in the Nine Hells is this?" Boult said, throwing the ball of paper at Harp.

"What do you mean?"

"Those are orders from Cardew," Boult said, answering his own question.

"He must have hired Bootman and told him where to find us," Harp agreed.

"It's from Cardew," Boult repeated again.

"Yes," Harp replied slowly, resisting the urge to make a jest. Harp wasn't the best at social interactions, but even he could tell that making light of the situation might be dangerous to his health.

"When you said that Avalor wanted us to come to Chult, I assumed it was to find Liel and her husband, Cardew," Boult said with barely contained fury. "If Cardew is lost in the jungle with Liel, how is he sending mercenaries to kill us?"

"Because he isn't lost in the jungle."

"Well, where is the bastard?"

"The Hero Cardew is alive and well," Harp continued. "He showed up at the Court of the Crimson Leaf—the only survivor of an unnatural attack in Chult, at least so he says. And that's when Avalor contacted me."

"Custard-swilling, dog-kissing, demon-loving, boil-on-a-halfling's ass," Boult muttered.

"I'm going to assume that's directed at the illustrious Hero of the Realm and not me," Harp said when Boult had finished his tirade. He considered Boult. "This isn't about my . . . relationship with Cardew, is it?"

Boult snorted. "Relationship? Like you two strolled through a field of violets holding hands?"

"You know what Cardew did to me," Harp said. "And while it makes my heart feel all tingly that his name brings out such violence in you—"

"It isn't about you!"

"Gee, Boult, even with the intellectual capacity of a loaf of bread, I managed to work that out," Harp said pointedly. "Normally I'd have no interest in prying in your past. But it seems like I'm not the only one in the room keeping secrets, and at the heart of the matter is a man named Cardew. You're right. I owe you an explanation. But I think you owe me one too."

"You should be put in a catapult and launched over a cliff," Boult told him.

"It's your turn to confess, Boult," Harp said quietly.

"I hate the day you came caterwauling into the world."

"Yes, yes, you despise me," Harp said. "Now talk."

"I was happier when I thought that son of a barghest was probably dead," Boult said. He sat down on the edge of the cot and glared at the crumpled missive on the floor. "Have you ever heard of Amhar, Scourge of Tethyr?"

"Of course. Who hasn't?"

"Who hasn't?" he repeated sadly. "That's the question, isn't it?"

CHAPTER FOUR

30 Hammer, Year of Splendors Burning
(1469 DR)
The Road to Windhollow

Amhar and the soldiers left the grounds of the Winter Palace and headed north up the dirt road. Each man carried a hooded lantern to ward off the gloom. During daylight hours, the pleasant track wound through the woods until it reached the foothills and climbed into the mountains beyond Windhollow. Queen Anais would have taken that road, had she not got stuck in Celleu due to the fog.

Fog wasn't a proper name for the weather, Amhar thought. Thick, fuggy, foul—it was as if gauze had enveloped the soldiers. Amhar's breath clogged his nostrils and throat, and the fog pressed on his ears, smothering sounds. Darkness he could have handled—his eyes were made for the gloom of deep tunnels—but the fog obscured everything past the end of his axe.

He tried to recall the name of the soldier trudging up the road beside him, but he couldn't remember. Or maybe he'd never known in the first place. None of the men on the road with him were in his regiment or stationed with him in Darromar.

Thinking of Darromar—right, ordered, well-built Darromar—Amhar wished he hadn't been sent to the Winter Palace. It was an honor, to be sure, to be entrusted with the safety of the realm's finest and the children of Anais and Evonne, the Heirs of Tethyr, besides.

But that night, in the presence of the abnormal weather, fear had wormed its way into his chest.

The groundskeeper vanished looking for the cook who disappeared with dinner unfinished. And why was that load of wood delivered in this weather? And then there were the guests themselves. They had managed to arrive before the fog settled, yet they were so fatigued they'd all begged off to their rooms to rest before dinner, without the usual preening and gossiping these sorts of events were full of.

Nothing made sense.

Preferring to be angry rather than afraid, Amhar focused his mind on Cardew, the idiot who was ignoring warning signs that were as plain as the nose on his face. Fussing about his dinner with an unnatural fog rising up and swallowing servants. And the children in the palace in that buffoon's care!

If anything happened, Amhar knew he'd blame Cardew's stubborn posturing for the rest of his days.

They reached the crest of the hill where they were supposed to rendevous with the man who had sent for reinforcements. The fog pressed in on them, smothering the light of their lanterns and deadening the sounds of their footfalls.

"Where did the scout go?" the man beside him asked, shivering in his uniform.

"He may be up the next rise," Amhar said. "Too foggy to see where you're at in this."

Suddenly a noise like a door being ripped off its hinges broke through the fog and made the soldiers startle and yank out their weapons. They moved into a tight circle with their backs to each other, tensely waiting for something to materialize out of the fog. Soon, they heard skittering noises coming from beyond the light of their lanterns. Amhar felt oddly claustrophobic, as if he were in a tiny room. The skittering noises faded away, but the soldiers held their defensive position until the silence seemed secure.

"The wildlife," Amhar said, his words sounding false even to his own ears. "They're probably as disoriented as we are."

Continuing their cautious walk up the road, they came to the foot of a steep rise where the ruts from cart wheels dug deep into the road's surface. There was still no sign of the scout, but the fog was a little thinner, and they could see the diffuse light of the moon through the clouds overhead.

"Ugh," a soldier said. "How come it got muddy all of a sudden?"

Amhar tried to lift a boot and found it stuck in wet earth where just a few moments before the ground had been bone dry. A dark liquid ran down the cart ruts, soaking the dirt. Amhar lowered his lantern and saw that the wetness wasn't water at all. Blood. He raised his eyes to the dark shape of the cart looming on the crest of the hill above him.

He motioned to the men to be quiet, although their lanterns would have given them away from a distance. They moved up the side of the road. The first corpse tripped the soldier beside Amhar.

The body of a man lay half on the road and half in the watery ditch that ran along it. Below the waist his body was a meaty mess, and his unblinking eyes were open to the night sky.

"Beshaba!" the soldier cried, scrambling back from the corpse.

"Swords up!" another whispered. "We've found our trouble."

The dark shape on the crest of the hill was a cart run off the road with a dead horse still harnessed to it. Amhar thought there were three more corpses beside the cart, but as he drew closer, he saw it was just one corpse hacked into three pieces. When the dwarf turned slightly to whisper to the soldier beside him, he saw horror on the man's face.

Something moved behind them. Amhar dropped and rolled to the ditch as three dark-clothed figures darted out of the fog, holding scythes in their gloved hands. Amhar's lantern went flying into the weeds behind him.

The attackers slipped in and out of shifting cones of light as his lantern flickered out. Men shouted, and swords clashed. Amhar gripped his axe and clambered to his feet as another soldier fell backward into the ditch, a sword in his chest.

Scrambling out of the ditch, Amhar rushed the attackers, his axe raised. He swung wildly into the murky fog, but the figures were quick and dodged his blade. The blunt end of a scythe flew out of the darkness, striking him between the eyes. Reeling backward, Amhar felt himself lose consciousness.

But not before he saw the distinctive curve of a pointed ear above a dark mask covering part of a man's face, limned in the faint moonlight.

He awoke to a misty morning. Even before he opened his eyes, he remembered where he was and what had happened. Traces of fog still clung to the low-lying areas, but as the sun appeared on the horizon, strong winds off the ocean cleansed the steely sky.

Amhar pushed himself off the ground. It was not a surprise to see the bodies strewn across the track, but the level of brutality was something more than he could fathom. He tried to count bodies, to determine how many had survived, but the road was littered with so many pieces—recognizable and otherwise—that he gave up.

Amhar made a cursory search of the empty cart. If there had been a tarp, he would have covered the bodies, or as much of them as he could. Shivering with cold and shock, he stumbled down the hill to the palace, blood soaking his uniform and fear soaking his heart.

CHAPTER FIVE

29 Kythorn, the Year of the Ageless One
(1479 DR)
The Marigold, *the Coast of Chult*

You're Amhar," Harp said, for the third time.

"Will you let me finish?" Boult said. "I made my way back to theWinter Palace. A new regiment had arrived and was dragging corpses out into the courtyard. They'd been . . . it was horrible."

"How many were killed?" Harp asked.

"Six guests, thirteen soldiers, and four children," Boult recited tonelessly. "Three survivors. And me."

"You're Amhar." Harp shook his head. "How did the attackers get into the palace in the first place?"

"The Inquiry said that the oldest boy, Daviel, stole away to see a village girl. He left a door in East Lion's gate open."

"Were you at the Inquiry?" Harp asked.

"In chains," Boult said bitterly. "It was a farce, of course. Daviel's body was found in the cellar. Why would the killer bring the body back to the palace?"

"A good question." They both fell silent. The Children's Massacre still weighed heavily on the hearts of Tethyr.

"You're Amhar," Harp said after a moment. "The infamous killer of children. Honestly, I don't know how I missed it."

Boult's eyes narrowed to slits, and a dark look passed over his features.

"Oh come on! I'm not serious, Boult," Harp said. "I know you'd never kill an innocent. But, you have to admit, it's a pretty strange thing to ask me to get my head around."

Harp wasn't exaggerating. After the massacre at the Winter Palace, Amhar the dwarf became notorious throughout Tethyr and even beyond its borders. The name Amhar became synonymous with the worst sorts of crimes. Every unsolved murder in Tethyr was blamed on him and his network of underlings. Many dwarves suffered for their alleged connections to Amhar even after he was sent to the Vankila Slab.

Harp led the way through the dank hold to the square of dusty sunlight at the base of the ladder.

"If you weren't even in the palace at the time of the massacre, how exactly did you end up blamed for it?" Harp asked as they weaved around the tools and ropes hanging from the ceiling.

"Cardew," Boult said. "He blamed me, and everyone believed him."

If Amhar the dwarf had become known as the Scourge of Tethyr after the tragedy, Cardew had emerged as the Hero of the Realm, savior of Ysabel, heir to the throne. He had ascended to a place of prominence in the Court of the Crimson Leaf and was said to carry Queen Anais's personal mark of confidence.

"You must be the busiest dwarf alive," Harp said, resting

his foot on the lowest rung of the ladder and staring up at the square of blue sky above him. "You managed to sail with me on the *Crane* and direct your minions' activities from the underworld at the same time? Pillaging, spreading plague, kidnapping—how do you find the time?"

"Don't forget Ranyt," Boult said sarcastically. "Amhar contracted a demon to plague that village. Oh, and supposedly I've trained a monster to sink ships in Lantan's Rest."

"Why didn't you tell me?" Harp prodded.

"About Lantan?"

"About Amhar," Harp said.

Boult hesitated. "Because you didn't need to know. No one needed to know."

"Until now?"

"Like you pointed out, I owed you an explanation," Boult said impatiently. "Especially since Cardew is involved. Are you planning on climbing out of the hold? Or shall I carry you up the ladder on my shoulders?"

But Harp didn't move. "Why did you take the name Boult?"

Boult sighed and looked away. After a moment, he said, "He was another dwarf in Vankila. For 'treason,' when 'treason' meant interfering with some lordling's trade."

"Does he know you're borrowing his name?" Harp said.

"He's dead, idiot. I was the only one who saw the ogres kill him. When they asked, I told everyone the ogres had killed Amhar and from then on I was Boult."

"That worked?" Harp asked.

"You remember how it was. We were so filthy we might as well have been made of mud. And no one looked at anyone else's face for long. Put the two of us in a pack of dwarves and no one could have said which was which."

"Didn't you want to clear your name?"

"Didn't you?" Boult said, glowering at Harp.

"Oh, I committed my crime, and I'd do it again. You, on

the other hand, are innocent. I would think you'd want the truth to come out."

"Amhar's dead, as far as I'm concerned."

"What does your family think?'

"He's dead to them as well." Boult gestured impatiently at the ladder, and Harp climbed one rung higher but stopped again.

"It's as easy as walking!" Boult said. "One foot in front of the other and you'll be topside in no time."

"You told me you were in prison for desertion," Harp said.

"I deserted the children."

"In what way? You went out to protect—"

"I'm done talking about it," Boult interrupted. "You know as well as I do that Cardew being here is no coincidence. Everything happens for a reason."

"I don't believe that," Harp replied and started climbing again. "Everything is coincidental. We're just blind men stumbling around in the dark."

"That's the stupidest thing you've ever said, and you know it."

"You're right. We're just hunks of meat being slowly boiled to death in the stewpot of existence."

"You're not as clever as you think you are," Boult growled.

Harp grinned and turned back to Boult. "Nope, but I'm still smarter than your average foodstuff."

"Tell me. If we're not searching for Cardew, are we searching for his wife?" Boult asked.

The grin disappeared from Harp's scarred face. "Avalor would like us to bring back her body. If there's enough left to bring to back."

Boult watched his friend climb up to the daylight. No man should have to talk about the woman he loved like that.

CHAPTER SIX

*30 Hammer, Year of Splendors Burning
(1469 DR)
Winter Palace, the Coast of Tethyr*

The night's formal dinner was a yearly tradition
even though the Winter Palace wasn't the ideal
place for entertaining, or the night outside the ideal
weather to do it in. An austere stone fortification
on a cliff overlooking the ocean, the palace had
survived the harsh winters and driving storms for
generations. It was notoriously drafty with cavernous high-ceilinged rooms and strange noises that
spawned endless stories of hauntings. The cold,
foggy weather only fed those old stories.

Even though the palace was chilly and damp,
her annual visit to the Winter Palace had always
been seven-year-old Ysabel's favorite because it
was the only time her cousins were all together.
Their family's nicest residence was the Violet
Stone House outside Riatavin, and her father's

ancestral manor outside of Darromar was much warmer. But the starkness of the cliff-top palace, with its black-roofed turrets, lion-headed gargoyles, and serpentine corridors appealed to Ysabel's imagination.

She walked down one of the corridors, trying to find the room her brother Teague had disappeared into. Room after room lay empty and cold, their doors locked.

Except one. Just past a suit of old armor, the door was ajar. She pushed the door open.

A shadow lunged from the darkness. Ysabel screamed and released the heavy wooden door, which swung back on its hinges, scraping against her bare foot.

"Teague!" she yelped.

Teague grabbed her arm to steady her as she stumbled backward in surprise, trying to catch her scraped foot. "Are you all right? I didn't mean to make you hurt yourself."

When she regained her balance, she punched him as hard as she could in the shoulder.

"Ouch," he said, laughing. "You've got quite an arm for a little girl."

"You're so mean," she said sulkily, glancing at the cut on the top of her foot, which was bleeding slightly.

Teague looked down at her smugly. "You fall for that every time."

"And you never get tired of the jest," she replied, giving him a shove. "Have you seen Cousin Daviel?"

"How should I know where he is?" Teague asked.

"I saw you two in the kitchen just a little while ago," Ysabel said.

"And yet I didn't see you," Teague said. "Little sneak. Still playing elves in the woods."

When Ysabel stood on the palace's eastern balcony on the occasional clear day, she could see the green tapestry of the Wealdath, the massive forest that had once stretched much farther inland. Sometimes she and her cousins pretended to be elves by sneaking around the courtyards and making mischief on the unsuspecting groundskeepers. But they had to be careful at such games. If someone discovered them and told their mother, Evonne, her anger would be as bright and as hard as the sharp edge of a blade. She never lashed them herself. But it might be better if she did because her manservant wielded the belt with an arm made of iron. Now that their Aunt Anais had been crowned Queen of Tethyr, it was less dangerous to play at being elves. But still they never knew who might be listening.

"You have to stop following us," Teague said.

"Why?" Ysabel asked, following him into the dark room. She heard him roll back the stone cover from the hearth, and soft red light from the fireplace filled the room. "Are you plotting something?"

"Did Mother and Auntie Anais arrive yet?" Teague asked, ignoring his little sister's queries.

Since the death of their father, Garion, a few years before, Teague and Ysabel rotated from palace to palace while Evonne remained in Darromar year round. Evonne was constantly busy with political work in Anais's Court of the Crimson Leaf—so busy that her children only saw her a few days out of every month. Evonne was beautiful to look at and had a quiet lyrical voice even when she was furious. But she frightened Ysabel sometimes, especially when she talked about the degraded races—the rotten ones who should be removed from Tethyr forever.

About a year before, Teague had whispered to Ysabel that their mother might actually be crowned the Queen of Tethyr. Ysabel worried that her Auntie Anais might be unhappy because she was actually next in line for the throne, at least according to the Line of Succession, a favorite topic of her boring tutor.

Evonne had sent Teague and Ysabel to an isolated farm to live with a silent old man who never let them out of his sight, which was strange because the brother and sister were used to little or no supervision at all. The old man was called Filgarth, and he had once been a warrior, or so said the scars on his arms and face. Filgarth was toothless, which troubled Ysabel—how did he eat?—and he had no duties other than to trail them as they played in the fields or forest. Despite their ever-present chaperone, Ysabel liked the run-down farm, which was close to an oak forest and had a leaky barn that was home to a litter of stripey kittens.

After a few months, one of their mother's servants appeared on the winding dirt road that led to the out-of-the-way property. He took them back to their mother's house in Darromar, as if nothing out of the ordinary had happened. A tenday later, they attended Auntie Anais's coronation, and Ysabel and Teague returned to their normal cycle of spending a few months at each of the palaces scattered throughout the kingdom.

"There's a fog," Ysabel told Teague, crossing to the slit in the wall where she could feel a wet mist creeping around the thick stones. "Mama and Auntie had to stop the night in Celleu."

"Because of a fog?" Teague asked, coming to stand beside his sister at the window. Outside, the sun had set even though it wasn't even dinnertime. It always got dark early on wintry afternoons, but that night the air was thick and white, almost as if it was snowing heavily. But there were no flakes falling from the sky, just light drops of water that moistened Ysabel's palm as she held her hand open against the night air.

"It looks . . . odd," Teague said uneasily. Peering out into the night, his thin face looked pinched with concern. It was so unlike him to worry about anything.

"Who's the baby now?" Ysabel teased. "Come on! Let's find Cousin Daviel."

"Why are you looking for him?" Teague wanted to know. "He doesn't want to play hide-and-seek."

"Master Cardew wants to see him," Ysabel said. She didn't like Declan Cardew, the haughty solider who served as Teague's chaperone. Cardew never talked to her. He acted like she didn't even exist.

"What's wrong with Cardew?" Teague asked her as they left the sitting room and padded down the cold flagstones to the spiral staircase that led to the kitchen area in the basement of the palace.

"Nothing," Ysabel said sullenly.

"Bella . . ." Teague began as he noticed his sister's wounded foot and the little blood tracks she'd left all along the corridor behind them. "You really hurt yourself! Go get a bandage. I'll find Daviel."

Ysabel stopped as if she were considering his offer, a look of serious concentration on her little face. She knew Teague thought she was slow, but she was really just careful. And she liked to irritate him.

"All right," she finally agreed, smiling at him brightly when he crossed his arms in frustration. "But when you find him, bring him to our quarters so we can get ready for dinner together."

"Are we still having dinner, even without Mother and Auntie Anais?"

"Oh, yes," Ysabel replied as she padded down the corridor in the direction of the infirmary. "Master Cardew said we had to."

CHAPTER SEVEN

29 Kythorn, the Year of the Ageless One
(1479 DR)
Chult

Harp and his men rowed the short distance through the choppy waves to the beach. He watched Boult working the right oar and grinned broadly. He'd been traveling with the most infamous killer in Tethyrian history, and had never known it.

Cardew had framed Boult for masterminding the entire massacre at the Winter Palace, with political implications that still resounded throughout Tethyr. Knowing Boult and his character, Harp decided there was a vicious irony to the situation. Life was such a travesty. A man had to learn to laugh about it, or he'd burn down the world for what it did to people who did nothing to deserve such pain. As if Boult could read his mind, the dwarf shot him an annoyed look and shook his head in disgust.

The skiff crested a wave, and Boult glowered at Harp over the top of his oar. "You're a goat, Harp. You're the son of a goat, and your children will be little, bleating goats," Boult said crossly.

Harp laughed, ignoring the surprised look on Verran's face, who had no idea where Boult's outburst had come from.

There were five of them in the skiff. Kitto and Boult were going with him into the jungle. Harp wanted to bring Verran onshore too, just because he wanted to keep an eye on him. At seventeen, the boy was a year older than Kitto, but he still had that wide-eyed look of most youths—scared, but curious. With his round cheeks and big blue eyes, he looked as if he'd just crawled out of a schoolroom. Verran was almost a head taller than Harp, with a stockier and more muscular physique. Most men of that size dominated any situation they were in. But Verran, who was almost as big as Cenhar, never seemed to know what to do with his body or how to use his commanding presence.

Cenhar and Llywellan had been with him on the *Marderward*. Both were older and capable in a fight, but Llywellan had the edge when it came to thinking, which made him a better choice to guard the ships. Besides, Cenhar carried a greataxe, and a jungle seemed like the kind of place where they might need to chop down a tree—or something more vicious.

"Don't worry, Verran," Cenhar said. "They're always like that. It's especially bad when things get hairy. Whenever Harp starts joking, somebody's going to get hit."

"Mainly because Harp thinks he's funnier than he is," Boult said.

"Kitto thinks I'm funny," Harp protested.

"Kitto thinks we're all funny," Boult said amicably.

From his place at the back of the boat, Kitto didn't say anything, but there was a faint smile on his lips. Kitto *was* easily amused by the antics of the world. Although he was quiet, Kitto seemed to be a master at picking up subtle things that Harp usually missed. Kitto could pick a cutpurse out of a crowded bazaar before the thief even made his move.

"Should we be worried?" Verran asked, when the boat reached the shallows. "I mean, are things going to get . . . dangerous?"

"It's Chult," Boult said. "What did you expect?"

Harp and Kitto jumped out and splashed through the waves as they lugged the skiff onto the narrow beach running along the edge of the cove. Kitto crouched down and scooped up a handful of fine white sand. He let it seep through his fingers while the others pulled on their packs and canteens.

"It's too hot," Harp groused. Sweat was running down his face and stinging his eyes, and his cotton shirt was sticking to his lower back.

"It's Chult," Boult repeated testily. "What did you expect?"

From the ship, the band of green that marked the beginning of jungle looked like a seamless wall of vegetation. Harp could see that the earlier assessment wasn't far off. The edge of the jungle was an imposing barrier of thorny vines, jagged leaves, and flowers in startling shades of red and orange.

"How in the Hells do you expect us to get through that?" Boult said, peering at the tangled undergrowth in front of them.

"Avalor said there was a path to the colony," Harp told him.

"He didn't happen to know where the path began, did he? There's probably a mile of beach along that cove."

"Well, we'd better start searching."

As they walked down the beach, tiny red crabs skittered

across the sand at their approach. There were no breaks in the wall of vegetation or paths leading into the darkness of the jungle. Except for their footprints in the sand, there was no evidence that anyone had ever discovered this pristine corner of the world. But as Harp and his men searched the beach, he began to hear sounds from inside the jungle. A faint vocalization, like the cry of a wounded beast, and a rumbling growl echoed out of the jungle. Even more disturbing were the rhythmic sounds that seemed too regular to be accidental.

"Is that drumming?" Verran asked nervously. They'd all heard rumors of what dwelled in Chult, the feral monstrosities that had survived for ages hidden in the tangled undergrowth that covered most of the island: yuan-ti, carrion crawlers, purple worms, plaguechanged horrors too terrible to consider.

"The colony is just a mile inland," Harp assured him. "Once we find the path, we'll be in and out before nightfall."

The men spread out along the beach, searching for what should have been seen easily. In his experience, forests were quiet, reverent places crowned by oaks and conifers, where man or elf could walk between the trunks of trees hindered by no more than the occasional blackberry bramble. The Chultan jungle couldn't be more different than the forests of his childhood. Listening to the distant, unfamiliar sounds, Harp felt as if he was faced with a creature he'd never encountered before. It was vicious and feral with only one purpose—constant growth toward the heavens.

A few paces down the beach, Kitto stood close to the edge of the jungle. With his eyes closed, he held his hands up with palms open to the tangled vegetation.

"Is something there, Kitto?" Harp asked.

"Heat," Kitto replied.

"Heat coming off the plants?" Sure enough, waves of hot

air pulsed against Harp's sweaty face. "What do you think it is?"

"The life of the jungle," Kitto told him, as the other men joined them. They waited there for a moment, feeling the flow of warm air against their faces, listening to the call of an unknown creature, and staring at the vegetation as if an easy passage through the mass of thorns and leaves might reveal itself.

"How bad can it be?" Harp said, mostly to himself. "We'll cut through, and maybe the way will get clearer as we get to higher ground."

"There's higher ground?" Verran asked.

"It's hard to see from here, but there are mountains inland," Boult said. "If we'd sailed from the north instead of the east, you would have been able to see the lay of the land."

Boult pulled out his short sword, and the other men followed his example. But it was Harp who took the first swing at the vines, quickly hacking a man-sized hole and stepping into the humid darkness. The foliage was thick above his head, blocking out most of the sunshine, with just the occasional patch of sky showing through the leaves.

"Stay close," Harp said over his shoulder.

The dull whack of his blade against the woody stalks and the rustle of leaves made talking to the other men difficult. The vines seemed to twist out of the way of his blade and regroup after each stroke. The farther Harp moved into the thicket, the slower he moved. The branches scratched his face, and he stumbled on the uneven ground. He couldn't help but think of Liel and wondered how anyone could make a home in a place as inhospitable as the jungles of Chult.

Harp remembered Liel standing in a grove of ash trees on Gwynneth Isle, shortly after they'd escaped the

Marderward. Although Liel had healed his injuries and fever, Harp had still been weak, and the short walk to the grove had sapped most of his newfound energy. Leaning against a tree to catch his breath, he'd watched Liel turn in slow circles staring up at the leaves, while the shifting pattern of light and shadow played across her face. She'd turned to smile at him. Her green eyes seemed to glow in the gathering twilight, and there was a pink tinge on her cheeks.

"The forest makes me powerful," she said.

There was no arrogance or pride in her words, and for an instant he envied her. Liel could convert the very structures of nature into magic, while he was bound by his mortality, his commonplace mind, and his workman's hands. But his envy vanished, and he felt awe that the beautiful creature could have cast her eyes on him and liked what she saw. The memory of Liel gave him hope that she might have survived her time in Chult. Who knew how the wildness of the jungle would affect Liel? It might keep her safe and cast her mind places he couldn't imagine.

"There has to be an opening soon," Harp said over his shoulder as he hacked through a snarl of sticky vines that reminded him of spiderwebs. "It can't be so thick all the way to the colony."

When Boult didn't answer, he turned around, but the rest of his crew was nowhere to be seen. He couldn't see the beach, and the passageway that he'd cut through the underbrush seemed to have reverted to its original state. Surrounded by a tangle of plants, Harp suddenly felt disoriented. He tried to listen for the ocean, but he couldn't hear the crashing of the waves through the dense plants. Harp resumed his hacking, moving slowly back to the beach—he hoped—but without making much progress. If his boyhood forest was a cathedral, the Chultan forest was a demon's playground.

The air around him was hot and close, and he felt dizzy as if he had been working without water in the hot sun for hours. He realized he had no sense of how long he'd been alone in the thicket. The sunlight world of sand and crashing waves was long gone as Harp struggled against the stranglehold of plants.

"Boult!" he shouted, surprised at how little his voice carried. He might have been yelling from inside a closet for all the sound he made. "Kitto!"

He attacked the vines with renewed vigor. They'd all left the beach at the same time. Surely they couldn't have gotten too far apart, not when they were all fighting through the same twisted undergrowth. Harp saw a beam of light flash across the ground. Bending down, he saw an opening at knee height. He sheathed his sword and scrambled on his hands and knees into a low, narrow passage through the thicket.

As he crawled along the ground, he felt his hands squish into something soft. The ground beneath his fingers was slick with white fungal growth. He crawled faster, sinking deeper into the thick mat of mold, the putrid smell of decay making him gag. A netting of black moss hung from the branches above him, tangling around his face and neck. Harp felt panic rising in his chest. It would be a miserable place to die.

Up ahead, he saw a clearing in the thicket. He lunged forward and tumbled into the open, pausing to wipe the slime from his hands on the leaves on the ground.

"Harp!" Cenhar called with relief. The old warrior stood at the edge of the clearing, his axe raised high above his shoulder. His long, gray hair was matted with leaves. Cenhar's massive biceps twitched as he gripped the handle tightly, and his eyes darted wildly as he scanned the undergrowth with unnerving concentration.

"What's wrong?" Harp asked. Usually Cenhar was as

steady as a boulder, but Harp wouldn't be surprised if the jungle had spooked even the veteran warrior.

"I heard something," Cenhar said.

"Animal?" Harp noticed that his sword's sheath was coated in white slime. Crouching down to wipe it off, Harp sensed movement behind him. He spun around, but nothing was there.

"Did you see that?" he asked.

"No, but I hear something over there," Cenhar said. He used the edge of his axe's blade to part the leaves and peer into the bushes.

"Let's get back," Harp said. "We need to find the others and regroup on the beach."

"Yeah—" Cenhar began. Something long and narrow snapped out of the undergrowth, cracked through the air, and retreated into the thicket with a hissing sound. Cenhar sidestepped out of the way and moved to join Harp in the center of the clearing.

"What in the Hells was that?" Cenhar said. "A whip?"

"I think it was a vine," Harp replied. The leaves on the ground began rustling as if a multitude of snakes were slithering toward their feet.

"Since when do vines move?" Cenhar shouted as the two men leaped away from the mysterious onslaught. A mass of dark green tendrils rose out of the loam. They undulated back and forth rhythmically before lashing simultaneously across the clearing. Harp and Cenhar scrambled away as the vines snapped against the ground.

"Welcome to the jungle," Harp said, pulling a flask with a cloudy orange liquid off his belt and flinging it at the vines. The bottle smashed, splattering the tendrils with acid, and making them drop to the ground and retreat out of sight under the fallen leaves. Cenhar and Harp moved to run, but the vines snapped into the air again. Cenhar dropped to the ground, yanking Harp down as the vines lashed over their heads. They clambered to their feet and plunged into the underbrush. Beside him, Cenhar gasped in pain. But when Harp paused to see what had happened, Cenhar shoved him to keep moving.

"Kitto!" Harp yelled. "Boult, you bastard! Answer!"

He heard Boult shouting at him, but the dwarf's voice sounded muffled and distant. Harp's skin itched. He looked down and saw small dark shapes swarming over his hands and legs. He yelped and tried to brush them off, but the swarm clung. He and Cenhar blundered in the general direction of Boult's voice. They stumbled out of the vegetation and onto the beach, as thousands of tiny insects swarmed over their clothes.

Wincing in pain, Cenhar stumbled and nearly fell, but Harp half-carried him down to the ocean waves where they frantically scrubbed off the creatures, some of which were already burrowing into their skin. Harp yanked off his shirt and scrubbed his face and the back of his neck. As they cleaned off the last of the insects, Cenhar groaned in pain. Harp helped him back ashore, and the old man collapsed on the beach.

"What happened?" Boult asked as he loosened the shoulder straps on Cenhar's leather chestplate. The warrior took ragged breaths between his gritted teeth. A green vine had wound tightly around his upper arm; hooked burrs curled deep into the inflamed tissue.

"It jumped on him," Harp said.

"The vine jumped on him?" Boult repeated, "I don't like that sound of that."

"How long were we in there?" Harp asked.

"Not very long," Boult replied. "But we all came out onto the beach in different places."

Harp pulled his dagger out of his boot and began to slice through the vine, sparking cries of pain from Cenhar.

"Damn," Harp said, sheathing his dagger. "We have to

get him back to the ship. Help me lift him."

But when they tried to pick Cenhar up, his body went rigid, and he seemed to stop breathing.

"Poison?" Boult asked.

"His lips are blue," Harp said. "We have to move."

Verran laid his hand on Harp's shoulder. "Let me try," he said, but he looked terrified.

"Try what?" Harp asked suspiciously. But he moved away so Verran could kneel beside Cenhar.

Verran held his hands over Cenhar's chest and began to chant under his breath. As his trembling fingers moved through the air, the barbed plant began to twist and writhe around Cenhar's arm. The warrior cried out, and Harp moved to stop Verran, but Boult stayed Harp with a hand on his shoulder. The dwarf pointed to the vine, which began smoking as if it were burning from the inside out. With a hissing sound, it blackened and dropped to the sand. Small puncture wounds remained in Cenhar's arm, but the redness vanished, and Cenhar flexed his huge gnarled hand with a look of relief.

Boult helped Cenhar sit up, and both of them stared at Verran, who looked like he wanted to crawl into a hole and hide.

"Stop looking at me like that," he said defensively. "I saved you."

"Uh, thanks." Cenhar swayed on his feet, and Harp thought the behemoth of a man was going to faint back onto the sand.

"We didn't know you were a sorcerer," Boult said to Verran.

"I'm not. I got rid of the vines, that's it." Verran jutted out his chin defiantly.

"You used magic!" Boult said.

"You should have told us," Harp said.

"I'm not . . . It doesn't matter," Verran said shakily.

"Magic always matters," Boult insisted.

"It's complicated," Verran said, kicking at the sand beneath his boots. "And private."

"If you want to be on the crew, you have to be honest with us," Boult continued angrily.

"Really?" Verran said. "Does that just apply to me? The captain can keep whatever secrets he wants?"

"What do you mean?" Harp asked.

"You have a massive secret. Not even a secret. It's all over you."

"What do you want to know, Verran?" Harp asked quietly.

"How'd you get the scars?" Verran demanded.

When he saw how the other men reacted to the question, Verran lost his adolescent bravado. "They're all over your body. I even saw them on your feet. You get those kind of scars from a demon pact."

"There are ways to get scars like mine," Harp said quietly, "that make a demon pact look like a stroll down the dock. I'm no warlock."

"What then?

"It's a long story I promise to tell you another time," Harp said, "but now. . . ." Harp stood up and brushed the sand off his knees. He caught Verran's eye and held it. "Where did you learn about demon pacts, Verran?"

Verran looked away from Harp and rubbed his eyes with his fists. "I don't know anything," he insisted. Harp could tell he was lying—and doing it badly.

"I'm not angry," Harp said. "Whatever your story is, you've clearly got skills we need. Besides, you wouldn't believe what Boult told me earlier."

Boult coughed, and Harp continued, "Men are entitled to their secrets, sure. But when it affects the safety of your crew, it's time to put it in the open."

"My father . . . was a warlock," Verran said and stopped.

Harp noticed the tears forming in the boy's eyes and decided the topic should be discussed with fewer people around.

"Good enough," Harp said, raising his hand. He turned to talk to Cenhar. "How are you feeling?"

"Like I been dragged through all Nine Hells . . . No offense to you, Verran," Cenhar said.

"Can you row the skiff back to the ship?" Harp asked.

"I don't need to go back."

"You're ill," Harp said firmly.

"My arm's all right," Cenhar said. He waggled his fingers as if to prove that everything worked. "But I don't want to—"

"Sleep on the ship," Harp insisted. "Tell Llywellan what happened. He'll keep an eye on you."

"What if you have trouble?"

"We're going to find the colony. We'll come back to the ship and figure out our strategy together. No time for trouble."

For a moment, Cenhar looked like he wanted to argue. Changing his mind he said, "Aye, captain."

"Kitto, Boult, help him get the boat on the water."

When the three men had moved away, Harp turned back to Verran.

"Your father was a warlock?" Harp prompted.

"Not at first. I loved my father, but he was . . . easy to persuade. He began studying with a man who had traveled everywhere searching for lost magics and artifacts. My father idolized him."

"A sorcerer?" Harp asked.

Verran gave a non-commital shrug. "He was very charismatic, and his followers were utterly devoted to him. I'd never met someone who was so . . . strong-willed. Just a few words could convince you of things that, as I look back on it, made no sense."

"You knew the man?"

Verran wiped his sleeve across his eyes. "Yes. My father used to take me to their gatherings, in the guts of a derelict building. I was always the youngest one there." He looked up at Harp. "They said it made me special."

"You were a child, Verran," Harp assured him. "You couldn't have known any better."

"Some things are horrible no matter how old you are."

Harp took a deep breath. He and Verran had more in common than the boy thought.

"The man offered my father a deal," Verran said.

"It's one of the oldest stories," Harp said grimly. "Men sell their freedom for power."

"And it worked," Verran said bitterly. "My father became very powerful. But he also changed. He'd been so happy, so cheerful, and suddenly it was like something black replaced his heart."

"Spending too much time around death will do that to a man," Harp agreed.

Verran shook his head. "It was more than that. I saw scars on his hands one night. Scars just like you have, only they were fresh," Verran continued. "My father was so proud of them. Whatever he'd done had been a major accomplishment. Mama got so angry. I'd never seen her like that. She saw marks on his back. There were five of them, all in a row. Like . . . silhouettes of a shape that's just a little too far away to recognize. The night when he got those scars, one of the . . . silhouettes . . . took a new shape. It was finished."

"I don't understand, Verran," Harp said patiently. He knew the boy was trying his best to explain, but finding the right words to describe something evil was hard. Harp knew that as well as anyone.

"It was the pact. My father was given power. And he was expected to do certain tasks, part of a larger plan that none of us understood."

"And one of those debts was paid that night?" Harp pressed.

"Yes. My mother was clever. Once she saw the mark on his back, she knew what he had done. She took me away from him."

"Where did you go?"

"A relation's farm in Cormyr. Mama and I were both relieved to be away from him. We missed who he had been, but we were happy there," Verran paused. "He found us a year later, after he'd had a change of heart. I'm amazed he found the strength to get away from them. But he couldn't escape the demon at that point, just fight it. He was a broken man. He'd sit in the fields for hours staring at the sky.

"I was in the village when . . . something came to the house and killed him and Mama. Our neighbor found me and told me what happened. They smuggled me out of the province that very day. There's no reason for it to be looking for me, but still I wonder. It's why I joined the *Crane*."

Harp laid his hand on Verran's shoulder. "None of us have an empty road behind us."

"No, I guess not," Verran said, but he sounded unconvinced. He turned sharply as Boult and Kitto walked up to them. Behind them, Harp could see Cenhar rowing the skiff across the waves to the *Crane*.

"Did you do the spell on the ship?" Boult asked abruptly. "The one that melted the captain?"

Verran looked at his fingers. "I'm not sure."

"How could you not know?" Boult demanded.

"It seems too powerful for me. Once we left home, my mother wouldn't let me try spells anymore. She was too scared."

"And do you try spells now?" Harp inquired.

"Sometimes," Verran admitted. "And sometimes things just happen."

"Has anyone ever gotten hurt?" Harp asked.

"You mean besides the dead captain?" Boult reminded him.

"I've never hurt anyone . . . who didn't deserve it," Verran finished slowly.

"That's comforting," Boult said sarcastically.

"It's been useful to us so far," Harp pointed out. "Verran, I don't supposed you have another useful spell that can locate the path?"

Verran looked sheepish. "It's over there."

"Did you just figure that out?" Harp asked.

"Um, a little while back. Before Cenhar was attacked. I was on that side of the trees when you shouted," Verran replied. "And there's something else."

"I hope it's a welcoming party," Boult said.

"No. I think there's a body on the other side of the trees."

A mesh of woven branches hid the path. Without Verran's luck, there was little chance they would have discovered it. And without the path, there was little chance they would have made it very far through the twisted undergrowth, fungus slicks, and flesh-eating vines.

"You think it was Bootman's crew who covered the path?" Harp asked Boult as they made their way down the narrow channel through the dense vegetation. It was more like a tunnel than a path, with leaves and branches intertwining over their heads. Without regular travel across the ground, the jungle would soon retake the unnatural highway that allowed intruders to enter its confines.

"Doubtful," Boult said. "That wasn't done yesterday. There was new growth mixed in with the cover. Plus, someone shaped the vines. I don't think they formed that latticework naturally."

Boult glanced at Harp out of the corner of his eye. Kitto and Verran were ahead of them on the path, and Boult wanted to know what Verran had told Harp. Boult had been suspicious of Verran from the moment they met him in a waterfront village south of the Amn border. A cold, stinging rain had fallen in sheets, soaking the shivering boy. At first glance, it was obvious the boy was unprepared for whatever he was dealing with. Boult barely gave him a second thought, but Harp had stopped and struck up a conversation.

Harp had bought the boy a hot meal in a nearby inn, and before Boult could kick his captain under the table, Harp had hired the strapping lad to help on the *Crane*. Despite the fact that he said he didn't know how to sail. Or use a sword. Or work a trade. Boult didn't have much use for such helplessness. But Harp was drawn to a needy person like a moth to a flame.

"You'd hire a plague rat to sail our ship," Boult grumbled as he stomped through the jungle. He glared up at Harp, hoping to get a rise out of him.

"Huh?" Harp asked.

"A plague rat," Boult repeated impatiently. "And you wouldn't be able to see his dagger at your throat."

Harp looked at Boult like he'd lost his senses. "Since when do rats have daggers? What are you babbling about?"

"I'm talking about Verran," Boult said.

Harp's brow furrowed. "He's had a hard time of it, Boult. Give him a chance."

"He's a wild shot," Boult said with annoyance. He should have known that Harp was going to defend him.

"Sometimes wild shots hit their mark," Harp said. "He took out Bootman. That was helpful."

"He could have just as easily taken you out," Boult said. "That doesn't make you a little nervous?"

"He could have. He didn't," Harp said. "And if we find Liel's body, I'll be grateful to him."

"How can you say that?"

"Because I'd know for sure," Harp said. "I'd know that she was gone."

Boult sucked in a mouthful of air, mainly to keep himself from saying what he wanted to. Harp's pining for Liel had gotten old years before, and he hoped the trip into Chult would end it, in whatever way necessary.

"Do you actually think we're just going to stumble on Liel's body as soon as we walk into the huge, highly dangerous jungle? Do you know how many people die in the jungle every day?"

Harp rolled his eyes. "No, and neither do you."

"It has to be a lot. Do you know how many ways there are to die in the jungle? Animals, disease, cannibals . . . Did I mention they have a disease down here that turns your tongue into an actual slug. In your mouth. Did you hear me? A slug."

"Ugh," Harp shuddered. "Tell me why I took the job again?"

"Cause you're a drunk who can barely keep his ship."

"Again. Not helping."

"And I'm not trying to. You were a good sailor once," Boult said.

"I was good," Harp said. "That's why you made me captain."

Boult snorted. "We made you captain because no one follows a dwarf who gets seasick."

"Particularly not one as charming as you."

"There's another way," Boult said, after a moment. "We could signal the crew and sail the ships to port."

"No. I told you already. We have a job to do."

"We're not prepared for the jungle," Boult said quietly. "And selling the *Marigold* will equal the rest of Avalor's payment."

"I'm going to the colony."

"There's a good chance that Liel is dead, Harp. What do

you want to find? Her decomposing body? Bring it home to her father in a box?"

"Cardew survived somehow," Harp pointed out. "And I'll wager Liel is mountains stronger than her pitiful excuse for a husband."

"Unless he killed her. That's what Avalor thinks happened, isn't it?"

Harp hesitated. "He wants proof. And when I find it, it will give me every justification to cut Cardew's throat."

"Vankila's not enough?" When Harp didn't respond, Boult continued. "Why would Cardew bring Liel all the way down here to kill her?" Boult said. "Why not just kill her in Tethyr? Or just have her kidnapped. Again."

"Too much protection? Avalor is well connected. And it's more than that, anyway. Avalor thinks Cardew has his heart set on something else."

Boult stopped in his tracks. "Avalor thinks so? So what does that sniveling blot of a man have his sights set on?"

"Not much," Harp said pushing a large fern frond out of his way. "Just the kingdom of Tethyr in the palm of his hand."

It had been Boult who insisted that Harp answer Avalor's summons in the first place. Harp and Avalor had never met in person, but the powerful elf had summoned him, and him alone, for a reason. If Avalor offered them a paying job, they would have to take it. Otherwise they were going to lose the *Crane*. If Harp was being summoned for another reason, he would just have to deal with whatever news Avalor had for him.

"And about time you started dealing with things too," Boult often said to him. "Kitto looks up to you. And there isn't much to look up to. Not anymore."

So Harp hauled himself to the designated meeting place, a pub called the Broken Axe. Although Harp had walked past the shabby building many times, the sign above the front door showed only a war axe cleft in two pieces; there was nothing to show that it was an alehouse.

Harp had a few pints while waiting for Avalor to arrive—just enough to get almost drunk, but sober enough to have a conversation and keep up appearances. It was the best he could possibly expect from himself, given the nature of the situation.

"Don't drink anything," Boult had told Harp before he left. "You want to keep your wits about you."

Then Avalor should have picked an establishment that served tea and sweet cake, Harp thought, taking another drink from his pint and staring out through the dirt-smeared window at the crowded market street. It was late afternoon before some festival to some druid or cleric. Harp couldn't care less, but it looked as if every wife and daughter from the quarter had turned out to buy a chicken.

"Must be the festival of the chicken," Harp muttered, earning dark looks from the two scabby men at the table next to his. The pub was only half full, and the two goons had been paying too much attention to him. Harp sighed. If years of hard living hadn't been enough to dull his senses, he wasn't sure what would.

"You blokes need something?" he asked in as amicable a tone as he could muster.

The bigger man grunted. "You look familiar."

That was nothing new to Harp. Whenever he went into a town, a certain element noticed him. Or rather they noticed the spider-web scarring across his face and hands. The scars had faded since the Vankila Slab, but the white lines were still noticeable, particularly if his skin was tanned from days at sea on the *Crane*. If someone recognized the distinctive scarring, it meant they were familiar with a particular kind of necromancy. As soon as recognition clouded their eyes, Harp hated them for it.

"I don't think so." Harp said evenly. It usually played out in one of two ways: The idiot got the hint and shut up, or he insisted on continuing the line of inquiry, in which case Harp usually had to punch something, which wasn't a good idea. It wasn't a good idea because Avalor was due to arrive at any moment. It particularly wasn't a good idea because Boult wasn't there to back him up. In all the brawls inspired by Harp's scars, Boult had always been there to back him up.

The men exchanged glances. "You sailed on the *Marderward*."

That was not what Harp was expecting. Since they had made no assumptions about his scars, he wasn't sure what to say to them. But just the mention of the *Marderward* made him want to get blinding drunk.

One of the men raised his glass. "To Captain Predeau." And his comrade raised his glass too.

Harp took a big drink. "May the scars of his victims never heal."

"Hear! Hear!" the men said appreciatively.

Harp took another drink. "May his enemies tremble at the sound of his name."

"Hear! Hear!"

Harp drained the last of his ale. "May the cries of the children he orphaned never be silenced!"

The big man set down his glass. "Something tells me you're not speaking well of the dead."

"Hard to do when the dead ain't well," Harp said as he stood up abruptly and shoved back the table.

The men were on their feet at the same time, fists raised and fury in their eyes. The well-dressed gnome who had been drying glasses behind the bar appeared out of nowhere and thrust himself between Harp and the other men.

"You have a visitor," the gnome said firmly to Harp. "Through there," he added, pointing to a door behind the bar. "And if you gentlemen will take your seats, I'll refill your pints on the house."

Harp bent over to pick up his pack, happy that the world wasn't spinning as he made his way across the floor. Since he'd got out of prison, he'd spent way too much time in places like the Broken Axe, throwing words around with men like that.

The back room was a dimly lit storage room, packed with jars of pickled food and barrels of ale. A light was coming from under the door on the other side of the room. Harp opened it, half expecting to see the alley. But the dirty cobblestone streets and shabby storefronts were nowhere to be seen. Instead, Harp was standing in the middle of an old-growth forest. He was surrounded by black-barked trees with strands of long red leaves that whispered in the wind. There was the distinctive slant of the shadows and the buttery light he remembered from the harvest season of his childhood. Harp heard a rustle in the underbrush and spun around. On the other side of the clearing was a great tawny stag with reddish horns branching from its head. It paused when it saw Harp, and leaped into the undergrowth.

Enjoying the quiet noises of small animals hidden in the underbrush, Harp followed the stag and saw a narrow path winding through the trees. He tried to remember the last time he enjoyed the quiet of a forest, but it had been years, before he was imprisoned in the Vankila Slab. He had spent too much of his adulthood in the city.

The path rounded a bend, and in the clearing in front of him, he saw an auburn-haired, copper-skinned elf alone at a mahogany table that was simple in design but polished to a glossy shine. Dressed in unadorned gray robes, the elf's hands were folded on the table, and his eyes were closed as if he were meditating. A roughly hewn staff rested against the table beside him.

It was Avalor, Treespeaker of the Wealdath Forest and member of Queen Anais's privy council. And father of Liel, Harp thought, again wishing he were drunker than he was. Avalor didn't move or give any sign that he recognized Harp's presence. In fact, he seemed to be in some kind of a trance. From his reputation, Harp knew Avalor was an older elf, although his unlined face and lean body betrayed no signs of aging.

When Harp reached the table, Avalor opened his eyes, rose to his feet, and extended his arm. Harp shook his hand, and the elf looked into his face and smiled gently. Staring into Avalor's bright green eyes, which were very much like Liel's eyes, Harp relaxed. The knot of tension in his belly faded away.

"Please sit, Master Levesque," Avalor said, nodding to a chair.

"Harp," Harp told him. He'd not used his surname for a long time.

"Thank you for coming," Avalor said. "I have wanted to meet you for a while."

"Is this . . . Are we in the Feywild?" Harp asked, taking a deep breath. The air smelled of honeysuckle and freshly turned earth.

"No, no," Avalor said. "It's just an illusion. We are actually in the barkeep's rather unremarkable garden. Much less pleasant. But we are alone, and the high walls keep away prying eyes. So you may speak freely. I thought we would be more comfortable. I have a keen dislike for the city."

"It's remarkable." Harp shook his head in wonder. "I could swear I'd walked into the heart of a forest." He looked back at Avalor. "I appreciate it. I, too, have a keen dislike for cities."

"And yet you frequent them as if you can't help yourself," Avalor pointed out.

"I never got a chance to thank you for getting me out of Vankila," Harp told him.

"And I never got a chance to thank you for saving my daughter," Avalor replied.

"I didn't save Liel."

"I think you did."

They sat quietly for a moment, and Harp could feel the elf's eyes inspecting the lines of scars crisscrossing his hands.

"I'm regretful that I couldn't get you out of Vankila before—"

"I'm grateful for what you did," Harp broke in. He didn't want to talk about his scars with Avalor. Someone powerful enough to create such an illusion in the barkeep's garden was sure to see through his nonchalance. Harp still had nightmares that one day the scars would unbind themselves and his body would fall apart into pieces on the ground. He had no interest in discussing his past with such a living legend.

"I was surprised to receive your summons," Harp continued.

"Yes, it is a matter of some delicacy," the elf began.

Harp snorted. "Are you sure I'm the one you want? Delicacy isn't my strength."

Avalor studied him. "I believe I can trust you in the matter. Let me begin by saying that we will pay you two thousand gold. Half of it on acceptance of the job, and the rest when you return with the information I need."

Harp frowned. "That's a lot of coin. You already had my attention."

"Yes, but I need your secrecy. You're a man of strong loyalties. The general nature of the task may be shared with your crew. But I'll ask you to keep the specifics to yourself, at least in the early stages of the venture."

"You want me to keep information from my crew?" Harp asked.

"At first. At least until you're away from our shores. If you don't feel like you can do that, we can end our conversation right now."

"It's not my way to keep secrets from my men," Harp said slowly. He knew that the coin from the advance itself would let them pay their debts and keep the ship. And without the ship, there wouldn't be any crew anyway.

"I know," Avalor said sympathetically. "But I need to make certain this information does not find the wrong ears."

"All right. But if there comes a time that I have to tell them for their safety, I will."

"Agreed."

"So what's the job?"

"Liel was murdered. I want you to find evidence of the crime and . . . bring her home."

Avalor's words hit Harp like a fist to his throat. He found himself coughing uncontrollably, as if he had swallowed water wrong. When he finally got control of himself, he looked at Avalor, whose angular face betrayed a hint of anger and sadness.

"I'm sorry to be so blunt. There's no way to soften a truth this hard."

Harp nodded, still trying to master his shock at the news that Liel was dead.

"I apologize if I upset you. I don't know the extent of your relationship—"

"I haven't seen her in years," Harp interrupted.

"But I know she cared for you deeply and had many regrets after you went to prison. It was at her request that I sought you out in the Vankila Slab. I would have on my own accord, had I known the situation. But, of course, I did not. Until she told me."

"Why me?" Harp managed to say. "Why of all people do you want me to look for her?"

"Isn't that is obvious?" Avalor said. "You of all people will take the matter to heart."

"Who do you think murdered her?"

Avalor reached for the nearby staff, his hands gripping the wood until his knuckles were white. "Do you even have to ask?"

"Why would Cardew want his own wife dead?"

"He's quite involved in the Branch of Linden. They're backing him for a powerful position on the Privy Council, but having an elvish wife is an embarrassment."

"How could you let her marry him?"

Avalor laughed. "Let? She knew I didn't want her to marry him. But she thought their marriage would help the tensions between elves and humans in Tethyr."

"She did?" Harp asked. Liel never told him that.

"I told her it wouldn't make any difference, that she shouldn't sacrifice her happiness for such an unlikely possibility. It became such a raw issue between us, that we stopped talking about Cardew."

"Still, why kill her? There are other ways to end a marriage," Harp pointed out.

"Not if you want to marry a queen."

"Cardew wants to marry Queen Anais?" Harp said doubtfully. The queen already had a consort, who was rumored to be perfectly weak-willed and unambitious enough for her tastes.

"Her niece, Harp. He wants to marry Princess Ysabel."

Maybe if Harp had been sober, the wheels of his mind would have spun a little faster. As it was, he didn't comprehend what Avalor was implying.

"Ysabel is just a girl . . ."

"Impressionable and easily manipulated."

"What about the queen we already have?"

"As you may or may not know, there have been plots to remove her since The Children's Massacre. With coordination and cleverness on the part of her masters, Ysabel could become queen of the realm."

"Which would mean that Cardew . . ."

"Would be royal consort and have the ear of the queen."

At that thought, Harp automatically reached for a drink that wasn't there. "What do you have in mind?"

CHAPTER EIGHT

29 Kythorn, the Year of the Ageless One
(1479 DR)
Chult

We have to stop him," Boult said when Harp had finished. "I knew Ysabel. She was a sweet child. She used to follow us around the castle yards, pretending she was an elf. Just a tiny little thing with a huge gap-toothed smile."

"She's not a child anymore," Harp said.

"Her brother and mother were murdered on the same night. Granted, her mother was as bad as the daughter of Asmodeus himself."

"So you're with me?" Harp said. "We'll do it for Princess Ysabel?"

Boult shot him a look. "We'll do it for what Cardew did to you."

Despite himself, Harp winced. "And to you."

After a quarter hour of walking along the path through the thicket, the ground opened up, and they found themselves in a stand of towering trees. The ground was nearly devoid of plants between the massive buttress roots, and sunlight filtered down in streams through the ceiling of leaves above them. There was an unnatural silence in the grove, as if the wildlife saw them approach and found places to hide.

"The thickets must have been the outer band of the jungle," Harp said looking up at the towering treetops hundreds of feet above them. "Have you ever seen trees that tall?"

"Captain?" Verran asked, walking up behind him. "The body's over there."

"Could it be an animal carcass?"

"Possibly," Verran said, but he didn't sound very convinced. "I didn't look too closely."

"Everyone have a look around," Harp said. "Keep an eye out for more . . . plant monsters."

Verran led him to a spot beside a buttress root. When Harp reached it, he could see that the root was partially hollow and someone was tucked inside.

"Can you get Boult?" Harp asked Verran. The boy nodded and headed across the grove.

When Harp bent down, he could see that something had been gnawing on the body and most of the face was gone. And there was something odd about the remains. It was as if sections of the corpse had disintegrated down to the bones while other parts were untouched by decay. A netting of skin bound the corpse into human form, and as soon as those skin-strands broke, the body would fall into an unrecognizable heap. Harp had seen many bodies in various states of decay and dismemberment, but nothing quite as disconcerting as the one before him.

He could see strands of reddish hair tucked under a green hood and a gold necklace hanging around the neck. He heard Boult come up behind him and pulled back so the dwarf could see inside the hollow.

"Let me," Boult said gruffly. Harp wandered a few steps away and stared up at the towering trees as the light glittered through the spaces between the rustling leaves. He could feel every muscle in his chest as he took each breath. He'd wondered about Liel so often in the past ten years that it seemed impossible that the Chultan jungle would be the place he found her, curled up in a hollow like a frightened animal.

Suddenly he didn't know if he could take it. He wasn't a sentimental man. Those who were close to him called him cold. And he wouldn't have admitted it to another soul, not to Boult or Kitto, who were the only family he had. But the first time he Liel on the deck of the *Marderward* was frozen in his memory like a painter's still-life. If it was possible to love someone from the first moment you saw them, Harp had loved Liel starting then.

Harp had been twenty-nine years old when he first set foot on the *Marderward*, a three-mast ship with a glossy black hull edged with gold. The carving of a raven-haired maiden graced her prow, her painted arm outstretched as if she were leading them across the treacherous seas. The ship's decks shone, and her sails were as white as snow. The crew's quarters were spotless, and a collection of well-fed cats kept them free of vermin.

But the ship's impressive exterior hid a rotten core. After only a few days aboard the ship, Harp regretted the night when he shared a few pints with some of the crewmen of the *Marderward*. Harp had just ended a charter on a filthy, ill-run boat that ran stolen goods up and down the Sword Coast. He'd been on pirate vessels for nearly ten years and had a vague notion that he wanted a legitimate life away from the pirating that had marked his sailing career thus far.

The *Marderward's* sailors assured Harp that their captain was a fair man who ran a tight ship. The crewmen paid for round after round of ale, and before the night was up, Harp signed a year's contract under Captain Taraf Predeau. He woke up with a headache and hoped for the best.

The red-haired, broad-shouldered captain had a deceptively boyish face and friendly grin. On Harp's first day aboard, the captain shook his hand and personally showed him around the immaculate ship, explaining the tight schedules and rigid discipline that was expected from his sailors. Despite his easy-going manners, Harp felt uneasy around the captain, with his booming voice and biting humor.

From the beginning, Predeau made fun of Harp's name, calling him Lute or Whistle. At first, Harp thought the captain was trying to get a rise out of him, but he soon realized the captain viewed Harp as a kindred spirit. And after a few tendays on the ship, it turned Harp's stomach that there was something about him that was appealing to a man such as Predeau. By that point, Harp understood that Predeau's clean-cut appearance was nothing but a façade. And it was his blood-encrusted whip and his steel-toed boots that told the true story of his depraved nature.

Although he had a joint license from the Houses of Amn, Predeau was far from a merchant seaman, despite what the sailors had led Harp to believe. By the time Liel was kidnapped and brought aboard the ship, Harp had seen how Predeau's kidnap-and-ransom scheme worked several times over. It soon became obvious that Predeau didn't kidnap arbitrary people off the street, but he did so at the request of the politically well connected. Mostly, it was perfunctory—haul them out of their beds at night, take them to the ship, and lock them up until their kin paid the coin. It wasn't pretty, but it wasn't cruel either. And there was a certain amount of satisfaction in watching a silk-robed nobleman spend a few days locked in the hold until the price was paid.

But Predeau hadn't been exaggerating when he'd said he ran a tight ship. He issued beatings or withheld the crew's payment for the slightest infraction. Still, Harp could have tolerated the conditions, except for the fact that Predeau treated the youngest members of his crew worse than the older sailors. Boys as young as eight who were purchased from parents who were desperate for any coin they could get their hands on. The so-called cabin hands were indentured until they were eighteen, and many were weak and ill from untreated maladies.

Harp was expected to organize the boys into work crews, but he wasn't their keeper. Predeau's henchmen monitored them constantly and locked them in their quarters whenever the ship made port. The boys slept in a dark, squalid room in the depths of the ship and ate the scraps left from the older sailors.

They'd been on the water for a few days when Harp awoke to the sounds of scuffling above his head. He rolled out of his hammock and climbed the ladder. The sun hadn't fully risen, but a handful of the boys were on deck, their hair and clothes damp from the spray of the rough waves. They were grouped around a small black-haired boy who was on his hands and knees scrubbing the boards. When the black-haired boy paused in his work, a lanky boy named Merik would kick at him or call him a name.

"What's going on?" Harp asked Merik. Even though he'd been onboard for less than a tenday, Harp had figured out that Merik was Predeau's pet. A few of the boys were handpicked as henchmen-in-training, with Predeau taking much pleasure in goading his favorites until they abused the younger and weaker ones of their own accord.

"Predeau said Kitto wasn't working hard enough," Merik explained. "He gave us all more shift time."

Harp looked down at Kitto, who couldn't have been more than eight or nine years old. The kid's arms were shaking with fatigue.

"How long have you been out here?"

Merik shrugged. "Not long enough."

"He's supposed to finish the deck?" Harp asked, looking down the length of the ship. Usually it took a crew of five several hours to finish the task.

"Yeah, then we get out of our extra time," Merik said, kicking at Kitto again. "Work faster, rat-face."

Harp looked down at Kitto, whose gaze never wavered from the brush in his hands. He scrubbed the deck rhythmically, as if he were some kind of machine. His blank features had no more expression than a mask.

"All right, get back to your jobs," Harp said firmly. "I'll take care of it."

Most of the boys looked relieved, but Merik looked suspicious. "Are ya going to make him finish so we can get out of our time?"

"I'll tell the captain you did your jobs."

As the days passed, Harp saw it happen again and again. Merik led the charge against Kitto, who never complained or cried. And hardly spoke, Harp noticed. Merik took his cue from Predeau, who seemed to have a particular dislike of slender, quick-footed Kitto, even though the boy had a reputation for being the best picklock and pickpocket on the crew. Predeau's men took Kitto with them whenever there was a tricky lock or the need for quick hands in a crowded bazaar. Despite these successful ventures, Predeau hounded Kitto more than anyone else on the ship.

Harp never heard Kitto say a word. After his day's work ended, the boy would find a quiet corner and hack away at a hunk of wood with a little blade that was barely sharp enough to cut butter. On the few occasions Harp tried to talk to him, Kitto scurried silently away, although Harp once found a crude whistle stuck in the laces of his boots. It played a surprisingly sweet tune.

On the night before Merik's eighteenth birthday, Harp found him sitting behind a row of barrels, smoking a pipe, and rolling a bone-carved die over and over on the boards beside him. The die landed on the jack-side every single time.

"Have you ever heard Kitto talk?" Harp asked, sitting down beside Merik and pulling out his tobacco pouch.

"Nah, he's a mute," Merik said, looking pleased that Harp had joined him. He sat up straighter and tucked the die into his pocket.

"Why does Predeau hate him?"

Merik shrugged. "Cause Kitto's too stupid to live, you know? All he's got to do is simple. But he always has to make things hard on himself."

"How?"

"You know those 'tails Predeau's got to use on the prisoners?"

Harp nodded his head. So far he hadn't witnessed one of the notoriously brutal beatings Predeau unleashed on crew members and prisoners from time to time, but he'd seen the cat-o-nine tails' distinctive scars on Kitto's back—Predeau's fingerprint that the child would bear his whole life.

"Usually he likes to do it himself, but sometimes he asks one of us to do the lashes. And you better do it, you know? Kitto had been around. He knew that. But there was a little boy got nabbed with his da. Not like a baby, but you know, younger than Kitto. Predeau hands him the 'tails and tells him to lash the boy. I think he stole a crust or something. But Kitto wouldn't even hold the handle, just let it drop to the ground. You should have seen the captain's face. Three times he put the 'tails into Kitto's hand, and three times Kitto lets it drop. Between you and me, it was kind of strong of him to do it, but it was stupid too. He took the kid's lashes and some more. Captain was furious and made us all pay for what Kitto done, and we hated him for it."

"Captain Predeau?" Harp asked.

"Kitto. It was his fault."

"What happened to the boy?"

"The kid? His coin got paid," Merik said, looking surprised at the question.

"Do you plan to leave after your birthday?" Harp asked, pulling out the small flask of brandy that was the boy's allotment for the tenday and handing it to him.

Merik shrugged again and uncorked the flask. "I've been on the boat since I was thirteen. I hated it so much, I thought I'd die. I was sure I'd leave the day I turned eighteen But now I'm not so sure."

"There's nothing for you on the ship."

"Where would I go? I hate it, but it's my home, you know?"

Harp sat quietly for a moment before checking over his shoulder to make sure there was no one in sight. They were sitting near the bow of the ship, both of them having finished their shifts before the dinner call. Harp pulled out his dagger and began to clean his fingernails. At the sight of the knife, there was shift in the mood. Merik, used to violence, felt it.

"I don't think you're stupid, Merik. I might be wrong, but I don't think so. Who bought you?"

"What?" Merik asked in confusion.

"Who bought you? Who beats you? Who makes you work like a dog for no pay?"

The boy made a move to get up, but Harp grabbed his wrist and yanked him down hard.

"Who, Merik? Is it Kitto?" He whispered, digging his fingernails into the boy's dirty arm.

The boy shook his head quickly, obviously shaken by Harp's unusual intensity.

"Say who it is," Harp said.

"The captain," Merik whispered.

"That's right. And who should you hate?"

Merik tried to wrench his wrist out of Harp's grasp, but Harp tightened his hand. There were tears in Merik's dark brown eyes. Harp felt bad about making him cry, but he felt relieved at the same time. At least Merik could still feel something. It might not be guilt exactly, but it was a stone's throw away from being so.

"Who should you hate? Kitto?"

Merik shook his head again.

"You've become a little captain, which makes you more whipped than Kitto. Don't you get that?"

Merik stopped struggling and slumped against the railing.

"Do you know what you're going to do on your birthday? You're going to walk off the ship a free man. And you're never going to look back. Find a girl, get married, and forget about Captain Predeau. Otherwise he'll be the voice that whispers in your ear for the rest of your life."

Harp put his dagger away and helped Merik to his feet. When the boy walked off the ship in the morning, Harp was the only one at the railing to watch him go.

With Merik gone, Predeau searched half-heartedly for a new ringleader. But with Harp around, the other boys were reluctant to turn on each other. They stopped targeting Kitto, kept quiet, and did their work. When Predeau unleashed his wrath, it was at the lot of them, and that seemed easier for the boys to take. Harp counted the days until his tenure was up and worried what would happen to the young sailors when he left.

And then Predeau kidnapped two elves: a blond male and a coppery-haired female. There'd never been any ransoms of anything but human men before, but from his perch in the rigging Harp saw the distinctive slant of the prisoners' ears, and a feeling of certain dread rose in his chest. Everyone knew that Predeau viewed elves as little more than vermin infesting the land. Harp slid down the mast rope for a better view of the elves, but not far enough to attract the attention of Predeau.

Predeau strode out of his cabin to the elves lashed to the center mast. Without speaking, he pulled out his sword and slit the throat of the male, an older elf who had a look of calm acceptance on his face when he died. In later years, Harp wondered why Predeau picked that elf, if he knew of him specifically, or if he was simply closest to the captain at the time. As if he'd heard Harp's involuntary gasp, Predeau looked up and grinned at Harp, who was still perched in the rigging.

"Get down here," he bellowed as the blood from the elf soaked into the boards around the mast.

Harp slid down, landing softly beside Liel, who was trembling visibly. She was shorter than Harp, and slender with a pixieish face. A delicate pattern of flowering vines was inked along her jaw and disappeared along her neck under her coppery hair. There was a palpable sense of strength about her, as if she could strangle a man with either her hands or an incantation—had she not been bound. They must have taken her cloak and armor when they grabbed her. It was too cold for the thin shift she was wearing.

"We got ourselves a little elf whore. What do you think we should do with her, Flute?"

"I'll take her down to the hold," Harp volunteered.

"Eager, aren't you, boy." Predeau laughed, and Harp saw the elf flinch. As Predeau headed back to his cabin, Harp undid the rope from around the mast and led her to the hold.

"No one is going to touch you," he whispered. But he could tell by the loathing in her eyes that she didn't believe him.

That night, he organized the boys into a round-the-clock watch on the elf. If any of Predeau's henchmen came near her, one of Harp's boys made a diversion, and another ran to tell Harp. Harp made sure he was the one who brought her food. When she figured out that Harp was watching out for her, the hatred disappeared from her eyes, although she was still reluctant to talk to him. She took a shine to Kitto, however. One night as Harp started down the steep steps with a plate of food, he heard two voices coming from the hold. He hurried to see who had slipped in without his notice, and saw Kitto seated on a barrel outside the elf's cage.

"What are you talking about?" Harp asked casually. He handed her the plate of food, trying to hide his surprise that Kitto wasn't mute after all.

"Flowers," she said, with no trace of humor.

He paused. "What kind?" he asked, as if it were the most natural thing in the world that they would be discussing gardening in their wretched surroundings.

"Violets." She smiled, and he decided it was the sweetest smile he had ever seen.

Soon it became obvious that Predeau was in no hurry to ransom Liel. When they were docked at ports, couriers brought letters almost every day, but Liel remained in the cell. One of the older sailors told Harp that he'd heard there wasn't going to be an exchange made at all. That Predeau had kidnapped her for political reasons and was waiting for the right moment to kill her and leave her body in a public place.

One day as Harp worked on the sails, he heard one of the boys screaming his name. Although he was much to high to make it safely, he jumped down out of the rigging and landed painfully on the deck where one of the boys named Mallie waited for him.

"Captain said that Kitto was trying to free the elf," Mallie cried. "He's beating him to death!"

Harp sprinted across the deck to the open trapdoor that led down to the hold. But as he scrambled down the steps, one of Predeau's men grabbed him and yanked him off the ladder. Harp scuffled with the man, shoving him up against the wall as another sailor grabbed Harp around the neck. Harp flipped the man over his shoulder, slammed him down hard, and punched him in the face to keep him there. Two more sailors grabbed Harp from behind and pulled him back as Predeau lashed Kitto with the 'tails.

"Stop!" Harp shouted as Predeau raised his arm to hit the boy again.

Predeau wheeled around and glared at Harp. "Did you just give me an order?"

"You're going to kill him," Harp yelled. "He's just a little boy."

He stopped struggling and looked around the room, which had grown eerily still except for the tin lanterns that swung back and forth with the rolling of the ship. Almost the entire crew was there, and some of the older sailors looked uncomfortable, although none had raised a finger to help Kitto. Liel's cell was in the far corner, but the elf was obscured by shadows. He could see her silhouette, but he couldn't tell if she were injured. Kitto lay on the floor in a heap at Predeau's feet.

"You're killing him," Harp repeated quietly, shrugging off the hands of the men holding him back.

"I'm a fair man," Predeau said. "He's got more lashes coming to him. You can, of course, be his proxy."

"I'll take them."

Predeau grinned. "Fine. Up on deck."

"Let someone see to Kitto."

"That wasn't part of the offer," he said, stepping over Kitto's bruised body on the way up to the deck.

That night, the blood soaked through Harp's shirt, ran down his trouser legs, and stained the inside of his boots.

He couldn't lie down, and he could barely stand up. When he joined the boys in their quarters, Mallie held a flask of whiskey to his lips and told Harp that the captain had locked Kitto up in the cell with Liel, that there were murmurs among the sailors that Predeau had gone too far this time.

Through teeth gritted in pain, Harp whispered his plan to the boys. As he told them what he wanted them to do—if they were willing—his mind was on the key in the captain's quarters. He would take it from that bastard. Then he would get Liel and whatever was left of Kitto off that floating tomb forever.

"I'm not going to lie to you," he said in a hushed voice, looking down at the five grubby faces assembled in front of him. "What I'm asking isn't an easy thing. But he won't stop at Kitto. One day it could be one of you under that lash."

He looked carefully for fear on their features. But he didn't find any. What he saw gave him a sense of hope.

"Shaun, you're on the armory door," he said, and the boys nodded. "Mallie, you'll rouse the men. You know which ones will follow. Bristol, you ready two boats. If nothing else, just get away.

"When you see the light in the captain's window, then you'll know what to do."

Standing behind Predeau, Harp pressed his dagger against the big man's throat. Grabbing a handful of the captain's long hair, Harp yanked Predeau's head back till he could see the thick blue vein pulsing on the side of the man's neck. Despite the precariousness of his position, Predeau didn't seem concerned, and was still issuing orders to Harp as if he were in control of everything that was happening.

"If you touch that lantern, boy, I'll see to it that your skin is flayed off your back and hung on the mast to dry."

Harp's face was swollen and cut, and he felt like he was bleeding from both eyes. He could barely stay on his feet, much less keep the blunt dagger in his hands from shaking. Harp had been on the short end of several beatings in his younger years, and the shame of being hit was something no man talked about—how taking that first punch makes you feel like an idiot. Harp had taken his first punch at age seven, from some of the older kids in the village. Horrified at the tears that had filled his eyes, he had launched himself at his attacker, only to be smacked down. The second punch had knocked him to his knees, but had brought out a rage that had him on his feet again, charging head first into the older boy, who was twice his age.

He'd put his attacker down that day, earning a reputation among his fellows. Quick on his feet, with a fist that could knock a man unconscious in one blow, Harp had rarely lost a fight since. But Predeau outweighed him and wore metal rings on his fingers that had split the skin on Harp's face wide open.

"I had high hopes for you, Harp," Predeau said. "You might pretend to be noble. But inside you're just like me."

After months of watching the captain inflict pain on the weak purely for pleasure, Harp had grown to despise Predeau. But that night, with Kitto bleeding out in the darkness of the hold, Harp felt a hatred for the captain like nothing he'd ever experienced. It felt like a burning poison flowing through his body, and killing was the only antidote. Being compared to the vile captain was worse than an insult. It was a terrifying reminder that Harp was just a few sins away from having a rotted, irreplaceable soul.

"I'm nothing like you," Harp said, pressing the blade harder against Predeau's neck. The big man didn't even flinch. Maybe Predeau was toying with Harp, the way he toyed with all his victims before he stomped the life out of them. Harp's eyes darted from the lantern on the desk beside him to the high windowsill, trying to gauge how he was going to keep Predeau at bay long enough to lift the light to the window.

Suddenly the captain began to chuckle, a maniacal sound that made the hairs on Harp's arm bristle.

"I know what's keeping you, boy. You can kill me and get out alone. Or you can go for the lantern, and hope your fellows are waiting below for your signal to rise up and take my ship. But you have doubts, don't you? They might be tucked up like little bedbugs, not caring one bit about you, the lantern, or your whore."

Harp cursed the captain under his breath. Predeau was speaking the truth. Harp had no idea if the sailors would find the courage to step out in the brewing storm and take up arms. Predeau ruled them with an iron fist, but at least they knew what to expect every day. Once they unsheathed their swords against their master, all that lay before them was the unknown.

Who was Harp to make them choose? Shouldn't he let them be idle in their familiar lives, as meek as fawns? Normally, he would have bowed to the slow momentum of change and done nothing. But his decision had a leyline that was guiding Harp toward the rising sun. It was Kitto who was waiting for him, like a son trusting that his father wouldn't let him down. And, more than anything, Harp wanted Kitto to have a life.

"You're always alone," Predeau said in his booming voice. "There's no one out there in the rain and wind. And if you let me go, I'll slaughter you like a pig. Take the kill and be done with it."

But Harp wasn't sure he could get a kill with the blunt dagger. For all he knew, Predeau veins were made of metal, and the bastard was just baiting him. And whether the others rose up was out of his hands now. He'd given them the choice, and if they wanted to live like chattel for the rest of their lives, he couldn't make them fight. Harp had the key to free Kitto and Liel in his pocket. He would get out, or he would die trying.

As Harp shoved Predeau's head toward the table, he sliced the knife back against the captain's throat. Predeau's face slammed into the edge of the wooden tabletop, and he crashed to the floor. Harp dropped the dagger, grabbed the lantern, and hoisted it to the high window. He just had time to shove it on the ledge and leap toward the closed door before Predeau was back on his feet. With a sadistic grin, Predeau grabbed a heavy wooden chair and hurled it at Harp with no more effort than if he were throwing a bread roll to a dinner mate. Harp dodged the chair, rolling out of the way as it splintered against the wall. The impact knocked the lantern off the ledge where it smashed onto the floor into glass shards, oil, and flame.

Though the lantern was gone from the window, it should have been enough. If the sailors were in the darkness waiting, they would have seen the light and recognized Harp's signal. Both Harp and Predeau froze, even though the fire was spreading across the floor as the lamp oil seeped into the wooden planks. All they heard was the hiss of the flames, the sails cracking in the wind, and the rain hammering against the deck.

Predeau loomed over him. "You made the wrong choice." He raised his foot and stomped on Harp's hand. Harp cried out at the impact. He heard a cracking noise; it felt like every one of his fingers had been broken under Predeau's steel-toed boots. Then Harp felt a pounding vibration through the deck of the ship. The rhythmic pounding increased in volume as he heard voices shouting Predeau's name. In two strides, Predeau crossed the cabin and threw open the door. Outside, the men stood defiantly on deck as the ship tossed in the rough waves and the rain pounded the boards. It wasn't just Harp's boys either, but many of the older men as well. Swords in hand, they were about to take their freedom.

"Harp!"

Harp didn't turn toward Boult's voice. His hand was resting on the tree, and his thoughts were firmly elsewhere.

"Harp!" Boult marched up beside him and glared up at him. "Stop daydreaming," he ordered. "It's not her. Unless she shrunk to dwarf size and gained a substantial amount of weight."

That snapped Harp back to the present. "It's a dwarf?"

"Didn't I just say that?"

"No, you said she shrunk to dwarf size."

"The corpse is a dwarf. It's not Liel."

"How do you know?"

Boult stared at Harp in frustration. "Because it's dwarf-sized," he sputtered. "She's got dwarf-sized bones and a dwarf-sized head, and it's a dwarf's corpse. This is the stupidest conversation we've had with each other in a decade of stupid conversations."

"Couldn't it be a small human?"

Boult rolled his eyes. "I'm going to forgive you for asking such a ridiculous question because you're distracted by thoughts of your long lost love."

"She's not my long lost—"

"Blah, blah, blah. You're only lying to yourself."

"Where in the realms did a dwarf come from?" Harp said ignoring Boult's comment. "There weren't any in the colony."

Boult shook his head. "They *live* here."

"In the jungle?"

"You think we all live in mountains digging for gem stones?"

"Well . . . yes."

Boult glared at him. "Shows what you know. We live everywhere. We live in the mountains. We live in the cities. We live in the jungles. We sail the oceans."

"No, you don't. You're the only dwarf in Faerûn who'll set foot on a ship, and you do a piss poor job of it."

"Well at least I can tell a dwarf from a human. You're dumber than a starving ship rat."

Harp's demeanor softened. "It's not Liel," he said, as if he finally believed it. "It's not Liel. Which means we haven't actually found what we're looking for."

CHAPTER NINE

30 Hammer, Year of Splendors Burning
(1479 DR)
Winter Palace, Tethyr

Tresco Maynard had seen the dense fog roll across the courtyard and cover the earth like a shroud. He hoped Evonne was safe within the walls of the Winter Palace, but couldn't take time to find her because he was obligated to search for his student Daviel, who had disappeared for the third time in a tenday. Tresco wasn't worried about Daviel, who was probably sneaking off to see a village girl, but he had to keep up the appearance of concerned tutor or risk losing his position entirely through rumors.

Outside the door of the kitchen, Tresco adjusted the brown cape on his shoulders and tucked it over the crook of one arm. If the cooks gave him any lip, he would have them all sent packing, he thought angrily as he shoved open the door.

But the warm, sweet-smelling room was deserted. Puzzled, Tresco walked past long tables laden with steaming dishes full of meat, soups, and spiced fruit. There were loaves of soft bread cooling on wooden racks, and the fires were stoked high in the massive ovens. But where were the cooks? Dinner was slated to begin despite Queen Anais's absence, and the servants should have been loading the silver serving carts. Suddenly, a cold breeze swept across the room, making Tresco's hands ache and putting a chill in his bones.

A door had been left open somewhere. Tresco pulled his woolen hood over his graying hair and flexed his stiff fingers. He was twenty years past his youth but still a powerfully built man and handsome despite his years. The infirmity in his hands was the first thing that truly made him feel old.

Tresco pulled a red leather pouch embossed with the circular crest of Kinnard Keep, his ancestral house, from under his cloak and took a pinch of black leaf. He placed it between his gums and cheek and waited until the tingling spread into his fingers. There were many things he didn't like about getting old, but that was no matter. He must find Daviel before dinner, if indeed there would be a dinner that night. Tresco was supposed to be a tutor, not a nanny. Keeping up with an active prince was a job for a younger man.

Tresco left the kitchen area and moved into the workshop where the blacksmith and coopers worked during the day. The forges were dampened, and only a few lanterns cast light on the sawdust floor. He left the workshop and continued down a narrow corridor. The air seemed wetter the farther he walked down the passageway, so the open door must be somewhere up ahead. Tresco had been to the Winter Palace many times and had a vague recollection of the haphazard floor plan—each generation built new additions to the sprawling palace without anything but temporary functionality in mind. The result was a maze of low-ceilinged walkways and dank storage rooms with mossy walls.

He'd been to the lower levels of the palace on several occasions in years past when he had been tutor for one of Daviel's uncles. In fact, Tresco had been a tutor for young men of the noble bloodlines for years. Yet even as one of the most sought-after tutors for royalty in Tethyr, he was underestimated by his peers.

Tresco remembered the days of his youth when ideas used to catch his mind and hold it like a vice. The hours of study would pass from day into night before Tresco looked up from a book or noticed the gripping pain of hunger in his belly. Unfortunately, those days were long past. Tresco's mind wandered aimlessly, like a lost traveler in an inhospitable land. Except for a few personal projects, Tresco had given up study altogether. Teaching had simply become a necessary, if unwanted, pastime. Daviel was bright enough, but unfocused, and Tresco barely had the will to keep him at his books.

Besides, he had more important things to think about. Like Evonne and all her talk of death, the jungle, and those disturbing tales of the sarrukh and their penchant for eating the flesh of the lesser races. Evonne had a vivid way of expressing herself, which was not appropriate for a woman of her stature, in Tresco's opinion. She was strong-willed, a quality that intrigued Tresco, almost despite himself. But she was the woman who should be queen! Evonne shouldn't concern herself with such disturbing things.

The last time he saw Evonne was a month before, when they had spent a few days together at Lindenhall, north of the Skyhart Waterfall. One night after dinner, she had begun talking about her impending death and how there was nothing anyone could do to stop it. It was the first time he'd ever seen Evonne cry, and it made him want to take her someplace far away—a place with thick walls and towers to the sky and locks no one could ever breach—and keep her safe forever.

After the emotional tenor of the evening, Tresco had felt closer to Evonne than ever before; it may well have been the most intense moment of his life—outside of the violent brawls of his youth. He and Evonne had been lovers for almost a year, but it had been sporadic, and at her insistence, secret. Before those days at Lindenhall, an afternoon was the longest he'd ever spent with her. Whenever they were together, it was always brief and always at her convenience, leaving Tresco with the unfortunate impression that Evonne saw their companionship as a token of her generosity.

But the night he'd held Evonne while she confessed her fear of death, everything had changed. Since his youth, Tresco had viewed women with little more than disdain. As soon as a woman fancied herself irreplaceable, he invariably grew weary of her company. He thought he was happily committed to an uncommitted life. But Evonne was unique. For the first time, he wanted a woman with a lasting, perhaps unceasing, desire.

So his tasks for the evening were to round up Daviel, change into dress attire for dinner, and spend the evening with a crowd of influential nobles, none of whom were in on the delicious secret—that Tresco was the secret lover of one of the most beautiful and important women in all of Tethyr.

Suddenly, a strong blast of frigid wind swept through the corridor extinguishing the lanterns and throwing Tresco into darkness. He stood quietly for a moment, his body trembling more from the chill than fear. He could hear rustling nearby. Whether it was vermin or something larger, he couldn't determine. After a few moments, he mumbled under his breath and moved his hands sharply, and the lanterns along the corridor flared with orange flame.

Tresco was no innocent. He had seen things, particularly in his adventurous youth, that were seared into his memory, as bloody and as horrible as the very day that he had first witnessed them. But in the instant after the light bloomed from his hands, he saw Evonne in the corridor in front of him, her long blonde hair loose on her shoulders, and her flowing white dress stained with blood.

Tresco's heart skipped. His vision cleared. It was not Evonne, but her daughter, Ysabel, in the bloodstained dress, her bare feet and heart-shaped face smeared with something thick and dark. How foolish to mistake the child for her mother. But Evonne had been in his thoughts at the moment the darkness fell.

"Ysabel!" Tresco said, choking on her name. He knew all the cousins by name, and they all referred to him as Uncle, a familiarity he begrudgingly permitted. "What are you doing here!"

"Looking for Cousin Daviel," she said, peering up at him intently.

"As am I," Tresco said. "But this is no place for a child. Go back to the main corridor and wait there. I will continue to search for Daviel."

"It's no matter, Uncle," she said quietly, her blue eyes unnaturally wide. "I've found him already."

Evonne Linden was killed in Celleu the same night that the children were massacred in the Winter Palace. After a lengthy discussion in their private chambers in the palace at Darromar, the men of the Inquiry settled on "unbelievable irony" over "unprecedented coordination." Their official position was that a bandit climbed up the trellis to Evonne's second-story window, unlatched the shuttered window, and suffocated her as she slept. Then he stole an embroidered bag that servants had seen her carrying earlier in the day—it was the only thing missing from her quarters—and disappeared into the night without the guards in the hallway ever hearing a sound.

The explanation satisfied Queen Anais's followers, but left Evonne's supporters screaming for the queen's blood. There was a door connecting Evonne's quarters and the queen's quarters, and many believed that Queen Anais had killed her own sister. Anais had reason to hate Evonne, of course. Had Evonne's revolt against Anais been successful, she would have seized the crown for herself. Evonne's husband, Garion, had been a powerful man with many secret followers. When he died, his substantial network switched its allegiance to Evonne and was ready to take up arms at her call.

After Evonne's death, there were several skirmishes between the queen's regiments and Evonne's die-hard proponents, who had begun calling themselves the Branch of Linden. After a particularly bloody skirmish on the black rocks of the Ebenspy Plateau, the Linden fighters were driven into Ebenspy Keep, an ancient castle on a rocky spike of land jutting out of the obsidian encrusted flatlands. With strong wards protecting the walls, the fighters held out for days before a coughing sickness killed half of them, and the queen's soldiers successfully blasted under the thick walls of volcanic glass and took control of the Keep. With the ringleaders swinging by their necks in front of the High Palace at Darromar, Queen Anais was satisfied that the Branch of Linden had been eradicated.

Still beautiful in death, Evonne was buried with state honors in the hillside mausoleum with a view of the sparkling ocean in the distance. The guardianship of her daughter,

Ysabel, was given to Queen Anais, in trust of Tresco Maynard. The child would live at Tresco Maynard's ancestral home, Kinnard Keep, on the edge of Kinnard Heath, a desolate expanse of gorse and heather.

CHAPTER TEN

29 Kythorn, the Year of the Ageless One
(1479 DR)
Chult

A leaf-strewn path led them out of the grove and up a vine-tangled slope toward the heart of the island. They left the corpse tucked in the tree hollow because it seemed a better grave than a shallow hole on the open floor. Although he couldn't see the sky through the leaf canopy, Harp judged it to be late afternoon. He found it hard to breathe in the heavy, moist air, and soon his clothes dripped with sweat and his flask was empty.

Their previous plans of a quick survey—in and out before nightfall—were looking less and less likely with every step through the brush. They would have to find a place to camp soon. The heat under the trees was rising, and the sunlight beat down through the green of the leaves, casting the world in a pale yellow glow. As the temperature rose, an eerie silence fell as if the jungle's creatures had retreated into a quiet, shady spot to wait out the worst of the heat.

Beside Harp, Kitto was whistling a tune softly to himself. It was a tune Harp recognized from the *Marderward,* and the words had stayed with him all these years: "Bitch Queen take my soul away to the depths of the sea. Don't make me stay one bleeding day. This world is not for me."

"So what do you think of the jungle?" Harp asked. "Lots of plants, huh."

Kitto stopped whistling and smiled down at his boots. Since Kitto never had much to say, it had become a joke to talk to him about mundane things, topics that other people would consider normal conversation, but Kitto seemed to think were hilarious. But then, most things that were normal to other people amused Kitto.

"Quite the weather we're having," Harp continued. "Did I tell you about the mule? She's got the mange. We had to put her out of her misery."

Boult piped up from behind them. "Got a bit of the ache in my neck. Oh, but the crops are quite good."

"Can you believe the price of eggs?" Harp asked. "And did you hear about Lady Arello and the Captain of the Guard? Scandalous!"

"You're all insane," Verran said. "Kitto, you should just tell them they're all insane."

They settled into an amicable silence. But their easy trek along the open floor didn't last long. As the incline became steeper and the vegetation grew thicker, the men spread out as they struggled up the hill, their feet slipping on loose stones that seemed to be only held together by a mat of roots on top of very shallow soil. Kitto stayed close to Harp, which meant the boy had something that he wanted to say.

They were at the back of the group, and Harp found himself breathing uncomfortably hard. Kitto waited with him as Harp paused to catch his breath.

"I need to take better care of myself," he said, taking a drink of water from Kitto's waterskin. "Maybe I'm getting too old for this."

Kitto didn't look tired at all. The wiry boy was all lean muscle, athleticism, and startling grace. Sometimes Kitto and Boult would have rope-climbing contests up the shroud ropes on the *Crane*. Boult was agile for a dwarf and much stronger than Kitto, but he couldn't best the boy's unparalleled displays of dexterousness.

"Too much ale," Kitto said in his soft, lilting voice. "And not enough sleep."

"Yes, I'm sorry about that. But don't give me too much trouble. That's Boult's job."

Kitto tipped his head back and looked up at the sky, and for the millionth time Harp wondered why the boy chose to tag along with him when there were thousands of people of better quality than Harp could ever hope to be. Kitto was perfectly capable of taking care of himself. He just didn't seem to be in a hurry to go anywhere.

"I told you that Liel was one of the colonists and that her father was worried that something had happened to her. I just want to make sure you're all right. I know you and Liel were friends."

"I'm all right," Kitto replied flatly. Harp tried to gauge the emotion in the boy's face, but Kitto was unreadable. With Harp breathing easier, they resumed climbing up the hill after Boult and Verran.

"She took care of you, right? After you left Gwynneth Isle and went to the Wealdath with her."

"She said I could stay in the Wealdath."

"Why didn't you?"

"I hated Cardew."

"That makes three of us," Harp said wryly as they scrambled up a rocky embankment.

"He knew you were in Vankila," Kitto said. "I heard him say he was going to make you pay."

That wasn't news to Harp, who was fully aware how Cardew had directed the events that transpired during his imprisonment at the Vankila Slab. With a single directive, Cardew had altered the course of Harp's life irrevocably.

"I tried to make Cardew tell me where you were. But he wouldn't."

Harp laid his hand on Kitto's shoulder. "You couldn't have gotten me out by yourself. It was better you didn't know."

"I should have been there too," Kitto said softly.

"No, that's the last place in the world you should have been. Come on, or I'll make you talk about the latest dress fashions. Ribbons or bows, Kitto? I just can't decide!"

By the time they caught up to Boult and Verran, it was obvious they had lost the path, or maybe they'd been following the wrong one all along. The ground flattened out again, and they trudged through stands of massive fern-like plants, their leaves covered with a white fuzziness that looked deceptively soft, but on closer inspection was actually made of razor-sharp barbs.

Even the flowers impeded their progress through the jungle. The ground had been overrun with a variety of pinkish blooms that grew on reedy stalks and sent out crimson tendrils to envelope whatever vegetation surrounded them. The tendrils from a single plant could overtake entire sections of jungle floor, engulfing everything in a lumpy red mesh. When the back of Harp's hand brushed against one of the crimson tendrils, his skin puffed up painfully.

"First lesson of the jungle," he told his crew as he rubbed salve on the rash and wrapped his hand in cloth. "If it has color, avoid it."

"Second lesson of the jungle," Boult replied, picking thorns out of the leg of his pants. "Avoid the jungle."

"And miss the glorious views?" Harp joked, gesturing ahead of him at the dense wall of thorns that formed a barrier to the north and west. The eastern route was no easier because of a steep vine-covered embankment.

"Have you noticed how the flat land is always followed by a sharp rise?" Verran said. "We've been climbing higher since we left the beach."

"Like we're climbing a massive staircase," Kitto said. His comment was followed by a long moment of silence. Harp tried to imagine what such a land formation would look like from a bird's eye view.

"Or maybe it's like a pyramid with the steps on all sides," Kitto continued.

"Either way begs the question," Boult said. "What's at the top?"

Although it wasn't very high, the embankment was nearly vertical. Ropey yellow vines draped the length of it, making it easy to climb. About halfway up, Harp reached for a handhold. His hand touched something reedy, and a blast of orange exploded into the air. Startled, Harp lost his grip on the vine, slid down the embankment, and crashed into Boult. The dwarf managed to keep hold of the cliff despite the weight of his captain and the flock of orange birds that flapped into the sky, screeching their indignation at the disruption.

"Hullo, Boult," Harp said, who had landed across the dwarf's arms. "Your assistance is most appreciated."

"Get off me, you lout," Boult grumbled. "You're the worst climber I've ever met. You could break your neck walking across a field."

"Nonsense," Harp replied, hauling himself upright and resuming his climb past the deep hollow where the cliff-dwelling birds nested. "I'm very agile."

"Agile like a cave slug," Boult retorted. "Is there anything you do well?"

"He makes good soup," Kitto called from below them on the cliff.

"No, he doesn't," Boult said. "Didn't you eat dinner last night? What did you do, Harp? Boil oranges in dirty water and call it food?"

Verran laughed. "I glad that's not the normal fare on the boat. I was worried I'd starve to death."

"Kitto liked it," Harp said as he reached the top of the cliff and pulled himself onto a small rock plateau. "The rest of you have no taste."

"Not after years of eating your cooking," Boult said, climbing onto the rock beside Harp.

"Damn, that's beautiful," Harp said as they stared out across the horizon at their first unencumbered sight of the open sky since they had left the *Crane* earlier that morning. In the gathering twilight, the ocean was a deep dusky blue, and they could see the two ships in the cove, surprisingly small in the distance.

"It's getting dark," Harp said. "We need to find a place to sleep."

"I doubt the jungle floor is a good spot for napping," Boult replied.

"What about here?" Harp asked, looking around. The flat rock was surrounded on three sides by tangled undergrowth. The side that opened to the ocean was level with the crowns of the towering trees they had walked under earlier that day.

"We'd never see anything coming up on us," Boult said shaking his head. "We might as well slice open our bellies and ring the dinner bell."

"You're so dramatic," Harp sighed. "How dangerous could it be?"

"In a place where the vines can eat you, I think the

meat-eaters can probably kill you with a sneeze," Boult said dryly.

"Poor, delicate Boult," Harp said, as Verran and Kitto reached the top of the cliff, climbed on the plateau, and laid down their packs gratefully. "Take a rest. I'll look around."

Harp pushed his way into the undergrowth on the far side of the plateau. Once he was inside the thicket, he followed a finger of rock that stuck out among the treetops. The rock jetty ended just a few feet from the top of one of the soaring trees. The wide leaves and thick branches above him hindered his view of the sky, and it was a substantial drop to the ground. But from where Harp stood, he was close to the thick woody vines that he'd noticed from the ground. They grew between the trees, lacing the branches together and forming paths in the air wide enough for a man to walk more or less comfortably, if he had any sense of balance.

Harp squatted down and held very still; soon wildlife began emerging from the tree cover. A little monkey-like creature with dark golden fur and an extremely long tail moved slowly along the vines, sniffing the air as if he knew that something wasn't quite right. The creature reached one of the wide, rough-barked trunks, gracefully scampered up into the leaves, and disappeared overhead.

Maybe it knew a safe place to spend the night. Harp stretched out to grab the nearest vine. Grasping it with two hands, he swung over the expanse. He kicked his legs, trying to get a footing on a wider vine below him. His shoulders aching, he overshot it twice and was very glad that Boult wasn't there to see his clumsy moves. When he finally found his balance, he walked carefully along the springy vine. The leaves were mere inches from his head, but the distance to the ground made him surprisingly dizzy. Harp had spent a good portion of his life working the tall sails of ships and had never had a problem with heights.

Maybe the heat of the jungle was getting to him.

When he reached the trunk where the golden monkey had disappeared, Harp had a harder time climbing up the trunk, but he shimmied up and poked his head unceremoniously through the leaves. In front of him was a natural floor formed by a tight mat of branches interwoven as they sought the sun and tangled on the roots of canopy ferns. Holding onto a vine, Harp jumped up and down on the floor to see if it would break under his weight. But jumping on it did nothing but sway the branches and disturb a few birds.

The natural platform was surrounded on all sides by leaves, and on one edge was a white flower the size of a boulder. With the palm of his hand, Harp scooped up some of the water that had collected in the petals and refilled his flask. The sky had dimmed from blue to purple. As for places to camp in the jungle, the leafy platform was more comfortable than they deserved.

As he made his way back to collect his friends, Harp could see a band of blue river cascading down from the inland mountains. Based on Avalor's information, he knew that the colony was less than half a mile from the river and only a mile inland from the cove. From his vantage point, Harp had a sense of where the colony should be. They must have taken the wrong path out of the grove. After a night's rest they would make their way to the river and head up the northern bank. The colony should be easy to find from there.

"You got lucky," Boult said, when he saw the treetop hideaway that Harp had found for them.

"Nah, I'm just smarter than you."

"What did you do? Follow a monkey?"

"Shut it, dwarf," Harp said. "You would have just shot it. And then where would we be?"

"Eating dinner," Boult replied.

In the gathering twilight, they ate a quick meal of hard

bread and dried meat. No one talked much as they stretched out to sleep on the springy branches. As the moon rose above them, none were prepared for what the jungle became after darkness fell. It was the noisiest night any of them had ever experienced. It seemed as if every creature in the jungle was agitated, angry, or just generally homicidal. Harp wasn't sure about the other men, but every time he dozed off, a sound of crashing, hissing, or gnashing startled him awake. It happened so many times, it was almost amusing, except for the fear he felt when the treetop shook under the heavy footsteps of some night wanderer who prowled the jungle below.

At some point in the night, Harp dozed off and rolled on his side. Awakened by a growling noise that sounded inches away from his ear, he opened his eyes. Through the gaps in the branches under him, he could see a black shadow lumbering across the forest floor below. In the faint light from the moon, the creature looked like it was tall enough to reach up and grab him through the canopy if it wanted to. Ambling between the buttress roots, it suddenly stopped and took several raspy breaths, as if it were tasting the air. The dark shape twisted, and Harp could see two yellow eyes glowing through the gloom. Still half-asleep, Harp reassured himself that getting eaten by a forest beast wasn't the worst way to go.

"Put me out of my misery," he whispered to the monstrosity below him. "I haven't had the guts to do it myself."

But the monster seemed to lose interest and moved into the shadows. The way it vanished from sight made Harp wonder if it had been more spirit than flesh. In the last moment before dawn, the din of the jungle finally ceased. The nighttime chaos was banished with the dawning of the sun, and a serene quiet accompanied the first rays of morning light. Finally, Harp dropped off to sleep.

And then the screaming began. Harp jerked awake, as

the high-pitched wails rang across the jungle, reverberated against the mountains, and echoed back across the valleys. A call of feral pain, it was loud enough to leave a ringing in his ears and primal enough to make his blood run cold. He heard the splintering of wood as something massive crashed through the undergrowth, followed by a thud that rattled the ground and jostled the branches under them.

"What is that?" Verran asked, his eyes wide and fearful. "What makes the ground shake like that?"

"Let's get out of the tree before we're tossed out," Harp said. They hurriedly gathered their things and made their way back to solid ground.

They left the tree crown and climbed back onto the rocky plateau. As they climbed to it, two unseen adversaries faced off somewhere in the direction of the river. They could hear the sounds of ripping skin, snarls and gnashing, and giant bodies flattening the landscape as they fought.

"What's that sound?" Verran asked. "Is it coming toward us?"

"Verran!" Boult snapped. "Why do you keep asking us? Am I not standing beside you? Do you see a spyglass in my hand?"

"You don't need to bite his head off, Boult," Harp chastised him. "What, a little rumble in the jungle makes you crabby before your morning cup of tea?"

"If I had a cup of tea in front of me, I wouldn't be in the stupid jungle," Boult shot back just as the sound of a bone snapping echoed across the clearing. As the thrashing between the beasts intensified, the birds in the trees screeched a harsh cacophony of warning calls. Kitto covered his ears as an unnatural screech of pain pierced the air. Then something very large fell very hard, shaking the ground again, and it was quiet.

"Did it die . . ." Verran started to ask, but he caught Boult's glare and shut his mouth.

Harp motioned for the others to follow him and scrambled through the undergrowth and down a rocky slope in the direction of the river that he'd seen the night before. As they neared the river, the ground leveled out, and he could hear the rushing of water. They came out of the trees at the edge of a small valley and the place where one of the monsters had met its end in the morning's battle. A gargantuan lizard, easily twenty-five feet long from the tip of its spiked tail to the front of its fanged maw, was sprawled across the ground. Its pebbly yellow skin had black stripes branching out from its spine, and given its muscular haunches and tiny front legs, it must have walked on its hind legs.

"If that's not at the top of the food chain, what is?" Harp said as they walked down the slope to the corpse of the monster. The monsters had felled several of the large trees that ringed the valley, and as Harp crawled over one of the massive trunks, he saw claw marks slashed deep across the bark. When they reached the corpse, they stopped and stared in wonder at the massive creature splayed out in the crushed and bloodied underbrush.

"I thought they were nightmares," Kitto said quietly.

"What were, Kitto?" Harp asked.

"The monsters I saw last night," Kitto told him.

"No, I saw them too," Harp said as he circled around the lizard. Bony frills stuck out around the base of its skull, which was twisted sideways on its neck. Gaping wounds bisected the lizard's back, and thick blood still oozed out of the claw marks, although the creature was decidedly dead.

Verran was standing near the lizard's head with a thoughtful look on his face and his head cocked as he inspected the lizard's blank yellow eyes. Each was bigger than a man's head and had a dark, vertical pupil that reminded Harp of a snake's. In death, a thick, cloudy shroud covered the eyes, and buzzing insects were amassing along their edges.

"Whatever killed it had to be bigger," Verran said. "Look at the way the neck is snapped."

"And why didn't it stay to eat it?" Boult asked, swiping an insect away from his face. Carrion bugs were moving into the sticky gashes and buzzing over the bloody ground.

"It could have been a purple worm," Verran suggested. He sounded almost excited at the idea of seeing monsters he had only heard about. "Or maybe a basilisk. Did you know it can petrify you?"

"I know that I don't want to spend another night in the jungle," Boult said. "Let's get going."

"A hydra!" Verran continued. "What if it was a hydra? The only way to kill one is to cut off all of its heads. Did you know that?"

"If we run into a hydra, I'm going to kill you, Harp," Boult said.

"If we run into a hydra, I'm going to kill myself," Harp told him.

They had just reached the other side of the depression when Kitto turned around and looked behind them with a puzzled expression on his face.

"What's wrong?" Harp asked him.

"What's that noise?" Kitto asked. "Is that the water?"

Harp heard it too, and it wasn't water. It was a punctuated clicking that sounded like something he'd heard before, but he couldn't quite remember when. Before his mind could settle on what it was, it grew louder. A large ant appeared at the top of the slope on the other side of the depression. About the size of a dog, with curved tusks like a boar, and a segmented body. The ant hesitated for a moment. Its beaked jaw clicked together rapidly, sending an almost metallic sound ringing through the trees.

"Why is everything huge in the jungle?" Boult asked.

"At least there's just one," Harp pointed out. He was disconcerted by the enormity of insect too. But before his words were fully formed, another ant appeared on the horizon followed by two more. Boult glared at Harp accusingly.

"You can't hold me responsible . . . " Harp began as a flood of the shiny black insects surged over the slope and skittered across the ground. Before the men could make a move, the ants engulfed the lizard's corpse until none of the yellow and black skin could be seen through the writhing ants' bodies.

"We're all right," Harp said in relief. "They just want the meat."

"Look at that!" Verran gasped as a much larger ant made its way down the slope and into the depression. The size of a small horse, the ant's reddish shell was the shade of rusted metal. Like the smaller ants, the queen ant had an armored body and spindly legs that looked too skinny to hold up the bulk of her body. Unlike her soldiers, she had the tattered remains of papery wings. The queen didn't participate in the feasting frenzy but instead skirted the edges of the swarm as her bent antennae quivered rapidly.

Flashes of white appeared through the swarming mass of black, and Harp studied it curiously for a few moments. Then he understood exactly what he was seeing—the white was the lizard's bones picked clean by the ants. Looking at the horrified faces of his companions, they had all reached the same conclusion. Even a lizard that large wasn't going to satisfy the ants, not when there was something else available, namely three men and a dwarf. As they turned to run, the queen ant swung her head in their direction with her beaked mouth clicking open and closed. As if of one mind, the army of ants skittered across the clearing toward the crewmates, leaving only a pile of bare bones in their wake.

"To the river!" Harp shouted as they sprinted across the uneven ground toward the sound of rushing water.

But when they came closer, they saw the river was far

below them at the bottom of a narrow ravine. The fast-flowing water had carved a channel deep into the earth, and there was no obvious route down the dirt banks. Jumping was possible, but it would be easy to break a leg on the narrow lip of dry ground at the edge of the water, or get swept into the rushing current of the river. They ran north along the ravine with Kitto leading the way as he leaped effortlessly over the clumps of ferns and rocks scattered on the ground. The ant soldiers seemed to have fallen back.

"The bastards are flanking us," Boult shouted. Through the gaps in the trees on their left side, Harp could see that Boult was right. A line of ants had moved ahead of them on their left, forming a half-circle around them. Once the ants overtook them, they would be trapped against the edge of the river with no means of escape.

"Since when are ants so smart?" Verran gasped as he ran beside Harp. Harp was equally shocked that the ants could execute such a trap, but he was breathing too hard to respond. As they ran, Harp saw a tree with vines dangling down to the ground. Up a tree was better than over the edge of the ravine, he thought. At least it would give them time to come up with a strategy of their own.

"Climb!" Harp shouted, grabbing a vine and pulling himself up as his feet scrabbled for traction against the bark. Boult was close behind him, while Kitto and Verran scurried up another tree that was across the clearing.

"Can ants climb trees?" Verran called from the other tree.

"Not sure," Harp gasped, as he perched on one of the branches and surveyed the ground below. These trees weren't as tall as the ones they'd slept in the night before, and the vines weren't as thick. At the moment, the ants weren't climbing; they were just milling around the bases of the trees. Boult and Harp climbed to the widest branch and waited to see what the ants would do. In the moment of calm, Harp realized he was trembling, not only from fatigue but from fear as well. As a younger man, he'd been stronger and faster than most men his size and went into battle with no hesitation. There had been too much comfort in his life in recent years. His body didn't remember how to react to danger.

"Look at the big ant, Harp," Boult said after a moment. "I think it's giving orders to the smaller ants."

"How can you tell?" Harp asked. The red queen paced back and forth across the clearing below them, moving between the two trees where the crewmates had taken refuge.

"Just watch," Boult said impatiently.

The queen moved through the swarm, its jaws clicking loudly. It would pause, change directions, and resume the rhythmic noise again. Harp recognized a pattern in the clicks—Boult was right. The queen was telling the soldiers what to do. The smaller ants began to methodically move up the trees. They didn't climb quickly, but in answer to Verran's question, they could definitely climb trees.

"Kill the big ant," Harp urged.

Boult pulled his crossbow off his back, loaded a bolt, and fired it at the queen. The bolt hit square at the base of her neck, but it bounced off her shell harmlessly. Boult tried two more times, and while his aim was dead on, the shell was too thick to penetrate.

"She's got to have a weak spot," Boult said in frustration. "But I'm not hitting it from this angle."

"What do you need?" Harp asked.

"The underbelly," Boult said. Immediately Harp began to move down the trunk and grabbed the longest vine.

"Don't you dare!" Boult shouted when he realized what Harp was intending to do.

But Harp was already sliding down the vine. "If I can't flip the big one over, then I'll lead her to the cliff," he called. "All of you fire at once, and we'll knock her over the edge."

"Get back here!" Boult shouted. "The small ones will eat you first!"

But when Harp dropped to the ground, it was the queen ant that charged him while her troops continued their methodical climb up the trees. The queen was so fast that Harp had to scramble backward to get away from her, tripping over the underbrush and falling on his back. The ant lunged at him, her tusks slicing through the air and her beaked mouth easily capable of snapping his head off his neck. Harp twisted out of the way, scraping his chin against a rock and getting a face full of mud. Pushing himself to his feet, he pulled out his sword and ran to the edge of the ravine.

"Maybe flipping her isn't such a good idea!" Harp yelled.

"Get her between you and the cliff," Boult shouted.

But that was easier said than done, and the ant seemed to have the same idea about knocking Harp into the river. Every time Harp tried to switch their positions, the ant lunged, forcing him to go on the defensive. Harp got the unsettling impression that she was toying with him, and as soon as she tired of the game, he was going to be the one squished on the ground.

"Last try!" Harp yelled. "When I go down on the ground, shoot at the same time!"

"No, Harp!" Kitto shouted.

Harp dodged as the ant lunged at him. With a burst of speed, he sprinted away from the ant to the edge of the ravine. Planting himself a few paces from the drop-off, he let the queen charge him. In the instant before she smacked into him, Harp dropped backward onto the ground, raised his sword, and plunged it into her underside just as she barreled over him.

When they saw Harp fall backward onto the ground, Kitto and Boult fired arrows that struck the ant's back, but they bounced harmlessly off the hard shell. Instead, it was the ant's own momentum that propelled her to the very edge of the ravine. The creature struggled against gravity, her legs skittering for a hold on the muddy bank before she flipped over the edge, taking a smattering of loose earth, Harp's sword, and Harp with her.

"Harp!" Kitto screamed, as Harp disappeared off the edge of the ravine.

"Hold him, Verran," Boult shouted. Verran grabbed Kitto's arm, but the boy jerked it away.

Kitto started down the trunk, and Verran grabbed his elbow again. Kitto glared up at him furiously and pulled away.

"The ants will leave," Verran assured him. "And we'll go after the captain."

Kitto looked doubtful, but he hesitated. Just as Verran said, the rank-and-file ants didn't know what to do without their leader. The ants on the tree trunks dropped to the ground and milled around in confusion, eventually wandering in different directions into the underbrush. A few walked directly off the edge of the ravine and into thin air, following the path of the queen. As the horde dispersed, the crewmates scrambled down the tree trunks, but the few remaining ants didn't seem to notice them.

Kitto ran to the edge where Harp had disappeared, dropped to his knees, and peered over the side.

"Do you see him?" Verran asked.

Boult stood at his shoulder. "It's not a vertical drop, Kit. He could have grabbed onto something. And I can't see his body."

"Let's find a way down," Verran said. A few paces up the river, a faint path traversed the bank down to the river. Halfway down the trail they could hear Harp calling to them over the rush of the river.

"See Kitto?" Boult said. "You're not going to get rid of him that easily."

Kitto's head was tipped forward, so his shaggy black hair covered his face, and he didn't say anything until they reached the bottom of the ravine. Harp was waiting for them by the river, wincing as he rubbed his shoulder. His face was muddy, and blood from his chin had dripped onto his sweat-stained shirt.

"Are you all right?" Kitto asked.

"Hah, stupid ant," Harp said. "Lost my sword, though."

"Bad luck," Boult said.

"Maybe not," Harp said, pointing downriver. "I found something else."

CHAPTER ELEVEN

30 Kythorn, the Year of the Ageless One
(1479 DR)
Chult

Set into the face of the riverside bluff, the wooden door was half-covered in flowering vines. The edge of the river was just paces away from the door, and there were watermarks halfway up the planks as if there had been recent flooding. A narrow path, just wide enough for a single person, led from the door to the river.

"Doesn't look much like an ancient ruin," Boult said, looking at the sturdy metal hinges and door-frame set into the bank. Between Bootman's attack and the ants, Chult's surprises were nothing to underestimate. The door was one more thing. What hid behind it?

"There's something here," Verran called from where he'd wandered down the bank. A short slope led down to the river, and a ring of three boulders formed a pool of calm water. Judging from the smattering of tracks along the slope, it was a popular watering hole for animals.

"I've never seen half these tracks before," Verran said, kneeling down and poking at the ground with a stick. "See those hoof prints? I'd say they're wild boar. But look, they've got an extra toe."

"What do you know about wild boar?" Boult said dubiously.

Verran looked embarrassed. "My father liked to go hunting. Before he died, he used to show me things."

Boult glared at Harp, who avoided his gaze. It would take an act of outright treachery for Harp to see that there was something suspicious about a boy who could unintentionally melt the skin off a man. Boult wasn't fooled by Verran. He might act like he was lost and confused, but he was taller than Harp and built like a blacksmith. A youth didn't have muscles like that unless he had done something hard to earn them.

"I can see . . . six different cat tracks," Verran said excitely. Kitto knelt down beside Verran to inspect the mud.

"I used to have a cat," Kitto told Verran.

"So did I," Verran said. "It was a fat tabby."

"Mine was gray," Kitto said.

Boult couldn't believe what he was hearing. At this rate, the boys would be skipping stones and laying out a picnic. Boult looked at Harp incredulously and saw that Harp was trying hard not to smile.

"Is that what you wanted to show us, Verran?" Harp inquired gently.

"There are human footprints. There," Verran told him.

Boult looked closer and saw a series of tracks that were unmistakably from a barefoot humanoid, and a smallish one at that.

"Another dwarf?" Harp asked. "Like the one we saw in the hollow?"

Verran shook his head and crouched down for a better look. "I don't think so. Usually they have a lower arch and the bone below the big toe sticks out more. Look, they go back up." Verran followed the tracks up the muddy slope in the direction of the door.

"And just what was young Master Verran doing tracking dwarves through the wilderness with his father," Boult said in a low voice.

Kitto frowned. "Verran's all right," he said.

"Yeah, Boult," Harp said. "Keep your wits about you. Maybe it was perfectly innocent."

"Sure, they were all going to frolic together like wood nymphs," Boult snapped.

"Can't a man just stalk a dwarf for the joy of it?" Harp said. "Why do you have to make it sound all nefarious?"

"Why don't you go chew on the pointy end of your sword, Harp?" Boult growled.

"I lost my sword, remember?" Harp replied.

"Quit it," Kitto said sternly. They trudged up the slope to where Verran was waiting.

"Well, there's nothing to do but go inside," Boult said after Verran pointed out how the footsteps disappeared on the dry ground in front of the door.

"Someone needs to wait out here and watch the door," Harp said. "Any volunteers?"

"I will," Kitto said.

"No, I will," Verran said. "I don't like dark, enclosed places."

"All right," Harp said. "Shout if you see something."

Stepping off to one side, Harp pushed gently against the door. It wasn't locked and swung open with a loud squeal.

"Another stellar move by Captain Harp," Boult sneered as they stared into the gloom of the cavern. "Nothing like rusty hinges to announce your presence."

"Oh, I'm sorry," Harp said sarcastically. "Of course, you would have thought to put a spot of lamp oil on the hinges first."

Harp took a step forward, but Boult shook his head. "You've got the night vision of an old man. Let me."

Harp put out his arm to stop Boult. "And you're about as stealthy as a cat in heat. Let me."

They hadn't gone more than a few steps down the passageway when they saw an open doorway on the left side of the corridor. A long line of thick-barred, low-ceilinged cages lined one wall of the dank room. Shackles were bolted to their slick floors, and bones and hunks of fur—some of which still had rotting flesh clinging to them—littered the cramped cages. Harp's haggard face had gone from tan to pale, and the ruddy scars crisscrossing his features stood out against his wan skin. Harp leaned one hand against the wall as if he were trying to regain his balance. Boult understood—he was having some unpleasant recollections of the Vankila Slab himself.

"I swore I'd cut out my own eyes before I'd go back to prison," Harp said to Boult. "Particularly before I'd go back to prison with you."

"But then you'd be stupid *and* ugly," Boult replied. "And if you'll notice what side of the bars we're on, we're not in prison."

"Yet," Harp said grimly.

The Vankila Slab was a prison in the sky. Built by a joint effort of the Houses of Amn, it had been constructed on a barren mote, a massive slab of earth floating above Murandinn. The ogres who were charged with running the prison were given enough gold and slave labor to construct four sky-scraping round towers connected by raised walkways. Without anything except the sky to offer perspective, the towers looked taller than they were, almost as if they might slide off the edge of the mote and go smashing into the ground hundreds of feet below without turning once. More than one prisoner held onto that fantasy—that the filthy walls of their prison tip into the airy abyss, taking their captives with them.

Originally, the Vankila Slab housed spellcasters who had defied Amn's ban on using magic or members of well-connected families who had fallen out of favor with Amn's ruling houses. But within ten years of building the prison, the political sensibilities in Amn shifted, and the Vankila Slab fell into the hands of a single faction that had its fingers deep in the murky politics of both Amn and Tethyr. Soon the prison became a mercenary operation that took the most dangerous criminals off the hands of the law and political prisoners off anyone who would pay.

Around that time, the wardens of the Vankila Slab discovered that the floating mote under their prison was filled with gemstones, and with an endless supply of free labor at their disposal they began to unearth the unexpected riches. From then on, the prisoners spent their days mining the gems with hand tools or spoons or their bloody fingernails—whatever they had on any particular day. Within a few decades, the gems were mostly mined out, but the overseers didn't want idle prisoners, so they kept them digging. On average, a prisoner came across a gem once a month, which earned them a hunk of meat with their gruel and little else but an early death from constant work in the scorching open ground known as the Turf.

By the time Harp left Liel and Kitto in a cove on the Moonshaes and turned himself over to the Amnian agents, the Vankila wardens were pursuing other uses for their prisoners. The faction that controlled the prison allowed select mages access to their prisoners, but only mages who practiced a certain kind of magic that might be useful to the wardens in the future. The mages needed space to study and conduct their experiments, so the wardens constructed a fortress high above the surface of the mote using the four existing towers as a foundation. From the ground, the prisoners could see only the bottom of the fortress—a rectangle that spanned the distance between the towers and cast half the mote into darkness. The prisoners resented the loss of the sun, and soon rumors of dark rituals and sacrifices swept through the inmates, who called the soaring fortress the Sky Tomb.

It was in the Sky Tomb that an elder mage known as the Practitioner set up shop. He wasn't always in residence at the Vankila Slab. Rather like a traveling scholar, he came and went, but his experiments were legendary. Like most of the mages, he wasn't interested in the criminally minded, who were too hard to handle. Rather he turned his attentions to the inmates who were in prison for political reasons, almost all of whom were some race other than human.

When Harp had turned himself in to the authorities, he had known nothing about the Practitioner or the Sky Tomb, although he had heard fireside tales of a floating prison so brutal that even birds wouldn't approach its shores. After he was taken from the Moonshae Isles in chains, Harp was put in the hold of a prison ship, which sailed to Amn. Harp expected to face a tribunal and be given the standard punishment for mutiny—a year of hard labor. Instead, he was brought to the Vankila Slab without ever seeing a magistrate. When the hood was taken off, Harp found himself among the notorious and deranged in the very prison that had housed Amhar, Scourge of Tethyr, and Mencelas the Reaper, to name the worst of the worst.

During his first days on the Turf, Harp noticed that the guards patrolled the edges of the mote more carefully than anywhere else. When he asked the emaciated man next to him why that was, the man startled at the sound a human voice. Pawing at the open sores on his neck, the man glanced at Harp suspiciously. His bleary gray eyes darted from side to side with seemingly involuntary jerks that made Harp wonder how the man could see anything clearly.

"Keeps us from jumping, doesn't it?" the man whispered before returning to his digging.

During his first nights in the Vankila Slab, Harp's mind settled on Liel in a way that was both comforting and disturbing. He couldn't keep his mind from replaying the days he was with her and the nights he spent in her arms. Sometimes it was simply too much, like a noose that slowly tightened around his throat. He alternated between regret and anger, and the undeniable hope that she would figure out where they had stashed him and find a way to get him out of the hellhole in the clouds.

A tenday after he arrived, the Vankila Slab still seemed like a brutal dream, and Harp kept expecting to wake up and find himself back in the sun-dappled forest on Gwynneth Isle with Liel and Kitto. He had been digging under the red sun for a couple of hours when an ogre approached him barking orders. Although he didn't know the language, it wasn't hard to figure out that the ogre wanted Harp to stand up and follow him. Harp happened to be working near a group of dwarves that morning, and he saw them exchange glances.

The ogre tied Harp's hands behind his back, and all the while, the clutch of dwarves watched with great interest, surprising and unnerving Harp. One of the gaunt dwarves spoke up.

"Look for me later," the dwarf said. "I'll help you."

The ogre raised his fist and cuffed the nearest face, not caring whether he was the dwarf who had spoken or not. Then they headed for the nearest tower as the ogre jerked Harp along behind him. Knowing the risk the dwarf had taken in speaking up, Harp felt a chill despite the heat of the day. The ogre walked Harp off the Turf and into the darkness of the gated yard below the Sky Tomb. As he had done many times before, Harp tipped his head back to look at up the fortress and wondered what went on so high above the ground. He was about to find out.

After climbing the long staircase to the Sky Tomb, the ogre led Harp into a spacious, attractive anteroom—the exact opposite of the conditions on the Turf. With golden struts framing walls of rose-colored glass, the anteroom looked more like a sanctuary than a tomb. The morning light filtered through the glass ceiling and cast the air in a soothing red glow. It would have been beautiful if there hadn't been such a sinister feel to the silence.

The ogre took him through a door, up a flight of stairs, and into a circular room covered by a rose-colored dome. Judging from the unspoiled view of the landscape and the heavens, it was the highest point in all of the Vankila Slab. An older, gray-haired man sat at a large wooden desk with his head bent over a parchment, the curled ends of which were held flat with blue crystals. He wore a black skullcap and wire-rimmed glasses perched on the end of his nose. When they entered the room, he peered at them momentarily over his spectacles, but he returned to his reading as if he had little interest in his visitors.

Except for the glass walls, the room reminded Harp of a study at an academy of arcane teaching. There were bookshelves set into trenches along the floor and ladders to get down to them. A long table laden with pots filled with yellow and red flowers ran the length of the eastern window. In the center of the room was a simple wooden chair.

The ogre shoved him into the chair and tied one hand and his feet to the rungs of the chair, which was bolted to the floor. The ogre clamped a leather cuff lined with matted fur around Harp's other wrist. The cuff was attached to a long chain that was also bolted to the floor. The chain allowed Harp some movement of his arm, but not enough to strike out. As the ogre checked the knots on the ropes, Harp noticed a strange scent like a mixture of burning hair and honey. After the ogre left, the older man continued to sit at his desk, sipping tea and reading until Harp got tired of waiting for something to happen.

"You got problems with birds hitting the glass?" he finally asked.

At the sound of Harp's voice, the man closed his book and gave him an amused smile.

"So, Master Harp. You made some people very angry."

"Apparently."

The man picked up a ceramic bowl from the table and carried it over to Harp. Inside, a white cloth floated in soapy water.

"Please wash your face and hand," the man said, still looking vaguely amused.

At first, Harp thought about refusing, but decided against it. It was just water after all.

"Are you my judge or my executioner?" Harp asked, tossing the grubby cloth back into the bowl. The man set the bowl next to the flowers and turned back to Harp.

"Maybe a little of both," the man said, sounding appreciative at Harp's question.

"Since when are mutineers put in Vankila? It's overkill, don't you think?"

The man tipped his head and peered down at his prisoner. "Are you guilty?"

"Of mutiny?" Harp asked.

"Of anything."

"Are we having a philosophical conversation? Because I've got to warn you, I've never had much use for books," Harp said. He had a feeling the conversation wasn't a discussion on the nature of a guilty soul.

"A pity. Books offer so much. There are some who find enough joy in learning to last an entire lifetime. It's such a pure way to spend one's time. Don't you think?"

Harp said nothing. The man walked over to his desk, rolled up the parchment that he had been reading, and tucked it inside a drawer.

"I expected to devote my life to study, but instead I became distracted by other pursuits. But you haven't answered my question. Are you guilty?"

"Is my confession necessary for whatever is about to happen?"

"No, I just find it interesting how people handle pain."

So there was going to be pain. Harp wasn't surprised, but that didn't make it any easier to take.

"Life is pain," the man told him with the same amused expression on his aged face. "Have you learned that yet?"

Harp took a deep breath. He'd seen Predeau torture enough people to have an idea of what was coming. Oddly, it was the serene surroundings that unnerved him the most. He wondered if the ogre was coming back and if he was bringing tools.

"If someone else is the cause of your pain, you feel as though you are a martyr. But if you have caused your misery through your own actions, then you are complicit in the agony. The men who are murderers, well, they know they deserve it. But the men who are here for their beliefs are different. The pain builds a self-righteous fire in them—at least at first."

"I don't deserve to be tortured for my crime."

"And which crime is that?"

"Mutiny."

"Ah. And what about the crime of adultery?"

"I didn't . . ." Harp stopped short when he realized the man was talking about Liel. It made him ill to think that the man would know that Liel even existed. And worse, that he would know about her and Harp. Liel was something precious, and their relationship was something that should have remained secret and safe. Only Harp and Liel knew what they had been to each other. So if the man knew, then Liel must have broken the secret.

"Master Cardew would say differently," the man said gravely. "In my opinion, a betrothed woman is the same as a married woman."

"Not everyone would agree with your opinion."

"Then they are mistaken. There is a natural order to the world, and ignoring it doesn't make it go away. Men should rule the world. Women and the lesser races must submit. There is no other way."

"I'd say there is. But considering our situation, I'm not in a position to argue with you," Harp said numbly.

"Indeed." The man stood up and crossed over to Harp. "Please give me your arm your arm, and turn your palm up." Harp complied. "Master Cardew said you should have kept your hands to yourself."

At first, it felt like a warm stone had been placed between his fingers. Mild at first, the sensation was concentrated in the palm of his hand. There was an unpleasant tingle at the top of his wrist, and then a burst of angry red lines shot across his skin, branching slowly across his palm and creeping up toward his fingernails. It took him only an instant to fathom the pain—it was like his skin was splitting from the inside, cut to shreds by invisible, white-hot needles. He'd never known pain like that. He'd never imagined it could exist. Then he couldn't understand why it didn't kill him.

"I'm fascinated with how things are put together," the man said thoughtfully. He pulled his hand back, and Harp slumped over in the chair gasping for air. "And how the right spell can reveal the structures of life itself."

Liel had done that, Harp thought as the room spun around

him. Liel had told Cardew about her relationship with Harp. His whole body ringing with pain, Harp willingly gave in to the blackness that closed around the edges of his vision. But as Harp's eyes drifted shut, the man brushed Harp's forehead with his fingers, and Harp jerked back into consciousness. Liel knew exactly where he was and what was happening to him, he thought. Her betrayal was absolute.

The skin on his hand began to disintegrate into a mass of tiny cuts, each deeper than the last, until the end of his arm looked like a bloody stump, nothing like a hand at all. Harp heard himself sobbing for the man to stop, to cut off his hand, to cut off his head, anything to make it stop.

"You see, I think there are building blocks that make up every living thing," the man continued. "The miniscule bits are smaller than you could ever imagine, but they are the fabric of everything. It may not give you comfort, Master Harp, but my work is for a purpose greater than yourself."

Harp had no memory after that, but when he awoke in his cell, the gaunt dwarf was sitting in his cell with him holding a flask of water to his lips. Harp was surprised to see that his hand was still attached to his arm. The cuts were closed. Flaming red scars showed where the chunks had been ripped apart and put back together.

Harp and his friends left the room with the low-ceilinged cages and headed down the main passage. As the tunnel sloped deeper into the cavern, pale yellow bricks had been used to shore up the walls. Holes in the wall where bricks had crumbled to the floor revealed dirt instead of rock. One wall bulged dramatically as if the soil were trying to force its way into the tunnel. The passage ended at a wooden door, which was open slightly with only darkness beyond.

"If there's anyone in there, they would have seen the light from our torches," Boult said as they hesitated outside the door.

Harp pushed the door wide open, and they entered a dark, cold room. Judging from the echo of their footfalls, it was a large room with a high ceiling. Kitto lit the torches on either side of the door, illuminating rows of cages lining the north and south walls. They were larger cells than the ones they'd seen near the entrance of the cavern, and there were no bones or carrion littering the cobblestone floors. A wide ceramic trough ran along the front of the bars.

"I don't think there's any place I'd rather be less than here," Harp said under his breath.

"And what do you suppose that charming substance is?" Boult asked, looking down at the dark, sticky stains that coated the bottom of the trough.

"Sweet molasses?" Harp suggested. "Bottled sunshine? Goodness and love made into a tasty draught?"

"I was going to say chopped-up bits of local wildlife, but that's just me," Boult replied.

Holding his torch low to the ground, Kitto followed the trough to the mossy stones of the far wall where it disappeared through a pipe.

"There's a door," Kitto said. The light from his torch barely lit the dark corner that was obscured by the line of cages. Harp and Boult moved to join Kitto when a grating whine blasted their ears and made them freeze in surprise. Kitto grabbed his sensitive ears and darted away from the wall. As the sound faded, there was a moment of silence, and then a hum and clank of gears reached their ears.

"A machine? Here?" Boult looked dumbfounded. Kitto hastened to join his friends as the ground shook under their boots. The cobblestones jostled, and dust fell from the ceiling, covering them in a gray powder.

"Harp, look," Kitto said softly, pointing at the dark corner.

A light shone from under the door—a light that hadn't been there moments earlier. Before Harp could answer, the sound of smashing glass and metallic reverberations rang out from the other side of the door. Someone or something was in that room.

Before Boult could stop him, Harp raced to the far wall and jerked open the door. A wave of heat and light made him shield his face with his hand and blink his eyes. When his vision recovered, he saw a tall, black furnace on the wall across from the door. Between the grates, he could see a green fire raging inside the metal cylinder. The unnatural green of the flames cast the room in indigo shadows and illuminated the towering machine that dominated the rest of the room.

The beehive-shaped machine had been split down the middle as if cleft in half by a giant's sword. Framed by curved metal braces, the inner workings of the contraption were a haphazard array of glass tubing and bundles of fleshy red cords twisted around a central black-lit core. Only half of the machine was visible, with the upper portion concealed in the darkness above them where the light from the furnace couldn't reach.

On the other side of the wreckage of the device, something shattered against the floor. Harp dashed around the machine, startling the slight figure that was clutching a wooden stick in his bloody fingers. He swung the stick at Harp, who easily knocked it out of it his hands. Harp grabbed his arm and twisted it up behind his back, and forced him to his knees just as Kitto rushed around the corner. Harp saw Kitto's eyes widen in surprise.

"Let her go!" Kitto cried.

At Kitto's unexpected command, Harp dropped the writhing body like a stone and backed away. Instead of fleeing, the person crouched on the ground like a cornered animal. Now that the figure was still, Harp could see that it had an unmistakably female form. Kitto crouched beside her and brushed back the red hair from her face.

"Liel?" Harp asked, recognition hitting him like a physical shock. At the sound of her name, she looked up at him in confusion. The elf hadn't changed since he'd seen her years before. Her hair was still the reddish color of a sunset. She had the same graceful curve of her jawbone, the same sea green of her eyes. But she was smeared with blood, her body trembled, and her feet were bare and muddy.

Despite the years, despite her disheveled condition, despite her betrayal, Harp wanted to reach out and touch her. He wanted to carry her through the jungle to the relative comfort and safety of his ship. He wanted a lot of things, but uncertainty kept his hands firmly at his sides. It had been so long since he'd seen her, and she had become a stranger.

"Harp? Kitto?" she implored. "What are you doing here?"

"Looking for you," Harp managed to say as Kitto helped her to her feet.

Liel stared at them with bloodshot eyes. "How did you know where I was?"

"Your father hired us."

"Avalor hired you?" She stared at Boult as if he had just said something.

"That's Boult. He's with us," Harp said. "Come on, let's get outside."

"What about the machine?" Liel asked.

"Yes, what about the machine?" Boult looked up at the half-destroyed contraption and back at Liel.

But Harp didn't care about the machine. He wanted to get Liel out of the place and away from the bars and sticky troughs, and machines made from fleshy cords. But when he tried to lead her to the door, she shied away from his touch.

"We can't leave it," Liel said urgently. "We have to destroy it."

"It's been split in two," Harp told her. "I think it's destroyed."

Liel hesitated and then allowed him to put his hand on her back and lead her up the passageway. But as they neared the entrance, she grew more and more agitated, casting furtive glances behind her and slowing her steps until she was barely walking at all.

"It's all right," Kitto assured her. "We're close to the ship."

Liel shook her head. "I can't leave."

"Why?"

"I just can't!"

"What is that machine?" Boult asked gruffly. "What does it do?"

At his question, she stopped walking and turned back the way they'd come. From where they stood, Harp could see the entrance to the cavern. The door was ajar, and outside he could see Verran leaning against a sunlit boulder, looking back at the entrance to the cave. Hearing the rush of the river made Harp want to be gone from the cavern immediately.

"Give me a reason," Harp said quietly. "Tell me why you can't leave."

"Cardew," Liel said promptly.

Boult frowned. "Cardew what?"

"Cardew's not in Chult," Harp told her. "He's back in Tethyr."

"Tethyr?" Liel repeated.

"Avalor wants to see you. We'll take you to the Wealdath."

"I can't leave," Liel repeated. "You don't know what Cardew has done in the jungle."

"Show us what he's done," Boult said, surprising Harp. But when Harp started to ask why Boult had suddenly had a change of heart about staying in the jungle, Boult silenced him with an abrupt gesture. "Show us the colony."

"What?" Harp said. "You're the one who wanted to leave."

But Boult's declaration had calmed Liel down. Her shoulders relaxed, and she stared at the dwarf with unblinking eyes. "You won't believe what he's planning to do."

CHAPTER TWELVE

1 Flamerule, the Year of the Ageless One
(1479 DR)
Kinnard Keep, Tethyr

"I'm so sorry about your wife, Declan," Ysabel said quietly, reaching out and resting her fingers lightly on Cardew's hand. Cardew gave her a sad smile and her small fingers a quick squeeze. "When did she die?"

Before Cardew could answer, Tresco coughed into his napkin. Excusing himself, he reached for a glass of water. Cardew turned back to Ysabel. Her cheeks were pink from the warmth of the fire. He hadn't seen her in nearly a year, and she still wore her long blonde hair in a girlish braid down her back. It was very becoming, but an unusual choice for a nineteen-year-old who would be marrying soon.

"She grew ill on the journey to Chult," Cardew said. "She died our first night on the island. It's been almost a year. I still think about her, of course."

"Of course," Ysabel said. "What was the jungle like? Was it horrible?"

"And how did you ever manage to survive?" Tresco asked. "I heard the colony was attacked by wraiths."

"No, no," Cardew said, shaking his head. "Nothing that . . . supernatural."

Ysabel and Tresco waited patiently, but Cardew was quiet for an overly long time.

"You don't have to give us details," Ysabel said. "I shouldn't have pressed you. It must have been dreadful."

Cardew nodded gratefully. For months, rumors had circulated that every colonist had been slaughtered in Chult, including the Hero of the Realm, Declan Cardew. His unexpected and miraculous return to the Court of the Crimson Leaf had caused much excitement among the nobles of Tethyr. How Cardew alone had escaped death and returned home with only a bruised head and a gaunt frame was not yet clear. When pressed, Cardew was a bit hazy on the details of what exactly had happened to him in the dark jungle.

"I heard Queen Anais ordered you to convalesce in Hulen," Ysabel said, reaching for her glass of red wine. The black-haired serving girl came through the door with a silver tray and laid bowls of thick broth before them.

"Yes, but it had been so long since I'd seen you," Cardew replied. "I couldn't wait any longer."

"We thought you were going to arrive two days ago," Tresco said.

"But we're just as happy to see you now, aren't we, Uncle?" Ysabel said hurriedly. "How long do you plan to stay?"

"Several days, if you'll have me," Cardew replied.

"Of course," Ysabel said happily. "Just as you said, it's been an age since we've been together."

"Yes, how long has it been?" Tresco asked, tapping his finger against the edge of his china bowl thoughtfully. "I believe it has been almost two years."

"Has it really?" Ysabel asked. "I remember fondly those nights that we played Scaffold Knights. And what was that other game you liked? Routacelle, wasn't it?"

"You won nearly every game," Cardew said, shaking his head in mock disbelief.

"I don't remember that," Ysabel protested. "You won far more than I did. Perhaps we can have a game after dinner. The set is around somewhere."

"Maybe another night," Cardew replied. "I'm afraid I'm not up to my former glory. You would slay me for sure."

"I like the orderliness of the game," Ysabel mused. "You know who your enemies are. There's no deception."

"Games were your favorite pastime when you were young," Tresco interjected. "I could barely keep you at your studies."

"You were away often, Tresco," Cardew said. "I would come to visit Bella, and you were at the academy or wherever your studies took you."

"Yet it was so hard for you to break away from court," Tresco countered. "You had so many responsibilities. We rarely saw you. But we understood, didn't we, Ysabel?"

"I was so concerned for you, Bella, in the years after the massacre," Cardew continued. "You were very much changed from the lively little girl I once knew."

"Those were dark years," Ysabel agreed. "You both were a great comfort to me."

"Did I ever tell you that I've been to Chult?" Tresco said abruptly.

"Have you?" Cardew asked. "No, I didn't realize that."

"Yes, I went on an expedition with a group of scholars from Candlekeep. We were searching for a type of poisonroot with healing properties."

"Uncle has the most interesting stories about the jungle, Declan," Ysabel said. "Tell the one about the giant lizard. That story gave me nightmares for days!"

"Oh, I don't intend to bore Cardew with my tales of adventure," Tresco said. "After the death of his wife, I'm sure the jungle is a horrible memory."

Blushing, Ysabel looked at the floor in embarrassment. "I'm sorry," she said. "My tongue gets away from me."

"It's no trouble," Cardew reassured her. "Your uncle is just thinking of my welfare."

"The soup is cold," Tresco declared with distaste, throwing his spoon into the broth, which sloshed onto the tablecloth. "I'll tell the cook to bring us something else."

Throwing his cloak over his shoulder, Tresco swept out of the room. As soon as the door clicked shut, Ysabel stood up. Lifting her skirt to her thighs, she straddled Cardew and hugged him tight around the neck.

"I thought you were dead," she whispered.

"Ysabel," he breathed as he clutched her back. He could feel the bones of her rib cage through the silk of her dress. "I've thought of you constantly since I left."

Gripping the back of his chair, Ysabel pressed her body down against his until he took a shuddering breath.

"No," he said. "Not when Tresco could walk in."

"Did you bring me something special?" she whispered coyly, her lips brushing his ear. "Did you bring me something from the wilderness?"

"I'd go to the ends of the world to get you whatever you want," he said. She cupped his face in her hands.

"Did you bring me anything?"

"I brought you another spellbook," Cardew whispered, gazing up at her. "I'll leave it behind the tapestry the way I used to."

"And I'll reward you, the way I used to," she promised, pressing her face against his neck.

"You make me . . . desperate," he told her.

"When can we be together?"

"Soon," he promised. "Soon you'll be my wife."

Ysabel kissed his mouth hard. Then she pushed away from him, smoothed her skirt down, and sat primly in her chair just as Tresco swung open the door.

"Cardew was just asking me about the portraits," Ysabel told Tresco, pointing to the wall at the collection of ten paintings, all of Evonne Linden. There was Evonne as a child, sitting on a swing under a massive oak tree. Evonne at her wedding feast, the day she married Garion. Evonne standing in the marble hall outside the judges' chambers in Darromar. "I told him that it had been our personal project. We hired the best painters in the realm, didn't we Uncle?"

"Indeed," Tresco said heartily.

"I didn't know Evonne liked horses," Cardew said dryly, looking up at a painting of Evonne riding a chestnut stallion.

"Well, you didn't know Evonne well at all, did you?" Tresco replied, motioning impatiently to the servant who had arrived with plates piled with lamb. "Did I ever tell you that it was Evonne who gave me the idea of exploring Chult in the first place? She had done all sorts of research on the sarrukh and said they had wealth beyond imagination in the ruins of their . . ."

As Tresco droned on about gold plates and copper goblets, Ysabel gave Cardew a secret smile. Cardew maintained a perfectly calm façade, but inside his chest, his heart was pounding.

CHAPTER THIRTEEN

1 Flamerule, the Year of the Ageless One
(1479 DR)
Chult

From the outside, the colony looked more like a military outpost than a village. Fashioned from roughly hewn planks and mud, the perimeter walls seemed as tall as the *Crane's* mast and were crowned with long black thorns. Creeping vines had engulfed several areas as the jungle reclaimed the colony. But the ground in front of the gate was muddy and barren, making the compound seem even less hospitable.

"Welcome to Cardewton," Liel said, without a trace of irony. The gate was slightly ajar, and Liel ducked inside and disappeared from sight without another word.

As if waiting for an invitation to enter, the men remained outside. Looking at the isolation of the spot, it seemed strange that Cardew chose to name the colony after himself. Only a man with Cardew's limitless ego could perceive a mudhole in the jungle as a prize worth claiming.

"Having seen her, I can see why you've been so moody so long," Boult finally said. "But, does she seem odd to you?"

Harp shrugged. "She seems subdued. The Liel I knew was like . . . a force of nature."

Boult snorted. "She's a druid. She *is* a force of nature."

"You know what I mean."

"No, I don't. And neither do you."

"It was like she had raw power that could barely be contained by her body," Kitto said quietly. "It was like heat came off her in waves."

Harp snapped his fingers. "Exactly. That's what I meant."

"I don't feel any power in her at all," Kitto said. "Just coldness."

Boult shot Harp a smug look. Harp had no idea what Boult should be smug about, but Boult rarely needed a good reason to feel superior.

"Don't start," Harp snapped. "It's been almost a month since Cardew showed up in Tethyr. We don't know what's happened to her since he left her behind."

"Then what are we doing standing out here?" Boult said. "Let's go find out."

Once inside, they could see that the space inside the walls was limited, not much larger than a city block in Darromar, with only a few permanent structures. A shabby wooden building with a thatched roof stood in the center of the encampment and had probably been the common area for the colonists. Near the eastern wall, a sturdy hut had been built in a grove of goldenfruit trees—a grove that had stood long before someone built a wall around the area.

"How long were the colonists here?" Boult asked as Harp and Kitto struggled to close the heavy gate.

"About three months, I think," Harp said, inspecting the locking mechanism on the gate, which consisted of a flimsy metal hook. It didn't look very secure, but then maybe the night creatures weren't interested in breaking and entering, just stomping and eating.

"They didn't get much done, did they?" Boult said, surveying the motley array of buildings.

"What do you mean?" Harp asked.

"If you were building a colony, what would be your first priority?" Boult asked.

"A dry place to sleep," Kitto said.

"Exactly," Boult agreed. "But look at those hovels."

Harp looked around at the handful of rudimentary lean-tos scattered along the perimeter. Made from sticks braced against the outer wall and covered in dried grasses, the lean-tos looked about as cozy as the low-walled pens that were clustered along the back wall of the encampment.

"Those aren't the dwellings of people who are planning to stay," Boult pointed out.

"What about that house?" Verran asked, gesturing to the hut in the grove of trees. The mud walls of the hut had been built on a wooden platform several feet off the ground, probably to discourage snakes and rodents from seeking shelter.

"I'll bet you the first round that is Master Cardew's house," Boult said under his breath to Harp. "Is that where Liel went?"

"Let's give her a few minutes to herself," Harp said.

"To do what?" Boult asked grumpily.

"Maybe find some shoes," Harp said pointedly. "We'll look around. Kitto, will you keep an eye on the gate? If you see any sign of Liel, give us a shout."

Kitto nodded and settled down on a stump near the wall while the others headed for the common building. They could see holes in the thatched roof, and the roughly hewn planks used for the walls were warped and graying. As they opened the squeaky door, the stench of rot was sharp in the air.

"Dead colonists?" Boult asked.

"It's not human," Verran blurted out. Then he looked as if he wished he'd kept his mouth shut.

"What are you, a dog?" Boult asked incredulously. "How do you do that?"

"Down, Boult," Harp said easily. "Identifying corpses by smell could be a useful skill."

"What? Knitting is a useful skill. Cooperage, definitely handy. No offense, Verran, but that's just . . ."

"Boult, enough." But Verran had already moved away into the gloom. "It's not his fault," Harp whispered angrily.

Boult jutted out his jaw unapologetically. "Maybe not, but it's still unsettling."

"Fine. Be unsettled in the privacy of your thick skull. He's just a kid. I'm sure he didn't ask to be that way."

"Oh, it's just a family trait? Like curly hair?" Boult hissed.

Harp shrugged noncommittally. "Well, in a way."

"In what way?" Boult demanded.

"His father was a warlock," Harp said softly, watching as Verran inspected a row of shelves at the far end of the room. "Maybe that has something to do with it."

"If his father made a bargain with something dark, then he would get the power, not his son," Boult informed Harp.

"Unless giving power to Verran was part of the bargain," Harp replied, suddenly feeling uneasy. He'd hadn't had a chance to ponder his conversation with Verran on the beach or consider the implications of what Verran had told Harp about his father.

"Maybe," Boult said. "Or maybe Verran's making all that up. Maybe he's the one who asked for the bargain. Maybe he made up the story about his father."

"And maybe this is all speculation," Harp said. "It could be . . . something else entirely."

"Let's hope so," Boult replied as Verran called to them from across the dusty room. He was standing near a low table that was still set with empty wooden bowls and cups filled with water. A rotting haunch of meat hung over a cold pile of ash in the fire pit.

"Dinner ended abruptly," Boult said. "I wonder what happened at lovely Cardewton? Did Avalor tell you what its lovely leader reported, Harp?"

"No, and I'm sure whatever Cardew said at court bears little resemblance to the truth."

"But Liel knows," Boult said gruffly.

"And we'll ask her. But be patient," Harp said. "Let her get some clothes, clean the blood off herself. She's not going anywhere."

"Patience is an excuse for the dull-witted," Boult retorted.

Harp opened his mouth to reply, but changed his mind. Between Liel and Verran, he had too much on his mind to banter with Boult. Having found Liel, he wasn't sure what to do next. If there were more hints to Cardew's plans here, Avalor would want to know what they were. But Avalor would also want his daughter safe in the Wealdath. Usually he could count on Boult for solid advice, but after Boult's revelation about Cardew, he wasn't sure the dwarf was thinking clearly either.

They headed to the door at the west end of the building, which opened onto a scrubby patch of ground. Nearby was a small shack with a padlock on the door, and there was another cluster of lean-tos near the outer wall. While Verran wandered over to check out the huts, Harp slammed his boot against the door of the shack. The entire frame splintered as the door went flying back and clattered against a weapons cabinet, knocking several swords to the dirt.

"Why even bother with a lock?" Harp said, looking at the splintered remains of the door.

The men replenished their bolts, and Harp checked the small selection of swords, most of which were rusted or slightly bent. There was only one that looked promising—a long sword with a golden hilt. An engraved serpent curled around the blade, and there was an empty space on each side of the pommel where jewels had been removed.

"Feel better?" Boult asked as Harp hefted the sword in his hand, sizing up the length and weight of the weapon.

"Isn't having a sword always better than not having a sword?" Harp asked.

"It depends on your definition of having."

Harp recognized a warning in Boult's tone. "Do you have something you want to say?"

"Maybe."

"Then just get it off your chest, dwarf."

"I have doubts that Cardew could mastermind anything as complex as an omelet, let alone run such an operation in Chult from his precious little estate in Tethyr."

Harp was genuinely surprised. "We know what Cardew is capable of. Why would such a thing be beyond him?"

"He's capable of lying. He's capable of having someone else do his dirty work. He's capable of taking orders. That's what we know."

"You don't think he organized the Children's Massacre?"

Boult snorted. "No, I've never thought that."

"Who do you think did it?"

"I have my theories."

Harp gestured impatiently. "The skillet's not getting any hotter, Boult. Throw on the butter and go."

"All right, but you won't like it."

"Just tell me."

"Remember I told you about the attack on the road outside

the Winter Palace. Well, here's what I didn't tell you: the assassins were elves."

"Elves? That doesn't make any sense."

"Not if the Branch of Linden set up the attack. But there's others—"

"The elves in Tethyr are solidly behind Avalor. He's had their allegiance for years. Are you implying that Avalor—"

Someone tapped lightly on the doorframe, and they both jumped.

Kitto cleared his throat, "Liel wants to talk to you," he said.

A late afternoon rainstorm forced them to take shelter inside the small hut that Liel had shared with her husband. The mud-and-straw walls were intact, but there were gaps between the floorboards and holes in the roof where the rain came through. Birds had nested in the thatch; they twittered and rustled as the wind lashed against the hut.

Before the storm came, Kitto had boiled a pot of water over the open fire pit outside. They sat on logs set around the fire by the colonists and drank tepid tea in mugs that Verran had found in the common building. With their packs pushed up against the driest wall, they sat on the floor and waited for Liel to speak. A crack of lightning crashed into the jungle nearby, but she didn't seem to hear it. She passed the cup from one hand to the next, staring intently into it.

"Things had been wrong with Cardew and me for a while. He spent all his time at Anais's court, maneuvering for position and playing the political games he loved so much. I left him and went back to living at my father's house in the Wealdath. After several months, Cardew came to me full of apologies. He had news of a venture in Chult, a venture that Queen Anais had handpicked for him. He was so excited, and it sounded like the perfect chance for us to do something together, to build something up—away from the intrigue of the queen's court.

"Cardew told me that we were going to Chult with a large contingent of adventurers and their families. But when we arrived in the jungle, it was just me, Cardew, and a handful of men and half-orcs. They were mercenaries hired from Baldur's Gate, and as soon as I saw them, I knew they weren't planning to make a home. We sailed to Chult in two different ships—Cardew and I on one ship, and the mercenaries on another. I first saw the men while we were standing on the beach as the ship sailed away. And I knew that Cardew had lied to me about what was going on in Chult.

"Minutes after we landed, a man was bit by a sand scorpion and died there on the beach. Another was almost killed by something ten feet into the jungle. I thought about leaving them and trying to find my way to Nyranzaru, but I wasn't even sure which direction to go. And I still had hopes that Cardew hadn't lied to me intentionally.

"The next day one of the half-orcs drank water from a muddy stream and began choking. I tried to help him, but he suffocated on his own tongue. I don't know where Cardew got the coin to pay the mercenaries' fees, but it must have been extensive. Nothing deterred them, not even after the first night when something came into the camp and dragged away another man.

"Cardew had a map that he consulted obsessively and wouldn't let anyone else see. I glanced at it once when he was sleeping. It was a map of the isle, and there were a series of sites that he'd marked, maybe eleven or twelve in all, all around the area. They were the hidden ruins that he'd come to search, but I didn't know it until later. There was something in the ruins that Cardew was determined to find, and he spent his days with a select group of men systematically searching the jungle.

"But that was harder than he expected. The jungle likes her secrets, and most days they simply wandered in the wilderness with nothing to show but rashes and scratches. Cardew hardly spoke to me, just gave me orders for what I was supposed to have the men do the next day. Each morning when I woke up he was gone, and he would arrive back just as the sun was setting. You have to understand, there was nowhere for me to go. There were no ships, there was no contact with outsiders, and to be honest, I wanted to know what he was up to.

"One day I followed them to the ruins on the north end of the valley beyond the waterfall. I guess one of the guards told Cardew that I had left the colony, because after that, he kept a guard with me at all times. It was unbearable. Then one day he arrived back to the camp early and called me into the house. He said that he had found something very important and showed me a parchment with a spell for opening a portal. He told me to make the portal and have it ready for us to go through the next day.

"But I was unwilling to do the magic. The spell had been translated into Common, but it was obviously something very old and powerful, perhaps something that he had found in the ruins. I decided that the portal was the reason he had brought me down to Chult in the first place. I was supposed to open it for him. But I'd seen enough to know that once I did it, I would have served my purpose and would no longer be useful to him. I was afraid what would happen to me if I complied.

"The next day Cardew arrived back at the camp bloody and alone. When I told him I hadn't finished the spell, he went into a rage. In our years as husband and wife, he had never laid his hands on me, but he hit me so hard I blacked out. When I woke up, he was gone.

"I've been here ever since, trying to figure out what he was doing and find a way home. The machine you saw must have been part of his plan. I was intent on destroying it, and that's when you found me."

Liel seemed exhausted after she told her story, and by an unspoken understanding, none of the men pressed her for more information. The rain stopped, and Harp fell asleep listening to a steady wind rustling the leaves. A few hours later, Harp heard Liel stir, pad softly across the floor of the hut, and go outside.

"Can I join you?" he asked, pulling the door shut behind them so the others wouldn't be disturbed by their voices. He laid his cloak over her shoulders.

"Of course." She pulled the cloak close around her body as if she had been cold. "I changed my mind about Tethyr. I want to go back."

"To Darromar and the court?" Harp asked in surprise.

"No, to the Wealdath," she explained. "I want to see the forest."

So some things had changed, Harp thought. The Liel he'd known would never have described the Wealdath as part of Tethyr. But it was to be expected that marrying a statesman and being in the Court of the Crimson Leaf would have changed the way she saw the world.

"What about Cardew?" Harp asked.

"Let him do what he will," she said softly. "Who am I to stop him?"

Harp watched her profile as she talked. Her face was tipped up to the clear, dark sky where the space between the stars looked more deep blue than pure black. Liel hadn't aged a day, which was not surprising considering her elf blood. She was beautiful to him in a way no one else had ever been, and he found something beautiful in most women.

He wanted to reach out and touch her jaw, to brush his fingers along the delicate vine-and-leaf pattern the way he had so many times before. Instead, he asked her the question he'd been waiting to ask for years.

"Why did you tell Cardew about us?" he asked.

"I didn't tell him. He just knew."

Harp wasn't sure what to say to that. He'd long forgiven Liel for telling Cardew about their relationship. She couldn't have known how Cardew would retaliate against his rival. But the news that Liel had never told their secret to Cardew at all was a surprise. Harp wanted to believe her, but he wasn't sure that he did.

"Did you know where they sent me?"

"No, I didn't. When I left the Wealdath, my father promised to find you and free you, wherever you were. Months later, he wrote to me and told me it was done. I asked where you were, but he never told me."

"Were you happy with Cardew?" Harp asked. "In the beginning at least?"

"Yes," she replied. "But it didn't last long."

"It never does," Harp agreed. Liel shifted beside him, and he sensed a change in her body, like an animal that glimpsed a predator and was preparing to flee.

"How could you turn yourself in like that?" she demanded suddenly. "You knew you would go to prison. You knew you would lose Kitto and me."

"It was the right thing to do," Harp said. "They were attacking elves indiscriminately, just for hiding us. They were using me as an excuse for the violence."

"Why didn't you just run away? Disappear into the North or go inland with Kitto? Once you'd got far enough, they never would have found you."

"But they might have found you," Harp said.

"Stop it," Liel said abruptly. "You're lying to me now, just the way you did then."

"I never lied to you." Harp's head was beginning to ache, and his brain felt sluggish.

"It was all a lie. From the very beginning. You used me."

Harp took a deep breath, unsure of why the conversation had suddenly veered in the direction it had. "I've wanted to apologize for something for a long time. I shouldn't have said that you were marrying Cardew for power and influence. I knew you better than that. I wasn't careful with my words. But I never lied to you."

Liel was quiet for a moment. "That was the breaking point?"

"Wasn't it?" Harp was shocked at the lack of emotion behind Liel's question. It had been the moment that had snapped them in two, the thing that had felt irreversible. It was as if he had triggered her memory, but none of the emotion about the argument itself.

"I guess it was," she finally said. "I remember."

"I never forgot," he said, disconcerted by her nonchalant manner.

"After we left the *Marderward* with Kitto, we were in that little boat for two days before we got to Gwynneth Isle," she continued. "And you were barely conscious. I'm not sure how we managed to get all the way to the island."

Between the lashes and Predeau's beating, Harp had been in bad shape when they left the *Marderward*. By the second day aboard the little skiff, he'd developed a high fever, and his wounds were inflamed with an infection that Liel couldn't heal. Those days were a blur for him. He remembered being frantic to keep Kitto and Liel near him, as if he would lose them forever if they were separated for even an instant. When they reached the safe haven, their host mistook Liel and Kitto as his wife and son.

Liel stared at the sky again. "What happened, Harp? You were there, and then, just like that, you weren't."

"What do you mean?"

"We were close. And then you just retreated from me."

"We talked about it being over from the moment it started," Harp reminded her. "I wasn't sure how you felt."

"You should have talked to me. You should have told me that you felt like what we were doing was wrong. But the fact that I wasn't even worth it to you . . ."

Harp started to speak, but she continued.

". . . It can only mean you never had any regard for me in the first place."

"That isn't true," Harp protested.

"Isn't it? It wasn't ever about anything but your convenience. Do you know what that makes me? Your whore."

"I'm not sure what to say," Harp said, managing to keep his voice steady despite the shock that she remembered their relationship in such a way. "You wanted it to be uncomplicated. You knew you were going back to Cardew."

"But it became something we didn't intend. You should've made an effort, not just left me without an explanation."

"I should have done a lot of things."

"I hated you. No, it was something different. I regretted ever knowing you. I wished that it had never happened."

"I didn't want to hurt you," Harp assured her. "That was never my intention."

"But you did."

"I'm sorry."

"It's easy to apologize. Those are just words."

Harp had a sense of vertigo as if he were sliding down a steep slope, and there was nothing to grab onto and stop himself. He felt exhausted and had no idea how to make things right.

"I didn't think you loved me, Liel. You never said you did."

"Why love someone you're never going to be with?" Liel said bitterly.

"If it means anything, you stayed in my head in a way I never expected."

"You were in prison. Holding onto a fantasy is expected."

"It was more than that," Harp said. "Even after prison. In life, I think you only get a few people who stay in your heart, whether you want them to or not."

"And I'm one of those?"

"This many years later, I think it's safe to say yes."

"I don't want to hate you anymore," she said, after a moment of silence.

Harp felt bruised, as if he'd just been hit with something very heavy. He wasn't sure if he wanted to drink himself blind or simply go to sleep and never wake up. He'd never felt so alone, even locked in the Vankila Slab, when her absence felt like a wound that wouldn't heal. He thought nothing could make him feel worse until she moved close against him. He put his arms around her, and even though it made no sense, the warmth of her body made him miss her in a way he hadn't for a long time. He spent the night with her sleeping in his arms and wondered if the loneliness would ever go away.

CHAPTER FOURTEEN

1 Flamerule, the Year of the Ageless One
(1479 DR)
Chult

Two shadows moved quietly through the unquiet jungle. A torrent of rain had fallen as the sun was setting, and a humid fog laid heavily on the hot night air. The figures moved carefully, disappearing into a strand of brush or behind a large root whenever a branch shook above them or they heard the sounds of large feet padding across the jungle floor. When they reached the edge of a clearing, one held back while the other scuttled across the open ground, moving as silently as a spider traversing a leaf.

The moon broke through the canopy, casting silver light on the young male dwarf who had entered the clearing. The dwarf known as Zo froze, the way a deer might if caught in a place it hadn't meant to be spotted. Zo pulled his hood over his long dark hair to obscure his face. He wore a leather breast-plate under his thin black cloak, a crossbow slung across his back, and a sheath belted at his waist.

A tenday before, Zo's chieftain father had been killed in a skirmish with the Scaly Ones, and Zo had taken the mantle of leader, even though he was too young to be married and still went by his childhood nickname. "Zo" meant "happy" in that particular dialect of the Chultan dwarves—or Dwarves of the Domain, as they called themselves.

When the moon disappeared behind a cloud, Zo made a low noise that resembled the call of a hawk. At the sound, another dwarf—an older female dressed in layers of color-fully embroidered cloth—scurried into the clearing. The elder dwarf, called Majida by her tribe, ducked into a thicket of crimson flowers that brushed against her bare hands and feet without irritation. After checking the clearing one last time, Zo followed her into the floral-scented undergrowth. The dwarves were so used to the crimson nettles that they could easily navigate the tangled thickets while most creatures had to walk around or suffer painful rashes. The two dwarves crouched down and stared at the high mudthorn walls in the clearing in front of them.

"Did they build the walls to keep something out or something in?" Majida asked. "Stupid humans. Don't they know about the Jumpers?"

Shorter than their northern kin, the tribe of Chultan dwarves were small enough to avoid the big predators, clever enough to avoid the traps and barbs of the jungle, and humble enough to be happy in their Domain, an extensive network of grottos and caverns. The dwarves avoided cities and other trappings of civilized life, but they were hardly feral, and would have had objections with anyone who described them as such. The Domain dwarves had a written language and a long memory, particularly about the savagery of the Scaly Ones and their abominations that still roamed the jungle thousands of years after the sarrukh had vanished. The serpent-abominations retained all of the cruelty and none of the finesse of their makers.

"Are you sure about this?" Zo whispered.

Majida glanced at him, surprised that her chief had expressed doubt. Majida had read the signs, and they had been obvious—or at least as obvious as anything in the realm of prognostication could be. She had discussed that with Zo and the tribal leaders—several times. Zo was like an infant when it came to leadership, but Majida was in her autumn years and had been shaman since before Zo's father was born. Her spell wouldn't be difficult, but the rest of the plan depended on Zo and his dwindling band of warriors. If Zo couldn't handle it, the whole plan would fall apart.

"I'm sure," Majida assured him. "Besides, we don't have a choice. We've lost three more in the past tenday."

"We'll fight harder."

Majida sighed. Typical male, thinking all the answers came from how he handled his sword.

"We've endured many things," she said. "But he is a particularly bad man, Zo. We have to stop him before he goes any further."

"How do you know they are any different than the others?" Zo asked.

"I only need to be sure about one."

Zo jutted out his chin. "I want to think about other plans."

Zo began to speak, but Majida touched his forehead in silent warning moments before a green-scaled jaculi slid out of the gloom. They waited in silence as it slithered by, the sickly glow of its eyes scanning the underbrush for prey. It paused just outside their thicket, the sound of its hissing breath uncomfortably close.

From where Majida was crouched in the underbrush, she could see that it was an exceptionally large snake, and she had no interest in tangling with it. The clever jaculi were much faster than either she or Zo, so there was no point in trying to run from it. It would simply overtake them, immobilize them, and eat them while they were still alive. The jungle had thousands of gruesome deaths to offer, but being slowly digested by a jaculi was one of the worst ways to die that Majida could think of.

Zo was trembling beside her, and Majida could sense the fear cresting in him. Soon he would bolt and run like the child he was. She laid a restraining hand on his shoulder and pressed her finger to her lips. She whispered a few words, and an indistinct form appeared in the palm of her hand. At first it was just a circle of blue light. But soon there was an outline of a wing, and she felt the distinctive feel of feathers against her hand. Smiling faintly, Majida hunched her shoulders over the glow and held it close to her chest. When she felt the little body grow warm, she opened her hand to reveal a perfect white bird with a crown of golden feathers.

Majida slipped a dagger out of the sheath she wore strapped to her upper arm. Holding the trembling bird tightly in one hand, she pushed the tip of the dagger into the skin just under its wing. When she pulled the knife out, blood flowed down the bird's breast and stained its white feathers. Majida held the bird up, and it fluttered from her, out of the thicket, and directly past the jaculi, who caught the obvious scent of blood. An injured bird was easy prey, and the snake followed the bird away from the nettle thicket back into the gloom. As soon as it was out of sight, Majida felt Zo relax beside her.

"Poor bird," she said sadly.

"You can make another," Zo told her.

Majida wanted to chide Zo for such a statement—as if the bird were no more important than a hood or a new breastplate—but she held her tongue.

"Let's go around to the southern wall," she whispered. But when she moved, Zo caught her elbow.

"Do we have to go tonight?" he asked. "Why can't we wait and see what happens tomorrow?"

"They're vulnerable for an attack. They might as well cut their own throats. That's how safe they are in there."

"You said they weren't going anywhere until morning," Zo reminded her.

"So I did. Which means tonight is the perfect time to sit here and weigh our options," she said sarcastically.

Zo looked at her with a hurt expression. "I can't tell if you're serious or not."

Immediately Majida felt bad. She liked Zo well enough. When his father died, their tribal customs had thrust leadership on him, even though there were other dwarves more qualified to lead than he. Majida thought that he would be a good leader in a few years, if he lived that long and was smart enough to learn from his mistakes. The dwarves of the Domain were particularly shortsighted when it came to embracing talent and recognizing the accidental nature of a person's birth. At different points during her long life, Majida's tribe had considered her a miscreant, a seditionist, and a rescuer. Several times, she had thought her tribe would exile her from the Domain, except she was the best healer and caster the tribe had ever produced.

"There are two ways the conflict can end: We can be picked off one by one until the Domain is empty. Or we can move."

"Move?"

"Find a new Domain."

"Where would we go?" Zo asked. "I hadn't thought of that."

By the look on his face, Majida knew he was imaging some green and verdant land just waiting for them. Majida had meant the last option as a farce, something that would bring him back to his senses, but he was actually considering it. Most of the dwarves of the Domain hadn't strayed far from the hidden caverns they called home, and Majida was one of the few to have traveled extensively outside of Chult.

"They don't want our kind anywhere else," she said firmly. "This is where we belong."

Zo scrubbed his stubby hands across his face. "All right. I'm putting my trust in you. What do you need me to do?"

"Follow me."

The sun hadn't broken the treeline when Boult woke up, but he could see well enough in the dim light to know that Harp and Liel were not in the room. And by the snoring coming from opposite sides of the room, he was sure that both boys were still sound asleep. Keeping an eye on the door, Boult began a systematic search of every inch of wall, floor, and ceiling. Shaking his head in disgust at the shoddy craftsmanship of the hut, Boult ran his fingers along the timbers at the base of the roof and poked at the seams between the boards on the walls.

On one side of the room was a chest filled with clothes. Boult slid it away from the wall and saw a cracked floorboard. Using his grubby fingernails to pry up the broken piece of wood, Boult saw that a small box had been nailed under the planks. He pried it open and pulled out a rolled-up parchment. A circle of red wax had sealed the parchment before being broken, and Boult took special care to examine it. He held the parchment to the light, examining the waxy ridges of the seal.

"An otter? Or maybe a weasel?" he murmured to himself.

Boult unrolled the parchment and held it up to the dusky

light coming through the uncovered window. After reading the parchment several times, he put it back into the small box under the planks, replaced the chest, and headed outside.

Stepping around Harp and Liel, Boult trotted down the stairs. He stopped mid-step when he noticed something on the trunk of the nearest tree. Glancing back over his shoulder at the sleeping figures intertwined on the porch, Boult inspected the ground between his feet and the tree. Besides a few rotting goldenfruit buzzing with flies and some patches of scrubby grass, the ground revealed nothing interesting.

Boult moved closer to the trunk where three runes had been seared into the bark. The marks were still fresh—a wisp of smoke hung in the air as if the bark still smoldered under the mystical mark. Boult stood in front of the trunk for a long time as he analyzed every nuance of the scorched lines. Slowly, he made a circuit around the house and found runes on trees every few feet around the hut. Behind the house, where the vegetation was thicker, it took him longer to locate the runes, but they were there. When he was done, he paused for a moment, watching as the streams of sunlight angled across the tops of the trees and flooded the grove with rose-tinted light.

Boult lit his pipe. He made a slow walk around the perimeter of the fence, chewing on his pipestem and standing for an overly long time in front of the goat pens. Then he returned to the front of house and sat on one of the logs around the cold fire pit. Boult puffed on his pipe, turning his griffon-head tamper around in his hands. When he saw Harp stir, he tamped out the pipe and secured it in his pouch.

"You look terrible," Boult said as Harp sat down across from him on a log.

"Thanks," Harp said, resting his head on his hands. "Kit and Verran still inside?"

"Yes," Boult said, taking a closer look at Harp. "Didn't get much sleep, did you?"

Harp shook his head.

"She did a number on you and not in the good way."

"Shut it, Boult," Harp said in a low voice.

"What did she do? Guilt you for ever daring to touch her precious body?"

"I'm not having that conversation with you."

"Women. They're right in it with you, and then they change their minds, and somehow you're a monster."

"What the hell are you talking about?"

"Wasn't that the gist of the conversation? How could you treat me like a such a whore?"

"Were you listening?"

"I didn't have to. I just imagined what she would say to get you to look like that."

"I should have done things differently."

"Maybe so. But not with that girl."

"Watch yourself, Boult. I still care about her."

Boult looked over his shoulder at the porch where Liel was just sitting up, her long hair tousled and her dress falling off her shoulder. She saw them looking at her and straightened her clothes. Then she pulled on her boots and came to sit beside Harp.

"If you're going to show us those ruins, we should leave soon," Boult said, leaning forward and resting his elbows on his legs. "Before the sun gets too hot."

"Maybe we should just go to the ship," Liel said after a moment.

"You don't want to go to the ruins?" Boult asked.

"Maybe you could take me home," Liel said.

"We can do that," Harp said with relief. "If that's what you want, I think that's the best plan."

"I don't know," Boult said. "I'd like to see the ruins."

"You don't care about the damn ruins," Harp said.

"I've seen that disease you talked about last night, Liel," Boult said, abruptly changing the subject.

"Which disease?" Liel asked with confusion.

"The one that swells up the tongue and chokes its victim," Boult reminded her. "You didn't have time to heal him?"

"No, he died within moments," Liel said.

"You've seen a lot of people die in the jungle," Boult said.

"I'd rather freeze to death in a snowfield than spend another day here," Liel said.

"What about Cardew?" Boult asked. "Yesterday you said you wanted to get proof of what he'd been doing."

"She's changed her mind," Harp said irritably. "And just wants to go home."

"Where do you think Cardew got the map?" Boult continued, ignoring Harp's obvious frustration.

"The one with the sites marked on it?" Liel said. "Queen Anais must have given it to him."

"But why would she issue a writ for a colony? Why not just send down mercenaries to search the ruins?"

"To keep up appearances? To satisfy her accomplices? How should I know? I wasn't privy to those discussions."

"Accomplices. That's an interesting word."

"The queen has interests that she keeps well hidden," Liel said in a monotonous voice. It sounded like she was reading a line of text from a book.

"Is that so? You learned a bit while in Cardew's keeping, then?"

"Boult," Harp warned.

"You said he discovered the parchment with the portal spell in the ruins?"

"I have no idea where he found it," Liel said. She looked perplexed, but there was no anger in her voice. It was same thing Harp had noticed when they were talking the night before. It was as if all her emotions had been extricated from her body. Harp remembered wishing there was a way to do that in the months after he got out of prison. He had wanted to hollow out his insides so that he was just a shell without any painful memories or recollections of joy.

"But you said it was ancient magic," Boult continued.

"That's what I thought," Liel explained.

"I don't understand why he dragged you to Chult when he could have hired a sorcerer the same way he hired the mercenaries."

"Why does it matter?" Harp said, suddenly feeling more alert. Boult was being annoying, and the direction of his questions was unnerving.

"Appearances," Liel repeated. "Cardew will do everything to keep up appearances."

"Were the mercenaries killed?" Boult asked

"I don't know," she replied. "Cardew came back from the ruins alone."

"Do you think he used the portal?" Boult was firing questions so rapidly that Liel barely had time to answer. Harp couldn't help wonder why Liel kept answering them, why she didn't tell Boult to shut his mouth. But she was so compliant. That was another part of her personality that had not been there during their time in the Moonshae Isles. The Liel he had known was anything but compliant.

"I think so."

"How did you find the cavern with the machine?" Boult asked.

"I was getting water from the river."

"There are closer watering holes to the camp than that one," Boult pointed out.

"I've been looking all over the jungle."

"For ruins?" Boult asked.

"For whatever Cardew has been planning," Liel said.

"Had Cardew been to Chult before?"

"No. Yes. I'm not sure."

"But you're his wife. How could you not know?"

"He would go away sometimes," Liel explained. "I

thought he was at Anais's court, but he could have been anywhere."

"Even running around the jungle? Constructing machines that operate using skin and blood?"

Liel's eyes widened, and Harp laid a hand on her arm. "Stop it, Boult," he warned. "She doesn't know all the answers."

"Are you sure, Harp?"

"What are you getting at? Because you are starting to—"

"Here's what I know," Boult interrupted. "I know that Cardew didn't build the machine or the cages. He probably didn't even know about them."

"You don't know that," Harp said, staring at the dwarf. "Do you?"

"I think whoever sent Cardew to Chult has been here for a while, making things, collecting things, generally doing bad things in the jungle," Boult continued. "What do you think about that theory, Liel?"

"That might be true," Liel said slowly.

"Who do you think that is?" Boult asked.

"Queen Anais," she said promptly.

"What does Queen Anais want with ancient magic?"

"I don't know."

"Speculate," Boult ordered brusquely.

"The Torque is very powerful," Liel said. "The queen wants the Torque."

"What Torque?" Harp asked.

Liel's coppery skin grew pale. "Torque?"

"You didn't mention that last night," Harp said.

"Didn't I?"

"What did Cardew say about a torque?" Harp asked.

Boult piped up before Liel answered. "Liel, Harp got a nasty sting from some bastard flower. Do you think you could heal him?"

"It's nothing," Harp said, annoyed that Boult had distracted Liel from answering his question.

"When we go to the ruins, we should be as strong as possible. What do you think, Liel?"

"I think he'll heal on his own," Liel murmured, looking at the ground.

"So, what about the cups?" Boult asked.

"What cups?"

"And the food on the plates?" Boult continued.

"Stop asking me questions," Liel said in a low, tense voice. For the first time in the conversation, there was an unmasked warning in her tone. But that didn't stop Boult. From the smirk on the dwarf's face, Harp knew that getting a rise out of her was what Boult had wanted all along.

"Have you even been in the dining hall? Cardew left almost a tenday ago. I'd think you might have cleared out the rotting meat before the maggots moved in. Except you're the maggot, aren't you?"

"Boult!" Harp said.

"And no one used the portal spell, Liel. I found it in the house."

"Give it to me," she ordered, glaring at the dwarf.

"Why don't you use some magic and take it from me?" Boult taunted. He would have expected Harp to snap at that, but instead Harp seemed to taking a closer look at the slender elf sitting next to him, her body rigid with tension and her hands clenched into fists as they rested on her knees.

"Harp, she isn't the Liel that you knew," Boult said.

"And you're going to listen to *him,* Amhar, the Killer of Children?" she said, turning her head sideways to address Harp. As her gaze drilled into him, he felt a chill go up his spine. She'd spoken in such a placid tone that it took a moment for the implication of her words to hit him. When it did, Harp leaped to his feet and backed away from her as if she'd spoken with the hiss of a forked tongue. Boult's face darkened, and he looked at the elf with pure hatred.

"He's been deceiving you all those years, Harp," Liel continued in that flat voice. "If he's innocent, why didn't he tell you who he was? He's in league with Queen Anais. They killed all those children to secure her power. There is no one to challenge her anymore. And once she gets her hands on the Torque, there will be no one to stop her."

"I don't even need to ask the question, but reassure me," Boult asked. "Did you tell her about my past, Harp?"

"I did not," Harp said quietly. He had felt beaten when he woke up that morning, but suddenly it felt like his body was being crushed under a heavy weight.

"Why the head games, Liel?" Boult demanded. "Why torture Harp with guilt?"

"You've kept your freedom so far, Amhar. But you'll die a miserable death at the Vankila Slab, the way you already should have died."

"If you know Vankila, then you knew where I was all along," Harp said taking a ragged breath. "Did you know what they did to me at Vankila at the request of your husband? Did you know?"

Liel started to run, but Boult launched himself at her. He tackled her, knocking her off the log and onto the ground. He tried to pin her down with his body, but she slammed the palm of her hand into his face. He managed to turn his head just in time to avoid a broken nose, but when his weight shifted, she twisted out from under him. She tried to scramble to her feet, but Boult lunged at her again, pinning her down. Liel struggled ferociously, but the dwarf outweighed her, and he managed to catch her arms and hold them.

"Harp!" Boult said, straining with the effort of keeping Liel's long limbs in check. "Grab her!"

Awoken by the sound of shouting, Kitto and Verran appeared on the porch, looking sleepy and confused. The boys stared wide-eyed when they saw Boult tussling with the elf while Harp looked on passively, as if he didn't care about the scene that was playing out in front of him.

"Don't leave the trees!" Boult yelled to the boys.

Before anyone could respond, there was a harsh, guttural noise from outside the compound and movement above the wall. Harp saw a silhouette framed against the blue sky as something leaped over the barrier and landed on the ground in front of the gate. The creature had a humanoid body covered in green and brown scales and the elongated head of a snake. Leather armor covered its muscled chest, and it held a jeweled sword in its clawed hand. A twist of gold shimmered around each of its ankles.

The yuan-ti—serpentfolk of Chult. A forked tongue flicked in and out of its wide mouth. The creature crouched down and swayed back and forth as it scoped the inside of the compound. With its red eyes focused on the cluster of people in front of the hut, it bared its long fangs and hissed loudly in an unfamiliar language. Liel and Boult were still wrestling on the ground, but Harp felt too exhausted by Liel's treachery to move. It was as if he had grown roots, and even the imminent threat of an enemy attack couldn't incite him to action.

"Help me," Boult demanded angrily. Verran hurried down from the porch while Kitto dashed inside the hut to retrieve the sword that Harp had taken from the armory. Before Verran reached Boult, the compound's gate began rattling as if it were being battered by a strong gale. The hinges creaked, and horizontal cracks branched across the door like lightning flashing across a stormy sky. The wood groaned. The planks snapped in half and fell to the mud.

When the dust cleared, more yuan-ti wearing leather armor and golden bands around their ankles stood in the wreckage. Behind them, three massive warriors crossed through the remains of the gate and entered the courtyard. Although they had human arms, these warriors were more snake than human and three times the size of a man. The warriors slithered on long, serpentine bodies around the wooden fragments of the door. Their dark scales glistened in the light, and their cloudy blue eyes protruded from their diamond-shaped skulls. Two carried long swords and wore plates of banded mail on their chests. The third gripped a jeweled metal staff and wore a row of glass vials and metal spikes looped across his chest.

"Take your sword!" Kitto urged, pushing the hilt into Harp's hand. Harp took it, but he let it hang loosely in his hand, the tip dragging in the dirt.

"Why aren't they attacking?" Verran cried. He tried to help Boult pin Liel's arms, but she struggled with renewed energy. The yuan-ti stopped when they reached the edge of the grove, prowling just outside the trees and talking in a mixture of hissing and clicking sounds.

"Someone cast a ward of protection," Boult said, shoving his knee into Liel's stomach just below her rib cage. She coughed at the impact and stopped fighting as she gasped for breath. "Look at the marks on the trees."

"Who did it?" Verran asked.

"It's Dwarven. That's all I know. But as long as we stay inside the circle of protection, they can't come into the grove."

"We're just going to sit and wait?" Verran cried. "I don't like that plan."

"We sit here until Harp gets his head together," Boult said. "Get your head together, Harp. Now!"

"Please, let me go," Liel cried. She was shaking from exertion. "You don't know what they'll do."

"They're your friends," Boult growled, pressing his knee harder into her chest until Liel gasped in pain. "You told them we were here."

"No!" Liel protested, pushing ineffectually against the dwarf's leg. Boult lifted the pressure slightly so she could talk. "I hate the yuan-ti. They're monsters."

"Who's your patron?" Boult demanded. "And stop blaming the poor queen."

The yuan-ti left the edge of the grove and turned their attention to the common building. One of the smaller creatures jumped onto the roof and tried to light the straw with his flint and steel. But the straw was wet from the rainstorm the night before, and the sparks didn't catch right away. Another creature leaped up onto the house and dumped oil from a waterskin onto the roof.

"They're going to burn us out," Verran said. "Will that work?"

"How should I know?" Boult said crossly, yanking Liel to her feet. A small flame flickered on one side of the roof, but with the oil soaking into the straw, the entire roof would burn soon. While Boult was distracted by the yuan-ti, Liel jerked away from him. Harp saw her slip a dagger from a sheath under her arm and thrust it at Boult. Knowing the dwarf might kill Liel for such an assault, Harp tried stop her, but the dagger sliced into his forearm. The blade split his skin just below the wrist, and Harp felt the warm blood soak down the sleeve of his shirt to his elbow.

When he saw the dagger clutched in the elf's hand and blood running down Harp's arm, Boult lunged for Liel. Harp stepped between them and blocked the dwarf with his shoulder. The impact of the dwarf's weight sent Harp sprawling backward into Liel, and the two of them tumbled down the embankment into the main grounds of the compound.

When Harp and Liel rolled past the line of trees at the edge of the grove, Boult spun to check the trunk of the goldenfruit tree. Just as he feared, the runes were disappearing. The scorch marks faded from black to gray and then vanished, leaving no trace on the trunk. The ring of protection was broken.

At the bottom of the embankment, Liel landed on top of Harp, straddling him with her hands pressed against his bloody shirt. He stared up at her, waiting to see what she would do. Out of the corner of his eye, he could see that the yuan-ti had left the smoldering common building and were closing on them quickly.

"Who are you?" he asked staring up into her sea green eyes.

"Not who you want me to be," she whispered. She climbed off him and ran through the broken gate. Barely glancing at the elf as she disappeared into the jungle, the largest serpent warrior put his sword against Harp's throat. Harp remained prone on the ground, not bothering to lift his hands to defend himself. The warrior pressed his sword closer and hissed some garbled syllables at the crewmates standing at the top of the embankment. His meaning was clear even if his words were not: Drop your weapons, or your friend gets gutted.

"We'll make it," Kitto murmured to Boult and Verran as they threw down their swords.

"Really?" Boult said, as the yuan-ti dragged Harp to his feet and tied his hands. "Because if I had to imagine what 'the end' would look like, it might look a lot like our situation."

As they were being tied and gagged, the three crewmates watched their captain for a signal. But Harp did nothing. He'd found Liel and lost her in less than a day. It didn't matter where they took him. He just didn't care anymore.

CHAPTER FIFTEEN

2 Flamerule, the Year of the Ageless One
(1479 DR)
Kinnard Keep, Tethyr

The path to Evonne's grave was well tended. The gravel was freshly raked and the grass along the edges neatly trimmed and leveled. As requested, the gardener had planted stands of red and gold flowers—Evonne's favorite colors—along the path. It was a steep climb to the wooded grove at the top of the hill, and Tresco paused halfway up to rest. From that height, he could see the crashing waves of the ocean in the distance.

"Where is Cardew?" Ysabel asked, as she waited beside Tresco. It was windy, and Ysabel's hair was escaping from the sky blue cloth that she had used to tie back her hair.

"He rode into town on business," Tresco replied. "He'll be back in time for dinner."

"Thank you for taking me," Ysabel said as they

continued up the hill. "It's been too long since I've visited my mother's grave."

"Of course," Tresco said. When Ysabel became his ward after the massacre, Tresco ordered the guards not to let the child go anywhere unattended. There were many would-be assassins and many who would pay good coin for the head of the daughter of Evonne Linden. Technically, Evonne's grave was on Tresco's estate, but it bordered land owned by House Lahame, a viciously royalist family. Because of their proximity, Tresco refused to let Ysabel travel to the gravesite without him. While Tresco always made it a point to visit Evonne's memorial on his rare visits to the estate, he didn't usually bring Ysabel with him. He liked to be alone with Evonne, after all.

"How was the sanatorium?" Ysabel asked. "Did you have any interesting patients?"

"Not my past visit," Tresco said regretfully as they crested the hill and crossed under the wooden arch that marked the entrance of the memorial garden. "I think the usefulness of that arrangement is coming to an end."

A year after Evonne's death, Tresco suggested that Ysabel design her mother's memorial. When she came to him with the plans, he was taken aback at the scope of the little girl's vision. But Evonne had left the girl a substantial amount of coin, which Tresco was happy to spend. Ysabel requested a life-size marble statue of Evonne, her hair loose on her shoulders and wearing a flowing gown like a goddess. The statue stood on top of a marble ossuary where Evonne's bones were entombed. A hexagon-shaped reflecting pool lay at the foot of the tomb. A master stonemason crafted a red and indigo mosaic of a leviathan curled in a spiral on the bottom of the pool. When the wind rippled the waves, it looked as if the leviathan was swimming in circles along the floor.

"You seem distracted, Uncle," Ysabel said. "Is something wrong?"

Tresco sighed. Ysabel was a bright girl, but for her safety, he'd kept her innocent about the complexities of not only court politics, but the natural hierarchy of power in and out of Tethyr. Given she was of age to marry, he wondered if he had done her a disfavor by sheltering her from the world.

"Do you know of Avalor, Treespeaker of the Wealdath?" Tresco asked.

"The filthy elf who sits at Anais's knee and laps up her scraps?" Ysabel asked.

"Yes," Tresco said. "I've had word that he hired a mercenary to investigate the colony in Chult."

"Why would he do that?" Ysabel asked.

"Because he doesn't know his place," Tresco said darkly. "Evonne would have done something about it, if only she'd had the chance."

"What about my mother's supporters?" Liel asked. "Why aren't they doing something?"

"You've heard of the battle of Ebenspy Keep, of course. Many of your parent's closest followers died in that assault. But the Branch of Linden still grows. You may yet see the Tethyr that your mother worked so hard to achieve." A silence fell over them as they stood beside the grave.

"May I ask you a question, Uncle?" Ysabel asked.

"You may," Tresco replied.

"Why were you annoyed with Cardew last night at dinner?"

"You're very observant. I was annoyed with him. He failed me in a business venture."

"A business venture with the colony?"

"Of course not," Tresco said testily. "That was Anais's enterprise. It was another matter entirely. But I am a forgiving man, and I'll give him another chance to prove himself."

"That is kind of you," Ysabel agreed.

"Despite Cardew's shortcomings, he would make an adequate husband for you."

"It's not too soon since his wife died?" Ysabel asked.

"No, it's been almost a year. He's free to marry. And the sooner the better I say."

"You know best, Uncle. I know my mother would have trusted your instincts."

"Your mother was a brilliant woman," Tresco said, warming up to the conversation. Ysabel had heard him say those things before, but he liked talking about Evonne. "Before I met her, I never put much stock in the intelligence of women. So easily distracted. But Evonne was unique."

"How so?"

"She had a keen eye for politics. And for people. She surrounded herself with only the finest men. She had natural talent, as well."

"In magic?"

"Oh, I wasn't thinking about magic, but yes, she dabbled in spells now and then. She was always at her books, and I think she learned a great deal simply by force of will."

"Men underestimate both force and will," Ysabel said quietly.

Tresco peered down at her, "No child. I meant that she worked hard to achieve what she had. After your father died, she was all alone. Most women would have crawled into a bed and wept. But not your mother. She took up his mantle."

"You admired that? I wouldn't think you would approve."

"I didn't at first. Eventually, I saw the necessity of her political involvement. It was her other interests that troubled me."

"What do you mean?"

Tresco sighed. "There was a dark side to your mother."

"A dark side?"

"She was fascinated by macabre things. Had she lived, I would have made sure to direct her interests elsewhere. I've tried very hard to keep you away from such things."

"How horrible. I didn't know that about her."

"It wasn't dire. Ironically, it was her interests that made me what I am today."

"How so?"

"A few months after she died," he said, "I found one of her manuscripts in my study. I'd never seen it before. She must have left it during one of our visits. A bound manuscript filled with maps and theories the likes of which I'd never seen. They were very complex and involved ancient magic from the sarrukh in Chult. To my knowledge, Evonne never traveled to Chult."

"Chult? Where the colony is?"

"Actually, yes. There are things hidden in the ruins you couldn't fathom."

"Oh, do you have more stories of the jungle! Tell me, Uncle. Have you found something incredible?"

"Not yet," Tresco said. "But I will. And then you'll see some changes in Tethyr. But enough talk about such things. I'm going to let you and Cardew dine alone."

"Why?"

"Cardew and I are going fox hunting tomorrow. We will leave early in the morning and return very late."

"Can I come?" Ysabel asked. "I love a good chase."

"Not this time. We have politics to discuss."

"You never let me go anywhere," Ysabel pouted.

"When I make the world safe for innocents like you, then you may walk freely," Tresco promised her. "But until that time, I must keep you safe."

"There are safe places other than Kinnard Keep," Ysabel pointed out.

"It's not just the temporal realm, child," Tresco said

patiently. "The darker realms conspire against us as well. They assaulted your mother, and I was powerless to stop them."

"What do you mean?"

"In the days before your mother was killed, she talked about her death," Tresco told her. "It was as if she knew it was coming."

"How could she have known?" Ysabel asked.

"I don't know, child. I wish I could have protected her. I know that I've guarded you carefully. It's because I don't want anything to happen to you the way it happened to your mother. But I must let you go into the world and marry. It would be wrong to keep you a child forever.

"I have something for you," Tresco said. "I planned to give it to your mother the night she died. I've kept it with me ever since, but I want you to have it."

Tresco opened his hand and held out an amulet. A delicate golden chain held a circular crest embedded with diamonds.

"Oh, Uncle!" Ysabel cried, looking down at it. On the crest was the lithe, curving body of an ermine, the symbol of Kinnard Keep and Tresco's ancestral house. "It's beautiful!"

Tresco looked away from the delighted Ysabel to the statue of Evonne, who had a knowing smile carved on her stone lips.

"It is indeed," he replied.

CHAPTER SIXTEEN

2 Flamerule, the Year of the Ageless One
(1479 DR)
Chult

The yuan-ti stripped the crewmates of their weapons and possessions and tied them together with a single length of rope, so they were forced to walk in a line like pack animals. Verran was in the front, followed by Kitto, Harp, and Boult. Each of the men was gagged, which meant that Verran and his unpredictable spells were going to be of no help to them.

Across from the gate was a massive patch of the crimson flowers like the ones that Harp had blundered into the day before, and Boult noticed that the yuan-ti gave the poisonous blooms a wide berth as they headed into the underbrush. Surprisingly, Boult didn't feel panic about the direction things had gone in, although he would miss his pipe and griffon-head tamper. The situation hadn't played itself out yet. Somewhere in the jungle they had an unknown ally—the dwarf who had cast the ward of protection on the trees in the grove.

Despite the rope on his wrists and the gag in his mouth, Boult felt triumphant. He'd learned a few things from that treacherous elf. Even if Cardew was following the orders of a patron, the Hero of the Realm was still in the thick of things somehow. Since the Children's Massacre, Boult had devoted his life to exacting revenge on the man who had framed him for murdering the royal heirs. If being captured by crusty snake-faces was just another step on the path to vengeance, so be it.

As he marched behind Harp of the Slumped Shoulders, Boult asked himself for the millionth time why he traveled with a man whose biggest talents in life were self-pity, self-torture, and self-delusion. That Liel was an evil, conniving bitch did not surprise Boult at all. That Harp had spent years of his life pining for the elf was a little more surprising. There was no doubt that she was attractive. But ever since Boult had begun to piece together the story of Liel, he doubted that the elf had ever loved Harp.

Boult would never admit it to anyone, but it wasn't compassion that drove him to help Harp in the Vankila Slab. Once he had figured out that Cardew hated Harp specifically, Boult reasoned that there must be ways to use the situation to his advantage. But if it wasn't compassion that made him take Harp under his wing, it soon was guilt. As Harp endured session after session, every part of him systematically killed and brought back, Boult wondered if that were a punishment that Cardew would have imposed on Amhar—had Amhar not switched identities with the real Boult and escaped the Practitioner's attentions.

That was something that Boult liked about Harp—his formidable refusal to die. Hopefully that would serve them in the Chult forest, seeing how they were trussed up and helpless.

The yuan-ti led them down a well-traveled path that headed north along the river gorge. As they crested a small rise and came out of the undergrowth, Boult felt droplets of water dampening his face and clothes. At first Boult thought it was raining despite the sun in the sky, but he realized it was mist rising from a waterfall that lay in front of them. The water rushed through a narrow channel dotted with boulders, over a sheer drop-off, and into a dark blue lake. The yuan-ti stopped and seemed to be arguing about something, giving Boult and the others a chance to stare in awe at the vista.

The rushing river drained into a deep, round canyon so perfectly formed that the smooth cliff walls looked like they were shaped by godly design rather than the chaos of the elements. Like the primary directions on a compass, four waterfalls drained into the canyon. Boult and the others stood on the the southern edge at the top of the smallest waterfall, which was at most thirty feet high. The height of the waterfall on the northern side was much more dramatic. Foaming water blasted down the northern waterfall into a wide canal, one of many canals that ringed the flat ground at the bottom of the canyon.

Beyond the northern waterfall, a range of six mountains blocked their view of the horizon. Huddled together in an unnatural circle, the mountains were like spikes jutting out of the tangled mat of jungle growth that covered the uneven landscape. The bare, silvery rock of the peaks made Boult think of sharp teeth taking a bite out of the sky. Dark gray clouds framed the tops of the mountains. Between the clouds, winged creatures glided on air currents, their shapes disappearing and reappearing in the mist.

On the eastern side of the basin, a golden dome shimmered in the sunlight like a coin at the bottom of a reflecting pool. A city had once flourished in the valley, but it lay in ruins and was partially obscured by years of rampant growth. Only the gilded dome was untouched by the creeping vines and unblemished by either the passage of time or the ravages of the climate. The domed palace had not entirely escaped the jungle, however, and the earth had opened up and swallowed the lower floors. Once the ground had settled, the bottom of the dome was level with the jungle floor.

Canals funneled the water from the four waterfalls into the mouth of a narrow gorge on the western side of the basin. The remains of a network of roads radiating out from the palace were visible between crumbling stone buildings. The city had been laid out in a series of circular sections with the walls and archways between the piazzas having since vanished beneath the jungle.

Tired of waiting for something to happen, Boult turned his attention to his captors. The more humanoid yuan-ti, with their fancy golden anklets, seemed to be arguing with the legless slitherers about the steep path that started at the head of the waterfall and traversed the slope down into the basin. It would be a challenging walk for anyone with feet, and Boult couldn't imagine the wide-bodied, heavily armored warriors making it along the narrow path.

As the argument between the Jumpers and the Slitherers intensified, a spear suddenly appeared above their heads. Although it was aimed in his general direction, Boult stared at it quizzically as it seemed to drift lazily across the gray sky. There was nothing threatening about it, just a pointy stick with a single blue feather and a metal tip. It hit one of the Slitherers, clattering uselessly against its armor and falling to the dirt.

Before anyone reacted to the spear, a much larger volley of darts whistled through the air. The cluster of tiny barbs soared out of the trees and hit the serpentfolk—but not Boult and his crewmates—with surprising accuracy. Even before all of the darts had found their targets, something short and wide barreled out of the underbrush, sprinting toward them at top speed and bellowing in a surprisingly loud and uncomfortably high-pitched manner.

Boult was the first one to register that it was a dwarf—a hairy, squat, overly confident dwarf. Despite the spear, the darts, and the dwarf running pell-mell in their direction, the serpentfolk seemed unconcerned, as if none of these things were worth a reaction. One of the Slitherers reached up to brush off the clump of darts that bristled across its back, but there was no collective effort to address the pending dwarven assault.

Boult was also the first one to register the words the dwarf was screaming, and when he did, he raised his eyebrows in surprise.

"What's he saying?" Harp mumbled around his gag.

Boult would have been happy to tell him, but the gag was pressed against his tongue, the noisy dwarf was nearly upon them, and one of the serpentfolk finally drew its sword.

"What's he saying?" Harp mumbled again, louder that time, as he tried to enunciate around the cloth in his mouth.

Knowing what was about to happen made Boult laugh. There was a good chance he would regret what he was about to do, but when such an opportunity presented itself, there wasn't anything to do but take the plunge—literally. With a mighty leap, Boult sprang into the fast-flowing water just as the screaming dwarf reached them and pushed them into the river from behind.

Being bound together with the same rope, the men were dragged into the current behind Boult. As the water closed over his head, he glimpsed Harp smacking face-first into the waves, a look of shock on his features. The rapids carried them to the edge, Boult's head bobbing above the waterline. Their situation was going to propel Harp out of his inaction or it was going to kill them; either way it was better than where they'd been just moments before. Besides, Boult had a feeling it was going to be the ride of his life.

Harp's head popped out of the water near Boult just as they reached the edge. He was screaming something at Boult through his water-soaked gag, and it sounded like some unkind things about Boult's mother. Boult gave him a wicked grin, and the world dropped away beneath them. It was an odd sensation, plummeting through the air surrounded only by an insubstantial film of water. Then he slammed into the lake, thankfully feet first.

That part was less fun. The impact took his breath away. All four crewmates hit at roughly the same spot in the lake, so body parts got tangled up, and Boult couldn't get his legs under him to kick for the surface. For a fleeting moment, Boult thought he was drowning. And then someone grabbed the back of his shirt and hauled him up to the sunlight. When they broke the surface of the water, the noisy dwarf who had jumped over the waterfall with them was whooping up a storm.

"That's the best idea you've ever had, Majida!" the dwarf yelled in Dwarvish. "I want to go again!"

An older, female dwarf was waiting at the edge of the lake. She waded into the water and helped drag Boult and the others out. The male dwarf began sawing through their ropes with a dagger while she loosened their gags.

"Damn, Boult," Harp said, coughing up water. "Next time you want to kill me, just stab me in the heart, all right?"

"Kitto?" Boult asked. "Verran? You all right?"

The boys nodded. Verran was white-faced and shaky—and he looked a little angry. But Kitto looked amused, almost exhilarated, and Boult had the impression he'd go for another jump as well.

"It's not over yet," the female dwarf said in Common, pointing at the top of the waterfall. The Slitherers had disappeared from sight, but two of the bandy-legged Jumpers leaped off the edge, moving easily between the slippery rocks that stuck out from the cliff-face. The water drenched the leather of their armor and rolled off their scales, but the hooked talons on their feet steadied them until they located the next rock. As they leaped down the waterfall, they moved like overgrown frogs hopping between lily pads, which might have been amusing except Boult was still attached to the other men, and none of them had any weapons to defend themselves from the serpentfolk.

"Keep cutting," Majida ordered.

"What are you going to do?" Zo asked.

"Just keep cutting," she told him. Then she steadied herself and began chanting under her breath. The Jumpers had made it halfway down the falls, but the rocks were smaller there and the flow of the water was stronger, which forced them to slow their descent. Boult saw movement on one side of the bank as vines undulated like snakes under a charmer's spell. When the first Jumper leaped to a lower rock, a vine lashed out and looped around its ankle. When it sprang from the rock, the vine yanked it backward and threw it off balance. Unable to adjust its body, it smashed headfirst against the boulders. The Jumper's body hung limply on the edge of the rock before slipping headlong into the churning water.

The other Jumper paused as its dead companion was swept down the waterfall, almost as if it were in shock that the dwarves had managed to take out one of its kin. Having seen how ineffectual the darts and spears were against the Slitherers when they were at the top of the waterfall, Boult suspected that the yuan-ti considered the dwarves more of an annoyance than a threat. Hissing angrily, the Jumper glowered down at Majida, who glared back defiantly.

The Jumper leaped into the air, deftly avoiding another vine that cracked against the rock near its leg. In a flash of speed, it bounded to a higher rock and out of reach of Majida's writhing vines. The Jumper coiled its body low and used its powerful legs to vault across the wide expanse to a muddy path on the side of the falls. Sprinting down the slope, the yuan-ti moved with startling speed. Just before it reached flat ground, it hurled itself into the air at Majida with its fangs and claws bared. Since Boult's hands were still bound, he had the inclination to close his eyes. He couldn't help Majida, and he'd rather not see the dwarf get her heart ripped out by the furious Jumper.

But Majida didn't flinch at the sight of the creature soaring through the air. Just as it was about to crash into her, she reached down and yanked a spear off the ground. The Jumper couldn't change the direction of its flight and rammed into the spear. It punctured its throat and slid out the back of its neck. The creature's weight knocked Majida flat on her back and its blood splattered across her face and clothes. The dead Jumper slid down the spear and landed on her.

"Majida!" Zo said as he finished cutting through the soggy ropes. "Use a spell next time!"

"Force was called for," Majida said nonchalantly, shoving the Jumper off to one side.

"We should hurry," Zo told them. "The other Scaly Ones will be here soon."

"Why are you helping us?" Boult demanded crossly, rubbing his raw wrists. He wasn't going anywhere until the jungle shaman was a little more forthcoming. Having seen her vine spell, he had little doubt that she was the one who had put the runes on the trees back at the compound.

"What he means to say is thank you for helping us," Harp said, bowing slightly. "I'm Harp. That's Verran and Kitto. And that's Boult. He's always suspicious. Don't take it personally."

"I am Majida," Majida replied. "And that is Zo. We'll take you someplace safe."

"Why did you cast the protection spell?" Boult demanded, crossing his arms. He had a right to be suspicious. There was more to the runes than Harp knew. "Why are you helping us?"

Majida smiled faintly. "I heard your question the first time, Outsider. But I don't have time to answer it. Unless you want to wait for more Scaly Ones?"

"Let's go, Boult," Harp said. "You can get your answers later."

"She knows my name, Harp," Boult said. "She wrote it in the runes."

"What? Why didn't you tell me?"

"Oh, I'm sorry," Boult said sarcastically. "Somehow amid all the treachery and capturing, it completely slipped my mind."

"What do you want from Boult?" Harp questioned.

"I wanted his help," Majida said. She turned to Harp. "Although I was seeking Boult, I now find that I recognize you as well."

"Me?" Harp asked. "How do you know me?"

"I know how you got those scars."

She took a stick from the ground and scratched a symbol in the dirt. It was a curving animal in a circle, and the sight of it made Harp go white.

"That is the symbol of a man we call the Ermine," Majida told them. "A powerful wizard and a cruel man. I think you both have seen it before."

"At Vankila, the Practitioner wore an amulet with that symbol," Harp said quietly.

Peering around Harp at the ground, Boult recognized it as well. "Nine bloody Hells," he said.

CHAPTER SEVENTEEN

2 Flamerule, the Year of the Ageless One
(1479 DR)
Chult

Having lived for centuries in the lethal jungle, the dwarves of the Domain had perfected survival tricks to give themselves an edge over the many predators who threatened their existence. Good mobility and escape routes were essential, so the dwarves cut secret pathways through the jungle. Hidden throughout the dense vegetation, the pathways tunneled through stinging thickets, walls of vines, stands of massive rhododendrons, and anything else the dwarves could use as cover from hungry eyes. If the path-cutters came up against a natural barrier such as a ridge or a river, they tunneled their way through or under it.

Like a labyrinth hidden in plain sight, the paths wound in laboriously long routes so as to never cut across open ground. Designed to accommodate dwarves and nothing larger, most of the paths were narrow and low so the men had to stoop while they walked, which made progress slow and conversation easy.

"The Ermine has been coming to Chult for years," Majida told them.

"So the Ermine and the Practitioner are the same person," Harp said. "He's the one running operations in Chult. He must have built the machine in the cavern even before the colony was set up."

"I told you that Cardew couldn't mastermind this," Boult said smugly.

"Yes, Boult, let us all bow down before your infinite wisdom," Harp said irritably.

"We didn't know about his flesh machine until recently, not until Liel told us," Majida explained.

"You know Liel?" Harp asked in surprise.

"Did you know she betrayed us?" Boult asked.

"The elf in the colony was not Liel," Majida said.

"What do you mean?" Harp said.

"She was . . . doubled," Majida said slowly, obviously searching for the appropriate word in the Common tongue.

"Doubled?" Harp asked in confusion.

"The Liel you spent time with was not Liel," Majida told Harp.

"She looked like Liel. She had her memories."

"But it was not Liel."

"Was it an illusion?" Harp asked doubtfully. Liel had been cold and aloof, but they had talked about things only the two of them knew.

"No, the body was real, and the memories were true," Majida said. "But her creation was false, and her actions were plotted by another's will."

"How is that possible?" Verran questioned.

"A dark ritual. That's what the flesh machine does," Majida said. "It takes blood and distills it to make another body, a double of the original. We call them husks."

"It seemed so much like Liel," Harp said, trying to get his head around what Majida was saying.

"How does the Practitioner direct her actions?" Boult demanded.

"The husks are childlike in their desire to please and to take instruction. The creator imposes his will on them at the moment of their creation, but it only lasts for a finite period of time. Then the husk's own will asserts itself, and they are not so easily controlled."

"I've seen copies of people before," Verran said. "But they were mute and dumb, like their skin was just a covering and the inside was hollowed out."

"Usually that is so," Majida said. "But your Practitioner is very good at making husks, and he filled it with many things from Liel herself."

"How could he do that?" Harp asked.

"With Liel's blood and the right magic funneled through the flesh machine, it's possible," Majida replied.

"I've heard of that," Verran told them. "From my father. But I didn't think it could be done anymore. I thought the magic was lost."

"To most of Faerûn, the magic is lost," Majida agreed. "But the sarrukh, the progenitors of the Scaly Ones, had the knowledge, and the Practitioner focused his will on getting it."

"My father said that blood copies are the pinnacle of what necromantic magic can achieve," Verran said.

Majida had stopped abruptly and touched the center of her forehead, which Harp took as a sign for him to keep silent. The group held still and listened to the jungle intently, but there were no sounds save the chirp of birds and the drip of water onto the buttress roots.

"The pinnacle of necromantic magic," Majida repeated finally, as if she had been musing on the phrase. "I find that to be an inherent contradiction. Necromancy is the lowest and most depraved sort of magic."

"I didn't mean anything," Verran said, abashed. "It's just what my father said."

"What's your name, child?" Majida asked. Her voice didn't waver from kindliness, but her dark eyes flashed under the indigo scarf that covered her hair.

"Verran," the boy mumbled. A blush had crept onto his cheeks, and he'd crossed his arms tightly over his chest.

"Did your father ever tell you what happens to the husks, Verran?" she prodded. Verran shrugged his shoulders slightly but didn't respond. Harp was annoyed by the boy's surliness at Majida, who had probably saved their lives by helping them escape.

"By the time emotions and free-will emerge in the husk, its life-cycle is almost finished. For a fleeting instant, they experience what it means to truly live, and then death reclaims them. Husk-making is cruelty and humiliation beyond reckoning."

"How long do the husks last?" Harp took a closer look at Majida. She might look like a provincial shaman, but her manner revealed experience and education that went beyond the boundaries of Chult.

"It's different for each husk body, but never more than a few months," Majida replied as she turned and continued down the leaf-locked path.

They reached the base of a tree so large that it would have taken half a dozen men to encircle its trunk. From the branches above them, a collection of white-furred monkeys looked down with distaste as Majida led the group up a buttress root wide enough to walk two abreast, and up into the trees that thrived under the dense canopy. They continued along thick woody vines that were braided together to form a hidden walkway through the papery leaves of the trees.

At the end of the vines, they dropped to the ground in the middle of a thorny thicket growing at the base of a ridge of silver colored rocks. The ridge, which seemed too sheer to climb, was covered in pockets of dark green moss that bulged off the rock. Tiny, gray-furred mammals with long tails and big round eyes scampered up and down the moss.

"If that's how we're getting to the top, Boult has to go first," Harp said, watching the antics of the cliff dwellers.

"I'll go," Kitto volunteered.

"No one has to climb," Zo said, pointing to an opening in the rock hidden behind the undergrowth. Wooden struts supported the entrance, and as they followed the path down into the darkness, Harp saw that runic markings had been etched into the support beams.

"Where does the tunnel go?" Harp asked.

"It takes us to the other side of the mountain," Zo said. "It's much easier than climbing up and over."

The tunnel dipped into the rock and then leveled out. With a low ceiling designed for small travelers, it was only wide enough to walk single file. Crouched in the narrow space with solid rock hanging above his head, Harp decided to avoid caves in the future even if he had to climb a mountain to get where he needed to be. Fortunately, he could already see the light at the end of the tunnel.

"So why would the Practitioner make a husk of Liel?" Harp asked, his voice muffled in the confined space. "How does she fit into it all?"

"I don't know, Harp," Boult replied testily.

"So you admit to being an idiot, just like the rest of us," Harp said.

"I admit nothing," Boult said. "But I wonder if the dwarf we saw in the glade was a husk."

"What dwarf?" Zo asked, stopping abruptly. Verran, who was walking behind him, bumped into him.

"We saw the body of a dwarf in a glade near the beach,"

Boult told them. "She had red hair, but she was badly decomposed."

"Red hair?" Zo asked, looking over his shoulder at Majida. "That doesn't sound like one of ours."

"You've seen husk dwarves before?" Boult asked.

"They sent a husk dwarf into the Domain to spy on us," Majida said. "Our home has been secret for centuries. It took several days before we realized that he wasn't who he said."

"How did you figure out what he was?" Verran asked.

"Husks that are made from a spellcaster's blood are easy to spot because the copy cannot cast spells," Majida explained. "It's harder to spot non-casters, like Brill. You have to look for subtler clues."

"Majida noticed that Brill liked foods that he didn't before," Zo said. "None of us would have noticed, and the husk would have led the Ermine straight to us, had we not cut the husk's head off before he had the chance."

"You killed him?" Kitto asked.

"He was a spy," Zo said.

"But . . . It wasn't his fault," Kitto protested.

"He was a spy," Zo repeated. "A mockery of the natural order."

"Did you find the dwarf . . . Brill?" Harp asked. It was very dark in that part of the tunnel, and Harp felt it was an awkward place to stop and have a conversation. Presumably all sorts of skitter-critters used the short cut through the mountain even if the serpentfolk had not discovered it.

"No, he was dead. They killed him when they took his blood."

"Is that what they did with Liel?" Harp asked bluntly. "Do you think she's dead?"

"I don't think so," Majida said, shaking her head.

"But you said . . ."

"They usually take the blood and kill the original, yes. But they had other plans for Liel, so they kept her alive."

"How do you know?"

"I was the last one to see her."

"When was that?" Harp said in surprise, jerking his head to look at Majida and banging it against the rock ceiling.

"Three days?" Majida said thoughtfully. "No, it has been four days."

"What!" Harp asked, feeling a jolt of hope at the unexpected news. "Why didn't you tell us?"

"I'm telling you now, if you'll listen," Majida said patiently. "She had escaped from the cavern with the flesh machine. She was weak from the bloodletting. She said that the Ermine, or Practitioner as you call him, had learned the location of the Torque. She wanted to stop him before he reached it."

"Did she tell you where she was going?" Harp asked, blinking at the sunlight when they reached the other side of the tunnel.

"She did. And she told me other things as well."

The wail was animalistic, almost innocent in its desperation and confusion, even though it came from a man who was far from blameless. With her back pressed against the wall of the hut, listening to the sounds of the mercenaries being slaughtered outside, Liel found herself contemplating the nature of guilt and justice. It was easier to think about such philosophical questions in a detached manner rather than listen to the incessant pleas for mercy and sickening sword strokes outside the window. Liel wasn't one to weep, and she had no love for the mercenaries. But even with all the foul acts they had committed in their lives, they didn't deserve to die like this.

As if he were a glass statue, Cardew had stood motionless in the middle of the room since the attack started. Liel stared at him, feeling the hatred for him curl inside her belly.

"Why do you do nothing?" Liel hissed, peering over her shoulder through the open window although she couldn't see much in the darkness—just the flash of a blade in the moonlight, or the submissive crouch of a man as he fell to his knees in supplication before his death.

"What would you suggest I do?" Cardew said dully. There was no anger in his voice. No cocky directive or thinly veiled threat either. The arrogant man who had dominated life in the colony for months—and restricted her every movement—was gone. Her husband simply sounded defeated.

"They're your men. Why don't you help them?" Liel knew that what she was saying was ridiculous. Without her spell to protect them, she and Cardew would be killed just like the mercenaries in the camp.

"They're not my men. You know that."

"No, I don't," Liel said angrily. "I don't know anything."

"Liel, this wasn't supposed to happen."

"I don't believe you," she hissed as another sobbing cry of pain rose up in the courtyard.

"Killing the men was never the plan."

"What was the plan?" Liel demanded.

"We were supposed to be gone. With the Torque."

"We who? You and me? Or you and them?"

"All of us."

"Your life is a farce, and you are fraud, Hero of the Realm," Liel scoffed.

"I saved Ysabel," Cardew said, his voice shaking.

"Poor, sweet Ysabel. Take care that she never finds out what you've been up to in the jungle. She might not idolize you in the same way."

Something slammed up against the thin wall of the hut with a wet smack, jostling Liel away from her position by the window.

"Is your spell holding?" Cardew asked worriedly.

"Yes, but it won't stop them from hurling corpses at us. It's just your basic keep-the-coward-safe spell."

"I'm not a coward," Cardew shouted, and Liel took pleasure in having made him angry enough to yell. "I stayed married to you, didn't I?"

"You bastard. You expect me to thank you for that?"

"Liel," Cardew said, his voice softening. "You know that my patron is part of the Branch of Linden. For me to be married to an elf . . . Well, you can imagine what they thought about that."

"Is that supposed to make me feel bad for you?" Liel said incredulously.

"No, it's supposed to make you understand how much I love you," he said, taking her hands in his. "Don't you remember how it used to be? In Darromar? Weren't we happy? I still love you, the way I did before."

Liel jerked her hands away. "Is everything that comes out of your mouth a lie? Tell me one thing that is true. Just one thing."

"I never meant to hurt you."

"The Branch of Linden exists to hurt me and all my kind. How can you say that?"

Outside, the screams of the men were growing less frequent.

"Listen to me," Cardew began.

"No, you listen to me," Liel said angrily. "You wanted me to make the portal so we could bring the Torque back to Tethyr. Who wants the Torque?"

Cardew shook his head. "I can't tell you, Liel. But he's coming. You can't let him find you."

"How do you know he's coming?" Liel demanded.

"As soon as all the men are dead, he will come. You have to be gone. Please, Liel. There's no reason for me to lie about that."

"Where exactly do you want me to go? We're in the middle of Chult, in case you hadn't noticed."

"You're clever. I know you've been out in the jungle many nights. The guards told me. I don't know how you're doing it exactly, but you have to do it. Quickly."

Liel wasn't going to admit it to Cardew, but she couldn't do the spell and transform the way she had so many times before. It took time to become the ocelot, a cream-colored cat with dark-brown rosettes that she had encountered when she first came to Chult. With its grace and speed, the ocelot quickly became her favored animal form, and she had used it on many nights to steal out of the camp and wander freely through the jungle.

"Why did you even bring me to Chult?" she demanded. "Why couldn't you have left me in the Wealdath? I wouldn't have stopped you from marrying anyone you wanted."

Cardew looked pained. "I thought we could make it right again."

"I believed that when you asked me to come with you. I really did. Now, I think it was just another lie. It's obvious your patron, whoever he is, is more powerful than me. From the looks of what he's doing outside, he could make a portal to see Sseth himself."

The camp had grown eerily quiet, and Cardew tugged Liel to her feet and looked out the window. The mysterious assailants had vanished, leaving only the bloody remains of the mercenaries in their wake.

"If you want to live, Liel, leave," Cardew said urgently.

"I hate you."

"I know. And I'm sorry. But you must get away as quickly as you can."

"Turn your back," Liel insisted, but Cardew hesitated.

"If I wanted to cut your throat, *husband,* I would simply let down the spell and have them do it."

Cardew was still facing the wall when Liel slipped through

the narrow gap between the floorboards and the wall. There was a hole in the tall fence that Liel used when she was in her cat form. But as an elf, she was too large to fit through the opening and escape into the jungle, and it would take too long to perform the ritual that let her change. Instead, she crawled under the floorboards of the house to wait. From her hiding place, she could see body parts strewn around the courtyard, and the smell of blood was heavy in the air.

Almost immediately, her sensitive ears heard someone approaching the colony. A lone figure strode through the half-open gate and crossed directly to the hut. It was a man, but he wore a long brown traveling cloak with a hood obscuring his face. Above her, she heard the front door swing open, and Cardew hurried onto the porch and down the steps into the yard. Liel couldn't see the men clearly, but she had the impression they clasped hands briefly, and she heard the stranger speak.

"So that is the colony. I'm not sure it is what Queen Anais had in mind."

"I'm sure it's not," Cardew said in a strained voice. Liel had been married to him long enough to know that it was fear in his voice. She inched forward on her belly to try and see who made her husband cower.

"I know where the Torque is," Cardew told his patron.

"Considering I gave you a map of the ruins, that is no accomplishment."

"You merely gave me a map of the jungle," Cardew protested. "There's a network of cities in that one quadrant. I had to search them all."

"And is the Torque in your possession?" the man asked icily. "I see nothing but dirt on your hands."

"I know where it is, but I can't get to it," Cardew said in a shaky voice.

"I'm very disappointed in you," the man said regretfully. "You had a vast well of resources."

"I tried. But it's well protected," Cardew protested.

"Yes, yes. I'm sure you made many ingenious attempts to secure one small object," the man sneered. "However, at the moment, there is a more pressing issue. I've heard rumors that your wife is still here in the world of the living."

"She's gone now," Cardew said.

"Gone? Gone as in rotting-in-the-ground gone? Or gone to tell her father about my operation in Chult?"

"She's gone . . ." Cardew began.

"In our bargain, you were to kill her when you arrived," the man reminded Cardew. "Her blood was supposed to stain the jungle floor. Those were your choice of florid words, if I remember correctly."

"It's difficult to kill your own wife."

"Yet it was your idea to begin with," the man pointed out.

"I know, but . . ." Cardew stuttered.

"An idea that was crucial to our overall plan," the man hissed. "If you couldn't do the act yourself, you should have had one of the men do it. I'm beginning to think you are incapable of handling anything except the court maidens."

"We cleared off the dome. We just haven't been able to get inside," Cardew said, the pitch of his voice rising to a whine. Liel shuddered at the thought that she had married such a man.

"Quiet, man," Cardew's patron said with contempt. "It's most annoying. Do you think a King would stutter so?"

"How is Ysabel?"

"Unspoiled and in the bloom of youth," the man replied.

"Ysabel is more to me than that."

"Women are nothing more than that. I'm going to give you one more chance, Declan. But believe me, it is your last."

"I can't just walk in and take it," Cardew protested. "I told you that."

"My personal guards will assist you, given that they have finished cleaning up your mess."

"What are you going to do?" Cardew asked.

"I have some hunting to do," the man replied.

"Hunting?" Cardew repeated.

Liel felt an invisible snare wrap around her wrist and drag her from under the house. She fought against the tether, twisting her shoulder painfully and digging her heels into the mud. But she couldn't break the hold, and found herself at the feet of the man whose face was still in shadows under his hood.

"If you would be so kind as to bind your wife's hands?" the man said to Cardew, throwing down a cord from his pack. Liel saw Cardew hesitate, and the man give him a thin-lipped smile.

"I won't ask you again," the man warned. "Either comply, or our arrangement is finished."

Cardew moved behind Liel and tied her hands behind her back. As she felt the ropes digging into her wrists, Liel burned with contempt for Cardew, a man who believed himself to be so powerful yet was nothing but a trained monkey dancing for his reward.

"What's going to happen to her?" Cardew asked his patron.

"She is no longer your concern. Bring me the Torque, Cardew. Don't return to Tethyr empty-handed."

With a final look at Liel, Cardew hurried out of the encampment, leaving his wife to whatever fate his master had planned for her.

CHAPTER EIGHTEEN

2 Flamerule, the Year of the Ageless One
(1479 DR)
Chult

They emerged from the tunnel to the edge of a barren, rocky chasm surrounded by a ring of jagged peaks. A sheer cliff of bluish-gray stone towered to the west. On the other side of the chasm, Harp could see a crevice through the rock—presumably the path that would take them to the entrance of the Domain. But there wasn't any obvious way across the chasm. Below them, a gradual slope of loose gravel dropped off into nothingness. From where they stood, Harp couldn't tell how far it was to the bottom of the chasm.

"That is Boneyard Canyon," Majida told them as she and Zo started climbing down the slope. "Don't fall."

Crouching and using their hands to steady themselves, the two dwarves slid at an angle down the slope to the cliff of bluish-gray stone. Their descent loosened a torrent of gravel that disappeared over the edge. The dwarves skidded to a stop against the cliff and clambered onto a narrow ledge that spanned the length of the rock wall. It was apparently the only way across the chasm short of sprouting wings.

Majida and Zo looked expectantly back at Harp and his crewmates, who stood agape having watched the dwarves' precipitous descent down the slope to the ledge. They made it look easy, but one misstep would result in a plunge into the crevice.

"That's suicide," Verran said in disbelief. "Jumping off the waterfall was safer than that."

"Don't take it slow," Zo called from the cliff. "That just makes it harder to steer yourself to the cliff without slipping off the edge."

"Well, we saw them do it," Harp said resolutely. "It's obviously possible to make it safely."

"At least for dwarves," Boult said.

"Then you should go first," Kitto said to Boult.

"Ah Kitto, you're always thinking of me," Boult growled, crouching like Zo and Majida had and angling himself to the ledge. Kitto waited until Boult reached the ledge safely and shot Harp a mischievous grin.

"Don't do anything stupid . . ." Harp began, but Kitto was already sliding down the slope—only he did it standing straight up. With an artful twist of his body, he stopped himself just as he reached the ledge and gracefully climbed up beside Boult.

"What, no somersault?" Harp called, relieved to see Kitto safely on the ledge.

"Next time," Kitto said cheerfully.

"You're a cagey one, aren't you," Majida said to Kitto. "I'll take you up to the nest of Horizon Eagle. I'd bet you could steal me a feather."

"I can steal anything," Kitto said without a trace of arrogance.

"It's you and me, then," Harp said to Verran as the two of them began to crab-walk down the slope. "I suppose there are worse fates than falling to your death."

"Worse than falling to your death in a pit of rotting corpses?" Verran asked.

Partway down the slope they could see that the chasm wasn't deep—only twenty feet down at its lowest point. But it was filled with half-rotted carcasses of animals and various humanoids, and the stench of decay hung heavy in the air. There were rib cages larger than a horse and skulls twice the size of a dwarf. Faded shreds of clothing and the rusted metal of ruined weapons could be seen among the piles of corpses.

"Look at that spine," Verran said appreciatively, pointing at an enormous backbone that curved around the perimeter of the chasm. "I want to see what kind of creature has a spine that long."

"Not me," Harp said peering down at the carnage below him. "I like my monsters dead and gone."

By the time that Harp and Verran reached the ledge, ominous clouds were moving across the sky. No one wanted to be caught on the outcropping of rock when the storm hit. With their chests to the cliff and hugging the rock with their arms, they made slow progress over the chasm. Harp looked over his shoulder at the grisly display of decaying meat and bleached bones breaching out of the pitch-black soil.

"What happened down there?" Harp called to Majida

"It's a dumping ground for a clutch of drakes that live on the mountaintops," she called back.

"Why do they dump fresh meat?"

"They're picky eaters," Majida said. "All the better for us. It keeps visitors away from the entrance to the Domain."

"I guess if you don't mind living on top of a clump of

carrion . . ." Harp mumbled under his breath as he slid one foot next to the other. The ledge was slightly longer than his boots, but not much, and Harp had the sense that he was going to topple off the edge. Fortunately, the cliff face had little nubs and outcroppings he could grab onto. His fingers probably weren't strong enough to actually keep him on the cliff, but it gave him the illusion of stability.

Beside him, Kitto turned his head and stared into the crevice. Harp's calves ached from standing on the balls of his feet, and he didn't want to dally on the cliff face.

"Uh, Kitto?" Harp said. "Are you all right? You're holding up the line."

"Harp?" Kitto asked. "What's down there?"

Harp looked down into the pit and movement in the chasm below them. Something twitched along the far edge followed by a slow undulation under one of the heaps of corpses. A stack of loose bones rolled down off the heap and clattered onto the dark earth.

"Boult!" Harp called.

"What?" Boult and the other dwarves had almost reached the other side.

"What's wrong?" Zo called.

"There's something in the pit!" Harp shouted. Something began inching under the rot to a spot in the center of the crevice.

Majida's head jerked toward the chasm just as something long and white whipped out from under the carrion and looped around Kitto's waist. Harp tried to grab the boy, but Kitto was yanked off the cliff. It looked as if fragments of bone from the pit had been knitted together by some unseen force to form a spiny tentacle. Kitto cried out in pain as the bones tightened vice-like around him.

"Give me a damn weapon!" Boult yelled. Three more tentacles, strips of flesh dangling from them like macabre decorations, rose writhing from the muck.

A mass of bones welled up in the middle of the pit. The remnant of a shattered lizard skull perched on top of a mish-mash of rib bones. Other pieces of bones lodged in the spaces between the ribs to form the body of the beast. The long backbone that Verran had noticed earlier jutted out from its back.

Shoving his sword into Boult's hands, Zo pulled his bow off his back and charged up the incline to higher ground. At the top of the slope, he fired four arrows rapidly at the creature's torso, but the arrows ricocheted or lodged harmlessly between the bones.

"Harp!" Boult shouted, leaning out to toss the sword to Harp. In one fluid motion, Harp caught the sword and leaped off the cliff. Jumping onto one of the tentacles, Harp braced his feet in the gaps between the bones and looped one arm around what looked to be a femur. With the other hand, he hacked at the tentacle lashing back and forth, but the blade scraped against it ineffectually.

On the ledge, a flaming scimitar erupted from Majida's hand. When the tail cracked against the cliff between her and Verran, Majida swung the sword against the bone. The fiery blade cleaved the spine-tail in half, and loose bones clattered against the cliff as they fell. But the loss of the tail didn't seem to slow the beast as another tentacle crashed against the ledge and nearly knocked Verran into the pit.

"This is futile!" Boult yelled, waving his empty hands in frustration. "We're not hurting it!"

"What the Hells is it?" Harp yelled as the tentacle he was riding swung at the wall of the pit. Letting the sword slip out of his hands, Harp dropped to the ground just as the tentacle slammed against the rocks. He landed on his knees on the slick ground and searched frantically through the piles of rot for the lost sword.

"Unnatural," Majida said. The flaming sword in her hand burned out into a wisp of black smoke.

Still suspended above them, Kitto cried out again. Pushing with both hands, he'd managed to raise himself higher in the tentacle's crushing grasp, but it still had a grip around his legs. When the bony appendage plummeted toward the cliff, Kitto flopped like a doll in a child's hand.

"Look at me, Verran," Majida said firmly to the boy beside her on the ledge. Verran was looking down in horror as the scene played out below him. With his face scrunched up like a little kid who was trying not to cry, Verran turned his head and looked at Majida.

"You have to do something, Verran," she said in a calm voice. "You have to do something now."

"What's he supposed to do?" Boult said.

"I can't!" Verran cried.

"Can you see it?" Majida said. "In your mind, Verran? Can you see what you're supposed to do?"

"It'll just make it worse!"

On the ground, Harp scooped the sword out of a pile of rancid blubber and charged at the beast's core. He jammed the weapon through the bone into an empty cavity where it lodged in place. Ducking as one of the bony appendages swung above his head, Harp tried in vain to pull the sword back out.

"My spells can't hurt it like that," Majida said urgently to Verran. "You have to make it alive!"

"What!" Boult said in disbelief. "He has to what?"

Verran shook his head desperately.

"Make it live. Do it, Verran!"

"You want to bring that thing to life?" Boult shouted. "Majida! That's insane!"

"Sit on the ledge," Majida said. "Don't think about the creature—I'll protect you. Think about what you need to do." Kitto finally managed to loose himself from the grasp of the tentacle. But just as he freed himself, it swung wildly, flinging the boy into the air. Tumbling to the ground, Kitto smacked against the rocks before landing with a dull thud. Harp left the sword stuck in the beast and sprinted to Kitto, who was just getting up off the ground. As Harp helped him to the edge of the pit, he saw Verran looking terrified on the ledge above him. The boy's lips moved silently, and his face seemed swollen and bruised as a dark blue tinge crept around his eyes.

With a sucking noise, the carrion that was spread out across the bottom of the pit oozed across the ground to the beast. It slid along its tentacles and up the bony core to the top of the shattered skull, until every inch of the monstrosity was covered in a gray, fleshy coating. Reddish-blue veins branched across the outside of the new skin, lacing the hunks of meat onto the skeletal frame. For a moment, the creature froze. From his position on the floor of the pit, Harp gawked at the creature above him, a monster that now resembled a marine animal, landlocked in a lake of decay.

In the moment of silence, Harp heard a low thud and then another. Kitto turned to him wide-eyed as the noise increased into a constant rhythm. Harp could feel each stroke pulse through the ground into the soles of his feet.

"What is that?" he asked breathlessly.

"The beating of its heart," Kitto said awestruck.

"Oh, Verran, what have you done?" Harp whispered. The creature shuddered as it took its first breath and expanded until it almost filled the pit. Looming above them, it cast Harp and Kitto into darkness. As it rose higher into the air, its four tentacles towered above Verran, Boult, and Majida, who were still on the ledge.

"Get out of there," Majida yelled down to Harp and Kitto, who were huddled in a corner of the pit. But the smooth walls of the chasm offered no handholds. The two men skirted the edge of pit until they were directly below the others on the ledge, but the creature's ever-expanding bulk threatened to crush them against the rock.

The meaty tentacles flailed in the air uncontrollably, and one of the appendages crashed down on the ledge between Boult and Majida. Boult kept his footing, but Majida was knocked off balance. She lunged across to the slope below Zo, but slid down the gravel and almost fell into the pit. Digging her fingers into the soil with her legs dangling off the edge, she managed to hold on until Zo climbed down and hauled her up to higher ground.

Using his crossbow as a club, Zo swung at any tentacle that came near them while Majida pressed her palms into the ground and recited an incantation. As her lips formed the ancient words, a snarl of shiny black thorns sprang out of the ground at the bottom of the pit. As long as arrows and as wide around as a man's wrist, the hooked thorns radiated like a starburst in the dirt surrounding the monster.

"Those are Banethorns," Zo warned the others. "They're poisonous."

"We've got to get them out of there!" Boult shouted, stepping quickly along the ledge to Zo and Majida. "Get me rope!"

Zo threw his pack on the ground, and Boult rummaged through it. When a tentacle flailed dangerously close to the dwarves, Zo slammed the wooden crossbow against it and deflected the blow. The tentacle retreated momentarily and crashed down again.

"Where's your damn rope?" Boult demanded, turning the pack upside down and dumping the contents onto the gravel.

Zo didn't have time to answer as he batted another assault away from Majida, who was still kneeling on the ground. Below them in the pit, spiky green leaves and mace-headed brambles rose out of the soil, twisting into thick, knotted vines that looped around the fleshy creature like chains. The hooked tips of the thorns dug into its skin while the poisoned sap seeped into its exposed veins. The creature struggled against the vines and thorns, and hunks of its flesh ripped away as it was pinned down under the clawing plants.

"Get off the ledge!" Harp called up to Verran. Verran didn't move. Muttering to himself, he leaned down and touched the wall above Harp's head. Under Verran's fingers, strands of the emerald vines flowed from brambles surrounding the monster and up the cliff to the ledge. Instead of black thorns, they were adorned with delicate yellow flowers.

"Climb!" Verran urged them.

Harp and Kitto scrambled up the vines, reaching the ledge just as the pit below was overtaken by the poisonous plants. The brambles engulfed the creature, and the men joined the dwarves on the other side of the chasm. With all four tentacles grasping the edge of the pit, the creature made one last effort to pull itself free from the twisting brambles. But it couldn't free itself from Majida's thicket, and the poison from the thorns pulsed through its veins until it reached the beast's core and its beating heart was stilled.

When the chasm was filled to the brim with twisted black vines, and there was nothing but silence in the air, Harp checked to make sure everyone was still standing. Kitto was bruised and a little bloody, but he assured Harp that he was fine.

"What just happened?" Boult demanded. "Who should I thank, and who should I punch?"

"Thank Verran and Majida," Harp said. "They saved us."

But Boult wasn't in a thankful mood. "Did you know something lived down there?"

"Nothing lived down there!" Zo said indignantly. "Majida! Do you know where that came from?"

Majida looked at Verran. "No," she said finally. "I

don't know. But we should get below ground as soon as possible."

Majida and Zo turned and walked into a narrow channel in the rock behind them. With smooth walls streaked with glossy bands of red and pink, the channel was an old river-bed that twisted through the rock. Above them, the storm clouds had blown away, and the sky was blue and clear.

"Did something happen, Verran?" Harp asked quietly as they followed the others through the channel.

"I didn't do anything!" Verran said defensively. "If she says I did, she's lying!"

"Easy," Harp said.

"I hate Chult," Verran said angrily. "And I hate her."

"You saved me and Harp," Kitto reminded him, but Verran strode away from them. Harp thought about calling him back, but decided against it. As Verran stalked away, Harp saw a large circle of blood staining the back of his shirt, just below the base of his neck.

"Was he injured?" Harp asked, but neither Kitto nor Boult had an answer. Verran had been on the cliff through the battle, and Harp couldn't imagine what blow would form such a perfectly round wound on the boy's back. With Verran in such a state, he couldn't imagine getting answers out of him either.

The channel ended at the edge of a massive cliff. They stood on a small parcel of flat ground where a handful of rune-marked trees clung to the edge of the cliff, their silver-tipped leaves rustling in the light breeze. Below them, the carpet of green seemed endless—like the world went on forever, and the jungle owned it all.

"Those trees mark the beginning of the Domain," Majida told them. The circular basin with the golden dome was almost directly below them. They had circled through the jungle and stood on the spiked mountain range that they had seen from a distance earlier that morning. Harp couldn't see the ocean from his vantage point, so he knew that they must be facing south or southeast. The *Crane* seemed very far away.

"Is that where we just were?" he asked, pointing to the southern waterfall and the ruins.

"Yes, those are the ruins of Hisari. The mountains are called the Crown in, well, in most languages spoken in the jungle."

"Hisari lies at the foot of the Crown," Verran murmured.

"Yes," Majida said. "Hisari means City of the Royal Mouth in the language of the Scaly Ones.

"Royal Mouth?" Verran asked dubiously.

"A better translation would be City of Kings," Majida said. "So they are the Crown of the City of Kings."

"Which came first, the city or the mountains?" Boult asked.

Majida smiled sadly. "The Scaly Ones played with nature as if it were a toy. You've seen the husks. But flesh was not the only thing they shaped to their pleasure. There is a legend that each peak holds a gemstone so vast that a demon was enlisted to carry the jewels to the pinnacles and bind them into the rock."

Majida tugged a length of muddy rope and pulled up a trap door, its boards rotted and warped. They peered into a dark shaft with a rickety ladder leading down into the darkness. Majida lowered herself over the edge and began down the ladder.

"Go ahead," Zo said, looking at Harp.

Harp climbed down the shaky ladder. The sunlight from above illuminated the glassy black walls of the shaft where thousands of fossils were left from the time when it had been a sea. The soil of the seabed had been filled with tiny snail-like creatures and helix-shaped worms. After so many years, their forms were outlined by white quartz that glittered like ancient stars in the deep black of the walls.

At the bottom of the shaft, Harp stood next to Majida and waited for the others. In front of them was a wooden door without a lock, and Harp could see a faint glow of light under the bottom of the door.

"Do your scars hurt?" Majida asked.

"Sometimes," Harp replied. "They've faded a lot. You should have seen them right after I got out of Vankila. They used to split open all the time."

"Split?"

"Yeah, I could brush up against a doorframe and end up bleeding buckets. It took almost a year for the skin to really heal."

"I can help you with them," Majida told him.

"Thank you, but nothing works," Harp said regretfully. "I've tried everything."

"We'll see."

"Majida, do you think that Verran had something to do with that creature coming to life?" he asked. Above them, Kitto was halfway down the ladder, and the others would be right behind him.

"I don't know," she said. "But there is something about him . . ."

"What?" Harp prompted.

Majida smiled sadly. "He's at a crossroads."

"I don't understand," Harp said.

"It's very similar to the place you are standing," Majida said.

"Are you sure I'm at a crossroads?" Harp said. "Because I feel like I'm at the bottom of a well."

When everyone had climbed down the ladder and the trap door was closed above them, Majida pushed open the wooden door. An unexpected flood of sunlight made Harp shield his eyes. Blinking rapidly, he stepped into an enormous subterranean room. High above them, crystal-encrusted stalagmites hung from the cavern's dripping ceiling. A narrow streambed flowing with azure water bisected the cavern floor, which was composed of the same black rock as the walls of the shaft.

"Fire-rock and mud-rock in the same place?" Boult muttered to Harp. "Something incredibly hot exploded here to get that combination."

The walls of the cavern were slopes of gray, pockmarked rock that let water seep into the cavern as well as sunlight. The rock was so porous that Harp could see the silhouettes of vines and flowers dangling on the other side. In the center of the massive cavern, a bronze urn burned with a glittery orange flame.

"Welcome to the Spirit Vault," Majida said. They stared at the cavern.

"Why do you call it that?" Harp asked.

Majida smiled and pointed to the far side of the cavern. The wall was the same glistening black as the shaft, but in place of sea fossils, the crystallized bones of a giant creature protruded from the obsidian wall.

Spanning from floor to ceiling, the bones were at least double the height of a giant and more than four times the size of an average man. While the bones of the creature's torso, arms, and legs were humanoid, the slant of its skull was distinctly feline. Spiny filaments of wings jutted out from behind its back, and broken chains dangled from his shackled wrists. With its wings outspread and palms opened, the creature looked as if it had been blasted back against the wall by some immense force that had made the cavern into a tomb.

"What are those?" Harp said in awe.

Zo gave him a quizzical look. "Those are the bones of a god."

CHAPTER NINETEEN

2 Flamerule, the Year of the Ageless One
(1479 DR)
Chult

That's not a god," Verran said. "That's just some monster."

Zo's eyes widened, and he sputtered harsh words in Dwarvish, but Verran didn't look abashed at all. Harp thought he looked defiant, and a little pleased, as if he took pleasure in angering the dwarven chief.

"You know, Verran," Harp said as gently as he could. "You shouldn't judge something you don't know anything about."

"It's not a god," Verran repeated. Furious, Zo turned bright red under his beard.

Majida sighed. "Zo, would you ask Lethea to prepare a place for our guests to rest? And food for them to eat?"

After Zo had stomped out of the cavern and down

a tunnel in the wall behind them Harp glared at Verran.

"We're guests here . . ." Harp began irritably, but Majida interrupted him before he could chastise the youth.

"You're right, Verran," she interrupted, staring intently at the boy. "It's not a god. But there's no use trying to dissuade someone from their beliefs, is there?"

"What do you mean by that?" Verran asked petulantly.

Harp and Boult exchanged glances. Ever since the waterfall, Verran had been touchy. Harp wanted to attribute it to hunger and tiredness, but Majida's fears about the boy were worrisome. And there was the strange emergence of the the creature in the pit. Without proof, Harp didn't want to think that Verran had anything to do with it. But considering how he had melted Bootman, it was hard not to wonder.

"The Captive is not unrelated to you," Majida told them. "The Practitioner is searching for the Torque, which was created from one of the broken links of his chains."

"What does the Torque do?" Kitto asked.

"The Domain's legends say many things," Majida said with a touch of amusement. "Various myths assign it powers from dismemberment to the utter extermination of the dwarves."

"Can you narrow that down?" Harp asked.

"Only to a guess," Majida said. "I think it gives the wearer heightened protection. Like a shield, it gifts them with the Captive's endurance, if not his strength."

"But you don't know for sure?" Boult asked.

"I am unraveling our legends in search of answers," Majida said. "And as you know, in the realm of myth, truth is always suffocated by fear."

"If the Torque is so powerful, why don't the yuan-ti just use it themselves?" Boult asked.

Majida shook her head. "The Scaly Ones can't use it."

"Why?" Harp asked.

"I don't know how the magic was ordered around the

artifact, but in their hands, it's simply a twist of metal. Since they can't use it, I believe it's safest in their keeping."

While they talked, Verran became more and more agitated. He shifted his weight from foot to foot, and his eyes darted around the cavern as if he were watching the flight path of some invisible bird. Harp raised his eyebrows and frowned at the impatient youth.

"What is wrong with you?" Harp asked. "Are you feeling all right?"

"I'm hungry," he said, jutting out his chin as if he expected someone to disagree with him.

"Go down the tunnel into the hub and ask for Lethea," Majida said. "She'll find something for you to eat."

Before she finished speaking, Verran spun on his heel and hurried down the tunnel and out of sight. Watching him, Harp had the unpleasant feeling that Verran was like a pot of water, waiting to boil.

"We should go to the ruins and look for Liel," Harp said to Majida when her dark eyes found his. "Liel thought the Torque was important. Cardew and his patron obviously think it's important."

"Not until you've rested. Kitto looks as if he's about to fall over."

"I'm fine," Kitto insisted.

But Majida was right. Kitto looked tired and pale. On closer inspection, Harp saw that the boy was shaking, probably from hunger.

"Agreed," Harp said. "Come on, Kitto, let's go get some food."

"All right, you," Boult growled at Majida when Kitto and Harp were gone. "Talk."

Majida laughed softly. "Abrupt, aren't you?"

"You inscribed my name in the trees in the colony, as part of the ward."

"Yes," Majida admitted.

"Why?" Boult demanded.

"I've dreamed about you, that you were coming to the jungle. My dreams are puzzling at best. Horrifying at worst. I thought you were the key to the puzzle."

"And now you're not so sure?" Boult prompted.

"And now I'm not so sure," Majida agreed.

"What's changed?"

But Majida didn't answer. They stood in silence in the warm circle of air around the urn, and Boult marveled at the spectacle of the skeleton immortalized in the shiny rock. At first glance, the bones had looked like pure white crystal, but he could see veins of color—rosy beige, copper, and light blue—that reminded Boult of the inside of a seashell. The thin bones branching from its back showed a wingspan that was impressive, even for the creature's gargantuan size. Splints of metal jutted out from the remains of the shackles. The splints looked as if they had punctured the skin of the Captive and fused to his bones while he still lived. It must have been incredibly painful, and Boult wondered if the fire was a way to honor the massive creature that had suffered at the hands at the Scaly Ones.

"Is the urn's fire natural or unnatural?" he finally asked.

"Unnatural and perpetual," she said, the corners of her lips turning upward slightly.

"It's never gone out?" Boult asked.

"Not even when a young scamp snuck in and doused it repeatedly with water," Majida replied. "Still it burned."

"Were you the scamp?" Boult asked after a pause.

Majida looked momentarily surprised. "That secret dies with me," she said good-naturedly.

Boult took a closer look at the metal urn. Fashioned from

unadorned bronze, the shallow urn had a wide, circular base. Inside the urn, the flame burned on a plate of opaque glass.

"I once heard a story about a man who turned against his patron god, going so far as to deny the god's existence," Boult said. "One night, the man realized that he had made a grave error and begged for the god's forgiveness. The god forgave the man, but all he promised him in return was suffering."

"Suffering is the nature of the world," Majida said. "Honor is not."

"I used to believe in honor. When I was a soldier, I lived to serve my queen and country—my masters—faithfully. Do you know what my masters did to me?"

"They betrayed you."

"They forced me to suffer for someone else's crime."

"Humiliation is the backbone of evil. That doesn't make your honor a mistake."

"My honor is dead."

"And what has risen up in its place? Revenge?"

"It has brought me so far," Boult pointed out.

"It has determined the company you keep," Majida said gravely. "It has brought you to the ends of the earth. And for what?"

"If Cardew wants something, I want it more," Boult growled.

"Then you are serving a master, whether you realize it or not."

"You don't understand."

"Maybe not. But I know that you and your friends are close to finding the Torque, and that gives me pause," Majida said.

"Because you want it to stay hidden in the ruins?"

Majida gave a little shrug. "I'm going to tell you a secret. One that most of the dwarves of the Domain don't know."

Boult's eyes narrowed. " You don't know me. Why trust me with it?"

"Because you will appreciate the irony."

"That's a very poor reason," Boult pointed out.

"Hence the irony," Majida said. "Will you listen?"

"Secrets are the commerce of revenge, Majida," Boult said. "I'll listen, as long as you know what business I am in."

"I know what you are," Majida said. "And I'm telling you anyway. For centuries, people have died trying to get the Torque. The Scaly Ones have bent their will around protecting it. It has been the nexus around which life and death have spun. And it's powerful, no doubt."

Majida stopped. Boult raised his eyebrows. "Don't stop now. I'm more than curious."

"All that time, the dwarves of the Domain have had something more powerful. Something that overshadows the Torque and all it has done."

"What?"

"Him." Majida gestured to the Captive and looked at Boult with a resolute expression on her aged face.

"I don't understand."

"His blood. There is a vial beneath the urn filled with an elixir made from his essence. The flames keep his life force alive, and the wards around the Domain keep him hidden. As you have seen for yourself, both the Scaly Ones and the Practitioner have the skill to bring him back to life and to dominate his will, at least for a short time."

"Create a husk of the Captive," Boult said incredulously, staring up at the towering skeleton that dominated the cavern. "In the history of bad ideas, that sounds like the worst. Huh. I'm not sure that's information I wanted to know."

Majida smiled. "Yes, but it's information that Cardew—and his patron—would kill to have, is it not?"

Boult nodded slowly.

"You don't have to be his chattel anymore."

"I'm not—"

"Boult!" Verran called, surprising them both. Neither had heard the boy approach. "Harp is looking for you."

"You are very puzzling," Boult said to Majida. But he said it in a kindly way, in a voice he was not accustomed to using. Then he left with Verran.

"Just as long as someone has all the pieces but me," she murmured to herself when they were gone.

Someone shook Harp's arm roughly. He and his crew were sleeping in a narrow dormitory where Harp had shoved multiple cots together to make something long enough for him to lay in comfortably. Harp was well fed, clean, and warm—all the things that made a perfect night's sleep. Or they would have, if someone wasn't still shaking his arm.

Irritable at the disruption, he sat up and saw Majida standing by his cot. His exasperation disappeared. He couldn't imagine the elder dwarf disturbing him for something trivial. The room was dark, but the door was ajar and the torches lit in the corridor outside. In the shadows, he could see her motion for him to follow her. Kitto and Boult were snoring, but Verran stirred restlessly as Harp pulled on his boots and shouldered his pack.

So far, Harp hadn't seen much of the layout of the Domain except the common room, which was like the hub on a wheel with a series of tunnels rotating off it like spokes. With multiple fire pits and clay ovens, the toasty, cedar-scented room was where most of the day-to-day living took place. Harp had met a handful of the other residents the night before, but hadn't gotten a sense of how many dwarves actually called the Domain home. Apparently, the dwarves kept goats on the open passes between mountains, and it was the time of year that many dwarves were away tending the herds.

They crossed through the common room where small fires still smoldered in the fire pits. In the dim light, Harp could see wisps of smoke rising into slits cut in the rock ceiling. When he passed under one, he could see a slice of the starry night sky high above him. Harp couldn't imagine how the dwarves could have carved such long narrow shafts in the rock.

"Are those shafts natural?" he whispered to Majida.

"We have built everything you see," she replied, pausing to light a torch in the fire pit. "Everything except the chamber of the captive."

At the end of the tunnels, Majida stopped at a plain wooden door, which she unlocked with a key from the chain that hung from her belt.

"So much for communal living," Harp remarked, nodding at the key.

"My kin think books should be used for kindling," Majida said, pushing open the door with her hip. "And the only use for metal is for swords."

They stepped into a cramped chamber at the bottom of a tall, narrow shaft with spiral stairs leading up through the rock. As Harp followed Majida up the stairs, his head brushed the bottom of the steps above him. At the top, Harp climbed into a dome that was built on the top of a rocky peak. The walls of the mountaintop observatory were almost translucent—Harp could see the ridges and formations of rocks on the outside. The color and sheen reminded him of an ivory plate that was so delicate it seemed his breath alone could sunder it.

"What is that?" Harp asked, brushing his fingertips against the smooth walls, which felt cool under his touch.

"Actually, it's metal," Majida said. "I made some adjustments to it."

Majida turned a crank and half of the domed ceiling opened with a squeak that sounded very metallic. The little room was open to the air, and Harp had an unhindered view of the night sky. The observatory was the closest he'd ever been to the stars, and their vastness made him feel light-headed.

"Are we on top of the Crown?" Harp asked, staring out at the moonlight.

"Yes. I built my observatory on a drake nesting site. But they leave the mountains at night to hunt, so they shouldn't trouble us. Although a young bull tried to stick his snout in here once."

"What happened?"

"I left a scar, and he never came back."

Harp turned his attention to a brass contraption on the far side of the room. Almost as tall as Harp and twice as wide, it had a circular bronze base that held a series of concentric brass rings attached on the same axis inside a metal skeleton. Harp had seen similar devices—although on a much smaller scale—used for navigation on ships. Their purpose had something to do with shadows and angles—Boult had explained it once, but Harp had forgotten the extensive equations and numerology necessary to understand how it worked. Harp preferred to navigate with his own eyes and the polar stars. Of course, as Boult pointed out, that didn't work so well when there was cloud cover.

A low cabinet housed hand-held navigational devices, such as a metal quadrant and a handful of hourglasses, each with different colored sand. Shells and fossils were neatly labeled and ordered in a glass box with many small compartments, and there was a half-empty potion chest open against the wall.

"Your observatory is impressive," Harp told Majida. "Have you learned all there is to know about the stars?"

"Unfortunately, no," Majida replied. "I am coming to believe that the answers I seek are found inside the body rather than the vast planes."

Harp shuddered. "I've heard that before."

"Have you?" Majida said, not sounding surprised at all. She lit a stick of incense in a wooden bowl on the table, and the scent of flowers floated through the air. Majida sat cross-legged on the green threadbare rug in the center of the floor and waited until Harp sat down across from her.

"When the sun rises, we'll go back down. Zo will show you a hidden tunnel that will take you to the entrance of the ruins. There's a magical barrier around the ruins, but Verran will be able to get you inside. I don't know whether you'll find Liel or not, but I can tell you that the Torque is below the entrance hall of the golden dome. It won't be easy to get."

"If we get the Torque, should we bring it to you?" Harp asked.

Majida was quiet for a moment. "No," she said finally. "If you get the Torque, drop it in the deepest ocean you can find."

"I can do that. I just happen to have a ship."

"I know."

"Liel told you about my ship? When we were together on Gwynneth Isle, we talked about getting one. But I didn't think she knew that it happened."

"She knew."

"Why did she never contact me? I know her father helped get me out of Vankila, and I was grateful for that. But I don't even know if that was his sense of honor or hers."

"She asked him to help you. He didn't stop until it was done."

"Still . . ."

"Cardew threatened your life if she tried to see you."

"The Husk-Liel said some things. Things that only Liel knew, but they were twisted."

"Seeds of truth, Harp, but the fruit of manipulation," Majida said quietly. "Did you love her?"

"Yes."

"Did she know that?"

"I hope so," Harp said emphatically.

"I hope you get another chance to tell her."

The sun was inching over the horizon, casting the sky in deep purple and rose. A salt-scented breeze swept in from the opening in the roof, and Harp wished he were on the *Crane* listening to the crack of the sails and feeling the swell of the water rock the boat under him.

"I can rid you of your scars," Majida told him.

Harp shook his head. "Like I told you before, I've tried everything. I've been to casters up and down the coast. No one can get rid of them."

"Then I have something they don't."

Harp closed his eyes. Majida waited a long time for him to speak.

"I'm not offering because they are horrifying, Harp," she finally said. "I am offering because they were inflicted on you, like a brand. If you want to keep them—"

Harp's eyes flew open. "I want you to take them off. I want you to make me what I was before."

"Then what gives you pause?" Majida asked.

"I wonder when Liel saw me. I wonder what kind of man she saw."

It was four against one, and Harp was too drunk to defend himself.

"Ghoul," the biggest one said, slamming his fist into Harp's face. Harp fell back into another man, who held his arms behind his back while the big one punched him in the stomach. "So ugly they had to sew you back together."

When they had dragged Harp out of the pub into the back alley just minutes before, Liel had lost of them in the crowd. She caught sight of them from the street and strode down the alley to them. By the time they saw her approaching, a blast of fire had shot from her hand and singed the big man's shoulder. He stumbled back against the wall, clutching his arm and moaning while his friends backed away. They dropped Harp to the cobblestones. The four men bolted down the alley leaving Liel alone with Harp.

The narrow alley was filthy, and she could hear the rats scurrying behind the rubbish bins. It reeked of alcohol and rot, and was the last place she wanted to be. It was the last place she wanted Harp to be. She crouched down beside the body at her feet. Unconscious, Harp lay in a twisted heap, his breathing shallow and labored.

She had been trailing Harp through the city for a couple of days, trying to figure out what to do. She thought about talking to Kitto, but he was always with Harp or the gaunt dwarf, whoever he was. Liel had seen Harp's scars from a distance, but it was the first time she'd seen them up close—thick, red lines crisscrossing his face and hands like a grotesque jigsaw puzzle. His shirt was tangled around his chest, and she could see the scars on his back and stomach.

Cardew had done that to him. Her husband's threats had been real. The Branch of Linden had spies everywhere, and if Cardew even knew she was in that wretched city, he would come after Harp. Liel had never felt so trapped. She didn't know how far her husband's reach extended. If she left Cardew, he might focus his ire on her father and the elves of the Wealdath. Besides, she and Harp had parted in anger. For all she knew, Harp hated her. The safest thing she could do was to leave Harp in the safekeeping of his friends.

She pulled him close so his head rested against her chest. If she didn't help him, he would die in the alley, drunk and bleeding. She couldn't let that be the culmination of his life.

How the human had managed to take root in her soul, she would never understand. Until that moment, she had told herself that what she felt for Harp was just a construct of desire, something easily shattered or sacrificed. But she'd never been good at lying to herself, and as she held him, there was no denying what she felt for him.

She forced herself to block out the stench of the alley, the wretched buildings, and the filthy city that corrupted the force of life. With his warm body in her arms, she could finally hear the rustle of leaves, the call of the birds, and the pulse of the faraway forest. She found her strength to mend his broken ribs and to heal the shattered bones in his hands. The gash on his forehead closed, but still the scars remained. When his breathing was deep and even, she pulled him to his feet.

She half-carried him down the road to the dodgy boarding house where he was staying with Kitto and the dwarf. She lowered him onto the doorstep, knocked loudly on the door, and disappeared into the shadows before anyone saw her. Still, there was something else she could do. Liel headed to the docks, where she had seen Harp talking to a fat man about a boat called the *Crane*. That ship might be his best chance for something that resembled happiness.

CHAPTER TWENTY

2 Flamerule, the Year of the Ageless One
(1479 DR)
Kinnard Keep, Tethyr

Sitting in the soft chair closest to the fire, Cardew
rested his elbows on his knees. He stabbed at the
burning logs with the fireplace poker, making the
flames crackle higher and sparks hiss and pop
as they flew up the chimney. Cardew crossed the
room to the collection of liquor bottles and poured
a glass of the amber liquor that had been imported
from the midlands.

Enjoying the sweet, warm taste, Cardew looked
appreciatively at the wall tapestry showing a flock
of sheep in a green meadow, the high shelves filled
with leather-bound books, and the glossy mahogany
desk and matching chairs. Officially it was Tresco's
study, but he rarely used the room, and Ysabel had
long claimed it for her own.

"Why do you look so pensive, Master Cardew?"

Ysabel said from the doorway. She was dressed in a dark navy dress with a high neck. Gone was the girlish braid, and her blonde hair fell loose around her shoulders.

"You look beautiful," he told her.

She smiled and came to sit in the chair next to him. "How was your business in town?"

"Boring. Just details about an estate I plan to purchase near the capitol," he told her.

"I hear you and Uncle are going fox hunting."

"Is that what he told you?" Cardew said. "I hadn't heard what the old scoundrel had planned for us. What would you like to drink, Bella?"

"Whatever you're having," she replied.

Cardew poured a second glass of the amber liquid and came to sit beside her again.

"What time will dinner be served?" he inquired, glancing at the closed door.

"Shortly."

"Will Tresco be joining us?"

"No," Ysabel said tersely.

"How interesting."

"Isn't it?" Ysabel agreed.

"I don't know if I've ever been fully alone with you," Cardew mused. "Tresco has kept you so well guarded."

"For my own safety."

Cardew frowned at her coyness. "Can we speak freely or not?" He reached over and laid his hand on her thigh. "Are we free to do as we please?"

Ysabel pushed his hand away. "We can speak freely, Declan. But you are not free to do whatever you please."

Cardew was surprised and a little hurt. "Did you get the spellbook I left for you?"

"I did. It was quite elementary. Of the same level as the spellbooks you brought me when I was a child."

"Really? You must have advanced quite a bit since we

last talked. Does Tresco know what you've been up to?"

"Of course not," Ysabel said crossly. "You know how he feels about the subject."

"Well, maybe you've become so adept you don't need me to bring you any more books," Cardew said. He stood up to refill his drink. When he turned around, Ysabel was standing directly behind him. His drink sloshed over the side of the glass and onto his hand. Irritably, he set the drink down on the table and dried his hand on a linen napkin.

"I appreciate your attentiveness, but I am ready for something more . . . fulfilling," Ysabel said.

Cardew reached for her, but she stepped away. Cardew let his arms fall to his sides.

"Why are you acting this way, Bella? Last night . . . I thought . . ."

"Acting like what?" she said petulantly.

"As if you don't know me," he said reaching out to stroke a lock of her hair. He wound it around his finger and gave it a little tug. "As if we're not planning to be together forever."

"Forever?" she asked, arching an eyebrow.

"Yes, Bella. That's what people do when they're in love."

Ysabel turned away from him and walked across the room to the bookcase. She ran the back of her fingers along the row of colorful spines until she reached a black leather tome, which she pulled out and held against her chest.

"The history of the Dragon Coast," she announced, tapping the cover. "It was written by a bandit who lived near Nathlan and was more erudite than most so-called intellectuals of the court."

Cardew didn't give a fig about the Dragon Coast. "No one doubts you're a smart girl . . ." he began.

"Did you know that I've read all of those volumes?" she continued, gesturing at the shelves behind her. "Philosophy, geography, history. All of it very dry, none magical of course. Uncle keeps the good books locked away."

"What are you saying?" Cardew demanded impatiently.

"I'm tired of people treating me as if I were a child," Ysabel said, not bothering to disguise the anger in her voice. "Tresco's kept me as if I were a pet. I've been under lock and key and constantly watched by guards. He has restricted all my schooling and refused to let me develop my spellcasting."

"I helped you with that, didn't I?" Cardew pointed out.

"You did," she acknowledged. "And I'm eternally grateful. But we've reached a fork in the road, if you will."

"I don't understand."

"I am a good listener, Declan. I have heard and understood a great many things from my vantage point as a prisoner chained to the wall."

"You haven't been chained to the wall," Cardew said impatiently. "Don't be dramatic."

"This is not the time for that discussion," Ysabel said with a hint of bitterness.

"Then what are we discussing?" Cardew asked crossly. The conversation was not going in the direction he had expected. During his ride home from town, his mind had played through a series of tantalizing fantasies about what he wanted to do with the princess just as soon as he got her alone.

Ysabel sat down on the chair in front of the fire and patted the chair across from her. After a moment's hesitation, Cardew sat beside her, hoping to recapture the mood of the night before.

"I need to know some things, Declan," she said quietly. "About my Uncle and about you."

"What sort of things?" he asked suspiciously.

When she reached out and took his hand, he felt a jolt of energy surge through his skin. The desire before fulfillment, when a simple touch felt electrifying, was his favorite part of courtship.

"I know you plan to marry me, with Tresco's blessing. But if you want me to be your wife, I need you to talk to me."

Cardew took a deep breath, feeling as if his feet were back on solid ground. Such discussions seemed typical for women. He never understood how chatting made them more interested in rolling around in the sheets, but who was he to question why.

"Of course, Bella," he said agreeably. "If we are to marry, I want us to be honest with each other. Ask me anything you want."

"I know that this is delicate. But I need to know about your first wife. How did you meet?"

"Liel?" Cardew was surprised at the question. "I met her after the massacre. I was wounded, and Anais sent me to be healed by her father, Avalor. I spent several months in their care."

"Did you love her?"

Cardew signed. "Queen Anais felt that our marriage would help heal the rift between men and elves. She was wrong, of course. But how could I refuse the queen?"

"Queen Anais is naïve," Ysabel agreed. "But you didn't answer the question. Did you love Liel?"

"I was bewitched by her beauty, which was substantial, although nothing compared to yours. Of course, you were just a child then. So you can't be jealous."

"I'm not," Ysabel assured him. "She was kidnapped by pirates, was she not?"

"Where did you hear that tale?" he asked "Yes, while we were engaged, but before we married, she was kidnapped and taken to sea."

"Who instigated it?" Ysabel asked.

"We never found out."

"Was her coin paid?"

Cardew hesitated, not sure why any of it would matter, but there didn't seem any harm in answering.

"No, it wasn't. As fate would have it, one of the pirates mutinied against the captain and fled the boat, taking her with him. They traveled to the Moonshae Isles and then she was returned safely to her father."

"How fortunate! You must have been grateful to the man for saving her life."

"Well," Cardew said, hesitating as he sought the appropriate words. "I may have misrepresented his intentions. He took her with him as capital. He planned to barter her freedom in exchange for a pardon of his crime of mutiny. It was less than honorable, you see."

"Yes, I see. What happened to him?"

"I have no idea," Cardew said, his brow furrowing. "Why does it matter?"

"It doesn't. It's a sweet story, though. A pirate saves a beautiful elf and returns her safely to the loving arms of her fiancé. Don't you see the appeal?"

"Dear Ysabel, you are so innocent. There was nothing sweet about it. It was sordid and unfortunate."

Ysabel frowned. "I don't understand . . ."

"And I'll say nothing more about the matter," Cardew said firmly. He was not about to share how a ruffian had cuckolded him. Cardew intended his tone of voice to chastise the girl and stop her from asking questions, but she stared at him without a trace of regret.

"Why did you tell the Inquiry that you saw me upstairs by Teague's body? And that you saved me from the masked assailants? And that we hid together in the woods until morning?"

"Because that's what happened," Cardew insisted. "Don't you remember?"

"I remember a lot of things, but not that."

"Bella, it was a horrifying experience. You were a mere child. You can't trust your memories."

"Why did you blame the dwarf? Are you such a coward that you had to direct attention away from your incompetence?"

Cardew was shocked into silence. That he was Amhar's accuser was a well-kept secret. He and the ministers conducting the Inquiry agreed that it might sully his reputation as Hero of the Realm if he were also the prime witness against the dwarf. In fact, he'd been paid a large amount of coin to let the Inquiry take the credit for discovering the identity of the culprit behind the massacre.

"Who has been filling your head with such nonsense?" he demanded angrily.

"Did you find what you were looking for in the jungle?" she asked innocently.

"Ysabel! What do you do! Listen at keyholes? Read letters not intended for you?"

"Did you find it or not?"

"I cannot believe that you . . ." Cardew sputtered.

"So you didn't find it. When Tresco said that you failed, he must have been speaking of the artifact."

"You are obviously not the girl I thought you were."

"And yet you are exactly the man I thought you were," Ysabel gave him a disarmingly sweet smile. "A weak-willed coward who blamed an innocent and condemned him to die, couldn't satisfy his wife, and couldn't uphold his end of the bargain in Chult. I would rather stay an unmarried crone than ever let you touch me again."

CHAPTER TWENTY-ONE

3 Flamerule, the Year of the Ageless One
(1479 DR)
Chult

Something banged shut with a ringing sound, and Harp opened his eyes. At first he thought it was the sound of the metal doors closing at the Vankila Slab. But when Harp opened his eyes, he was looking up at the apex of a pearly dome, not the gray stones of a prison cell.

Disoriented, Harp turned his head and saw the brass starscope gleaming beside him. He was in Majida's observatory. But where had she gone? And how long had he been unconscious? Waking up in an unfamiliar place and missing a few hours from his memory was nothing new in his life. It was usually accompanied by the onset of panic and the sickness that followed too much alcohol. But Harp felt unexpectedly calm as he pushed himself upright. Sitting on the green rug, he stretched his shoulders, trying to get an uncomfortable kink out of his neck. He tried to recall the last thing that had happened. Majida had lit the heavily scented incense. They had talked about Liel.

"I can't promise it won't hurt," Majida had said. "It depends on you."

"I don't care," Harp had assured her. "Believe me. I don't care."

When Majida began her spell, and Harp's vision slipped sideways, although he'd have sworn he hadn't moved from his position cross-legged on the floor. And there had been pain, at least at first. But then his mind had reached for comfort the way a drowning man reaches for something to keep him afloat. He remembered his mother, brushing the hair back from his sweaty face when he was ill as a child. He remembered the time he'd ridden on his father's shoulders, laughing with delight as they ran through a meadow filled with orange wild flowers. And there was Liel. Mostly his mind found its comfort with her.

In the early days on Gwynneth Isle, what he had felt for her was so fragile it seemed as if it would break if he thought of it too often. One night at sunset, they had climbed the Delmark, a stony plateau that rose above the treetops at the heart of the forest. Sitting on the edge of the rock with their legs dangling off the side, they watched the sun bleed into the distant ocean. It was windy on the hill. Chilly, but not unpleasantly so. Still, she leaned against him, and the warmth of her body was like a buffer against the cold. In that moment, he knew that she would be with him for the rest of his life, even in those times when they were not in the same place. It was as if she had become fundamental for him, an inextricable part of how he understood the world.

He wanted to touch her, to rest his hand on the small of her back or put his arms around her. But he was uneasy at the idea that their relationship had become anything but a diversion for both of them. He had not planned on falling in love with her. Considering she was engaged, it was inconvenient and complicated. He wouldn't let it happen, he assured himself. He wouldn't let himself love her. It would be enjoyable, and then it would be over. As if she sensed a shift in his mood, she turned and gave him a little smile. It was disarmingly sweet, unassuming in its beauty, and utterly innocent of the destruction that would follow in the wake of their affair.

"Do you miss the sea?" she asked, puzzled by his intensity. They had talked of him teaching her to sail, so her question was not unexpected.

"I miss you," he said.

"You're silly," she said, lying down and putting her head in his lap. The first stars were appearing in the twilit sky. "I'm right here."

He stroked the side of her neck where the delicate strokes of ink disappeared behind her ear. The artist had been a master—shaping leaves, vines, and flowers that were elegant in their simplicity yet somehow enhanced the beauty of an already striking woman. She sat up so she could lean her head against his chest and slip her arms around his neck.

"What?" she asked as he studied her face.

Telling her she was beautiful seemed trite somehow. That word would never convey the emerald color of her eyes, the curve of shadow under her cheekbones, or the way her upper lip was slightly fuller than her lower.

"You have a pointy little chin," he told her.

"Is that so?"

"Yes," he said, kissing it. "And pointy little ears. And pointy little elbows."

"Fortunately, you don't seem to mind."

"That's true. I don't mind at all."

He kissed a spot behind her ear and moved down her neck. Lightly, he laid his hand on her belly, feeling the ridges of muscles in her stomach as she arched against his hand. He traced his finger to the hollow at the base of her throat, which was half-hidden by the neckline of her silver cloak. The light was fading, but he could see a break in the design of her tattoo. The silhouette of a crouching cat encircled by twisting vines, it was so small that he couldn't believe the artist could capture the details down to its tiny eye, a splash of green among the other black stokes.

"You stopped," she protested. "Don't stop."

"What does the cat mean?"

"Cat? What cat?"

"Here, under your chin."

"Not now. It's complicated."

"Do you have somewhere to go?" he asked.

"No."

"Then we have all night," Harp assured her. "So go on, tell me."

"Tell you what?"

"What do the markings on your neck mean?" he asked. "The cat, the vines. They're beautiful, but what do they mean?"

"Are you always so easily distracted? Or is it just me?"

"Believe me, I'm not distracted. My attention is utterly, completely on you. And soon, I'll be happy to prove it. But for now, humor me."

"Fine," Liel said with mock exasperation. "But I expect due compensation."

"With pleasure," Harp said.

"It's the story of my life," she told him. "It was written before I was born."

"Really?" Harp said, intrigued by her answer. "What does it say?"

"Oh, that I'll save the world," Liel teased him. "And fall in love with an ill-bred pirate."

"Ill-bred pirates are the best kind. What does your pirate do?"

Liel took Harp's hand and began stroking his palm with her thumb. "He buys me a mast ship. One with a dragon-head and a golden sail."

"What a nice pirate."

"Yes," Liel agreed. "A very nice pirate."

Before he went back to kissing her, Harp pressed his fingertip against the cat silhouette. He could feel Liel's heart beating. "So they are a pirate, a green-eyed cat, and a golden sail."

"What are?"

"The keys to your heart."

"As if you need a key," she said. Tired of waiting, she kissed him instead.

Shakily, Harp pushed himself to his feet, bracing his hands on his knees until a wave of nausea passed. His life had been simple before he knew Liel. He'd had an innate sense of right and wrong that drove his actions—like a hidden compass that always told him which way to go. And all he had to do was make his way toward the horizon and things would work out all right. Take the *Marderward*. It was the obvious thing to get Kitto off that ship, and to save Liel in the process. No one was going to give him a crown for being noble, but he helped where he could and watched out for himself and his friends no matter what.

Being with Liel had mixed up the compass. Even after his moment of clarity that night on the Delmark, he'd opted for simplicity over truth. Keeping Liel at a distance, turning himself in to the authorities instead of fighting the mutiny charge—those were things that went against his instincts. He'd followed the wrong path, and it had landed him in the

Vankila Slab, the razor-sharp edge of death. And it had led him away from Liel, who took root in his mind as both the cause and the salvation of his eroded life. For the first time since he'd been chained to the floor in the Practitioner's study, Harp's directional sense had returned. Finally, he sensed true north.

If he were given the day on the Delmark again, he would tell Liel that he loved her—he might have lost her anyway, but at least she would have known. Harp paused in the center of the observatory, listening to the wind whistle through the hinges in the ceiling. The incense still burned in the earthenware dish, so Harp thought it must be the same day, the same moment almost, since he had come up the spiral stairs with Majida.

Reaching for the door handle, he jerked his hand back in shock. Slowly, he stretched out his arm again. His skin was as smooth and as unmarred as when he'd been a child. Majida had done it—she'd removed the scars. She'd healed him and erased the Practitioner's brand. How that was possible, he didn't know, but she'd done it.

Trembling, Harp flung open the door and stumbled down the staircase. With his heart pounding and his head spinning, he steadied himself against the wall. Harp couldn't fight the feeling that something was missing, that he had misplaced something important. He doubled over, fighting dizziness. And then he understood. What he felt was an absence of pain.

Since the Vankila Slab, Harp had lived with constant pain, like the incessant lapping of the tide. Now he felt the beating of his heart, the cool air against his skin, and the hum of his muscles as they moved. But nothing felt like claws against his skin, or needles into his muscles—nothing hurt at all. Harp continued down the steps, enjoying the loose-ness of his joints and the fluid way his muscles moved. He felt like he could run for hours, move a mountain, or swim to Tethyr. But first, he was going to find Liel, no matter how small the chance that she was alive.

When Harp walked into the nearly deserted hub, Kitto and Boult were seated at one of the long tables eating breakfast with Zo. All three stared at him in silent awe as he sat down on the wooden bench beside Kitto. There was a tray of eggs and chopped pork, and Harp heaped the plate with more food than he would normally eat in a tenday.

"Where's Verran?" Harp asked shoving the eggs into his mouth as the others gaped at him. "Come on now. Don't stare. You'll hurt my feelings."

Boult recovered first. "What happened to your scars, Harp?"

"Majida's healing touch," Harp said casually. "I guess you know how fortunate you are to have her, Zo. I know mages in Waterdeep who would kill to have her study with them."

"How did she do it?" Kitto asked, his black eyes abnormally wide as he stared at his friend.

"I'm not sure," Harp replied. "Where is she? And where's Verran?"

No one answered. They were still too busy gaping at him. Having seen his reflection in the sheen of Majida's observatory, he understood their reaction. While he still had crow's feet at the corners of his eyes and creases in the center of his forehead, most of the signs of aging brought on by too much ale, hard living, and days under the hot sun were gone. He looked as if he'd been reborn a much younger man.

"Suddenly I'm *not* a scarred freak, and you all can't stop looking at me."

"I don't know if you've seen yourself," Boult said, turning

his attention back to his food. "But you are very much changed."

"But that's a good thing, right?" Harp said, perplexed by the undercurrents of emotion in the room.

"Sure it is, Harp," Boult said, exchanging glances with Kitto. "We're just . . ."

"Happy for you," Kitto said with a little grin.

"Yeah," Boult agreed. "Since you have new skin, it's a great time to make a new start. You can stop being such an idiot."

"Ah, Boult," Harp said between bites. "You know how to make any occasion special."

"You're a drunken fool," Boult said sweetly.

"And you're a vengeful scoundrel," Harp replied, just as sweetly.

"Last son of a fat goblin," Boult said.

"Arrogant goat," Harp shot back, and Kitto laughed.

"What's so funny, boyo?" Harp asked Kitto amicably.

"Everything's changed," Kitto said, smiling down at his plate. "But nothing's changed too."

Zo had been watching the exchange curiously. "I have no idea what any of you are talking about," he said, pushing back from the table. "But if you're going to the ruins, we don't want to get started too late in the day."

"How far is it to the ruins?" Harp asked, finishing the last bite of his breakfast and standing up. He'd had enough of resting. In fact, he felt like he would never need to sleep again.

"It's not far to the edge of the Domain," Zo told him. "Beyond that, I'm not sure how far it is to the boundaries of the ruins itself."

"Is that where you took Liel?"

"Majida took her to the edge. But I won't leave the Domain. You'll have to make your way from there by yourself."

"So why doesn't Majida take us?"

Zo scowled. "Because *I'm* taking you. Majida's busy."

"So, don't make fun of me, Boult," Harp said. "But I lost my sword. *Again.*"

"How many is that?" Boult asked, shaking his head in disgust. "Two in less than a tenday?"

"There's an armory down that tunnel," Zo told them. "You're welcome to take what you need."

"I'll go round up Verran," Boult said. "Pick me out something nice."

"We'll pay you, of course," Harp said to Zo, as he and Kitto followed the dwarf into the armory. "You've shown us enough hospitality already."

Zo shook his head. "Kill Scaly Ones. Kill the man you call the Practitioner. That'll be payment enough."

If Verran was shocked by Harp's new appearance, he hid it well. Sullen and withdrawn, the boy trailed behind them as they followed Zo down the eastern tunnel. Harp's pack was filled with supplies, and it felt heavy on his shoulders as they walked through the dimly lit tunnel. He'd picked out two stubby swords, a sturdy but diminutive shield, and a crossbow that would have fit a child's hand. Not that Harp was going to complain. Even miniscule weapons were better than nothing.

"What do you know about the ruins?" he asked Zo as they walked.

"Hisari was the name of the city. It's been hundreds of years since the earth swallowed it. From what Majida says, it's still intact, just buried. Did you see the ruins when you were on top of the waterfall?"

"I saw the golden dome."

"That's the top of the palace. Until recently, it was covered by the jungle, but Cardew and his men cleared it away."

"That's what they spent their time doing?"

"Yes. But they couldn't get into the palace. Fortunately, they didn't know about our underground tunnels."

"They couldn't break through the dome?"

"They tried, but nothing worked. They weren't able to dig down into it either. Probably because of then magical barrier that surrounds it."

"Do yuan-ti live in the ruins?" Boult asked.

"They dwell above ground. There must be things living down there, but what, I'm not sure."

Up ahead the tunnel made a sharp right. Zo stopped, lit a torch, and handed it to Harp.

"The Domain ends up ahead," Zo said. "I've never been past that point, and I don't care to go."

"You said something about a barrier?" Verran asked.

"Yes, at the edge of Hisari."

"It's not a dwarven ward?" Boult asked.

"No, we have our own wards on the Domain," Zo replied. "You'll see our runes on the walls from here until you reach the edge of our territory. But the barrier around Hisari is something different. It's ancient."

"How did Liel get through?" Verran asked.

"Majida didn't tell you?" Zo asked in surprise.

Harp shook his head. "She didn't give us specifics."

"She didn't tell me either," Zo said. "I know that she and Liel spent hours trying to bring it down. What finally worked, I can't say."

"Can you get us through, Verran?" Harp asked.

"I'll try," Verran said, his eyes darting away as if he couldn't bring himself to look at Harp's unscarred face.

"If you need us, you know where to find us," Zo said, clasping hands with each of them before he turned and headed back down the way they'd come.

"Well, men," Harp said. "Any final thoughts before we head into the mouth of the beast?"

"I wanted to go back to the ship that first day," Boult said, snatching the torch from Harp's hand and stomping down the tunnel. "I said we should sail to Nyanzaru and sell the *Marigold*. If you'd listened to me, we'd be sitting on a pile of coin and drinking a pint."

"Ah, but you'd never have seen a giant lizard."

"It was dead," Boult said over his shoulder as they followed him into the tunnel.

"You'd never have seen a dead giant lizard get eaten by ants," Harp reminded him.

"Eh," Boult said, shrugging.

"You'd never have jumped off a waterfall," Harp said.

"Or been attacked by a creature made out of corpses," Kitto added.

"Or seen the bones of a god," Harp pointed out.

"It wasn't a god," Verran muttered, but everyone ignored him.

"And Harp would still have his scars," Kitto said.

Boult stopped. At first Harp thought it was because of what Kitto had said, but Boult was staring at the wall. In tiny writing from floor to ceiling, black runes were scorched into the rock and glowing faintly in the torchlight. Boult held the torch close to them and peered at the wall.

"Are those the wards of protection?"

"Those are what has kept the dwarves hidden all these years," Boult said in amazement. "But they're more than that. They tell the dwarves' history. Embedded in the writing are the names of everyone who's lived here. How people died."

"Like a genealogy?" Harp asked.

Boult read more. "No, more than that. Events are recorded too. The Spellplague. The history of the yuan-ti is probably written here as well, at least from the dwarves' perspective."

"Does it tell the future too?" Harp asked. "I'd really like to know if I'm going to die today."

"Come on," Verran said impatiently. "This isn't the time for a history lesson."

They moved slowly down the tunnel, with Boult trying to read as they walked. Finally, Verran lit his own torch and took the lead, moving much more quickly down the passage.

"Why are you in such a hurry?" Harp asked Verran.

"Do you want me to take down the barrier? Or are we going to sit around and read about Grandma Bushybeard? If we're going to do it, let's do it."

Verran stormed off down the passage while the others exchanged looks.

"He's grumpy this morning," Harp said. "Anyone know why?"

"Maybe he's hungry," Boult said "He didn't eat breakfast with us."

"Where did you find him?" Harp asked.

"I didn't. He walked into the hub after you went into the armory."

Verran had disappeared from sight, and Harp felt increasingly uneasy about the boy's mood. When the tunnel veered right, they saw Verran crouched in the middle of the tunnel and staring at a white mesh that stretched across the passageway. Swaying gently as if blown by a light breeze, it had the appearance of an exquisite tapestry that was woven from fine, almost translucent threads.

"Is it wrong for me to hope that's a spider web?" Harp said.

"It's the barrier," Verran replied. "It's a type of ward."

"It doesn't look very magical," Boult said doubtfully. "Can we just brush it aside?"

Verran reached into his cloak, pulled out a hunk of bread, and tossed it into the barrier. With a snap of light, the bread seared black and fell to the ground smoking.

"Toast anyone?" Boult said.

"My father's mentor called it a shroud barrier," Verran said. "He used them to contain dead bodies."

"Contain them from doing what?" Harp asked.

"No, to preserve them for later use," Verran said.

"Use for what?" Boult asked. "How come you know that?"

"I don't know *anything,*" Verran said ferociously, and he covered his face with his hands. It was such a childlike gesture that Harp felt the urge to comfort him, but then he realized that Verran's lips were moving behind his fingertips. His was not the stance of a penitent. Verran was casting.

A gust of hot air blew through the tunnel. It was dry and smelled like cinders, like air from the bellows of a distant forge. Faint rips appeared in the barrier as if an invisible hand were gently pulling apart the strands. Then red stains branched out from the separations, staining the white gauze with crimson. When all trace of white was gone, the barrier slid to the ground in a wet, bloody heap. Verran glanced at his crewmates with a self-satisfied expression.

"Do you even know how you did that?" Harp said in disbelief.

"Does it matter?" Verran said smugly. "It's down, at least for the moment. Do you want to chat, or go find your elf? Or at least another husk of your elf?"

Beside him, Boult bristled, but Harp laid a hand on the dwarf's arm. "Lead on, young master," he said to Verran with no trace of sarcasm in his tone.

"When we get back to the *Crane,* he needs a lesson in manners," Boult whispered to Harp as they stepped over the lumpy mass on the ground. When they reached the end of the tunnel, Harp stared at the scene in front of him with a sinking feeling in his chest.

"That's if we get back to the *Crane* at all," Harp said.

CHAPTER TWENTY-TWO

3 Flamerule, the Year of the Ageless One
(1479 DR)
Chult

Hisari had been a city of domed buildings, white-washed walls, and elevated roads that arched over fast-flowing canals. The focal point of the city had been the golden-domed palace and its surrounding open-air forums.

Then the earth swallowed half of the gleaming city, which came to rest in a sprawling underground cavern that had never been warmed by the sun. The rest of Hisari remained above ground to be engulfed by vines and creeping flowers, while the collapsed city stewed in the hot, moist climate until every brick and pillar was coated in a slick mossy growth. Over time, a latticework of roots and dirt formed above the ruins. It was not a seamless floor, and strands of murky light filtered into the cavern along with dripping rainwater.

"That is beyond disgusting," Harp said. "At least Vankila was dry."

They scrambled down the embankment and made a small jump onto the remains of a raised road that was constructed from stone and supported by stout pillars. The surface had once been covered in a smooth, glassy coating that had shattered into sharp fragments that crunched as they walked on them. From their vantage point, they could see that the road arched over a canal, just one of several channels of water radiating from the dome.

"I've never seen a road built that way," Verran said as they walked slowly down the slope. "Why elevate it? Why not just build bridges over the canals?"

"Maybe no one wanted to get anywhere near the water," Harp said, staring down at a bloom of pink globs floating in the thick, sludgy canal. There was movement under the surface as the occasional air bubble fought its way to the surface and popped. But whatever was writhing below them was hidden under a layer of black algae.

"Any ideas what lives down there?" Harp asked, covering his nose to block the stench of bloated dead things.

Verran shook his head. "Nothing pleasant, that's for sure."

Harp took a closer look at the boy, whose mood seemed to have improved after they left the Domain. In fact, Verran seemed downright cheerful, considering they were walking through the rotting remains of a hostile empire. They crossed the canal and walked past a row of crumbling round houses, the walls green with fungus. The trenches along the streets were filled with brown slime, and slugs as long as a human's leg writhed in the muck.

"You want to take a peek inside one of the houses?" Harp asked Kitto.

"No way," Kitto said grimly. "Do you really think Liel would have stayed down here?"

"I don't know," Harp replied. If she had stayed down here, it meant she probably had been trapped.

They had almost reached the end of the street when a shadow passed between the houses. Kitto saw it first and put his hand on his sword. Boult and Harp drew their weapons. Verran had been walking slightly ahead, but at the sound of the swords, he turned to them, and a look of curious concern crossed his features. Behind him, something darted out from around the corner, but Verran's body blocked their view of it.

"Verran . . ." Harp began. But the boy had already wheeled around to see a scaly doglike creature crouched behind him, its fangs bared, and its tail quivering. When Verran turned, the animal bristled, and a guttural hissing noise emerged from its throat. About the size of a goat but more heavily muscled, the creature was eyeless, with an elongated muzzle, an oversized jaw, and mud-colored scales. A plated tail curved over its ridged back like a scorpion.

"It's a nifern," Verran told them, amazement evident in his tone. "I've never seen one before."

"Back away," Boult warned him. "It's not a puppy dog."

"See that barb on the end of the tail?" Verran said. "It's poisonous. It can stop a man's heart in moments."

Instead of moving back as he had been instructed, Verran crouched down so he was face to face with the nifern. The growling intensified, and the animal lowered its head aggressively.

"Verran, move away," Harp warned again, but Verran ignored him. Boult rolled his eyes in disgust, and Kitto shifted nervously. The nifern could easily rip out Verran's throat before any of them had time to do anything to help him.

"Have you ever heard of self-preservation, kid?" Boult grumbled, inching slowly toward the hunched-over boy. Speaking softly in indecipherable words, Verran held out his hand. The nifern cocked his head as if it was listening. When the nifern whined and raised its head, Verran looked back at his shipmates, a pleased expression on his face.

"I think I tamed it," he said. But the animal sprang forward against the boy's chest and knocked him hard onto the ground. Verran cried out as the shards of glass dug into his back and the nifern's fangs sunk into his shoulder. Boult reacted first, rushing forward and swinging his sword just as the creature's tail dipped toward Verran. The tip of its tail went flying into the canal. A mass of black flesh with white fangs rose up out of the water and devoured the tail, before disappearing with a splash back under the algae.

Boult arched his sword around and plunged the blade deep into the back of the nifern's neck. The animal squealed and let loose of Verran's shoulder. The boy scrambled back on the roadway, slicing his hands on the shards before Kitto and Harp reached him and pulled him to his feet.

Yanking the sword out of the twitching animal collapsed on the ground, Boult wheeled on Verran, who was cradling his bloody hands against his chest.

"What the hell were you thinking?" Boult demanded angrily. "Don't you ever do what you're told?"

The dwarf started to say more, but Harp silenced him with a shake of his head.

"You have bandages?" Harp asked Kitto, who nodded and pulled off his pack.

Verran whimpered and held out his hands as Kitto wound the gauze around them. Boult stalked a perimeter, keeping an eye on the churning water in the canal.

"The spells I want to do, I can't," Verran said sadly. "And the spells I hate come as naturally to me as breathing."

"Yeah," Kitto said. "I know how you feel. The only thing I was ever good at was stealing."

The glass from the roadway had shredded the back of the boy's shirt. Through the rips in the dirty white cotton,

Harp could see a sliver of glass as long as a finger lodged in Verran's shoulder.

"I need to pull that out," Harp said, but Verran shook his head and twisted away from him.

"It's fine," Verran insisted.

"You have a huge shard of glass stuck in your back," Harp said. "How is that fine?"

"Leave it alone!" Verran snapped, turning again so Harp couldn't see his back. "It doesn't hurt."

The absurdity of Verran's claim made Harp instantly suspicious. He started to chastise the boy but stopped abruptly. With sudden clarity, Harp realized why Verran didn't want him to pull the glass out. Looking at the defiant boy, Harp felt fear for the first time since they set foot in the repulsive ruins of Hisari.

"Then let Kitto do it," he said nonchalantly, despite his growing dread. "But someone has to. You can't reach it yourself, and you can't wander around like that."

Verran seemed to consider the suggestion while Harp strolled casually over to Bolt, who was staring grim-faced into the canal.

"We got a problem?" Boult asked softly.

"I told you that his father was a warlock," Harp whispered. "His father had brands across his back. They marked the debts he owed his patron in exchange for power."

"Do you think Verran has them too?" Boult asked.

"It would explain how he can do spells beyond what you would expect a boy to handle," Harp said. He felt slightly ill at the thought of a father who would lead his son into a cult and let him make a bargain that would mark his child's life forever. Cutting his son's throat in ritual sacrifice might have been a less cruel fate.

"And if the patron is working through him . . ." Boult said. Behind them, Verran yelped as Kitto yanked out the glass. "Then who knows what Verran is capable of."

"Remember, we don't know anything for certain," Harp said as they went to rejoin the boys. "And I don't want to confront him down here—if we're wrong, we're just going to make him upset and distract him."

"And if we're right?"

Harp stopped and faced Boult."You really think he's a warlock—do want to fight him in this cesspool? We deal with it before we get back to the *Crane*. Let's find the palace. Hisari is a breeding ground for things I don't want to meet."

The palace wasn't hard to find. The wide causeway leading up to the dome was adorned with pillars, each with a white urn at the top that might have held flowers but were crumbling into dust. When the crewmates reached the carved doorway at the front of the palace, they could see a band of blue sky above them where the jungle floor didn't meet the edge of the golden dome.

They stared at the imposing façade, which had been constructed from dark red. An arched double doorway reached halfway up the front of the palace. Framing the sides and top of the door, three panels of redwood carvings depicted a creature with the body of a snake, the head of a bird, and horns like those of a ram. Both the stones and the ornately carved door were untouched by the dank growth that marred the rest of the fallen city.

"Look at those," Kitto said, pointing at the pattern of tiny interlocking triangles carved into the face of door. A shiny silver stone had been laid at the center of each triangle. Of the hundreds of tiny stones spaced across the door, not a single one was missing.

"The stones must not be valuable," Boult said as they approached the door. "Or someone would have stolen them."

"Thieves probably took one look at the ruins and ran screaming in the other direction," Harp said.

"Look, there's no handle," Kitto said, running his hands lightly over the door. "Or hinges. Or seam."

On closer inspection, they saw that Kitto was right. The door appeared to be a solid piece of wood. If there was a way to get inside the palace through the front entrance, it wasn't readily apparent. And it wasn't going to be easy to search the perimeter of the building for another way inside, either. Thick, black water had seeped over the banks of the canal and settled in the low courtyards on either side of the causeway.

The rectangular courtyards were home to bulbous swamp dwellers that oozed across the top of the water and around mossy bones jutting above the water line. Except for the elevated causeway, the stagnant water surrounded the palace. Occasionally black tentacles or the arch of a bloated back would crest the surface and then disappear.

"No one goes anywhere near that water," Harp said. "Just the sight of it probably takes years off our lives."

"Just the sight of you takes years off my life," Boult replied.

"Can we get up there?" Kitto asked. There was a narrow balcony high above their heads, its stone supports carved to look like snakes.

"We're not getting anywhere," Verran said after they had searched the front of the palace. Even Kitto couldn't locate any handholds or niches to climb up to the balcony.

"I say we go back into the ruins and try to circle behind the palace," Boult suggested.

"I agree," Harp said. "What do you think, Kitto?"

"I think we're in trouble," Kitto said, pointing to a nifern that was standing at the top of the causeway.

"Nah," Boult said. "They're like dumplings with legs. I killed the other one with one blow."

Before Boult had finished his sentence, several other niferns appeared. They milled around at the top of the causeway, raising and lowering their heads as if they were sniffing the foul-smelling air.

"Huh," Harp said as the pack continued to amass on the road ahead of them. "I don't think they liked you calling them dumplings."

"Your mother was a dumpling," Boult said.

"My mother was a saint."

"Your mother was a whore who left you in an alley for the rats."

"Your mother was a rat who left you in the alley for the whores," Harp retorted.

"Shut up!" Verran snapped. "Can't you be serious for once?"

"It gets them worked up to kill something," Kitto said. "You should try it."

"I don't think so," Verran said. "And I don't see you making a fool of yourself every time you open your mouth, Kitto."

"My house is in order," Kitto said. "I'm not scared to die."

"You don't have a house, kiddo," Harp said, smiling faintly.

"That's why it's so easy to keep it clean," Kitto replied.

"Well, that water's not clean," Harp said. The niferns had grown to a dozen, trapping them against the palace door. "I'm guessing fighting for the causeway is our best option."

"What are they waiting for?" Boult asked.

"Probably just sizing us up," Verran prattled nervously. "There's a type of wolf that hunts like that. They'll surround you and just watch. They won't let you leave, but it's like they want to see what you'll do. I don't know. Maybe they're not really that smart. There's also a kind of beast—"

"It's all right, Verran," Harp said gently. "We'll get through this. It might be a good time to try one of your spells."

"I don't think I can," Verran said worriedly. "I feel something strange. It's affecting my magic. If I do a spell, something awful might happen."

"Or you might melt some of those doggies," Boult said. "That spell you did on Bootman would be useful right now."

"Or it might melt you," Kitto reminded Boult.

"Fine, Master Thief," Boult said. "You have a better plan?"

"No," Kitto said honestly.

"Captain Harp?" Boult asked. "How about some orders?"

"Unfurl the sails?" Harp suggested. "Tack to starboard. Hold that wheel steady, boys."

"You are so useless," Boult growled. "Me and Harp in front. Kitto and Verran get behind us."

Harp knew the maneuver that Boult was suggesting, but usually it was done with a larger number of soldiers. The ones in front would brace themselves behind the shields, while the ones in back used long weapons to stab the oncoming enemies. Following Boult's orders, they grouped themselves into a defensive box to await the onslaught of the scaly dogs. Harp immediately noticed a flaw in the plan.

"Um, Boult?" he said, keeping an eye on the niferns still milling at the top of the causeway. "You do realize that we're holding the dwarven equivalent of frying pans and steak knives."

"Only if your hands are freakishly large."

"It's stupid," Harp said, standing up. "The boys are more likely to stab me in the back of the head than anything."

"What do you suggest?" Boult said.

"No time," Kitto yelled as the animals rushed down the road in unison. Kitto sheathed his sword, pulled his crossbow off his shoulder, and loaded one of the small bolts.

"What the hell are you doing?" Harp asked, waving his dagger-sized blade at Kitto. "Get your sword out!"

But Kitto leaped onto one of the pillars, curled an arm around it, and momentarily braced his feet against the square base. He jumped from the pillar onto the back of one of the niferns. Firing the crossbow directly into the back of the creature's skull, he killed it instantly. As the body of the nifern slumped on the ground, the rest of the hissing niferns surrounded them like a flood. Harp kicked one in the head, sending it reeling. Dazed briefly, the animal scurried back into the fray. As Boult stabbed one in the throat, another swung its tail and forced Boult to drop to the ground to avoid the stinger. Three niferns leaped onto his back, biting into him while Harp and Kitto rushed to pull Boult back to his feet.

"Verran, do something!" Harp called as he kicked another one in the jaw. Kitto sliced one across the back with his blade, but it rushed at him as if it didn't notice the wound. Kitto nearly lost his balance as he scrambled backward, but Harp bent low and brought his sword up under the creature's belly, slitting it open. He jumped back as the blood sloshed across the glass shards strewn across the ground.

"I can try, but it might just make them enormous and invulnerable," Verran shouted.

"Try something!" Boult demanded.

Harp and the others flanked Verran to keep the niferns away from the boy as he pressed his palms to his forehead, chanting under his breath. The niferns formed a tight circle around them, ready to rip the men to shreds as soon as they ran out of fight. Verran dropped his hands, and a yellowish haze began rising from the ground.

"Verran!" Harp exclaimed, looking at the mist around his boots. "What is that?"

"I don't know! It wasn't what I was thinking about at all!"

The haze drifted across the ground and pooled around the niferns' paws. As if the yellow clouds distracted them, the niferns stopped their assault and snapped at the wisps of

yellow air. When the haze reached the height of the niferns'
faces, the animals began to wheeze. One by one they dropped
to the ground as their sides labored up and down with shallow breaths. They shuddered and were still.

"It's poison," Verran said. "Fast poison. That's good!"

"Except it's not," Kitto said, pointing to the crest of
the causeway where more niferns were stalking back and
forth aggressively, safely out of range of the low-lying
poisoned air.

"If we run, we'll get eaten by the reinforcements," Harp
said.

"And if we stay, we'll choke on our own vomit," Boult said,
looking down at the haze that had reached his thighs.

"Up the pillars," Kitto urged, climbing up to the top
of the square base while the others followed. It got them
off the ground, but the haze was still rising quickly.

"I told you it could go bad," Verran said.

"It could be worse," Harp said.

"At least we'll be unconscious when they eat our bodies,"
Boult said.

"Harp! Do you hear something?" Kitto asked, twisting
his body around to look at the front of the palace.

"What?" Harp asked.

"I hear mewling, like a kitten," Harp said.

"I don't hear anything," Boult said. "Except the sound of
my upcoming death."

Harp jumped off the pillar and waded through the haze
to the palace door.

"What are you doing?" Boult shouted.

"Liel!" Harp yelled. "Liel, where are you!"

"Harp, there's no one there," Boult said.

"Liel!" Harp shouted again. Above him on the balcony,
a cat with cream-colored fur and dark brown spots had
appeared on the top of the stone railing. "It's Harp! And
Kitto!"

The cat jumped off the railing and disappeared from sight. Kitto jumped down and hurried through the haze after Harp.

"Are they both insane?" Boult asked Verran.

But then a figure appeared on the balcony above them. When she leaned out over the railing to look down at the crewmates, her coppery hair glinted in the sunlight, and her face was familiar to them all.

"Liel!" Harp said joyfully.

"Throw me a rope!" she called.

Kitto reached in his backpack and pulled out a coil of rope. With one skillful toss, he threw the rope up to her waiting hand. Quickly, Liel looped one end around one of the pillars, knotted it tightly, and threw it back down. Verran and Boult left their pillar and waded through the haze that nearly reached Boult's chin.

"Go!" Harp told Boult. The dwarf scaled the rope quickly and hauled himself over the railing on the balcony. Kitto scampered up the rope after Boult as easily as if he were climbing a shroud rope on a sunny summer's day.

"Your turn," Harp said, pushing Verran to the rope. Verran pressed his feet against the stones, leaned back until he was almost perpendicular to the ground, and walked up the front of the palace. Harp followed him, enjoying the newfound strength in his arms and clearness of his lungs. Clearly Majida had healed more than his skin. Harp pulled himself onto the balcony, dusted himself off, and grinned at Liel. When he'd seen her in the cavern by the river, he'd hesitated, not knowing what to do with himself, wanting to touch her but too unsure to reach out. He wasn't going to make the same mistake again.

"Hey, you," Harp said, putting his arms around her and looking down into her eyes.

"Hey, yourself," she said, slipping her arms around his waist and tipping her head back to grin up at him.

"You still have a pointy little chin," he said. "And pointy little ears."

"And you still talk too much," she told him.

"Did I tell you I loved you?" he asked.

"No, you never got around to it."

Harp shook his head ruefully. "My mistake."

And he kissed her.

CHAPTER TWENTY-THREE

3 Flamerule, the Year of the Ageless One
(1479 DR)
Chult

Boult cleared his throat. "I'm happy you kids are happy, but don't we have things to do? People to see? Artifacts to steal . . . I mean, recover?"

Harp kissed Liel one last time before he reluctantly broke away. "You haven't changed at all."

"But you have," Liel said. "Or rather, you changed back."

"I hate to break up your reunion, but Verran's haze of death is still rising," Boult told them.

"Actually, it's not," Verran said defensively, looking over the railing at the dead niferns slumped on the ground. "It looks like it's going away."

"Liel, that is Verran," Harp said. "You know Kitto, of course."

Liel embraced the boy. "Kitto, it's been so long."

"Good to see you, Liel," Kitto mumbled shyly.

"And that is Boult, a friend of mine from Vankila."

Boult and Liel shook hands. After spending time with the husk, Boult seemed a little disconcerted at meeting the real Liel, but Majida had vouched for the elf and that would be enough to convince Boult to trust her. Verran, however, wasn't as understanding.

"We've already met you," Verran said curtly. "We met your husk."

Liel turned white. "Oh no. What did it do?"

"Nothing," Harp said quickly. "There was little contact, and we learned the truth soon enough."

"We have to stop him," Liel said angrily. "Stop him from making more husks and stealing the Torque, and whatever else the bastard is planning."

"Cardew?" Harp asked.

"Cardew's just a puppet," Liel said bitterly. "He has a patron. A man named Tresco, who has been orchestrating events here in Chult."

Harp felt his heart beating rapidly in his chest. Just like that, his torturer had a name. The man who had chained him down and mutilated him had an identity, just like anyone else. When he thought of the gray-haired man as Tresco, his memory seemed less potent somehow. Harp had the irrational thought that it was easier to kill a man with a name.

Or at least it was easier to track him down and then kill him.

"Are you all right?" Liel asked, taking his hand. She was watching Harp's face closely.

"Tresco is the man who tortured me at Vankila," Harp said. "We knew him as the Practitioner."

"I knew that Tresco ran . . . affairs at the prison, but I didn't know he did it himself," Liel said, laying her hand on Harp's arm.

"Wait," Boult said. "Tresco Maynard? He was Anais's son's tutor."

"At the Winter Palace?" Harp frowned.

Boult nodded. "It was Ysabel, Cardew, and Tresco that survived."

"So, maybe Cardew's not just a puppet in this particular scheme," Harp said. "Maybe he's been a puppet all along."

"I wouldn't be surprised," Liel said. "Tresco wants the throne in the hands of a ruler he can control. One who'll chase anyone not human from Tethyr and give him all the power he wants. That's not a plan that happens overnight."

"Why does Tresco want the Torque?" Kitto asked.

"I'm not sure exactly," Liel told them. "It suppresses magic somehow."

"That doesn't seem very useful," Verran said dismissively.

"Majida told me that the Torque shields the wearer. But from what I've overheard it sounds like it prevents spells from being cast," Liel said. "It's possible whoever wears the Torque can cast spells, but no else can. That seems very useful to me. And to Tresco."

"Am I feeling the effects of the Torque?" Verran asked. "It feels like I wouldn't be able to cast a spell, even if I wanted to."

"I think so," Liel said. "I feel that too."

"Then we must be close to it," Boult said. "Let's quit chatting and get it."

"Can you take us to the Torque?" Harp asked.

"Unfortunately, I can't," Liel said. "Come and see."

A crystal clear lake blocked the path to the Torque. As if it were a giant cup filled with water, the vast hall under the golden dome was completely submerged. They'd entered the hall from the balcony and stood on a whispering gallery ringing the perimeter of the cylindrical palace.

Directly under the dome, the gallery was the highest point in the hall, but the water lapped gently under the walkway, making it feel more like a dock than a lofty perch.

"As you can see, there's a water problem," Liel said.

The dome was completely smooth on the outside, but he inside had slender golden trusses made from twisted metal that radiated from its apex down to the gallery where they stood. The base of the dome was so close that Harp could reach up and touch the metal, which had been enchanted to permit light to permeate its surface. The golden sheen radiating from the dome gave off heat, and the hall was as warm and as bright as if they were standing directly under the sun. Where other buildings were crumbling, the dome was solid, and kept the debris from outside out of the water that filled the hall.

Harp leaned over the crumbling railing and peered down into the water. It was clear enough to see all the way down to the blue and white floor of the hall. From where he stood in the gallery, he could just see the top of the arched doorway and the glitter of silver stones that had been set into it, a mirror image of what they had seen outside when they stood in front of the palace.

"No wonder the Scaly Ones didn't want anyone opening the door from the outside," Harp said. "They'd get a face full of water."

"They were serious about protecting the Torque," Boult agreed. "Even if we can get rid of the water, is there any way down from the gallery?"

"There's a ramp over there," Liel said, pointing across the water to a stone ramp that arched from the gallery to a large gilded pillar in the center of the hall. The ramp spiraled down the massive pillar, which was inlaid with a geometric pattern of turquoise and gold tiles. The ramp continued down through a circular opening in the floor below until it disappeared into watery darkness.

"Can either of you cast something and drain the water?" Harp asked Liel and Verran, who shook their heads.

"I've tried it," Liel told him. "Nothing happens. It feels so dead and cold."

"Majida said the Torque was below the entrance hall," Harp said. "Can we just swim down?"

"I don't think we can hold our breath that long," Verran said.

"Have you searched for a lever or a switch that might empty the water out of the hall?" Boult asked Liel.

Liel shrugged. "Thoroughly, but that doesn't mean much in this place. There's nothing obvious, but the sarrukh were clever architects. It could take a lifetime to find."

"It's all we can do. Let's spread out," Harp said. "Kitto and Verran, check along the railing. Boult and Liel, check the walls. I'll go over the floor. Go carefully. Anything that looks strange, call it out."

Mosaics adorned the wall of the whispering gallery, and the intricate tile patterns were unblemished despite the years since their creation. In a display of skillful artisanship, the rich array of colors illustrated the history of the sarrukh. They didn't seem to tell a sequential history, though. Harp passed one panel that depicted an army of serpentfolk sweeping across a grassy meadow like a plague of locusts. The next panel showed basking serpentfolk surrounded by piles of gold in a verdant jungle.

As Harp progressed down the gallery, the mosaics became more grisly, as the sarrukh chronicled their fondness for mass slaughter and mayhem—chained humans being decapitated, chained humans clearing rocks from a pit, and chained humans hauling massive stones up a mountain under a swirling gray sky while the overseers whipped them. Harp stopped paying attention to the walls and focused on searching the floor. But Boult couldn't take his eyes off the macabre scenes plastered on the wall.

"Those are pleasant," Boult said sarcastically.

Boult continued down the curve of the wall until he came to a panel that showed dwarves in bondage being led out of a cave by serpentfolk. A line of dwarf heads were mounted on pikes along a rocky ridge. Dwarf men were laid out on the ground in a line as yuan-ti prepared to roll a massive stone over them and crush them to death.

"Boult!" Harp called. He could see a thin, silver cord nestled in between two rows of tile and obscured by grit and dust. "I think I've found something."

Walking back to Harp, Boult leaned down and picked up a hunk of rock from the floor.

"What are you doing?" Harp asked. Boult tossed it up in the air and caught it as if to size up the weight of the stone.

"Expressing my disgust," Boult said vehemently, hurling the rock at the mosaic of the subjugated dwarfs.

There was a loud pop as the rock smashed into the mosaic. But instead of a crashing noise, they heard a short rush of air, like a sharp intake of breath. Then the mosaic rippled the way water does when a pebble is dropped into it. Harp only had time to register the strange undulation of the stones before the colorful tiles exploded off the wall in a spray of ceramic slivers and thick white dust. Like a wall of knives, the shards blasted into the air as Boult scrambled backward away from the projectiles. With no target to hit, the shards splashed harmlessly in the water.

"Everyone all right?" Harp asked after a moment of shock. Boult had been the closest to the explosion, but he had backed far enough out of range to avoid getting sliced. Liel, Verran, and Kitto had been on the other side of the gallery and safely out of range.

"I think I found a trap," Boult said dryly.

"Good thing you didn't hit it with a hammer," Kitto called across the water.

Harp walked cautiously up to the wall. The red stones of the outer wall were still intact, and there was no sign of the plaster that secured the tiles to the wall. It was as if the mosaic had never been there at all.

"Why would they trap the wall?" Boult asked.

"To keep anyone from breaking through it from the outside?" Verran suggested, walking up behind them.

"To keep anyone from throwing rocks at their precious artwork?" Liel said.

"It doesn't matter why, just don't touch any more walls," Harp said. "Or anything else."

"What were you trying to show me, Harp?" Boult asked. "Before I distracted you with my exploding wall trick?"

Harp pointed at the line that ran between the tiles. "I wondered if that was a trap. Having seen that, I'm going to say yes."

They continued the search of the gallery, but there were no levers to be found. When the group reassembled, they were dusty and disgusted by the atrocities immortalized on the brightly colored walls. But the hall below them was still filled with water.

"Any other ideas?" Harp said. "Did Cardew ever mention the water in the palace?"

"No, but I heard him tell Tresco that they couldn't get to the Torque," Liel said. "And with the Torque disrupting spells in here, I imagine that even Tresco would have had difficulty in getting rid of the water."

"Harp," Kitto called from the other side of the gallery. "Look at that one."

Kitto stood in front of a mosaic showing a serpent with the head of a bird and ram's horns. It clutched a black key in its hooked beak. Surrounded by blue water, the creature was swimming down through a shaft of sunlight to a familiar-looking arched doorway and the silver lock in the center.

"That's the door to the palace," Kitto said, pointing to

the image of the doorway. "And that's the creature that's carved on the panels outside."

"Maybe you can open the door from the inside, if you have that key," Liel said.

"But we don't have the key," Verran pointed out. "And we know it's not hidden on the gallery, because we just searched. And the door is still underwater. Maybe we should leave and look for a way to the surface."

"Without the Torque?" Liel asked.

"Unless you have the key, and you're not telling us," Verran snapped.

"Are you feeling all right?" Harp asked Verran.

"We're not getting anywhere," Verran said, a whine creeping into his voice. "I want to go back to the boat."

"It isn't over yet," Harp said patiently. "We have to try and see it through."

Verran stalked away, and Liel raised her eyebrows.

"He's exhibiting some powerful magic," Harp told Liel quietly. "I don't think he knows how to control it. I'm concerned about him."

"He's not going to be able to do magic inside the palace. I couldn't make a stone glow, not against the force of the Torque."

"I can do it," Kitto said.

"Do what?" Harp asked. "Make a stone glow?"

"Pick the lock and open the door. You know I can."

"Yes, you're amazing," Harp agreed. "On the safety of land! By the time you swim down to the door, you'll barely have enough air to get back up."

"I can do it, Harp," Kitto insisted. "You know I'm a good swimmer."

"Why don't we try to open it from the outside?" Harp asked.

"The niferns aren't just going to sit and watch me," Kitto pointed out. "Listen. They're going crazy out there."

The scaly dogs were making more noise than they had been, and it sounded like a large pack had amassed below the balcony. They were making scratchy, yelping sounds, and getting louder with every passing moment.

"I'll go see what they're doing," Verran said, and he walked outside onto the balcony.

"Besides, we checked the door from the outside," Kitto reminded Harp. "There was no lock remember?"

"He's right," Boult said.

"Then let me swim down and try," Harp said.

"You're not as good of a swimmer as me," Kitto said honestly. He loosened the clasp on his cloak and let it drop on the ground around his feet. Kitto leaned down to unlace his boots. "And besides, you're kind of old."

"I'm not old!" Harp protested.

"You know I'm right," Kitto said, pulling out a cracked leather case that held his lock-pick tools. "No one does locks like me."

"If it's sealed with magic, then you may need a magic key," Harp said petulantly. Kitto ignored him and emptied the contents of his backpack on the ground. He began stuffing large pieces of rock from the remains of the railing into his pack.

"What are you doing?" Harp demanded as he racked his brain for a way to keep the boy on dry land.

"Making sure I'll sink," Kitto said, looking up at Harp with his crooked little smile.

"Harp's right," Liel agreed. "The lock itself is probably enchanted."

"Then I get down there and can't open it. I'll just swim back up."

"Or drown trying," Harp said darkly when Kitto had finished filling the bag with rocks. "Which is what it looks like you're planning to do."

"I need both hands free," Kitto pointed out, shutting the

clasps on the backpack, and struggling to lift it onto his shoulders.

"I don't like it," Harp insisted.

"I can do it," Kitto said.

Verran came dashing into the room, sword in hand. "Whatever we're doing, let's hurry. There are four Jumpers headed our way."

"How close?" Boult demanded.

"They're at the top of the causeway," Verran told them. "They're nearly at the palace."

"Just let me try," Kitto urged.

Harp relented. "Don't be stupid about it. If it won't open, give it up. And come help us fight."

Kitto nodded and swung his leg over the railing where he paused for a moment. Harp felt a rush of protectiveness and opened his mouth to stop the boy, but Kitto was too quick for him.

"See you soon," he said and pushed off the ledge. Harp heard a splash as Kitto hit the water.

"I hate Cardew," Harp said under his breath. Tresco may have been the mastermind of the situation, but it was that arrogant miscreant Cardew that had brought them to their junction. "If anything happens to Kitto, I'm going to personally gut Cardew and feed his heart to a scaly dog on a platter," Harp said viciously.

"Welcome to the Land of Revenge," Boult said sounding surprised at the intensity in Harp's voice. "It's a beautiful country. I myself have a villa."

"Even if anything doesn't happen to Kitto, let's paint your villa in Tresco's blood."

"Red is a charming choice," Boult agreed as they drew their swords.

Even as a child, Kitto had been a good swimmer, the best among his three brothers. They would race each other across the wide river that ran through the valley near their homestead. It was a lazy river, filled with silt from the salt flats up north in the high country. When Kitto swam in it, he always felt as if the water was resisting him, and that no matter which direction he went in, he was swimming against the current. In mid-summer the salt deposits were so thick that he and his brothers could float effortlessly on the surface and not sink. It made Kitto feel as if nature itself were comforting him.

Although the sparkling water in the palace's entrance hall was untainted by salt or grime, Kitto had the same sensation now. If he stopped swimming and just let go, he felt he would float to the surface despite the heavy backpack and the rocks that were quickly dragging him to the bottom of the hall. Kitto had expected the water to be cold, but it was surprisingly warm. Almost like bathwater.

Kitto felt inexplicably sleepy, and he told himself that it must be part of the spell's effect. As he swam down, he forced himself think about the hardest locks he'd ever sprung. Like the hair-trigger lock on the red lacquered chest in the Baron's house, while Predeau breathed down his neck and the guards clomped up and down in the hall outside. Or the pinprick lock on the floor in Lady Charlotte's brothel; that one had taken him longer than he had expected. Predeau had lowered him on a rope through the skylight, so at least Kitto was away from the Captain's terrifying presence. But the sounds of a man rutting with a whore in the room next to him made it hard to hear the mechanics of the lock.

Dragged down by the rocks in his backpack, Kitto landed on the tile floor near the base of the pillar and trudged quickly through the water to the door. There were no carvings on the inside, only the silver stones embedded in the wood.

Just as the mosaic showed, there was shiny silver lock in the center of the door. It was larger than anything Kitto had worked before, but the keyhole was shaped like a teardrop. He'd opened teardrop locks before. His mind was already forming an image of what the inside must look like, how the mechanism fit together, and the exact spot where he needed to put pressure to spring the lock.

But his lungs were burning. Kitto slid his tools into the silver lock, using them as delicate extensions of his fingertips. Instead of the usual ridges and bars, Kitto felt nothing at all. Maybe a longer tool? Kitto fumbled with the leather case tucked in his belt. He let the smaller tools drift away from him and pulled out the longest hooks he had, ones he'd never used before. They felt very clumsy and without finesse, but as Harp always said, big problems called for big swords.

Kitto's chest felt like it was going to explode. He shrugged off the backpack and kicked for the surface. He would have to make a second try, if he could make it to the top before his air ran out. When Kitto broke the surface, he heard shouting, the sounds of quick-moving feet, and the clank of blades against one another. Kitto took a huge gulp of air and swam down to the door. It was harder without the backpack, and by the time he reached the door, Kitto felt sleepy and his muscles ached with fatigue.

When he reached the door, he looped his foot through the strap of the heavy backpack to keep from floating away and slid the long pieces of metal back into the silver lock. Finally he felt something, like a thin net of wire. Again, the burning of his lungs grew painful. But he wouldn't swim for the surface, he would stick it out. He twisted the piece of metal gently, searching for the pin. If only he could just . . . Blackness began clouding the edges of his vision. Kitto felt a lip of metal, twisted the tool sharply, and felt something loosen. Despite the water in his ears, he thought he heard the sound of glass breaking and a sucking noise. Then he gave in to the blackness.

The Jumpers sprang from the flagstones, leaped over the railing, and landed on the balcony. Liel anticipated the maneuver and swung while it was still in mid-air. The ruddy-skinned warrior twisted away from her blade, tucked forward, and somersaulted across the balcony. The Jumpers were smaller than the ones they'd encountered in the camp but more heavily armed and armored. Each wore a leather breastplate and carried two punching daggers with elongated hilts that covered their wrists.

Another Jumper lunged at Verran, who dodged and swung wildly. He cut his assailant across the cheek, but it was a superficial scratch. The yuan-ti advanced, swinging at Verran with its bladed fists. The ruddy-skinned warrior sprang to its feet, its milky blue eyes fixed on Liel. She raised her sword. With one pounce, it was on top of her, and her sword slipped from her hand. The warrior's clawed hands dug into her shoulder as it forced her to the railing, her back pressing against the stone painfully.

She struggled with the warrior, and it brought its fangs down on her neck, biting into her shoulder. Liel cried out as Verran slammed his sword down on the back of the warrior's neck. The creature's armor took most of the blow, but it let go of Liel's neck and jerked its head around, hissing at the boy. While the warrior was distracted, Liel pulled a shard of red stone from a pouch on her belt. When the yuan-ti turned back to her, its mouth open and fangs bared, she jammed the rough shard into its forked tongue, pinning it to the inside of its mouth.

Spluttering in pain as the shard slid all the way through its cheek, the Jumper reared back in confusion. Liel grabbed its elbow and yanked it back toward the railing. Sweeping her foot against its ankle, she knocked it completely off balance. It leaned precariously over the railing, and with a light push of Liel's hand, it went tumbling over the edge and slammed into the ground where a pack of hissing niferns were milling around in front of the palace door. Excited by the scent of the creature's blood, the frenzied animals ripped the yuan-ti's limbs from its body.

Still in the doorway between the palace and the balcony, Boult blocked a blow that came at the side of his head, stopping the blade just before it slid into his ear. Skirting the edges of the combat with his crossbow, Harp threw a dagger at Boult's attacker. The dagger sank deep into the yuan-ti's shoulder, just outside the edge of its armor.

With the dagger still protruding from its skin, the yuan-ti flicked its long tongue angrily. The fingers on its damaged arm twitched spasmodically as it pulled the dagger free. It hissed and let the dagger fell to the ground. Holding the other dagger straight in front of it like a battering ram, the Jumper charged Harp, who raised his sword in a sweeping upward arc, but he was too slow. The yuan-ti coiled its body low and drove its fist toward Harp's abdomen. Harp doubled up to protect his stomach, dropping his sword, and the dagger sliced into his arm just above the elbow.

With the blood from his arm dripping onto the ground, Harp slammed his boot into the yuan-ti's leg, right above what he hoped was the creature's knee. He heard a satisfying crunch as the leg twisted backward. The Jumper yelped and stumbled toward Boult, who had just parried a blow from another warrior.

"Boult! Spin!" Harp shouted

Without hesitating, Boult wheeled around, cutting Harp's wounded Jumper across the chest. The dwarf spun full circle and resumed his fight with another warrior, who was startled by Boult's sudden change of direction. Boult thrust his sword under the warrior's arm near the shoulder. As he felt the blade slide into skin, Boult yanked down with such force that the straps securing the breastplate snapped and the warrior's armor clattered to the floor. Boult's sword sliced from armpit to hipbone, and the warrior slumped to the ground.

Kneeling on the ground with its broken leg twisted underneath him and gushing blood from its chest, the yuan-ti was done for as well. But before Harp could finish it off, the Jumper hissed at Harp, raised the dagger in its right hand, and stabbed itself in the neck. The creature crashed onto the floor with blood jetting out of its neck.

"Anais's crown!" Harp swore. "Have I killed *anything* since we've been in Chult?"

"Of course you have," Boult said reassuringly.

Verran and Liel were two-on-one with the last serpent warrior, who was backed into the corner against the railing. It was missing an eye and barely able to hold its remaining dagger. Harp pointed at them, but Boult gave an unconcerned shrug. Liel and Verran clearly had the situation in hand.

"Who? Who have I killed?" Harp demanded.

"Bootman?" Boult suggested, watching Verran slam the hilt of his sword against the Jumper's skull. The creature crumpled to the ground.

"No, *you* shot an arrow through his throat." Harp grumbled. "And Verran melted him. I don't know who deserves credit, but it isn't me."

"Didn't you kill a yuan-ti?" Boult asked. Together, Verran and Liel pushed the dazed yuan-ti over the railing to the pack of niferns waiting below.

"At the waterfall?" Harp asked. "No, Majida killed both of those."

"I know," Boult said, snapping his fingers. "You killed an ant."

Harp gave him a dirty look. "Oh, thank goodness. For a

moment, I felt like I had lost my manhood. Now I feel like a brute. You're too kind."

"It was a big ant," Boult said.

Just as Verran and Liel turned away from the railing, a rumble shook the palace.

"Kitto!" Harp shouted.

But there was no sign of Kitto in the rushing, white-capped water, which rotated around the pillar, creating a giant whirlpool under the dome.

"We have to get him," Harp said, moving to jump in the water.

Boult grabbed him. "No! You're not going to find him in that."

"Wait! The waterline is falling," Liel said.

As the water disappeared down the hole in the floor of the hall, Harp shrugged off Boult and sprinted down to the ramp that led off the gallery and spiraled around the pillar. By the time he reached the dripping floor, the water was gone. Harp sprinted to where Kitto's body lay near the door, his foot still tangled in the strap of the heavy pack.

"Kitto!" Harp said, kneeling by the boy's body. "He's not moving!"

Liel crouched beside Harp and laid her hand against Kitto's cheek. "I can feel a heartbeat," she told him. "But something else is wrong."

Harp turned Kitto on his side to drain the water out of his mouth. But even then the boy didn't move.

"He's breathing!" Harp exclaimed. He could see a shallow movement beneath the boy's tattered shirt. "Why isn't he moving?"

Liel placed her hands on Kitto's chest and closed her eyes. A faint white glow appeared around her fingertips, but after a moment, she pulled away with a pained expression on her face.

"I'm sorry," she apologized. "I can't heal him inside. Whatever is blocking my magic . . . I can't do it."

"Please," Harp begged.

"It's some kind of curse, Harp," said Liel, reaching down and untangling Kitto's foot from the backpack. "It isn't a natural injury."

"Then break the curse!"

"I can't, Harp. At least not in the presence of the Torque."

"Maybe Majida could help him," Harp lifted Kitto off the ground as if he were a small child. "We can get him to the Domain, and she'll heal him."

"What about the Torque?" Boult asked. "We've drained the water; Tresco can walk in here and take it."

"I don't care about the damn Torque!" Harp snapped. "We need someone who can help Kitto. And if Majida can do it, then I'm going to find her."

"Wait!" Verran pulled a vial of red liquid from under his tunic. "I can do it. I can do it with this."

CHAPTER TWENTY-FOUR

3 Flamerule, the Year of the Ageless One
(1479 DR)
Chult

What is that?" Harp asked curiously.

"You can't do magic in here," Liel stated flatly.

"How powerful are you?" Boult demanded loudly.

All three had spoken at the same time, and Verran looked from one face to the next as if trying to decide whom he should answer first. Then he stared at the wet floor, looking very much like a schoolboy who had been caught doing mischief.

"It's all right. We just don't understand." Liel assured him. She peered at the vial clutched in his fist. She could see the ornate golden stopper, but his fingers concealed the rest of the vial.

"It's just something about the place." Verran's voice trembled. "I can feel the old magic."

"What do you mean?" Liel asked.

"It's revealing itself to me, just the way it did when I brought down the barrier in the tunnel. It's revealing how to use it."

"You know what these creatures were capable of doing," Boult sputtered. "You're channeling dark magic. What you're sensing is death."

"In death comes rebirth, you know that," Verran protested.

Boult glared at him. "Is that what your father said? Because that's how evil mages like to justify brutalizing the innocent."

"I can break the curse!" Verran insisted. "I can see how to do it in my head!"

"You're not listening to him, are you?" Boult asked Harp, who had gently laid Kitto back down on the tile floor.

"It takes incredible power to work any magic inside the palace." Liel told Harp. "And the curse is the product of ancient, potent magic."

"I couldn't do it by myself." Verran held up the vial. "But I can with an elixir."

"We don't even know what kind of curse it is," Liel said, brushing a lock of wet hair off Kitto's forehead. "We need more information, Harp."

"Enough!" Harp snarled. "Verran, will he be alive? Truly alive?"

"He will be," Verran assured him. "He'll be Kitto again. Just like he was."

"He doesn't know that!" Boult fumed. "It could be a trick! Or he's being misled by whatever is giving him access to his power."

"I don't think we can trust . . ." Liel began.

"Bring him back," Harp interrupted.

"There will be a price, Harp," Liel said. "There always is."

"I don't care," Harp said roughly.

"We don't know where Verran's power is coming from," Boult said. "We don't want Kitto to be used that way."

"So Kitto died for what . . . to drain a pool of water?" Harp leaped up and squared off with Boult. Harp's hands were balled into fists, and his body was rigid with anger. Liel had never seen Harp so furious. Even Boult looked surprised, but he didn't back away.

"Is that all his life is going to amount to? I took him off the *Marderward* to die in Hisari? For nothing?"

"He's not dead!" Boult shouted.

"He might as well be!" Harp shouted back.

"We'll get the Torque." Liel quickly moved between them. She laid her hands against Harp's chest and gently moved him away from Boult. "We'll save Ysabel from Cardew. We'll stop Tresco from overthrowing the Queen. And we'll find a way to help Kitto."

"Do it, Verran," Harp ordered. His gaze swung from Boult to Liel. "Kitto would die to save any of you. And he would do it without hesitation."

Liel let her hands drop to her sides. Harp was going to do whatever he could to help Kitto, and she wasn't going to convince him that there was a safer way. Even if she could stop him, she wasn't sure that she wanted to. Beside her, Boult shook his head in disgust but said nothing more. Verran crouched beside Kitto's limp body. He loosened the vial's golden stopper and tipped a drop of the red liquid onto his palm.

"Is that blood?" Boult asked, staring down Verran's hand.

"Quiet," Verran commanded. He smeared the blood across Kitto's blue lips and began chanting in guttural, hissing sounds. If they were words, then none of the others had heard them before. The blood pooled on Kitto's lips in unnatural droplets and then abruptly seeped into his skin.

Angry red lines branched out across his face, traveling down his neck and to his heart. Verran pulled open Kitto's shirt to reveal his chest. He poured another drop of the elixir on his hand and slammed his open palm onto the skin above Kitto's heart.

When Verran struck the boy so violently, Liel cried out. The spell she was witnessing was so different than her own healing, which drew on memories of old-growth forests and windswept cliffs, the warm dens of small creatures, and the infinite beauty of life's detail. Verran's spell was the antithesis of that. Here was life's bloodletting, murder in reverse. It called upon every catacomb, every ream of twisted flesh, and every layer of humiliation. That healing could come from such a place made no sense.

Verran jerked his hand away, leaving a bloody handprint on Kitto's chest. Again, the elixir pooled unnaturally on top of the skin, only it took the shape of a bloody, clawed hand. The clawed fingers rose off Kitto's chest and plunged deep into his skin. Kitto arched off the floor as the blood-hand clenched around his heart. Still chanting, Verran slammed his fist onto the blood-hand, sending red droplets across Kitto's body and onto the legs of the people standing nearby. The blood-hand evaporated into the air, and Kitto jerked upright, his head thrown back. His arms were up in a defensive posture, and his eyes rolled into his head.

"Kitto!" Harp said, dropping to the ground beside the boy.

But Kitto's arms shot out from his side, and his body jerked in seizure. Harp placed his hands behind the boy's head to keep him from slamming his skull into the tiles.

"Grab his legs," Harp shouted. But before anyone could move, Kitto became quiet and still. He opened his eyes and looked around in fright.

"Kitto! You're safe."

"What happened?"

"You drowned," Harp said, helping him sit up. "I told you not to drown."

"I had the worst dream." Kitto's eyes were watering, and he blinked rapidly as if to clear his vision. "I was in chains."

"You're all right now," Harp reassured him. "Can you stand up?"

"I was in chains," Kitto repeated as Harp and Boult helped him to his feet. "And there was an army of serpents."

Kitto turned to look at the door. The silver stones and lock had vanished, and all that remained was a plain door made from rough-cut, redwood planks. "Did I open the lock?"

"You did a great job," Harp told him, pressing the case of lockpicks back into Kitto's hands. "You got rid of the water."

"I drowned?" Kitto said in amazement.

"No, the pool was cursed," Liel explained. "But Verran brought you back."

Harp caught Verran's eye. Verran had an odd mix of emotions on his face. He looked like he wanted to cry, fight, and hide all at the same time.

"Thank you," Harp said to Verran.

"I owe you," Kitto said sincerely.

"Can we leave?" Verran pleaded. "I don't feel very well."

"That was quite a spell," Liel said, picking up Verran's pack and handing it to him. "You're going to feel drained for a while. What type of elixir was that?"

"Something my father gave me," Verran said, his expression suddenly closed.

Boult cleared his throat. "I agree with Verran. Let's get the Torque and get out as soon as possible."

They followed the ramp as it curved around the gilded pillar and through the opening in the floor. The ramp ended in a long room with a low, tiled ceiling. Two rows of flared columns supported the ceiling. Raised walkways divided the rectangular room into four shallow pools, each paved in a different color tile—crimson, royal blue, deep green, and violet—that stood out dramatically against the whitewashed walls. Water dripped off the ceiling, a sign that the area had been filled with water before Kitto broke the spell.

"Is it a bathing hall for serpents?" Harp asked. "Look at all the colors. It's as festive as a carnival."

"It's where they incubated their creations," Liel explained. "The crimson pool was for bleeding out the slaves to feed the new hatchlings."

"So, not like a carnival," Boult said.

"Not any carnival I want to go to," Harp agreed.

While they were talking, Verran wandered up the walkway and crouched down to look at something on the base of one of the columns. The stone pillars had been painted, but the water had eroded most of the plaster and pigment, leaving only clumps of color sticking to the surface.

"What do you think that does?" Verran asked, pointing to a metal square bolted to the wall with a round indentation in the center. "Do you think it's a trigger?"

"Whatever you do, don't—" Boult started to say, as Verran reached forward and pushed it. "Touch it."

"Verran!" Boult shouted angrily as the sound of a metal gear began grinding ominously from somewhere below them. Verran hurried away from the pillar sheepishly as the grinding intensified. A continuous clanking noise that sounded like chains running through a metal pulley echoed against the tiled walls.

"I'd say we have only moments before something really awful happens," Harp said, pointing to the black goo that was bubbling up from the drains in the middle of the pools.

"I don't think it's a trap," Liel disagreed. "It's too obvious."

"If it were a trap, would anyone be stupid enough to just walk up and press the button?" Boult asked. "No offense, Verran."

"Whether it's a trap or not, we should leave," Liel said. The gunk was seeping faster into the pools, covering the bottom, and rising quickly.

"There's only one way out." Harp pointed to the archway at the end of the southern walkway. "Unless we go back up the ramp."

"Let's go back up the ramp," Verran urged them.

"The Torque is close," Harp said. He gestured to the open door at the end of the southern walkway. "We can't leave it there for Tresco."

Without waiting for the others to follow, Harp strode down the walkway and disappeared through the door. Liel was close behind him. The gunk was already gushing out of the drain. Boult grinned at Kitto and Verran.

"Do it for Princess Ysabel!" Boult shouted.

"Do it so we don't get swallowed by that," Kitto replied as the sludge jetted up into the air. Kitto and Boult hurried into the tunnel behind Liel and Harp. Verran hesitated for a moment, looking longingly at the beam of sunshine streaming down into the pit. Then he ran after the others, moving through the door and into the tunnel just as the geyser of gunk coated the walls and ceiling in thick black sludge.

"What was that?" Verran asked as they stood a safe distance inside the arched tunnel.

"More proof that yuan-ti are the most vile creatures on the planet?" Harp said, shuddering.

"It was probably a cleaning system," Liel suggested. "They sprayed the room down periodically."

"With putrid sludge?" Verran asked dubiously.

"I imagine they used water," Liel said. "But it has sat in the tanks for a long time."

"They needed some way to clean up after the eviscerations," Boult said. He led the way down the short tunnel, which ended at a thickly lacquered door that was not much taller than Harp.

"Got those picks ready?" Harp asked Kitto.

"There's no lock," Kitto pointed out.

"Any thoughts on what's on the other side?" Harp tapped lightly on the door with his fingertips. "When you're planning your palace, what comes after the torture chamber?"

"Why don't you just knock and see if the monsters will let us in?" Boult scoffed as Harp gingerly tugged open the door.

The small door opened onto an unexpectedly enormous hall. Twice as long as it was wide, the hall had high, vaulted ceilings supported by two rows of slender columns along each side. Another gallery ran the along the perimeter of the hall. Instead of wall mosaics, stained-glass windows lined the walls of the gallery. When the palace had been above ground, sunlight flooding through the blue and red glass would have lit the hall in patterns of colored light. But now only dim shadows filtered through darkened windows that looked out on the dank subterranean remains of Hisari.

"I didn't think such an unassuming door would open onto something quite so dramatic," Liel said in awe as she gazed up at the lofty ceiling and cavernous space in front of them.

Unlike the rest of the palace, the hall had not been underwater, and everything was covered in a thin layer of jungle dirt. Part of the vaulted ceiling had collapsed, but the jungle had grown across the gap, keeping the ruins hidden from outsiders. Through the sparse root mat above their heads, they could see the tree canopy and patches of blue sky. A large pile of rocky debris and dirt from where the ceiling had collapsed blocked their view of the other side of the hall.

"All the work to get to the palace," Boult grumbled as he stared at the gaping hole in the ceiling. "And we could have just jumped down through the floor and come in anyway."

"Yeah, but we didn't know where the palace was," Verran pointed out. "You could probably walk over it and never know what was under your feet."

"How are you feeling, Kitto?" Harp asked.

"Better than ever," Kitto replied nonchalantly. He was investigating a marble statue near the columns to the left of the door. The statue was a massive serpent with humanoid arms riding in a chariot pulled by four life-sized humans. In one hand the serpent held a scepter inlaid with a red gem. A golden crown of intertwined serpents rested on its brow.

"Can I take the crown, Harp?" Kitto climbed partway up the statue to get a closer look at the serpent's carved face and leering obsidian eyes.

"Could that crown be the Torque, Liel?" Harp asked.

"No, Majida said the Scaly Ones hated the Torque," she said. "They saw it as the bane of their power. They wouldn't have put it in a place of honor."

Harp considered Kitto's request. "Let's wait until we find the Torque. I don't want to set off another trap. . . ."

"It wasn't a trap!" Verran interrupted angrily. "I saved Kitto's life, and you're mad at me for pushing a button."

"Don't worry about it, Verran," Harp reassured him. "Boult set off a trap upstairs in the gallery. Remember?"

But Verran stalked away and began climbing up the pile of debris. Kitto jumped off the statue and hurried after him.

"Verran," Kitto said as they climbed up the rocks. "You can have the crown . . ."

But when Kitto reached the top of the pile of rubble, he

wheeled around and looked down at Harp, who could see fear in the boy's eyes.

"What's wrong?" Harp asked, scrambling up to the top of the debris.

When he reached Kitto, he saw that the rest of the hall was intact and unmarred by its wet environs or the jungle. An enormous mosaic covered the entire north wall, by far the largest that they had seen in the palace. The mosaic chronicled an epic battle, and it was immediately familiar—they had seen the aftermath of the battle in Majida's Spirit Vault. The mosaic depicted the flesh-and-blood Captive in his last moments, the broken chains dangling from his arms and legs, his hands up in hopeless defense against an army of thousands of yuan-ti, and a blade of mystical flame that hurled through the sky toward him. It was the moment before his death, the moment when his bones would be forever locked in the black stone of the cavern.

"That's what I saw in my dream," Kitto said in amazement. "When I was under the curse."

"You saw the mosaic?" Harp asked. The mosaic's impressive proportions alone would have awed him. But the vivid color and startling details—from the runes on the serpents' golden helms to the veins on the Captive's iridescent wings—were breathtaking.

"No, I saw the army and the flash of fire that killed him." Kitto pointed a shaky finger at the Captive. "I saw it from my own eyes. As if I were standing on the battlefield. As if I were him."

"Isn't that interesting," Boult said, glaring at Verran, who glared back at the dwarf defiantly. "What else do you remember, Kitto?"

"Just that instant. And then I was back under the dome with you."

"Look at that," Liel called. While they were talking, she had climbed down the debris and crossed the marble floor to a white double-door under the mosaic. As she walked, her leather boots left narrow footprints on the grimy floor.

"Whatever is restraining my magic, I think it's coming from in there," Liel said when the others joined her in front of the door. The door was made from a pearl-like substance that shimmered in the dusky light.

"I can feel it too," Verran agreed.

"So the Torque is in there," Harp said.

"Most likely," Liel said. "We don't have a plan of action, do we?"

"Of course not." Boult said, rolling his eyes. "There's more chance of lightning striking me dead on a summer day than Harp actually thinking ahead."

"I have a plan," Harp protested. "Walk in there and take it."

"It's not going to be that easy, and you know it," Boult chided him.

"Ah, don't be such a baby," Harp replied. "They never thought anyone would get past their giant fishbowl. What else could they possibly have put down here?"

"You know you just doomed us," Boult groaned. "Now there's going to be something horrible waiting for us on the other side of that pretty little door."

"Silly Boult," Harp said dismissively. "As if you can change the world just by saying a few simple words."

"Have you tried to explain the basics of spellcasting to him?" Boult asked Liel. "How a few simple words can change the world?"

"I've tried, but it's beyond him," Liel smiled.

"I'm a simple man with simple pleasures," Harp explained. "I like tools, levers, skin. Things I can put my hands on. None of that ethereal nonsense for me."

When they opened the pearl door, they saw a cramped anteroom with stone benches carved out of the wall. An eerie red glow illuminated the tiny chamber, but a screen made of blackened wood blocked their view of the corner of the room. Harp put his fingers to his lips, but the aura of tension and malice was so profound, nobody wanted to speak anyway.

Harp moved quietly along the wall until he reached the screen. Peering around the corner, he saw a much deeper chamber, its walls cut from hazy red stone. At the far end of the chamber was an unremarkable wooden pedestal holding a circlet of unpolished silver. But it was the floor of the chamber that captured Harp's attention. Waves of light rolled off its glassy red surface, and Harp could hear a constant humming noise that made his head ache despite the low-pitched sound.

"The Torque is just sitting there," Harp whispered as he turned back to the group.

"Do you see anything else?" Liel murmured quietly.

"An ominous floor."

"What?" Boult whispered in confusion.

"Have a look." Harp said in a normal voice. There wasn't anything to disturb besides the Torque.

They walked out from behind the screen and stared at the expanse of red glass that stretched across the floor.

"What makes it glow?" Kitto asked.

"I have no idea," Liel said, looking worried. "I've never felt anything like it before."

"So, should I just walk over there and take it?" Harp asked.

"I don't think you should step on the glass at all," Boult cautioned. "In the jungle, isn't the color red supposed to be a warning to stay away?"

A voice came out of the shadows behind them. "Not for my loyal servants who come bearing the gift I have craved for too long."

They spun around in unison, their hands on their weapons, as a massive serpentine guardian slithered out of the shadows behind them. An illusion of a brick-and-mortar wall had concealed an empty room where the guardian had lain in wait and kept guard over the Torque. Like the warriors who had captured them at the colony, the guardian had the body of a snake and the torso of a human, but he was more than double the size of the largest ophidian warrior they had encountered so far. The thick plates and scales that covered his body were a mottled yellow and glistened with mineral deposits formed during the eons cloistered in the damp chamber. The guardian wore a jeweled breastplate and gold bands around his upper arms, but his hands were empty of weapons.

"Huh. I guess there was a fish in the fishbowl after all," Harp said.

CHAPTER TWENTY-FIVE

3 Flamerule, the Year of the Ageless One
(1479 DR)
Chult

The guardian slithered out of the shadows, driving them back onto the red floor and blocking the only exit out of the chamber.

"Loyal servants?" Harp said, gaping up at the serpent guardian. who was so large that his head nearly touched the ceiling. Once he crawled out of the shadows, he seemed to expand to fill the anteroom from wall to wall. He was everywhere at once; his serpentine body coiled around itself in constant motion like a wall of flesh, blocking the entrance.

"I am Shristisanti, Guardian of the Atrocity. I have been waiting, not asleep, not awake but in a constant state of watching. You've brought me to my end."

"Is that a good thing?" Harp asked Boult.

"I have no idea," Liel replied. "I have no idea what he's talking about."

"Bring forth the blood, and I will destroy the Atrocity."

With wide-eyed horror, Boult whirled around and stared at Verran, who gave a little whimper.

"You didn't," Boult exclaimed. "Please tell me that you didn't."

"Didn't what?" Harp asked, alarmed at the dwarf's expression.

"Steal the Captive's elixir from the urn in the Spirit Vault."

Verran looked terrified, and he pressed his hand against his chest where the vial hung from a leather strap around his neck.

"Majida told me about it," Boult said hurriedly. "It was very strange. She must have sensed something about Verran and wanted me to know about it."

"The Atrocity must be destroyed." The guardian slithered onto the glass floor and forced them to back farther into the chamber. "Give me the blood of the Captive."

"What Atrocity is he talking about?" Harp asked.

"The Torque," Kitto said quietly.

"What?" Harp glanced sharply at the black-haired boy, who was staring up at the guardian without fear.

"It's a link from the Captive's shackles," Kitto explained. "In my dream I saw it fall to the ground just before he was hit with the blast that killed him. The Torque is from a piece of his chains."

Shristisanti swung his head toward Kitto. "Are you the bearer of the blood?"

"No . . ."

"Then why are you tainted with it!" Shristisanti hissed, splaying his fingers out and holding his palm level with the floor. Under his hand, the red glass rippled like water. As Harp gaped at the fluid floor, a pulse of energy swelled beneath their feet. A wave of liquefied glass rose like a tidal wave out of the ground and flowed toward Kitto. The boy dived to the side, but it caught him below the knees, spinning him around and hurling him across the room. Kitto's back slammed into the chamber wall, and he fell forward onto his hands and knees. Kitto struggled to his feet as the rest of them drew their weapons.

"We just healed him," Harp growled, pulling out his sword. "There's no way you're hurting him again."

"Servant, step forward with the blood," Shristisanti commanded as a line of glowing spikes rose at the edge of the floor and surged toward them. "Or I will kill you and search your mutilated bodies."

"Get ready!" Harp shouted.

But Verran stepped forward. "I have the blood."

"What is your name, servant?" Shristisanti asked Verran. As the spikes dissolved back into the floor, a pulse of energy vibrated through the soles of their boots.

"I didn't know what I was bringing to you," Verran explained. "I thought it might be worth something in the city."

The guardian made a sound that seemed like a cross between a hiss and a laugh. "Worth something! As if you could ever comprehend the wellspring of power that flows from the Captive's essence. Give it to me."

"Don't even think about it, Verran," Boult warned. "Nothing he can offer you is worth it."

"Shut up, dwarf!" Verran shouted, spinning around to face Boult. "You hated me before I did anything wrong!"

"Nobody hates you," Harp assured him. "Boult's just a bastard. We all think so."

"And you think you're going to be able to help me by getting me a tutor?" Verran cried. "I'm corrupted already. They've got their claws dug into me, and I can't make them let go."

"We'll find a way to help you," Harp promised.

"You should have seen what I was like before I met Harp," Kitto said vehemently. "I was a walking corpse until he helped me."

"You saved Kitto," Boult said gruffly to Verran. "You can turn it around."

"It's too late for me," Verran insisted. "If you could see the things in my head, you'd kill me yourself." He turned back to Shristisanti. "What will you give me?"

The guardian's forked tongue flicked out of his mouth. "You will have a place of honor in the new regime."

"That's it?"

"I could kill you, eat your flesh, and take the blood for myself."

"I'll take the place of honor, then," Verran agreed.

While Shristisanti was distracted talking to Verran, Kitto backed to the pedestal where the Torque sat. With Liel blocking the line of sight between him and the guardian, Kitto reached behind his back and grabbed the twisted span of metal. But as he touched the Torque, he yanked his hand back in pain as the metal blistered his fingertips.

"The barrier that protects the palace also protects the Atrocity," the Guardian roared. "It will not come down lightly."

On either side of Kitto, waist-high walls of molten glass rose out of the floor and rippled toward the center of the room where Kitto stood. Just before they reached him, Kitto jumped straight into the air and pushed one foot off the top of the pedestal to boost himself higher. As the ridges of energy slammed against one another, the wooden pedestal completely disintegrated. The Torque tumbled to the floor as the waves of energy dispersed, followed by Kitto, who crashed onto the ground beside the Torque. He didn't move, and Liel hurried over to his body.

"I told you! Kitto's had enough abuse for one day," Harp

shouted. He charged at Shristisanti, but Verran grabbed his arm and yanked him back.

"I'll give it to you," Verran said, reaching into his shirt and pulling out the vial of blood-elixir. Behind them, Liel was helping Kitto to his feet. The boy's nose was bleeding. Kitto wiped his face with his sleeve, smearing blood across it.

As Shristisanti slid forward to Verran with his arm outstretched, Boult charged from the side, ramming his sword deep into the guardian's unprotected back. The sword plunged deep into his body. It should have been a serious blow, but the guardian's flesh pushed out the sword, healing itself despite the deadly wound. Shristisani picked up the blade and hurled it away.

Shristisanti whipped his tail against Boult, who reeled back across the chamber. Harp shook off Verran's grip and sprinted at the guardian. He managed to cut the creature's arm, but the blood didn't have time to seep from the skin before the wound closed. Liel pulled out her bow, but she was forced to drop to the ground and roll to one side to avoid getting hit by an arc of energy that erupted from the floor.

Verran stood in the middle of the fray as if in the eye of a storm.

"You can't hurt him," Verran told them. "He's invulnerable."

"Don't give it to him, Verran," Harp urged.

A water-like geyser of molten glass erupted from the floor, forcing the rest of the group to scramble deeper into the chamber and farther away from Verran and the guardian. Glassy red drops splattered against their clothes, leaving little holes in the cloth. The boiling floor that separated them from Verran seeped like lava toward their feet.

"I can't go back," Verran cried. "I think I killed Majida. She surprised me as I was taking the elixir out of the Spirit Vault, and I hit her. I think she's dead."

"Verran, please," Harp called to the boy. "Let us help you."

"No one can help me!" Verran said desperately. "Ask Kitto. He saw the marks across my back. You know why I have them, Harp. You know what they make me."

Verran held out the vial like he was presenting Shristisanti with an offering. The guardian slithered forward, but just as Shristisanti's hand would have grasped the vial, Verran darted under his arm and sprinted around the screen and to the door leading into the great hall. Surprised by Verran's unexpected quickness, Shristisanti whipped his body around and plunged after the boy.

When the guardian left the chamber, the bubbling floor hardened with a crackling sound, and a webbing of cracks laced the cloudy surface like ice that was about to shatter. By the time the others had dashed across the slippery floor and into the cavernous hall, the guardian was already on top of Verran. He lifted his hand and let the boy scramble to his feet before slamming him to the ground with his tail. Frantically, Verran twisted free and rolled away, but the serpent pinned him again.

"He's just playing with him," Boult said with horror as the grisly game continued.

Harp yanked his crossbow off his back.

"That won't hurt him," Boult said irritably, but he followed Harp's example.

They shot bolts into the guardian's back. When the bolts pierced his yellow scales, Shristisanti arched in shock. The guardian whirled around with his fangs bared, and the pupils of his red eyes narrowed to thin slits. Black blood oozed out from the arrow wounds, and Shristisanti's long body undulated rhythmically as if in response to the pain.

"He's not healing!" Harp shouted. Somehow the guardian's invulnerability had disappeared. Hissing furiously, Shristisanti yanked the bolts out of his wounded back. Leaving

Verran sprawled on the ground, the guardian coiled his body in a tight spiral. He splayed his fingers out the way he had done inside the chamber. But instead of liquefying into molten red glass, the dusty debris-strewn stones remained unchanged.

"The chamber was the source of his power!" Liel said. "He can't cast if he's out of it."

Kitto and Harp rushed forward, but the Guardian swung around and swatted them both away with a sweeping arc of his tail. Boult reloaded and launched another bolt that lodged in Shristisanti's shoulder. The guardian ignored it and swiveled around to face Harp. Liel rammed her sword into the base of the beast's tail, cleaving a large chunk of flesh off the top. She darted away as the bloody tail flailed wildly and crashed down on the spot where she had been standing.

"Keep him out of that chamber," Boult said, circling around the guardian to Verran and the debris pile.

"He wants the blood more than the Torque," Harp yelled back. He was between Shristisanti and the entrance to the Torque chamber, but he doubted he would be much of an obstacle if the guardian decided to slither back into his enchanted lair. The guardian curled and spiraled around himself as he swung back and forth, making him a very hard target to hit.

Shristisanti turned his attention back to Verran, who had scrambled to his feet and backed away from the guardian until he was pressed against the pile of debris from the collapsed roof. Dazed and bleeding, he stood there, staring up at Shristisanti's ruthless expression. If there were mercy to be had that day, it would not come from the ancient ophidian warrior. As if in a trance, Verran made no move to climb the rubble and get away from the guardian.

"Run, Verran," Liel called.

"Throw me the blood," Harp yelled as he and Kitto charged

the guardian again. Harp's sword sliced Shristisanti below the shoulder blade, and Kitto stabbed him in the side. Coiling around like a whirlpool, the undulations of the Guardian's body kept them at bay. Verran stood passively, as if he knew what was coming but had no will or inclination to stop it. Shristisanti reached forward and snapped Verran's neck, snatching the vial as the boy fell to the ground.

"Verran!" Harp screamed.

Shristisanti held his prize up to the sunlight flooding through the jagged hole in the roof. As he peered at the blood elixir, the red light coming through the glass vial stained the guardian's haughty, self-satisfied face. Harp knew that as soon as the guardian slithered back into the chamber with the Torque, they would be powerless against him. Staring at Verran's body slumped on the ground, his head twisted wrong on his neck, Harp was struck by an overwhelming sense of hopelessness—evil always won, and there was nothing he could do to change it. A flood of images filled his mind: Majida lying dead by Verran's hand, Tresco smugly leading Ysabel down the aisle of a cathedral to marry Cardew, Anais's palace in flames. Harp heard Liel calling his name and looked up to see Shristisanti moving toward him. Harp was overcome by a sense of desperation. He'd failed, yet again.

Boult screamed in Dwarvish and sprinted to the pile of rubble. In the instant that Harp understood what Boult planned to do, his hopelessness evaporated, and his survival instincts kicked him into action. Across the hall, Liel immediately grasped the dwarf's plan as well. She grabbed Kitto's hand, and everyone scattered away from the guardian.

Still holding the vial of elixir above his head, Shristisanti stared in surprise as they ran like frightened bunnies. With his loaded crossbow in his arms, Boult charged up the debris pile like he was being chased by a pack of flaming hellbeasts. Liel and Kitto dashed under the gallery and dived behind one of the marble statues. Since the guardian was between him and the debris pile, Harp bolted for the Torque chamber. Scrambling through the door, he skidded past the blackened screen, slid feet first onto the glassy floor, and smacked into the stone wall.

When he reached the top of the rubble, Boult leaped high into the air, fired his crossbow at the apex of his jump, and rolled down the far side of the pile.

"You missed," Shristisanti boomed as he watched the bolt soar harmlessly over his head.

The bolt struck the wall above the pearl door, precisely in the center of the mosaic depicting the Captive in the last moments of his life. The impact of the bolt against the hard tile snapped the wooden shaft in half, and the splintered pieces fell to the floor. In the heartbeat of silence that followed, Kitto sucked in his breath, Liel laid her hand on Kitto's arm, and the sound of a wire snapping echoed across the hall.

The mosaic swelled outward from the wall, like a giant hand was pushing it from behind. Licks of fire burned between the gaps in the tile. A flaming piece of ceramic blasted out of the mosaic, ricocheted and sank deep into the stone pillar near Liel and Kitto. With increasing speed and frequency, fragments of tile snapped off the wall, shot through the air with a whine, and peppered the cavernous hall with flaming projectiles. Most of them sailed over Shristisanti's head, but one shard winged him, piercing his flesh and carving out a circular hole all the way through his shoulder.

The remainder of the mosaic tiles exploded from the blackened stones of the wall behind them. The flames blinked out, and deafening noise, like the sound of a tidal wave crashing into a forest, swept across the hall. The mosaic exploded in a maelstrom of knifelike shards and choking dust. The torrent of blistering hot shards engulfed Shristisanti, slicing through his scales and shredding his body. The bloody remains of his body dropped to the floor with a wet thud while the shards continued on their trajectory. They sailed through the air until they hit the debris pile and stuck into the rubble like colorful spikes.

"Everyone all right?" Harp yelled from inside the chamber. When the gritty dust cleared, he saw the fleshy chunks of Shristisanti heaped on the floor.

Hearing his friends' voices call back in assent, Harp stood up and brushed himself off, every muscle in his back and neck complaining of misuse. The glassy floor gave off a faint red glow, but not as brightly as it had done before. At the far end of the chamber, the Torque lay unceremoniously on the floor. Harp leaned over and tentatively touched the band of metal. It felt cool and harmless against his fingertips. When Shristisanti died, the barrier around the city that had prevented their easy entry must have fallen, leaving the Torque unprotected.

Harp turned the Torque over in his hand and wondered at all the machinations that had gone on for a simple piece of tarnished metal, a shackle that had once bound the giant Captive. Had the plan already been in progress when Captain Predeau kidnapped Liel? When Cardew snapped his fingers and had Tresco torture Harp at Vankila? Was Boult right that everything was part of a larger order of events, and when Verran stole the blood elixir, he was acting in someone else's theater? Who was getting revenge on whom? And had it been the Captive's day of vengeance, above all else that had transpired during their tenday in the jungle? Harp shook his head. A man could go crazy thinking such thoughts.

"Harp!" He heard Liel calling to him. There was a tension in her voice that made him hurry out of the chamber to see what was wrong. As he crossed through the pearl door into the great hall, he saw ropes dangling down from the hole in the roof. Several masked archers perched on the side of the hole with arrows notched and pointed down at his friends.

CHAPTER TWENTY-SIX

3 Flamerule, the Year of the Ageless One
(1479 DR)
Chult

Liel, Boult, and Kitto stood in the center of the hall with their hands on their heads, surrounded by a dozen men in leather armor and dark tunics. A handsome, square-jawed man stood off to one side talking to a hooded man in a dark cloak. As Harp emerged from the chamber holding the Torque, the man pushed back his hood revealing long gray hair and a knowing smile. At the sight of the man's face, Harp's stomach clenched. The last time he'd seen the gray-haired man, Harp had been strapped to a chair in the Vankila Slab watching parts of his body die piece by piece.

"Master Harp," Tresco sounded pleased, as if he were seeing a friend after a long absence. "It's been so long."

Harp kept his mouth closed. If Tresco was

here, that must mean the soldiers were husks and the man beside him was Cardew. Harp had never met Liel's husband before. Involuntarily, he glanced at Liel and saw that she was looking at him already. When their eyes met, Liel gave Harp a gentle smile.

"You retrieved the Torque," Tresco said, clasping his hands in delight. "I must say I'm grateful."

Still, Harp didn't speak. He avoided looking at Shristi-santi's oozing remains where he'd last seen the vial of elixir. Instead, Harp looked at Verran's corpse with a strong sense of regret and sadness. Harp wasn't angry with the boy for what he'd done. If Verran hadn't stolen the blood, Kitto would still be cursed, maybe even dead. But then, Majida wouldn't have been hurt, or maybe even dead.

"Does anything happen for a reason?" asked Harp, looking past Tresco's archers at the blue of the sky. "Or is it just random events ramming into each other in search of a purpose?"

"There's a reason, Harp," Liel assured him, earning a dark glance from Cardew.

"Such optimism from someone who should already be rotting in the ground," Tresco sneered. "And yes, there is a reason. Apparently, you were meant to retrieve the Torque for me. With the barrier in place, there was no way through the ever-so-convenient hole in the ceiling that Cardew found. But once you killed the guardian, we were able to drop in, just like that."

But Harp barely heard what Tresco said. He was thinking about each of his friends, what might be going on in their heads, and how they might react to the situation they now faced. Kitto would be all right—he wasn't personally involved with Cardew or Tresco. Harp was concerned about Liel. Her husband had plotted to kill her, which was was bound to shake her sensibilities. But she had given Harp that serene smile, so he figured she was in control of herself.

Harp swung his glance to Boult, who looked stoic on the surface. Yet Harp knew that the dwarf must be ready to explode.

Cardew was Boult's accuser and the object of the dwarf's hatred for years. At its core, every action Boult had taken for a decade was a calculation on how to slay the man who had doomed him to a life in the Vankila Slab and had ruined his name. Boult must have figured out that Tresco was the mastermind of the Children's Massacre. Harp had no idea what Boult was about to do, but unless something shifted in their favor, it was unlikely that a dwarf on a rampage would accomplish much except another dead body on the floor.

"Your skin has healed since last I saw you . . ." Tresco began to say to Harp.

"What's this guy's name again?" Harp interrupted. "I can't quite keep it straight. Practitioner? Ermine? Treecow?"

"Murderer?" Boult asked.

"Scum?" Kitto offered.

"Coward?" Liel suggested.

"I prefer that one for Cardew," Boult said.

Cardew stirred angrily and opened his mouth to speak, but Harp cut him off.

"So that is Cardew," Harp said, nodding toward the tall man. "Liel, you could have done so much better than him."

"I did," she said, smiling at Harp again. "You."

"You have no idea what's going . . ." Cardew began.

"Cardew," Tresco warned. "I insist you keep your mouth shut, or I'll have to kill your whoring wife."

With his shoulder down like a battering ram, Harp launched himself at the cloaked wizard. But several of the masked soldiers intercepted him. They surrounded him, grabbing his arms, while one of the men punched him in the stomach. As they forced Harp to his knees, Liel slammed her elbow across the face of the nearest soldier. The soldier grabbed his nose, blood gushing between his fingers, while another man swung his sword at Liel. She sidestepped and knocked his hand away, then kicked the man's leg above the knee, forcing it back unnaturally, before two other soldiers grabbed her from behind.

They dragged Liel over by Harp and pushed her down beside him. Harp really wanted to stand up and gut Tresco. He really, really wanted to see Boult cut off Cardew's head with a meat cleaver.

"Hand it over, Harp," Boult said grimly. "There's not much you can do about it."

"Yes, Harp," Liel said in a monotone voice. "Give him the Torque."

Harp looked between Liel and Boult in surprise, trying to see if there was a hidden message in their acquiescence, but he didn't hear anything but defeat. He looked at Kitto, who shrugged noncommittally. Harp held out the Torque to the nearest soldier, who carried it to Tresco and bowed slightly as he handed it to his master. Tresco took an audible breath and accepted the Torque, his face lighting up as he touched the curved band.

"I did it, Evonne," Tresco said, cradling the Torque against his chest. "I did it for you."

When Tresco fit the Torque around his neck, the air yellowed and seemed to settle around him, as if it had tangible weight and definition. Tresco's body became indistinct, the way an object appears through a grimy window. He looked down at Liel and Harp like they were nothing but ants beneath his feet.

"You have no idea how powerful I am," he said to no one in particular. "No one will ever underestimate me again."

Tresco turned his back to his prisoners, and a dark shadow formed in the air in front of him. Wisps of smoke appeared, and an acrid smell wafted across the air, as if the shadow were burning the air as it materialized in the stillness of the hall. The shadow elongated and took the shape of a rusty doorframe with a barred metal door that looked like it belonged on a prison cell.

Through the open bars of the metal door, they could see a windswept moor and a castle on a hill in the distance. A cool breeze swept in from the desolate countryside bringing the scent of autumn to the sweltering ruins. The familiar smell made Harp long to be in the cool quiet of a real forest and not that hot, fatal jungle. He glanced at Liel's profile, but her attention was focused on Tresco and his portal back to Tethyr.

"Cardew, you have your instructions," Tresco said, turning his head slightly and speaking over his shoulder. "Bring me flesh tokens, and I shall embrace you. Ysabel may have given up on you, but I have not."

Tresco pushed on the door, which made a harsh grating sound as it opened onto the field of gorse and purple heather. Without a glance behind him, the old man stepped through the door, which closed with a metallic clang and dissolved into nothingness. With the ringing sound still reverberating off the walls, everyone looked at Cardew. Cardew looked vaguely surprised at the sudden attention, and then his shoulders slumped.

"Liel," he said, walking in front of where she kneeled on the ground. He stood in front of her and leaned down so he could look down at her face. "I'm very sorry to have to do it."

Liel looked up at him. When Cardew's eyes locked with hers, he took an involuntary step back, the fear evident on his handsome features. Liel's palms were open to the sky, her head tipped back to the sunlight, and from her lips tumbled the words borne of all the power the jungle had to offer.

"Idiot," she snarled at him. "You forgot that when the Torque left, my magic came back."

As Liel rose to her feet, her body quivered with ferocious energy and her presende dominated the hall. Cardew and the husk-soldiers shrank away from her presence, and she swung her head around to look at her friends.

"Get behind me," she commanded them, and they scurried to obey. Above the hole in the roof, the swatch of blue sky darkened into a vortex of black storm clouds. The soldiers on the edge of the hole lowered their bows and looked up in confusion as a volley of lightning cracked out of the sky. It slammed into one of them, scorching his body into a burned slab of flesh. The impact knocked the other archers off the edge and sent them tumbling down into the hall. When their smoking bodies hit the ground with a sickening thud, the soldiers on the ground turned and ran.

Before they could scramble up the debris pile and out of harm's way, gusts of air spun down from the sky and formed a wall in front of Liel. She rammed her arm straight out from her shoulder and, at her command, the currents of air swirled across the hall in an unavoidable torrent. Catching men both dead and alive in its wake, it tossed them across the hall as if they were no weightier than fallen leaves. Bodies slammed against columns, their spines breaking on impact. The stained glass cracked inside the window frame. As the wind died down, the loose glass fell from the frames and rained down into the hall in a cascade of red and blue fragments that smashed onto the rubble-strewn floor.

Unmolested by the wind, Harp, Boult, and Kitto gawked at the extent of the destruction wrought by Liel's spell. The rush of wind stilled, leaving only white currents of air that eddied around the bases of the pillars. Liel pressed her hands together, and the white currents joined together to form the links of an ethereal chain. One end of the chain wound itself around the leg of a body slumped at the base of a column. Liel jerked her arm backward. As if pulled by an invisible hand, the chain dragged the limp body across the expanse of broken glass where it came to rest in front of her.

"You've gotten some serious power since I saw you last," Harp said in awe, staring down at the broken body of Cardew lying at the elf's feet.

"He's not dead," Boult said as Cardew moaned and blinked his eyes.

"Liel," Cardew whispered, his blood-splattered lips barely moving. "Please help me."

"Don't even think about it," Boult insisted. "After that display of magical prowess, healing the bastard would be anticlimactic."

"Boult would be most disappointed," Harp agreed. "It's all right that Liel killed him and not you, right?"

"Oh yes," Boult said. "It just feels right, don't you think?"

"I'm going to give him a chance to save himself," Liel said quietly.

"What?" Boult sputtered. "You can't be serious."

"Tell us what we need to know, and I'll save you," Liel promised Cardew.

"Of all the idiotic . . ." Boult began.

"Just let Liel talk to him," Harp put a restraining hand on the dwarf's shoulder. "Go look for the elixir, why don't you?"

"Why don't you look for the elixir?" Boult said stomping off to the debris pile. "There's no reason in the infinite heavens to let that dog live."

"What is Tresco planning?" Liel asked.

"Overthrow Anais and put Ysabel on the throne," Cardew whispered.

"We know that already!" Boult yelled from across the room.

"Why did he say that Ysabel had forsaken you?" Liel asked.

"Somehow she figured out what we were doing in the jungle. It disgusted her. I disgusted her."

"You disgust everyone," Boult yelled again, kicking chunks of the guardian's flesh around on the floor as he searched for the vial.

"If Tresco finds out how much she knows, he'll kill her," Cardew moaned. "You have to protect her. She's an innocent in all of his plans."

"Did Tresco mastermind the Children's Massacre?" Harp demanded.

"I don't know," Cardew said. "He must have been involved . . . But I don't know."

"Where is Ysabel?" Liel asked.

"At Kinnard Keep. She's been in Tresco's care since the massacre," Cardew whispered.

"Does Tresco know about the elixir?" Liel asked.

"What elixir?" Cardew rasped. His breathing was labored, and blood seeped out from under his body, staining the dusty floor.

"The elixir I have," Boult said triumphantly, holding up the slimy, though unbroken, vial of blood. "Safe under Shristisanti."

"Poor Verran," Harp said as he watched Boult slipped the elixir into his pack.

"He *was* one, you know," Kitto said. "A warlock. I saw the marks on his back when I pulled out the glass. They looked like brands."

"So he made the pact," Harp said sadly. "Just like his father."

"But he wasn't all bad," Kitto said. "He just didn't know what to do."

"I need to get the elixir back to the dwarves," Boult said, covering Verran's body with a cloak. "I need to find out if Majida is all right."

"And we need to get to Tethyr and help Ysabel," Harp said.

"Can you reopen a portal?" Harp asked Liel.

"Only with the scroll," she explained.

"The spell scroll in the colony," Boult reminded them. "I left it under the floorboards in the hut."

"I know where you're talking about," Liel said. "But we'll have to get back there fast."

"Are you sure you want to split up?" Harp asked Boult.

"I have to get the blood back to the Domain," Boult said urgently. "It's the only place it's safe."

"Do you want me to go with you?" Kitto asked Boult.

"We need you," Harp told Kitto. "We'll probably have to fight Tresco while he's wearing the Torque."

"Which means that Liel won't be able to use her magic," Kitto pointed out. "If that happens, I won't be able to do much."

"Hit him on the head with a rock and steal the Torque?" Harp said after a moment.

"It's so stupid that it's brilliant," Kitto grinned faintly. "You've really outdone yourself, Harp."

"That's Captain Harp to you, sailor," Harp grinned back at him.

"What are you going to do about Cardew?" Boult asked Liel.

"I don't know," Liel said helplessly. "I guess I'll heal him and take him back to Queen Anais. Let her decide what to do with him."

"He can tell her what Tresco has been doing in Chult," Harp pointed out. "What do you think, Boult?"

Boult hesitated. "I've wanted him to suffer for so long. I wanted him to die as painfully as possible. And now that the moment's here, I just don't care."

"All right, we'll let Queen Anais decide," Harp agreed.

But Kitto stepped forward and calmly shoved his sword into the base of Cardew's throat. Cardew opened his mouth in surprise, but no words came. Kitto pulled his sword out, and blood welled out of the wound, flowed down Cardew's neck and chest, and stained his snow-white shirt. In the time it took for the others to comprehend what had happened, Cardew was dead.

"He tried to kill Liel," Kitto said unapologetically. "He framed Boult. He tortured Harp. What about what he did to me? The Branch of Linden owned Captain Predeau. Their coin kept him going. He treated me like a slave and nearly beat me to death. If you weren't going to kill him for yourselves, then he was going to die for me."

"All right, fine with me," Harp told him without hesitation.

"Good riddance," Boult agreed.

"I have an idea, Boult," Harp said as they prepared to climb up the ropes that had been left by Tresco's men. "Instead of Tethyr, let's meet on the Moonshae Isles."

"The cove?" Liel asked as a huge smile spread across Kitto's face. "Does Boult know about the safe haven?"

"Harp's talked about it so damn much, I could find it in my sleep," Boult said. "How long do you think it will take you to reach Ysabel?"

"As long as it takes to get to the camp and open the portal," Harp answered.

"Try to make it fast," Boult urged them. "You have to get to her before Tresco does."

"We'll hurry," Liel promised.

"Safe home, then," said Harp, extending his hand to Boult, who clasped it warmly.

"Safe home, brother," Boult replied.

CHAPTER TWENTY-SEVEN

4 Flamerule, the Year of the Ageless One
(1479 DR)
Kinnard Keep, Tethyr

Hello, Ysabel," Tresco said as he stepped through
the door and into the warm air of the atrium. The
glass atrium was on the western side of Kinnard
Keep, and Ysabel insisted that the gardeners keep
flowers blooming all year round, especially in the
cold winter months when the outside gardens were
barren and lifeless.

Surrounded by jade plants and hanging baskets,
Ysabel sat at a stone table near an ornamental tree
blooming with crimson flowers. She wore a light
blue dress with white embroidery down the sides,
and her hair was pulled back in a loose braid. The
leather-bound book on the marble tabletop looked
vaguely familiar—probably one from Tresco's
library—but she wasn't reading when he opened
the door. Instead, she'd been staring out at the

windswept heath through the condensation on the glass panes.

"Good day, Uncle," she said politely, her hands resting demurely in her lap. "Are you back from your business so soon?"

"Yes." Tresco set a leather case on the table in front of her. "I returned yesterday afternoon, but the servants said you had already retired to your quarters, and I didn't care to trouble you."

"Is Master Cardew with you?" she asked, glancing at the case and then up at Tresco.

"He is not." Tresco answered. "Am I to understand that the two of you quarreled?"

"It was merely a trifle, Uncle," she replied. "Please sit and tell me about your journey."

"Why do you sit in the atrium? You know it's the least protected room in the castle. And where are your guards?"

"They are merely out of sight," Ysabel replied obliquely.

"That is not acceptable," Tresco fumed. "They have orders to guard you at all times . . ."

"Won't you sit?" Ysabel said sharply.

"I do not wish to," Tresco said irritably. That wasn't true at all. He had planned on having a leisurely lunch with the girl. It was so unlike Ysabel to be anything but compliant.

"Then leave, Uncle." She looked away from him and opened the leather cover of her book.

"I'll remind you that this is my house, and you are my ward," Tresco said in a firm tone.

For a moment, Ysabel sat frozen and stared down at her hands. But when she looked up at Tresco, there was a placid look on her pretty features. Tresco felt his frustration ease. That was the expression he was accustomed to seeing on Ysabel's face. Now, they could enjoy a pleasant afternoon. "My apologies, Uncle. My thoughts weigh heavily on my mind."

"What is wrong?" Tresco asked, pulling out one of the

wrought-iron chairs. It scratched across the paving stones with an irritating metallic sound. "Are you upset with Cardew?"

"When I last spoke to him, he told me that you two were going to secure an object of great importance."

"Did he?" Tresco's anger reappeared instantly. Declan Cardew had to be one of the dimmest people he'd ever had the misfortune of working with, including the ogres at the Vankila Slab. "Well, Declan shouldn't have troubled you with such nonsense. It's none of your concern."

"Are you angry with him?" Ysabel asked.

Tresco sighed. "Cardew is useful, but not necessarily the brightest man in the realm."

"Useful how?" Ysabel prompted.

"Like a gilded sign above a merchant's door," Tresco replied. He enjoyed his quip although he didn't expect his ward to understand his private jest. But Ysabel looked at him without confusion.

"A merchant who sells flour sacks filled with sawdust," she replied.

"What did you say?" Tresco asked in surprise.

Ysabel gave him an accommodating smile. "I have begun to doubt . . . the quality of Cardew's character."

"That's interesting," Tresco said, with a sense of relief that her comment had been about Cardew and nothing more substantial. "I have as well."

"Do you still want me to marry him?"

Tresco pushed back his chair back from the table and paced up and down the flagstone path. Ysabel watched him patiently. It was too warm in the atrium, and there was an unpleasant scent of acrid earth and overripe fruit in the air, but neither guardian nor ward seemed to notice.

"Unfortunately, my plans have changed," Tresco said finally. "I don't think he is the right match for you after all."

"What a surprise." Ysabel didn't sound surprised at all.

"Yes, my dear. I have made other arrangements for you." Tresco stopped his pacing and came to stand beside her chair.

"Before we discuss your plans for my future," Ysabel said, "let's talk about what's in the case."

"Why should we talk about the case?" Tresco asked.

"Because that case holds the culmination of your *life's* work," she explained. "Work that was never yours to begin with. Evonne discovered something miraculous, and when you found her manuscript, her research propelled you to things far beyond your comprehension. She was the giant, and you just used her to become what you are."

Tresco narrowed his eyes. "Did Cardew tell you that? In some aspects, you are correct. Based on your mother's notes, I discovered the existence of a powerful artifact."

"That's what you brought back from the jungle—the artifact?" Ysabel asked, resting her fingertips against the old leather of the case. "And it's in here?"

"No," he replied with a self-satisfied smile. "It's around my neck." He adjusted the collar of his tunic to show Ysabel the twist of tarnished metal around his throat.

"What a pity," she mused.

"Why?" He was perplexed and unnerved by her manner. She seemed different. Her spine was as straight as an arrow, and her voice sounded deeper than the little-girl's voice he was accustomed to hearing from her.

"Why?" he demanded again.

"Look, Uncle." She pointed over his shoulder at the glass-paned door that led out of the atrium and into the inner courtyard of Kinnard Keep. "We have visitors."

"I'm not expecting anyone," Tresco said. He turned abruptly to see who would be fool enough to traipse across the moor in such nasty weather.

"Visitors who have come to save me, I imagine," Ysabel said in a pleased tone.

"Save you?" Tresco turned back to Ysabel in confusion.

"Those must be Avalor's mercenaries," she told him. "I can only hope that they are more clever than you. Perhaps they unearthed something more interesting than a broken chain."

Tresco wheeled around as the glass door crashed open, its panes shattering. Still covered in mud and blood from the jungle, Harp crossed the threshold with a sword in his hand. Tresco could see Cardew's elvish wife and the dark-haired boy directly behind him. Under the layers of grime, the sight of Harp's unblemished skin annoyed Tresco. So did the sight of the red-haired elf, who should have been long dead.

"Cardew failed again?" Tresco asked.

"Cardew's dead," Liel said.

"It's just the three of you?" Tresco scoffed. "You should have brought your father and his army. I would have enjoyed making Avalor the Great grovel under my boot."

Liel put her hand on Harp's shoulder as if to hold him back. "Tresco is wearing the Torque. We're too late."

"We can't leave Ysabel." Harp said. But he took a step backward like the coward he was.

"How foolish you are," Tresco said, jerking his hand through the air as if he were shaking off unwanted drops of water. "You know you can't hurt me while I have the Torque. Why did you even try?"

Liel, Harp, and Kitto moved to run, but Tresco's spell caught them before they could escape to the courtyard. Their breath curdled in their mouth, and they clutched their throats as the spell strangled them. Coughing and pawing at their throats as their lungs burned, Harp and Kitto fell to their knees, while Liel pressed herself against the wall to stay upright. But she couldn't find enough strength to overcome the overwhelming force of the Torque.

"Do you see the power it grants me?" Tresco asked as

he turned to Ysabel. She had stood up from the table to watch the intruders struggle on the ground as they slowly suffocated. "I shall be unstoppable."

"And what about me?" Ysabel said. The casualness of her inquiry struck Tresco as very odd. It sounded as if she hadn't noticed there were people dying on the floor. Hadn't she just witnessed Tresco's newfound power and dominance? Tresco sighed. Suddenly, he was very tired of Ysabel's company.

"I had a marvelous plan to marry you, the Rightful Queen, to Cardew, the Hero of the Realm. You would have captured the imaginations of all of Tethyr while I ran the kingdom. But with Cardew dead . . ."

"You had already given up on your plan of marrying me to Cardew," Ysabel reminded him.

"So I had," Tresco said smugly.

"What do you plan to do?" Ysabel inquired again. She had to speak louder to be heard over the gasps of the people writhing on the floor. Tresco wondered if Ysabel was familiar with the effects of the spell. In a few moments, the intruders would lose consciousness, if they hadn't already. And then they would slip gracefully into death, unaware of what had transpired around them.

"You have turned into quite a fetching girl," Tresco told her. "I envision a great funeral procession. Your coffin will be drawn by white horses down the grand boulevard in Darromar with me leading the way."

"You'll kill me, then," Ysabel said without emotion.

"I'm sorry, my dear. But beautiful girls make good martyrs," Tresco said regretfully.

Slowly, Ysabel raised her arm that had been hidden behind the table. On her fist she wore a massive, spiked gauntlet made of bronze. Emblazoned with intricate designs, it covered her skin up to her elbow and looked so heavy that it would have been difficult for someone twice Ysabel's size to maneuver it.

"What is that wretched thing?" Tresco asked, so startled by its sudden appearance on her slender arm that he forgot about the spell he was preparing to cast.

"It is the manner of your death," she replied as she rammed the gauntlet into his belly with surprising strength and speed. As the spikes shredded his insides, she twisted the metal glove. He howled as the pain engulfed him.

"But the Torque!" he cried.

"The Torque only grants a ward against magic," she said. "You stupid, stupid man."

"Ysabel!" He wanted to plead for mercy, but her name was the only word he could manage to speak.

"Where is the Captive's elixir?" she hissed.

Tresco had no idea what she was talking about. Blood was filling his mouth and nose.

"The manuscript I left you had all the information you needed to find the elixir," Ysabel hissed as Tresco's blood ran down her arm. "I spelled it out for you in small, simple words. Yet you come back with a . . . Torque? Such an inferior artifact? It has merely a fraction of the power in the vial. Is there anyone more miserable than you?"

Tresco's hands grasped futilely at the air around him as if he could steady himself with the ether itself. The pain was so incomprehensible that it felt as if it must be afflicting someone else. Tresco had inflicted so much suffering during his experiments at the Vankila Slab. For the first time, the words of his victims rattled through his mind as his consciousness blinked on and off like a torch about to burn itself out. And what words they had been: words of mercy, of remembrance, of forgiveness. His victims had pleaded for those they loved and those they had wronged. Their regrets consumed them and then flew from them like startled birds. Tresco had felt nothing but contempt for their unexpected compassion. He found no joy or hope to draw from within himself, and now he envied them. And he loathed the void of a life that he had lived.

"Hopefully, my so-called rescuers can lead me to the elixir," Ysabel said, glaring at the bodies on the floor. "Then it all won't have been in vain."

Reaching out with her free hand, Ysabel yanked the Torque off Tresco's neck and inspected the unpolished metal. Then she slipped it on her own neck, where it was hidden under the high collar of her dress. As soon as the Torque left Tresco's body, Harp, Liel, and Kitto stopped struggling as the invisible grip on their throats dispersed and air flowed to their lungs again. But none of them yet moved off the floor. Ysabel leaned close to Tresco so her lips were against his ear.

"You have kept me prisoner for a decade," she hissed. "You have kept me from my magic, forcing me to squeeze blood from a stone for every drop of knowledge and power that I possess. I should have been reborn with all that I had in my previous body, but no, I was forced to play the simpering girl to sniveling idiots."

Tresco could barely keep his head from falling to his chest. He shifted slightly for one last look at the statuesque profile of the girl who had been his ward.

"Evonne?" Tresco gasped with his last breath.

"You always were slow, Tresco. I have been there from the moment the lights went out in the Winter Palace the night of the massacre. I've been with you—locked in this useless body of a child. I should have been powerful despite the youthful vessel. I should've had all my magic at my disposal. But instead I was weak, forced to claw my way back to what I was. No thanks to you."

She twisted the gauntlet again. "And now I have returned to the pinnacle of my power," she said viciously. "Not you nor anyone else will keep me from my rightful place on the throne."

She yanked her hand out of the gauntlet, let Tresco's lifeless body fall on top of it, and turned around as the other three stirred.

"What happened?" Harp asked, as he stood up shakily and saw Tresco slumped on the ground and blood seeped into the cracks between the paving stones.

"He tried to cast a spell, I think." Ysabel's voice quivered. "His chest caved in . . . Blood was everywhere."

"The Torque did that?" Harp asked Liel. "Could it have killed him?"

"I don't know," Liel replied. "Maybe there was an enchantment on it?"

"Do you know where the Torque is?" Harp asked Ysabel.

"He said there was an artifact in here," she replied, picking up the case and holding it against her chest. "My guards have deserted me. Will you take me to Queen Anais? I have so much to show her."

"Of course," Harp assured her. "We have horses outside. We can go immediately."

"Thank you," Ysabel said appreciatively. "And on the way, you must tell me everything that happened in the jungle."

MARK SEHESTEDT

Chosen of Nendawen

The consumer, the despoiler, has come to Narfell. His followers have taken Highwatch and slain all who held it—save one.

Vengeance will be yours, the Master of the Hunt promises.
If you survive.

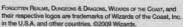

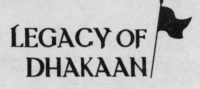

DON BASSINGTHWAITE'S

LEGACY OF DHAKAAN

From the ashes of a fallen empire,
a new kingdom rises.

The Doom of Kings

The Word of Traitors
September 2009

The Tyranny of Ghosts
June 2010

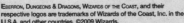

MAGIC
The Gathering®

Everything you thought you knew
about MAGIC™ novels is changing…

From the mind of

ARI MARMELL

comes a tour de force of imagination.

AGENTS
OF
ARTIFICE

The ascendance of a new age in the planeswalker
mythology: be a part of the book that takes fans
deeper than ever into the lives of the Multiverse's most
powerful beings:

Jace Beleren™
a powerful mind-mage whose choices now will forever
determine his path as a planeswalker;

Liliana Vess™
a dangerous necromancer whose beauty belies a dark
secret and even darker associations; and

Tezzeret™
leader of an inter-planar consortium whose quest for
knowledge may be undone by his lust for power.